**Nikki tumbled down right on top of Dallas.
Not that he was complaining.**

Another sob left her throat. "Hey." He wrapped his arms around her.

She raised her face and rested her chin on his chest, and that's when Dallas realized that last little noise wasn't a sob. "What did Bud eat?" The laughter in her voice sounded so sweet. If that's what it took to make her laugh, his bulldog might just be getting more people food after all.

Nikki shifted as if to move off him, and he wasn't sure what provoked him to do it, but he raised his head an inch off the floor and pressed his lips against hers. It was just a kiss, he told himself. Probably wasn't the wisest move, especially considering her knee had optimum placement and could achieve a direct hit.

But a little voice in Dallas's head said he probably should be more worried about the direct hit to his heart. The second he tasted Nikki's mouth, he told the little voice to take ~~~~~~~~~~ he wouldn't regret this

Raves for
Christie Craig and Her Novels

"Delightful...Craig hits all the high notes en route to happily ever after."
—*Publishers Weekly* on *Shut Up and Kiss Me*

"Funny, hot, and suspenseful, Craig's writing has it all. She's the newest addition to my list of have-to-read authors. Warning: Definitely addictive."
—Nina Bangs, *New York Times* bestselling author

"Craig is the jewel of my finds when it comes to new authors to add to my favorites list. Her characters draw you in immediately, make you care about them in no time flat, and her humor is to die for."
—GoodBadandUnread.com

"Christine Craig writes delicious sexy romances that are as addictive as a can of Pringles; once you start, you can't stop! Hilarious, romantic...entertaining from start to finish."
—NightOwlRomance.com

"Craig is like chocolate: addicting and good for you. I dare you to dive in and not get a good laugh."
—BookBitch.com

Also by Christie Craig

Blame It on Texas

Only in Texas

CHRISTIE CRAIG

FOREVER

NEW YORK   BOSTON

This book is a work of fiction. Names, characters, places, and incidents are the product of the author's imagination or are used fictitiously. Any resemblance to actual events, locales, or persons, living or dead, is coincidental.

Originally published by Hachette Book Group as *Don't Mess with Texas*.

Forever
Hachette Book Group
237 Park Avenue
New York, NY 10017
www.HachetteBookGroup.com

Forever is an imprint of Grand Central Publishing.
The Forever name and logo are trademarks of Hachette Book Group, Inc.

The Hachette Speakers Bureau provides a wide range of authors for speaking events. To find out more, go to www.hachettespeakersbureau.com or call (866) 376-6591.

The publisher is not responsible for websites (or their content) that are not owned by the publisher.

Printed in the United States of America

First Edition: September 2011

10 9 8 7 6 5 4 3 2 1

Acknowledgments

Writing is a solitary business, but I didn't, and couldn't, have gotten this far without my support system, a system that first and foremost includes my husband. I know the extent of his love when he comes tiptoeing into my office and whispers those sweet heartrending words in my ear: "I'll do the laundry." Thank you, Steve.

To my critique group and best friends in the whole world: Faye Hughes, Jody Payne, Suzan Harden, and Teri Thackston, whose support, laughter, and spelling and grammar abilities keep me going. To my newfound critique and walking buddy, Susan Muller, who allows me to rattle on about plot problems for about two miles every day. To my agent, Kim Lionetti, who knows just when to say, "You're overthinking it again." To my editor, Michele Bidelspach for helping me make my stories as good as they can get.

Only in Texas

CHAPTER ONE

"IT'S THE RIGHT THING. It's the right thing."

At five o'clock on the dot, Nikki Hunt drove past the valet parking entrance to Venny's Restaurant and turned into the one-car alley lined with garbage Dumpsters. She eased her car over potholes big enough to lose a tire in, and parked her Honda Accord. "It's the right thing," she repeated then rested her forehead against the steering wheel. After one or two seconds, she squared her shoulders and mentally pulled up her big girl panties. Letting go of a deep breath, she stared at the Dumpster adjacent to her car and hoped this wasn't a foreshadowing of the evening.

Though no one would guess it—other than that one bill collector, her bank, and the McDonald's attendant who'd waited for her to dig out enough change to pay for her sausage biscuit this morning—Nikki couldn't afford valet parking.

Her local gallery barely made enough money to cover the rent. Who knew that a little downturn in the economy would prevent the general population from appreciating art?

Okay, fine, she knew. She was financially strapped, not stupid. And yeah, she'd also known that opening the gallery had been risky. But at the time, she'd had Jack to fall back on if things got tough. Good ol' Jack, charming, financially stable, and dependable—dependable, that is, as long as one didn't depend on him to keep his pecker in his pants.

She pulled a tube of lipstick from her purse, turned the rearview mirror her way and added a hint of pink to her lips.

Please, Nikki, meet me at Venny's. I made some mistakes, but we can fix it.

Jack's words skipped through her head.

Was Jack really going to ask her for a do-over? Was she really contemplating saying yes? And was saying yes the right thing? The questions bounced around her brain, hitting hard against her conscience.

Rubbing her lips together to smooth the pink sheen on her mouth, she looked at the back of the restaurant—probably the most expensive restaurant in Miller, Texas. The one where Jack, the man she considered the love of her life, had proposed to her four years ago. This wasn't the first time she'd heard from Jack since the divorce. The flowers he'd sent had gone to her grandmother's retirement center. Someone should enjoy them. The messages where he begged her to take him back went unanswered. She hadn't even been tempted. Until today.

Today he'd called the gallery right after Nikki had received a call from the retirement home, reminding her that her grandmother's cable bill was due. Right after she realized she was going to be short paying Ellen, her one and only part-time employee. There'd been desperation in Jack's voice and it had mimicked the desperation Nikki felt in her own life.

She focused on the rearview mirror again and gave herself a good, hard look. She fluffed her hair, hoping her thick, blond curls would appear stylish and not impoverished. Nana's cable trumped her regular clip job. Her grandmother had spent thirteen years taking care of Nikki, so the least she could do was allow the woman to watch the cooking network.

And Ellen—how could she not pay the woman who'd become her best friend? The woman who singlehandedly dragged Nikki out of the done-wrong slumps kicking and screaming.

Nikki stepped out of her car. The heat radiating from the pavement assaulted her. She could almost feel her hair frizz. Humidity thickened the air, making it hard to breathe. Or maybe that was just the anxiety of seeing Jack, of making a decision to reenter the holy union—a union that turned out not to be so holy for him.

Passing the Dumpster, she wrinkled her nose and walked faster. The ring of her cell brought her to a stop. She grabbed the phone from her purse, and checked the number.

"Hello, Nana?"

"You're my one call," Nana said.

"Shoot." Nikki hurried her steps to escape the garbage smell. Common sense told her Nana was playing the timed crossword game with her Ol' Timers Club. A game that allowed the participant a single one-minute call to someone who might be able to help. But the first time Nana had used her one-call line, she'd been in jail. Sure, Nana had only been arrested once, but bailing your grandmother out of the slammer was not something one tended to forget.

"Name of the club you join when you get it on at high altitudes, twelve letters," Nana said.

"What kind of crossword puzzle is this?" Nikki asked.

"Smokin' hot."

Figures. The Ol' Timers Club members, on average, had a better sex life than Nikki did. "Mile High Club. Not that I belong." She cut the corner to the restaurant, welcoming the warm scents of Venny's menu items.

"You should," Nana said.

"Gotta go," Nikki said before Nana started ranting about Nikki's less-than-exciting social life.

"You're coming to the dress rehearsal tonight?" Nana asked.

What dress rehearsal? Then Nikki remembered. Her grandmother and several of the Ol' Timers had gotten parts in a small neighborhood theater show.

"I can't, but I'll come to the show." If she could afford the ticket.

"Where are you?"

"About to walk into a restaurant."

"A date?" Nana sounded hopeful.

"No." *Just possibly coming to get proposed to for the second time by the man I used to love.*

Used to? Nikki stopped so fast she almost tripped. Didn't she still love Jack? Weren't there still feelings underneath the pain of his infidelity? Because if she didn't really have feeling for him then...

"Who are you meeting?" Nana asked.

It's the right thing. "No one," she lied, flinching.

In the background, Nikki could hear Nana's friend Benny call out, "Five seconds."

"Gotta go," Nikki repeated.

"Nikki Althea Hunt, do not tell me you're meeting that lowlife scum of an ex—"

"Love ya." Nikki hung up, dropped her cell back into her purse and tried to ignore the doubt concerning what she was about to do. Instead, she wondered what the hell her mother had been smoking when she named her Althea. Then again, figuring out what her mother was smoking when she'd dropped six-year-old Nikki at Nana's with the request that Nana raise her was a much better puzzle. And not one Nikki liked to think about, either.

Walking into the restaurant, pretending she belonged in the rich, famous, and lawyer circle, Nikki was embraced by the scents of beef burgundy. Her stomach gave one last groan, then died and went to heaven without looking back. The biscuit she'd scraped change together for this morning was a forgotten memory.

"Meeting someone?" the hostess asked as Nikki peeked into the dining room.

"Jack Leon." Nikki spotted him sitting at the table—the same table where he'd proposed to her—talking on his cell phone.

"This way." The hostess started walking but Nikki caught her arm and yanked her back. The woman's eyes rounded.

"Just a second, please." Nikki continued to stare at Jack and waited. Where was it? Where was the heart flutter when her gaze landed on him? A light flutter would do. That's all she was asking for.

No flutters, damn it. The only emotion bumping around her chest was residual fury at finding him in her gallery office, on the sofa, banging her hired help.

Not a good memory to be hanging in her mental closet

tonight. Not if Jack was going to propose. Because if she said yes, then she might be the one banging her ex.

"Crappers," she muttered and her heart did a cartwheel, hitting the sides of her ribs. Nikki had no problem with sex. Not that she'd had any pleasure in a *long* time. A really long time. Like...since Jack.

The truth rained down on her. She wasn't here because she loved Jack. If she went back to him it wouldn't even be for pleasure. It would be for money. Sure, the money was to pay Nana's cable, to pay Ellen, and to keep her gallery afloat, but still...the hard fact was she'd be having sex for money.

"Oh shit!" Could she stoop that low?

My name is Nikki Hunt, not Nikki Name Your Price.

"I don't think I can do this," she muttered and tightened her hold on the hostess's arm.

"You don't think you can do what?" asked the hostess.

"Oh hell. It's not the right thing."

"What's not the right thing?"

Nikki stared at her feet. "How important are the cooking shows anyway?"

"Which one?" asked the hostess, still mistaking Nikki's muttering for conversation. "I like Rachael Ray."

Releasing the hostess's arm, Nikki turned to go, but stopped short when a waiter carting a tray of yeast-scented bread and real butter moved past. He left a wake of warm tantalizing aroma.

Crapola. She wouldn't have sex with Jack. She wouldn't remarry him, but could she sit through a dinner for some mouthwatering food? Yup, she could stoop that low.

Call it payment for defiling the much-loved antique

sofa in her office. No way could she have kept it after seeing him and her employee going at it doggy-style on the piece of furniture.

Mind made up, Nikki swung around and, without waiting for the hostess, shot across the dining room and plopped down at Jack's table.

Still on the phone, Jack looked up. His eyes widened with what appeared to be relief, and he nodded. Dropping her purse at her feet and, not waiting for a bread plate, she snagged a hot roll and smeared a generous amount of sweet butter on it. Her mouth watered as the butter oozed over the bread.

"No," Jack snapped into the phone and held up an apologetic finger to her.

She nodded, smiled, and took a bite of the roll. Her stomach growled as if it were saying bread alone wouldn't silence or satisfy it. She noticed a bowl of gumbo sitting in front of Jack. She'd kill for gumbo. Too bad Jack had a thing about sharing food.

"Fuck, no!" Jack seethed. "I can't do this."

The F word brought Nikki's gaze up from his gumbo. Jack, a refined lawyer trying to make partner and always concerned about public decorum, seldom cursed. Amazingly, from his viewpoint, screwing your wife's part-time help wasn't considered bad manners.

"Listen to me," Jack muttered.

Nikki recalled Jack taking offense at her occasional slip of "shit," "damn," and "hell"—a habit she'd obtained from hanging out with Nana and the Ol' Timers. Jack had almost broken her of it, too. Then, staring at his Armani suit and his hundred-dollar haircut, Nikki had an epiphany.

Jack had spent the entire two years of their marriage, not to mention the year they'd dated, trying to turn her into someone else—someone who would look good on the arm of a partner of the Brian and Sterns Law Firm. *Don't say this. Say that. Wear this. Do you have to spend so much time with your grandmother?*

Glancing down at her black pants and knit top, she knew he wouldn't approve of her wardrobe. How odd that she hadn't even considered dressing up for the event. Or maybe not odd. It should have been a clue that their reconciling was a joke. Seriously, she hadn't even put on sexy underwear. Her gaze shot back to his gumbo.

Screw Jack's apparel approval and his no-share policy. She reached for the bowl and, suddenly feeling lowbrow and proud of it, dunked her roll in the roux and brought the soupy mess to her lips.

Heaven.

Spotting a floating shrimp in the cup, and not lowbrow enough to use her fingers, she went for Jack's spoon.

He slapped his hand on top of hers and frowned—a disapproving, judgmental frown that pulled at his brown eyes.

Big mistake on his part.

Slipping her hand from under his, she fished out the shrimp with two fingers and ate it. Even made a show of licking her fingers. Jack's mouth fell open at her lack of manners. Not that she cared. Considering the way things were going, the gumbo and rolls were all she'd be having for dinner. She might as well enjoy them.

A tuxedo-wearing waiter ran up and placed a spoon in front of her. Nikki smiled at his pinched, disapproving look, which matched her husband's frown.

"Thank you," she said, proving she wasn't totally lacking in the manners department.

"Something to drink?" the waiter asked, his expression still critical of her lack of etiquette.

"A Budweiser, please." She didn't like beer, but it fit her mood. And just like that, she knew why. All this time—even after she'd caught Jack bare-ass naked with her employee, even after she realized how badly he'd screwed her with that prenuptial agreement—she'd never given Jack a bit of comeuppance. And why? Because she'd been more hurt than angry. Now, realizing she'd stopped loving him, the hurt had evaporated and she was just angry. And it wasn't altogether a bad feeling, either.

Jack stood up. Frowning, he pressed his phone to his shoulder. "Order for us," he said. "I'll be right back." He snatched up his gumbo and handed it to the waiter. "And she'll take a glass of Cabernet." He took off.

Nikki tightened her hands on the edge of the table and considered walking out, but another waiter walked by with a plate of chicken marsala. She inhaled and eyed the waiter clutching Jack's gumbo as if afraid she might fight him for it. And she might have but suddenly, she got an odd aftertaste from the gumbo. "Bring us one beef burgundy and one chicken marsala. *And my beer.*"

After one disapproving eye roll, the waiter walked away.

She'd already sipped from the frosty mug and devoured another roll when Jack returned. He sat across from her and frowned. She snatched another bite of bread, pretty certain her free meal had just come to an end.

His frown faded. "You have no idea how glad I am that you came."

Nikki nearly choked on her bread. What? No condescending remark about her lack of manners? Jack was playing nice. Jack never played nice unless he *really* wanted something.

Did he want her back that badly? It wouldn't change anything, but whose ego couldn't use stroking?

He picked up his linen napkin and dabbed at his forehead where she'd just noticed he was sweating. Sweating was right up there with playing nice. Jack didn't sweat.

Her pinching gut said something was up and it had to do with more than just her. She leaned in. "What's going on, Jack?"

Dallas O'Connor walked into the building that housed both his business and apartment. Stopping just inside the doorway, he waited. Five seconds. Ten. When Bud didn't greet him, Dallas looked over at the coffin against the nearby wall. Someone had opened the dang thing again.

He growled low in his throat, "Get out of there."

One soulful second later, Bud—short for "Budweiser"—raised his head from inside the coffin and rested his hanging jowls on the edge of the polished wooden box. The pain of being chastised flashed in his huge bug eyes. Bud, an English bulldog, hated being chastised.

"Out," Dallas said, lowering his voice. "It's not a doggy bed."

The prior owners of the building, which had been a funeral home, had left the damn casket when they moved out six months ago. Dallas had called and left numerous messages asking them to remove the dang thing, but no response. The last time he'd told them they had one more week, and he was going to sell it on eBay. He was tired of having to explain the casket to his clients.

The dog leaped out of the coffin and barreled over to Dallas. After one swipe over the dog's side, Dallas glanced at his watch and shot back to the office. He found Tyler, one of his Only in Texas Private Investigations partners, listening to the police scanner as he watched the television. Tyler's expression had worry stamped all over it, too.

"He hasn't called yet?" Dallas removed his gun from his holster and placed it in his desk—a habit he hadn't broken from the seven years he'd worked for the Glencoe Police Department. Seven years he wished he could get back. The only good thing that had come from those years was the friendship of his PI partners, Tyler and Austin.

Tyler glanced away from the television. "Not a word. Any luck at the park?"

"There were two female joggers, but neither of them fit the description Nance gave."

Frowning, Tyler leaned back in his chair. "I'm afraid we're not going to get anything to save this kid. He's going to go down for robbery."

"It's not over." No way would Dallas let that innocent boy do time. But right now, both he and Tyler should be worried about one of their own. Dallas motioned to the police scanner. "Have the cops been called out yet?"

Tyler nodded and concern pinched his brows, making the two-inch scar over his right eye stretch tighter. "Thirty minutes ago."

"Shit," Dallas said. "Why the hell hasn't he called?"

"You know Austin," Tyler said. "He's a lone wolf."

"That's not how we operate," Dallas said, but in his gut

he knew they were all lone wolves. Life had taught them that was the only way to live. Getting set up by a low-life drug dealer named DeLuna and then having almost everyone you believed in turn their backs on you—not to mention spending sixteen months in the slammer—well, it did that to you. It made you feel as if the only one you could trust was yourself.

Dallas glanced at the silent television. "Any media coverage?"

"Not yet," Tyler said. "But the cops called for another unit to help hold them back, so they're there."

"Have you tried to reach him?" Dallas dialed Austin's number.

"He's not answering." Tyler grabbed the remote and ramped up the volume. "We got something."

Dallas glanced at the redheaded reporter on the screen, but listened to his cell until the call went to Austin's voice mail and he hung up. The camera closed in on the reporter as she announced a breaking news segment.

"God, she's hot," Tyler said.

Dallas studied the redhead as she held a microphone close to her lips. "You need to get laid."

"Okay," Tyler said. "You want to give my number to that hot brunette I saw leaving here last week? Or tell your ex to pay me a visit. She could leave her underwear at my place, too."

"Funny," Dallas said, and regretted telling the guys about his screwup with his ex. Then again, he hadn't told them. His dog had. Bud had come traipsing into the office the next morning with a pair of red panties hanging from his jowls. Thankfully, Suzan—aka, the hot brunette—was careful to take her underwear with her when she left his bed.

And she didn't expect—or want—more than he was willing to give. The perfect relationship—pure sex. Twice a month, when her ex got her kids for the weekend, she showed up at his place. Most nights, she didn't even stay over. Sex and the bed to himself—what more could a guy ask?

The news reporter started talking. "We're here at the home of Blake Mallard, CEO of Acorn Oil Company. An anonymous caller said Mallard's dirty shenanigans, both with the company and his personal life, were about to be made public." The reporter paused.

"He had to have gotten out." Tyler traced his finger over the scar at his temple. He'd earned it during their stint in prison. While Tyler never talked about the fight, Dallas knew the guy who'd given Tyler the mark hadn't walked away unscathed. Rumor in the pen had it the guy hadn't walked away at all, but had to be carried out on a stretcher. Jail time was never a walk in the park, but Dallas suspected Tyler had had a harder time behind bars than both he and Austin.

The reporter started talking again, and a smile threatened to spill from her lips. "According to sources, Mallard was found handcuffed to his bed with a call girl. The missing files Mallard swore were stolen from his office were found in the room. We're told the cops were called to the residence by Mallard's wife, who was worried someone had broken in."

After a few beats of silence, the reporter continued. "We're told the girl found with Mallard is claiming a guy dressed in a clown costume handcuffed them to the bed and pulled the files from Mallard's private safe."

"Did y'all try to call me?" Austin's voice came from the doorway.

Dallas glanced up. "You..." Words failed him.

"I love it," Tyler said and laughed.

"You mean this?" Austin motioned at his bright red-and-blue polka-dotted clown suit and multicolored wig. Whipping off the wig, he tossed it up and caught it.

Dallas shook his head. "You love theatrics, don't you?"

"Theatrics? Are you kidding? This was brilliance. It's a gated community. I had to get past security. A birthday party was happening next door to the Mallards. They wouldn't let in a guy wearing a ski mask, but a clown? Not a problem." Austin looked at the TV. "Did I make the news?"

"Oh, yeah," Tyler said.

Austin tossed his wig on his desk. "It's not every day we get to solve a cheating-spouse case and a real crime at the same time. It felt good. And now we can put this case to bed and I can focus on proving Nance is innocent."

Dallas raked his hand through his hair. "I'll bet a hundred bucks my brother will be calling me within five minutes, wanting to know if we're behind this."

Austin dropped his clown-suited ass into a chair. "Tell him Miller PD owes me a beer for solving their case."

The reporter appeared on the screen again. Austin looked at the television. "She's hot."

"That's what I said." Tyler grinned.

Austin looked back at Dallas. "Did you get anything at the park?"

"Nothing," Dallas said.

"I'm going to try a few different parks around here," Austin said. "Maybe the chick swaps off and jogs at different places."

"Maybe," Dallas said.

"Did you hear from Roberto?" Austin asked Tyler.

"Yeah," Tyler answered. "None of his leads point to DeLuna."

"Then tell him to get some new leads," Austin said, his frustration clearly showing at having so much time pass since they'd had anything on DeLuna.

Dallas's cell phone rang. He checked the number. "See," he told Austin. "It's my brother."

"I thought pissing off the guys in blue was our goal." Austin crossed his arms.

"You're wrong." Dallas stared at the phone. "Pissing off the lowlife drug runner DeLuna is our goal. Pissing off the guys in blue..." He looked up with a grin. "Well, that's just an added benefit. My brother being the exception, of course."

As his partners chuckled, Dallas answered the call. "What's up, Tony?"

"Damn, Dallas, tell me that wasn't you," Tony demanded.

"What wasn't me?" Dallas shot Austin an I-told-you-so frown.

"Why do I think you're lying?" Tony came back.

"Because you're a suspicious son of a bitch."

Tony sighed. "Can you meet me for a burger at Buck's Place in half an hour?"

"Why?"

"To eat," Tony said.

Dallas wasn't buying it. Not that he and his brother didn't do dinner. They had weekly dinners with their dad. But something told Dallas that Tony wanted more than a burger and fries. To confirm it, Dallas asked, "You paying?"

"Sure," Tony said.

Yup, Tony wanted something. His brother never agreed to pay.

Nikki watched Jack rearrange his silverware in an attempt to avoid her question. "What's going on, Jack?" she asked again.

He shook his head. "Just trouble at work."

"What kind of trouble?"

He shifted his arm, knocking the linen napkin off the table. Scooting back in his chair, he reached to collect the cloth. Falling into old habits, she signaled for the waiter to bring a clean napkin.

"It's okay," Jack said, sitting up.

That's when she knew something had to be seriously wrong. Jack, a germ freak, would never use a dropped napkin.

"Look, the reason I asked you here is...I need a wife on my arm."

"A wife?" Had she heard him right? He didn't need *her*. He needed a wife. Anyone would do. As long as they were trainable and, damn it, she'd proven she was. Only not anymore.

"I realize I slipped up."

"Really, you think screwing my part-time help was a slipup?"

He frowned but before he could answer, his phone buzzed again. He looked at the caller ID. "I have to take this." He put a hand on his stomach and swayed when he stood up. Even though she was furious, she almost suggested he sit down, but then he grabbed her beer and set it down on a table that a busboy was cleaning.

Damn him! She popped up, tossed her napkin on the

table and went to rescue her beer. Eying the busboy, she grinned. "I think I lost this." Then she plopped back down in her seat. She wasn't Jack's to train anymore and when he returned she would, for the first time, tell him exactly what she thought of him. After, she enjoyed her dinner of course.

Five minutes later, dinner arrived but Jack still hadn't. Considering manners were optional tonight, she started without him. She even enjoyed some of Jack's beef burgundy. She'd been so involved in savoring the food, she hadn't realized so much time had passed.

"Is he coming back?" the waiter asked.

"Of course he is." Panic clenched her stomach and she nearly choked on the steak. "He has to."

She waited another twenty minutes, even had the busboy check the bathroom, before she accepted the inevitable. Jack wasn't coming back. The waiter returned with the check and eyed her suspiciously as if to say any woman who would stick her finger in her date's soup was thoroughly capable of the eat-and-run offense.

Glancing at the check, she muttered, "I'm going to kill him!"

"Kill who?" the waiter asked.

"Who do you think?" She peeked at the bill and moaned. A hundred and eighty without tip, then there was the fee the bank would charge her for overdrawing her checking account.

Her stomach roiled again, this time in a bad way. Snatching up her purse, she found her debit card. Thankfully, she had overdraft insurance. With anger making her shake, she handed the card to the waiter. Her stomach cramped. She considered complaining that something she'd eaten had upset her stomach, but she knew how that would look.

"Yup, he's as good as dead!"

"I'm killing him," Nikki muttered fifteen minutes later as she pulled out her already overdrawn debit card again.

The grocery store cashier scanned the Pepto-Bismol, Tums, Rolaids, and antidiarrheal meds before looking at Nikki. "Kill who?"

Why did people think just because she was talking, she was speaking to them? Was she the only one who talked to herself? Nevertheless, with the cashier's curious stare, Nikki felt obligated to answer. "My ex." She placed a palm on her stomach as it roiled.

Holding her purchases in a plastic bag, Nikki couldn't escape quickly enough. She darted out the door. The ball of orange sun hung low in the predusk sky. Her eyes stung. She almost got to the car when the smell of grilled burgers from the hamburger joint next door washed over her and the full wave of nausea hit. A woman with two kids dancing around her came right at Nikki. Not wanting to upchuck on an innocent child, she swung around in the opposite direction, opened her bag and heaved as quietly as she could inside it.

Realizing she'd just puked on her medicine, she lost her backbone, and tears filled her eyes. *Only the weak cry.* The words filled her head, but damn it, right now she was weak.

She rushed to her car, wanting only to get home. Tying a knot in the bag, she grabbed her keys, hit the clicker to unlock the doors and then popped open the trunk.

Tears rolled down her cheeks. Her stomach cramped so hard her breath caught.

She got to her bumper, was just about to drop the contaminated bag into the trunk when she saw . . . She blinked the tears from her eyes as if that alone would make the image go away.

It didn't.

There, stuffed in the back of her car, was a body.

She recognized the Armani suit first. Then she saw his face. His eyes were wide open, but something was missing.

Life.

Jack was dead.

Jack was dead in the trunk of her car.

Her vision started to swirl.

She tried to scream. Nausea hit harder. Unable to stop herself, she lost the rest of her two-hundred-dollar meal all over her dead ex-husband's three-thousand-dollar suit.

CHAPTER TWO

"BUT HERE'S THE best part." Dallas picked up his coffee and eyed his brother over the rim of the cup. "The wife came out of the bathroom and started beating him with a toilet brush. A toilet brush!"

Tony smiled, something he seldom did lately. Then his humor faded. "And this is what you want to do for the rest of your life?"

"We only take on a few of those. We're working real cases, too."

"Like the Mallard case?"

"Mallard?" Dallas feigned innocence, hoping to avoid lying, and looked out the window as a patrol car, lights glaring, pulled into the parking lot next to the restaurant.

"Okay, let's talk about the case you're not even getting paid for," Tony said.

"What case?" Then Dallas remembered telling his brother about the Nance case last week over beers. He probably should be less forthcoming—especially since it was a Miller PD case. Not that robbery was his brother's division.

Tony stirred sugar into his coffee. "Detective Shane called me."

"So you've been sent to tell me to back off." Dallas congratulated himself for knowing something was up.

"He's a good cop. He's certain he has the right guy."

"He's wrong."

"You're not even getting paid for this case, so I don't—"

"You think this is about money?" Dallas, Tyler, and Austin had all gotten a fat check from the state of Texas— as if the state could ever buy back their mistake. Not that they wanted to blow through the cash, but they'd all agreed that stopping another innocent man from going to prison came before getting paid. And Eddie Nance was innocent. Dallas would bet his right testicle on the fact.

Dallas leaned in. "The only thing Nance is guilty of is being black and wearing gray sweats like the guy who robbed who convenience store."

Tony dropped his spoon on the table. "The clerk pointed him out in the lineup. And the kid was picked up less than two miles from the store an hour later. He has priors."

"One eyewitness doesn't make a case. I'll bet there were fifty black men wearing gray sweats in that two-mile radius. And his one prior is for a fight with his buddy over a girl. He's not a criminal. The kid had a scholarship to go to college. Had!"

Tony shook his head, but didn't argue. Dallas wanted to believe it was because his brother knew he was right.

"I can't believe you really want to do this kind of work when you could be doing the real thing," Tony grumbled and pulled his coffee closer.

"It's real. We've even managed to get about six of DeLuna's drug runners off the street."

Tony's frown deepened. "That's why you're doing this whole PI shit, isn't it? To get DeLuna?"

Was his brother just now figuring that out? The way he, Tyler, and Austin saw it, if they kept poking at DeLuna's dirty little operation, sooner or later the drug lord would get mad enough to crawl out from the rock he'd hidden under and face them. When he did, they'd be ready.

"It's not the only reason." That was true, too. Dallas leaned back in the booth. Making sure others didn't get screwed by the system—the same system that had let him, Tyler, and Austin down—mattered as well. And as Austin mentioned earlier, if they managed to piss off the guys in blue, the men who had stood there and watched three of their own get sold down the river, well, that was okay, too.

"You're gonna get yourself killed. And when you do, I'm going to be fucking pissed!"

A second police car, siren blasting, whipped into the parking lot next door.

"Dying's not on my agenda," Dallas said. "Justice is."

"Damn it, Dallas. If you want to go after DeLuna, get back on the police force."

Dallas set his coffee down. "Yeah, well, cops and I don't get along anymore."

Tony pulled out his badge and slammed it down on the table in front of Dallas. "What do you think I am?"

"You're a pain in my ass, but you're family." Dallas wished he could say he didn't miss the job. He did—part of it. But the political bullshit that came with the job... well, they could shove it up their asses. Working cheating-spouses and missing-poodles cases was better than going back to a system that let three of their own get tossed to the wolves. And after all, he and his business partners could turn down the wacky cases. Hell, they did turn down most of them, but they had agreed that the small cases could lead to bigger cases. Plus, it kept some cash flow coming in and gave them something to do besides play spider solitaire.

Dallas's attention went back to Tony. "Besides, you're Miller PD, not Glencoe."

"Then come to work at Miller PD. I could get you on."

"Not interested."

"You're as stubborn as our old man, you know that?"

"Funny, that's what your wife said about you yesterday."

Dallas waited for Tony's reaction. He wasn't disappointed. Tony nearly came out of his seat. "You saw LeAnn? When? Is she okay?"

Dallas had dreaded mentioning his sister-in-law, but Tony would be pissed if he found out Dallas had seen LeAnn and hadn't said anything.

"She had some car trouble about a block from the office. She looked fine."

"Why didn't she call me?"

"Like I said, she was about a block from the office. Turned out to be a loose battery cable. I fixed it and she went on her merry way."

"*You* should've called me. I'd have done it. Maybe she would have finally talked to me. Did you know she won't return my calls?"

Yeah, Dallas knew. It was practically all Tony talked about when he wasn't chewing Dallas out about his new-found profession. But if he'd called Tony, LeAnn would have been pissed. Not that his loyalties went to LeAnn, but… "Weren't you the one who preached to me about finding closure with Serena? About just breaking ties?"

Tony's expression hardened. "That was you and Serena. LeAnn and I are different."

Dallas started to argue, but the pain in his brother's eyes had Dallas pulling back. Tony and LeAnn's situation was different. Heartrendingly different. Dallas wasn't sure that meant they had a chance in hell at reconciling, but what did he know?

Tony leaned in. "Did she ask about me?"

"Yeah, I think she did." She hadn't. But Dallas had told her that Tony had been in a piss-poor mood, that he probably missed her. Another police car whipped into the lot next door. "I wonder what's up," Dallas said more to change the subject than because he was interested in the drama.

"Don't know, don't care." Tony's frustration about LeAnn sounded in his voice. "If it's a homicide they'll call me. What did LeAnn—" Tony's cell rang. He snatched his phone from his belt loop and looked at the number. "Shit. It's a homicide."

Nothing like a little murder to help digest a hamburger. Dallas walked with Tony to the grocery store parking lot. They were met by Juan Bata, a patrol cop a few years younger than Tony. Dallas and Tony had grown up with Juan in the neighborhood a few miles north of town.

"You're fast," Juan said.

"I was next door at the restaurant," Tony answered. "What we got?"

"A no-brainer," Juan said. "Ex-wife."

He waved at a woman sitting on the asphalt in the

middle of a parking spot. She had her arms wrapped around her calves, and her head down on her knees. Her curly blond hair spilled over her legs.

"And dead ex-husband." Juan waved to the car with the open trunk. "Another case of marital bliss."

Tony and Juan moved in and Dallas followed.

"Nasty," Tony said. Dallas stared at the body covered in vomit. Peeking from under the man's expensive suit coat was a white shirt. Or what was once a white shirt. Blood always did a number on white cotton.

"CSU on the way?" Tony asked Juan.

Juan nodded. "Supposedly Blondie puked on him."

Tony took his pen out and lifted the suit coat up to inspect the wound.

"Looks like a knife wound," Dallas said.

"Yup." Tony looked at Juan. "Does Blondie have a name?"

"What we got?" Rick Clark, another homicide cop and one of Tony's friends, walked up. Dallas nodded. He didn't care much for hanging out with cops, but they were his brother's friends so he tolerated them.

"Looks like a stabbing. Found him in the ex-wife's car. And her name is . . ." Tony looked back at Juan.

Juan opened a pad. "Nikki Hunt. Dead guy is Jack Leon."

Jack Leon? The name bounced around Dallas's head and hit some familiar bells.

"She copping to it?" Tony asked Juan.

"Swears she doesn't have a clue how he got there. Said she had dinner with him at Venny's. That's a high-priced place that people like us can't afford. Supposedly, hubby skipped out and left her to pay the bill. Claims she left the restaurant and came here. But get this...she was talking about killing him with the cashier inside the store."

Tony glanced at the suspect. "I do love it when they make it easy for us."

Juan continued to stare at the blonde. "Why are the pretty ones always guilty?"

"She didn't do it," said Clark, sounding almost cocky. "Look at her angel eyes. A woman with those eyes—"

"Forget the eyes, check out that body," Juan said. "Black widows are always hot."

Dallas looked at the woman. She'd raised her head and her round blue eyes seemed to stare at nothing. Her shirt clung to curves. Juan was right. She was hot. Dallas envisioned another hot-looking woman with angel eyes. Betrayal hardened his gut when he recalled arguing with his ex last week.

"The eyes can fool you," Dallas said. "They can suck you in and then stab you in the back. And never even blink with guilt."

Clark looked at him and pulled out his pad. "You ready to put your money where your mouth is?"

"Money on what?" Dallas asked.

"On her guilt," Clark answered.

"Wouldn't be a very fair bet. Everything here points to her being guilty," Dallas countered.

"Everything but me," Clark said, and tapped his forehead.

"That's not the head you're thinking with right now," Dallas said.

"Maybe." Clark smiled, and let his gaze shift back to the blonde.

When Dallas didn't have a comeback, Clark continued.

"Give a guy a chance to win back some of the money you walked away with last weekend in that poker game. I'll make it easy—if we still consider her the main suspect in twenty-four hours, you win. If we're seriously looking into new leads, I win."

"Count me in," Juan said. "I'll go twenty."

"We got a job to do here." Tony, his professionalism showing in his actions, walked over to talk to the suspect.

"You in?" Clark asked Dallas, tapping the pen to the pad.

"You really want to give away your money?" Dallas's phone rang. He checked the number—Austin.

"Come on," Clark said. "You didn't mind taking my money during the poker game."

Dallas nodded.

"Twenty?" Clark asked.

"Fine." Stepping away, he took the call. "What's up?"

"I'm so damn good," Austin said.

"What? You got another clown gig?" Dallas teased and rolled his shoulders to get the tension he felt just from being back on a police scene.

"I found the girl Nance said he'd talked with the night of the robbery. She also jogs at Oak Park. She remembered Nance, confirms his story, said they talked a good twenty minutes."

"Freaking fabulous," Dallas said. "Is she willing to go to the police?"

"Said she was. I got her info. We're getting this kid off. Damn, that feels good."

"Hell, yeah." Victory stirred in Dallas's chest. Deep down, he knew this wouldn't completely prove Nance innocent. The DA would argue the kid had time to get from the store to the park, but it would give his lawyer something to work with.

An ambulance pulled into the parking lot, sirens roaring. Obviously, someone hadn't explained that the situation wasn't urgent.

"Where are you?" Austin asked.

"Would you believe a murder scene?" Dallas gazed back at the blonde.

"That's one way to round up business." Austin laughed. "Who's dead and who's being unjustly accused?"

The realization hit his conscience and went south, and Dallas felt as if it made a direct thump on his balls. He was doing to Blondie what everyone had done to Nance. What everyone had done to him. Hell, he'd even bet a twenty on her guilt.

"Damn," he muttered.

"What?" Austin asked.

"Gotta go." Dallas disconnected. He turned around to see Tony talking to the woman. She'd stood up and had her arms wrapped around her middle as if she was about to fall apart. Maybe it was because she'd killed her husband—maybe it was because she was being accused of a crime she didn't commit.

"Oh God." The blonde swung away from his brother.

Tony moved in front of her. "I asked you a question."

Blondie sprinted five steps, and ran smack-dab into Dallas's chest. When she bounced back a few inches, he grabbed her arms to steady her.

Her tear-filled baby blues met his gaze and, for some crazy reason, all Dallas could think about was how soft her skin was under his palms. They stared at each other, one, two seconds.

"You okay?" he asked, reading all sorts of panic in her expression.

"No." She shook her head and her curls bounced around her face. Then she doubled over and puked all over Dallas's shoes.

Stunned, he stared at his Reeboks and, before he came to his senses enough to move, she puked again—making a direct hit in the middle of his chest.

CHAPTER THREE

A WHILE LATER, Nikki lay back on the hospital bed and stared at the IV pumping fluids and meds into her veins. Her mind reeled. She glanced around for her purse, wanting to call Ellen, needing a bit of moral support. Then she looked at the clock. Ellen had already closed shop. Gone to teach her yoga class.

Gone. Gone. The word stuck in her head.

Jack was gone. Jack was dead. The image of his body being pulled out of her trunk flashed in her head. She remembered the blood and her stomach roiled.

She was probably going to have to get new carpet laid in the trunk of her car. When she'd first spotted Jack curled up in her trunk, she'd missed the blood. But when the coroner had gotten Jack's body out...

The image flashed again. Her stomach threatened to revolt. Not that it had anything left to revolt with.

The two-hundred-dollar dinner was long gone. She was down to dry heaves and felt certain she'd blown a lung in the process.

Jack was dead.

Now she wasn't sure if it was panic making her sick, or Venny's chicken marsala.

Finding out meant her overdrawn account now topped the thousand-dollar-mark. Yeah, she'd opted for the high-deductible insurance. Nikki seldom ever got sick. Plain and simple, she couldn't afford to be sick.

But she was sick now. So sick, she'd barfed all over her stomach medicine, all over her ex-husband's body, and all over the guy she'd collided with at the parking lot. Had he been a cop or just a bystander? The question rolled through her head as another wave of nausea roiled through her stomach. Clutching the pink plastic tub the nurse had given her to use if she got sick again, Nikki fought the desire to throw up.

She closed her eyes and could see the stranger back at the parking lot looking down at her—his blue eyes were darker than hers. But his dark brown hair and olive complexion made his eyes more noticeable—strikingly noticeable. And she'd noticed the look in those eyes— concerned and almost apologetic—even when she'd *obviously* been the one needing to apologize. But she didn't have a clue about the etiquette required in this situation. She'd never thrown up on anyone before.

First, she'd gotten his shoes. And then...Oh Lord, she didn't want to think about the mess she'd made of his shirt.

Or the look on his face. Or the laughter she'd heard in the background.

"Don't think about it." Her mind flashed to Jack's shirt—to all the blood.

Dead. Jack is dead. "Don't think about it."

Her chest ached. She hadn't felt one flutter for her ex when she saw him at the restaurant, but for almost three years she'd loved him. Adored him. Her world had revolved around him, trying to make him happy, trying to be the wife he wanted, and then he broke her heart. "Don't think about it."

"Don't think about what?" a male voice asked from the door.

Dallas, shirtless, parked between Austin's and Tyler's cars in front of the office. Grabbing his hurled-on shirt from the floorboard, he hurried inside. Bud, his tongue hanging out and his whole short and stocky body wagging in joy at his master's return, met him at the door.

"Hey, Bud." Kneeling, he patted the dog. "No!" Dallas said when the canine went straight for his shoes as if he smelled something appetizing. In a hurry, Dallas stood and walked toward the office where he'd heard voices. Bud followed—his paws clicking against the hardwood as they went, and his nose still sniffing the air.

Popping his head in the office door, Dallas said to his partners, "Do me a favor and Google a Nikki Hunt and give me the highlights of what you find. Then get me the address to Venny's Restaurant while I take a really, really fast shower." He met Austin's gaze. "Good job on the Nance case. I owe you a beer."

Tyler tapped into his computer. "Nikki Hunt, come to Papa." He looked up. "What's up? Did the woman steal the shirt off your back?"

"Not quite," Dallas said. He'd tell them later and give them a good laugh—not that he thought it was all that funny. But the guys at the scene hadn't stopped laughing when he left. Frowning, Dallas headed down the hall with Bud following. Home, sweet home.

When Dallas had found the building and approached Tyler and Austin about opening Only in Texas, their own PI agency, both guys had flinched at the price of the building. Dallas remedied that by paying the extra fifty thousand and having a portion of the building converted into a small apartment.

Stepping into his bathroom, he started to toss his shirt into the dirty clothes but tossed it in the garbage instead. Kicking off his shoes, he set them up on the counter, away from Bud. Undressed, not even waiting for the water to warm, he popped into the shower, lathered, rinsed, and then grabbed a towel.

Half-dressed moments later, he opened the door that led into the hallway back to the office. "Get anything?" he called.

"There's two Nikki Hunts," Tyler called back. "One's a dancer at a men's club—very hot—the other's an artist and almost as hot. Which is she?"

"You know which one we're voting for, don't you?" Austin called out.

Dallas slipped a shirt over his head and envisioned the woman back at the parking lot. She'd been hot, but was she the stripper kind of hot? Were strippers that soft?

"I don't know," he answered and ran a hand through his wet hair. "They both local?"

"Almost," Austin answered. "The stripper's in Houston."

"Blond?" Dallas offered.

"Both blond." Tyler's laughter rang out. "Wait, I know. Is she a C or double D?"

"C," Dallas answered.

"The artist wins," Tyler answered.

"Damn," said Austin. "I was hoping you knew the other one and would introduce me."

"Like I wouldn't keep her for myself." Dallas grabbed his keys and walked back down the hall, stopping at the office door. "What else did you get?"

Tyler looked up. "She has a gallery—sells her work and that of a few other artists in a shop on the square."

"Is this connected to the murder case you crashed?" Austin asked seriously.

"Yeah."

"Not the victim?" Tyler glanced back at the computer with sympathy.

"Nope. Her ex's body was found in her trunk."

"Did she do it?" Tyler asked.

"Not sure." Dallas mentally flinched when he remembered how he'd condemned her. "Did you get the address to Venny's?"

"Yeah, it's 2234 Walters Street. But you better put on a tie. It's upscale."

"I don't think I'll be dining." Something clattered at Dallas's feet. He looked down to where Bud had dropped his food bowl. "Is food all you think about, boy?"

"It wouldn't be if you let him get a little," Austin kidded.

"As soon as he proves he knows how to use a condom, I'll let him do that." Dallas started out.

"You need company?" Tyler asked.

Dallas looked back. "Nah. But could you walk and feed Bud? I might be late."

"Oh, speaking of Bud." The humor from Tyler's voice faded. "I forgot to tell you, you got some papers from Serena's lawyer."

"Shit!" Dallas spun around, walked into the office and snatched the envelope from Tyler's hand. He ripped it open and read the first few lines. "She's fucking doing it. Can you *fucking* believe she's actually doing it? Joint custody, my ass!"

Tyler leaned back in his chair. "It's you she wants, not the dog."

"You shouldn't have given her a taste of the good stuff," Austin said, smiling.

"It was revenge sex," Tyler piped in. "I wouldn't mind having a shot at revenge sex with Lisa. Screw her hard then tell her to go screw herself."

"It was a damn mistake." One Dallas sorely regretted, too. He'd just gotten the apartment finished and had a few guys over for a poker game to christen the place. The guys had left, and Dallas was finishing off the last beer—two past his limit. When Serena showed up claiming she wanted to check on Bud, he'd been just drunk enough to let her come in. Just drunk and horny enough not to fight off her advances. Though he clearly recalled telling her, *"If we do this, it doesn't mean a thing."*

He'd no more than rolled off her when he remembered the ring on her finger and realized he'd been wrong. It had meant something. It meant if Serena was capable of sleeping with him while she wore Bill's engagement ring, then maybe she'd been capable of sleeping with Bill, her boss for the past five years, when she'd worn his wedding ring.

When he'd confronted her about it, she'd admitted they'd had a one-time fling but, of course, she assured him that it hadn't meant anything at the time.

Right.

He'd been pissed. And not even because she'd cheated.

But because not once during his marriage—and damn if he hadn't turned down some nice-looking ass—had he cheated on Serena. And why? Because he'd been a friggin' idiot.

Dallas stared at the papers. He started to crumble them in his fist when the lawyers' names at the bottom of the stationery caught his eye.

Jack Leon. That's why the name had been familiar. The dead guy in Nikki Hunt's trunk was part of the hot-shot law firm Serena had used to get her divorce and was now using in a custody battle for Dallas's dog.

With his mind back on the murder, he tossed the papers on Tyler's desk. "Do me another favor. Do a search on Jack Leon, the lawyer, and call me. And don't forget to feed Bud."

"What is it you aren't supposed to think about?"

Nikki glanced up as Detective Anthony O'Connor strolled into her little curtained area. She almost thought it was the guy she'd used as a barf bag. But nope, just the head honcho cop who'd accused her of killing Jack.

Not that she was too worried. She was innocent. Only the guilty worried, right?

"Sorry," Nikki said. "I talk to myself a lot." The nausea pulled at her stomach and she pulled the pink tub closer and looked at the bag of fluid hanging to her left. The doctor said the meds in the IV would "*eventually*" calm her stomach.

"Maybe you can tell me what 'yourself' is saying about what happened tonight."

There it was again—the accusation in his tone that was mirrored in his expression. His eyes tightened, his right eyebrow arched slightly, and he pressed his lips together in a thin line. If he was trying to intimidate her, he could give himself a high five. His disapproving glare was downright daunting. Had they taught him that look in the police academy?

Maybe I should be worried. "You really don't think I did this, do you?" Her stomach roiled again. She eyed her IV. "Eventually" couldn't arrive soon enough.

"Did you do it?"

"No." She sat up and squared her shoulders, trying to come off as a person with strong character. Of course, that was hard to do when you wore a backless hospital gown and held a Pepto-Bismol–colored, hospital-regulation barf tub in your lap.

His arched brow said he didn't believe her.

What could she say to convince him? Or maybe she shouldn't say anything. She considered asking for a lawyer, but decided to just puke instead.

Or she should say, she decided to go through the motions of puking.

When the dry heaves passed, he handed her a damp cloth. She raised her eyes to his dark brown gaze, hoping the suspicion had vanished. Nope. Obviously, the detective could be nice to people he considered murderers.

"Why would I put him in my trunk?" she blurted out and used the cloth to wipe her face in case she had any residual drool from her newly acquired pastime.

His gaze grew colder. "Why don't you tell me?"

"Why don't you leave the room for a minute?" The nurse, a full-figured African-American woman, walked into the room. "I need to get some blood." The nurse shot the detective a cutting look and he left.

Nikki looked at the nurse. "I didn't kill my ex."

"Honey, the way I see it, if your ex was anywhere near as bad as mine, or as rude as that cop was to me when he brought you in here, you did the world a favor."

Watching the blood fill the vial, Nikki remembered Jack's shirt and fought another wave of nausea.

When the nurse left, Nikki leaned back and closed her eyes. She wasn't sure how much time had passed when she heard someone clear his throat. She opened her eyes and was hit again by the accusation in the detective's eyes.

"I think you were about to explain how your ex-husband's body got into your trunk."

"No, I wasn't about to explain that. Because I didn't put Jack in my trunk. I didn't shoot him. I don't own a gun. Don't even know how to shoot one." She looked at her hands. "Shouldn't you be doing one of those powder tests on my hands?"

He cocked his head to the side and studied her. Hard. He looked as if he was about to say something profound, something important. She held her breath and waited.

And waited.

When he didn't speak, she dropped back against the pillow. Who knew puking took so much energy?

He pulled a notepad from his pocket, jotted something down, and then raised his eyes again. "You know the grocery store cashier said you were talking to her about killing your ex?"

"I wasn't talking to her, I was talking to myself. She just assumed I was speaking to her. I mutter when I'm upset."

"Were you upset enough to kill him?"

"He stuck me with the bill at Venny's. Do you know how expensive that is? So, yeah, I was furious. Furious enough to say I wanted to kill him, but...but I'm not a killer. I even use catch-and-release mouse traps."

The crinkle in his brow confused her. Did he believe her or not?

He scratched his head. "What do you do when you catch them? Put them in your trunk?"

She blinked. "No. I take them outside and let them go."

"Oh." He continued to look at her. "Don't they just come back inside?"

She recalled Nana and Ellen asking her the same thing. "Probably, but my point is I don't kill them. Because I'm not a killer."

He didn't seem impressed. Obviously, using live traps wasn't considered evidence. Glancing back at his pad, he asked, "What were you and your ex arguing about at the restaurant?"

"We weren't arguing. He wasn't thrilled when I used my fingers to fish out the shrimp in his gumbo, but we didn't argue."

"Then why did he leave and stick you with the bill?"

"I don't know. He was on the phone when I got there. He left, then came back and told me he was in some kind of trouble. I asked what was going on, but his phone rang again and he said he had to take it. He asked me to order and walked away."

"She's telling the truth," a deep, male voice said from directly behind Detective O'Connor.

Nikki had to lean a good five inches to the right to look at the face of her much-needed, much-appreciated, supporter. Not that looks mattered. If she wasn't in desperate need of a breath mint, she would have kissed him. She really needed someone in her corner right now.

The moment her gaze met his blue eyes, her focus shifted downward to the dusty blue T-shirt stretched across his wide chest. Thank goodness he'd changed his shirt.

Detective O'Connor swung around and faced the newcomer. "Why are you here?"

"I just got back from Venny's Restaurant, spoke to the waiter." His blue-eyed gaze met hers again and he nodded.

"Damn it, Dallas," the detective said. "You're not a cop."

Not a cop. Dallas. Taking in the information, she watched the two men face each other.

Dallas stuffed both his hands into his jeans and frowned. "But I am a PI."

So not-a-cop Dallas was a PI. What was a private investigator doing here?

"This isn't your problem," Detective O'Connor insisted. "Don't you even start messing with my case."

"You mean helping, right? Because I just gave your boys the heads up on the real crime scene in back of the restaurant. I'm betting Ms. Hunt was parked back there." Dallas looked at her. "Right?"

Nikki nodded.

"Blood?" Detective O'Connor asked.

"Yup. There was also a set of keys, which I pointed out to your guys. I'll bet you'll find they belong to her ex. And if my hunch is right, you'll find he had a key to her car."

Both men looked at her to confirm. "He used to have one," she said, trying to understand what this meant. "You think he was stealing my car?"

"Not necessarily," Dallas said. "But it would explain how he got inside your trunk."

"Fine," Detective O'Connor snapped. "So you've managed to show up my men by getting to the restaurant first."

"Actually, they were there first. They just didn't check the parking lot in the back."

"Just get the hell away from my case." Detective O'Connor's grimace deepened.

The intimidating scowl didn't seem to affect Dallas. "Just trying to get to the truth."

"We'll get to the truth," the detective said.

"Oh, like the system doesn't make mistakes." Now, Dallas looked mad.

Detective O'Connor didn't back down. "This isn't the system, it's me. I don't make mistakes."

Ignoring the last statement, Dallas looked back at her. He seemed to focus on the Pepto-Bismol–pink tub in her lap. "Considering what else I found in the parking lot, it appears as if the vic was also sick. I'm thinking someone slipped something into their dinner."

"Someone poisoned me?" Nikki asked.

"She's not your client," the detective snapped, ignoring Nikki.

Dallas glanced at her. "She could be."

"Someone poisoned me?" she repeated.

Her question remained unanswered while the two men continued arguing. While she hated to be a pest, her question seemed kind of important. Didn't the doctors and nurses need to know if she'd been poisoned?

"Are you trying to piss me off?" Detective O'Connor demanded.

"No. I'm trying to help Ms. Hunt," Dallas said.

"Hey," Ms. Hunt said, her mind still on the possibility of being poisoned. "Was I—"

"You don't even know her," Detective O'Connor accused.

The PI smiled at her. "We bonded."

"Did someone really poison me?" she repeated again.

"Was that before or after she puked on you?" Detective O'Connor asked and the PI looked back at him.

"I think it was during." Dallas turned his grin toward her again.

"Bonded my ass. She puked on you. Next you'll tell me you consider that your retainer."

Dallas shifted his attention back to the cop. "Hey, that works."

"I asked a question." Nikki's stomach cramped and she put a hand on her middle. She felt sick, but how sick? What kind of poison had she ingested? Was it lethal? Was she bleeding to death on the inside while these two stood by arguing about God only knew what?

A cell phone rang. Detective O'Connor grabbed the phone from his belt loop, scowled at the PI then took the call. "Hello. You're breaking up. We have a bad..." He paused. "I know, Dallas just informed me. Get CSU down there. Hey...you're fading out again. Let me call you back." Detective O'Connor pointed a finger at Dallas and said, "Don't do this to me." Then he walked out of the curtained cubicle.

Nikki, hand still placed over her roiling stomach, watched the detective leave then refocused on the blue-eyed private investigator. "Did someone poison me?"

CHAPTER FOUR

TONY COULDN'T FRIGGIN' believe his brother would start this shit with him. Frustrated, he dialed Clark's number. Cell phone pressed to his ear, Tony walked down the hall until he got to the nurse's station. Clark answered.

"Hey, it's me again," Tony said. "Just get CSU there. Make sure..."

Damn! His phone started fading out again. Looking up at the glaring nurse, he snapped his phone shut and focused on her. "You need to run a tox screen on Ms. Hunt. There's a chance she might have been given something against her will."

"The other cop, the one with manners, already told me," the nurse said crisply.

Tony frowned. What had he done to piss *her* off? He recalled getting pushy to get the blonde brought back in the ER right away. Hell, she'd already puked all over his brother, and Tony hadn't wanted to be her next victim.

Staring at the nurse, he realized the nicer cop she alluded to had to be Dallas. Tony didn't bother correcting her. Instead, he started down the hall to find a place where he could call Clark back. He went the way he thought would have an exit, but didn't find it. He looked at his phone, found it had all the bars, then he spotted the visitor's room. He had one foot inside when he heard a familiar sound.

He stopped, thinking he'd imagined it. But the light-hearted, warm-the-soul kind of laugh sounded again. *LeAnn.*

Swinging around, he spotted his wife standing at the nurses' station, her back to him. He hadn't known she'd switched hospitals. His chest grew heavy and light at the same time. Damn, he'd missed her. He ran a hand through his hair, and took a step toward her.

Her hair hung longer. The soft brown strands bounced against her shoulders, and Tony's hands itched to touch them. He'd loved her hair long and begged her not to cut it. But she'd insisted that short hair would be less time consuming.

Had it really been nine months since he'd seen her? Not that he hadn't tried. He left messages on her phone once a week, telling her the same thing. He wanted to talk. He could understand why she was mad. But he was so damn sorry.

She had yet to call him back. He kept telling himself she would eventually give in—that the time away was his punishment for walking away from her when she'd needed him the most. Funny how back then he'd thought time away would help things. Now, he saw it for the mistake it was. He'd fucked up but, damn it, didn't he deserve a chance to fix it?

He almost got to the nurses' station when he realized she wasn't alone. A man, a doctor-looking sort, stood beside her. He stood too damn close, too. And the way he looked at LeAnn left little doubt of his intentions. Tony held himself in check. Or he did until the white-coated man touched his wife's cheek.

Tightening his fist, Tony hurried his last steps. Thankfully, LeAnn stepped back and the man dropped his hand.

Obviously hearing his footsteps, LeAnn turned. "Can I help..." Her bright green eyes widened. "Tony."

"LeAnn." He forced himself to unclench his fist and smile. Though he wasn't sure the smile came off real. At best it was probably rusty. He hadn't had a lot of reasons to smile lately.

The doctor said something under his breath. Tony met his eyes briefly and hoped like hell the man could read his mind. *Stay the fuck away from her.* As if he had picked up on Tony's thoughts—or maybe it was the murder in his eyes—the man left.

"Is everything okay?" LeAnn asked.

"It is now," he said, pushing his frustration back and hoping to make the most of this unexpected gift. "You look...fantastic." When she didn't reply, he continued. "When did you start working here?"

"Yesterday. I...I needed a change."

He nodded and, damn it, but he wanted to touch her so bad he had to stuff his hands in his pockets to fight temptation. "Dallas said you had car trouble last week."

"Is that why you're here?"

"No. I'm here on a case."

"I thought you worked homicide now."

So she'd cared enough to be curious about what he was doing. Did she also know he lived and breathed for the moment they could get back together? "I am. I have a possible suspect, but she's sick. We found her ex-husband dead in her trunk."

"That's terrible," she said, though Tony wasn't sure if she was really interested or just needed something to say. "Do you think she killed him?"

"I don't know yet." He studied his wife and opened his mouth to say something about the case. Instead the words, "I miss you so damn much," came out.

She looked away, but not before he saw frustration hit her eyes.

Damn it, he'd screwed up by moving too fast. Then he decided to go for broke. "I call and leave messages and you never call me back."

She continued to stare down at the desk. "I know." Opening one of the files, she studied it. "I'm not ready to deal with this yet, Tony."

"It's been nine months."

She raised her gaze and when he saw her eyes wet with emotion, pain ripped at his chest.

"You promised you wouldn't pressure me," she said.

"And you promised me if I moved out we'd see a marriage counselor."

"Why do we need go through this? Can't we just let it go?"

"Not if it means letting go of us!" he said. "That's the only reason I agreed to this separation, LeAnn, because you promised we would talk. I know I screwed up. When I took the job, I wasn't thinking. It wasn't supposed to last but a week, I thought a few days apart would—"

"Stop." She held out a hand. "I don't blame you for taking the job, okay? I could hardly stand being with myself."

Her words hit like an eighteen-wheeler without brakes. "Damn it, LeAnn, I didn't leave because of you. I left because..." Two more nurses walked up to the station.

"Later, okay?" There was a pleading in her eyes.

He leaned across the counter and said in lower voice, "When?"

"Soon," she said under her breath.

Unable to resist, and realizing the nurses had their backs to them, he reached across the counter and ran the back of his hand across her cheek. "I'm off Sunday," he whispered. "I'll be over around ten a.m."

The word "no" formed on her lips. He didn't give her a chance to say it. Swinging around, he left. His heart pounded in his chest. He looked at his watch, counting the days, and hours until Sunday. He knew he'd been pushy and yet, damn, he'd been patient for nine months. He wanted his wife back and maybe it was time for him to stop being patient and go get her.

He was almost back to the ER when his phone rang. Frowning, he stopped to see who was calling. It was Juan Bata. What did Juan want?

Tony answered the call. "What's up, Juan?" If the guy had just called to gab, he didn't have time.

"Something strange is going on," Juan said. "I think it's connected."

"What's connected?"

"Remember the barfer?" He chuckled.

"What about her?"

"Well... her place..." Static followed.

"Her place... what? Juan? You're breaking up. I'll call you right back." Tony ran off to find a place where he could get reception.

*   *   *

Nikki stared at the PI and waited for him to answer her question. "Was I poisoned?"

"It's a possibility," he said. "Did you two share any of the same food?"

"No," she said, shaking her head. "He didn't even eat. Wait—the gumbo. But I only had a bite."

"You're small." His gaze slid down her front as if measuring her. "It wouldn't take much."

Nikki instantly became aware of the thinness of the gown, of how little she had on beneath the cotton. Little as in nothing. Her stomach cramped and she remembered she might have been poisoned. She started looking around for a nurse's call button.

"You need something?" he asked.

"A nurse or a doctor," she said. "I think they should know that I might have been poisoned."

"I already mentioned it to one of the nurses."

"Oh." She settled back. He kept studying her and she kept checking to make sure the gown hadn't slipped off her shoulder. He made her nervous, jumpy, and aware of how terrible she looked. She ran a hand through her hair. Not that her appearance should be high on her list of concerns. Face it, puking on a man didn't tend to leave a great impression. And with her official barf bucket still in her lap, she doubted her second impression was much better. "I...I should apologize for throwing up on you."

He grinned. "I'll admit it's not the reaction I usually get from women."

She stared at his smile, at the way his mouth tilted a bit higher on the right than the left. She could guess what kind of reaction he normally got from women. The man oozed charm. The kind of charm that got a girl in trouble. *The kind of charm Jack has.*

Had.

Jack is dead.

She pushed that thought aside to deal with later. Right now, she needed to find out why the PI was here. Then again, it could only be one thing: money. He wanted her to hire him. Good luck with that. She was probably going to have to lay off her best friend, Ellen, from the gallery, and hiring someone else was out of the question. A pity he'd gotten barfed on for no good reason.

"So you're a PI?" she asked.

"Yup."

"What do you do, chase cops around to get cases?"

He grinned. "Actually, I was having dinner with the detective when the call came in. We were at the restaurant next door."

"So you know each other."

"Yeah, I'd say that."

The room became quiet again. Her stomach fluttered. Not the nausea kind of flutter, but the kind she'd been almost hoping to feel when she saw Jack. The kind fueled by either hormones or emotion, the kind that stemmed from either love or lust.

Since she didn't know diddly-squat about this blue-eyed devil, love wasn't in the picture.

That left lust. *Oh hell.*

The flutter hit again and her heart did a little dance to the theme song from *Jaws*. Sure, she'd known that sooner or later her ability to feel something for the opposite sex would return. And in another year or so, Nikki might even have been able to open herself to the possibility.

But today? Was the universe screwing with her on purpose?

Didn't she have enough on her plate being accused of killing her ex-husband and possibly being poisoned, not to mention the guilt of telling Nana her cable would be nixed and informing Ellen her part-time job was over?

"Shit," she muttered.

"What?" he asked.

"What, what?" She looked up at him, and fought the need to cry.

"You said 'shit.' I wondered what's wrong."

"I said that aloud?" She bit down on her lip as a morsel of panic stirred. Surely, she hadn't mentioned anything about lust or sex...had she? "That's all I said, right?"

He looked confused, but grinned. "What else did you think you said?"

"Nothing." She sat up straighter then, realizing "eventually" had finally come and the nausea had passed. She placed the pink tub on the bedside table. "Here's the deal. I appreciate what you've done. But..."

"Appreciate what?" His lips didn't show it, but his eyes smiled. "Are we talking about my retainer again?"

Her cheeks warmed. "I was thinking more along the lines of standing up for me to the cop."

"Oh. Yeah, it's nice to have someone in your corner, isn't it?"

Something about the sincerity in his eyes, said he'd been there, done that, and wore the T-shirt. "Yeah. It sucks."

He casually crossed his arms and leaned against the one real wall in the three-sided curtained cubical. And dang blast it, if he didn't have leaning down to an art form. He looked really good leaning—the pose made his shoulders appear like a solid lean-on-me wall of strength, the blue shirt pulled a bit tighter across his chest and hard torso, and, in the slightly slanted position, his biceps appeared flexed.

Her fingers itched for a pad and paper to sketch him. He'd make a great painting. Lots of body language that said, "bad boy" but at the same time whispered, "hero." While his features were completely different, his presence reminded her of the old images of James Dean, a movie star her grandmother swore had been the best-looking man alive.

Realizing she was staring, she spoke up. "Like I said, I appreciate it, but...I don't need a PI. I'm innocent."

He pushed away from the wall and tucked one hand into his jeans pocket—causing more flexing in his right forearm. For some totally illogical reason, she wondered what it would feel like to be held in those arms. In the last twelve months, she'd nursed her broken heart and damaged self-esteem. Plus, she'd managed to fall out of love and lust with a man who at one time she thought hung the moon and—truth be told—she hadn't missed sex a whole heck of lot. What she'd missed was having someone, a male someone, hold her. Dallas looked down at her. "Sometimes being innocent doesn't mean a hill of beans."

"I'm sure Detective O'Connor will figure it out. He's being a big jerk right now—don't tell him I said that—but...I trust justice will prevail."

All traces of his earlier smile vanished and he looked serious—even coplike. "You don't really believe in prevailing justice, do you?"

She took a deep breath. "I'm trying hard to. And

you're not helping." She nipped at her lip then decided to be completely honest. "Okay, here's the thing. I'm having a cash flow problem. I can't afford you."

"You don't know how much I charge."

"Does flat broke mean anything to you?" she asked.

She expected him to nod, wish her good luck and walk out. He didn't.

"Not an issue. I do payment plans."

"Yeah, well, I don't do payment plans. Not when the financial future looks bleak."

His blue eyes met hers and held. He didn't just stare, he searched...studied.

She clutched her hands together, feeling naked under the heat of his gaze. She sat up higher. Her unsupported girls swayed against the thin cotton.

His attention lowered for a fraction of a second to her unintentional bounce. "I'm not opposed to bartering."

Her breath caught. Okay, she'd misread the hero image. "I don't do *that,* either."

"Don't do...?" His eyes crinkled at the corners with suppressed laughter. He let go of a light chuckle. "I'm honored your mind took you there."

"My mind didn't take me anywhere. You did."

His grin didn't waver. "I don't see how, because I was talking about your paintings."

CHAPTER FIVE

IT HAD BEEN a while since Dallas had seen a woman blush. While he'd never thought of it as sexy, he was having second thoughts. Maybe even a few thirds. He found her...refreshing. He couldn't pinpoint exactly why. Perhaps because her emotions were so readable...or maybe it was her frankness, her unpretentiousness. Though, after you upchucked on someone, he supposed it was hard to be pretentious.

"My paintings?" Her big blue eyes seemed bluer when she blushed.

"You're an artist, right?"

She nodded.

Sensing he'd made her uncomfortable, he pulled back his smile.

She tugged at the sheet around her waist. "How did you know I was an artist?"

"I excel at my job." He hesitated. "I had one of my partners Google you."

She half-grinned. "Of course." She stared at her hands and, when she glanced back up, he spotted a determined glint in her expression. Then she squared her shoulders and her chin inched up.

She was planning to tell him no. And here he thought he'd spotted some intelligence in those baby blues. What a shame.

"Look, I appreciate the offer, but I...I don't think I need a PI. It's like you said, the waiter is going to confirm my story. When the detective talks to the waiter—"

"That's exactly why I think you need me."

"What?"

"I didn't mention this to the detective, but the waiter was more than eager to tell me that you told him you were planning to kill your ex."

"But—"

"No, let me continue." He moved closer. He couldn't force her to accept his help, but he'd be damned if he wouldn't tell her the facts. And no matter how refreshing she came off, he wouldn't sugarcoat it. "First, because nine times out of ten a person is murdered by someone they know, the cops always suspect the victim's spouse or ex. And statistics prove them right. Oh, and in this case, the victim's ex is...." He pointed at her. "You."

"Yes, but—"

"Let me finish." He stepped closer, and lost his train of thought when the hospital gown slipped down her shoulder, exposing what he knew would be very soft, feminine skin. So okay, in addition to refreshing, he found her sexy as hell but it meant nothing and he pushed those thoughts aside. "Then the cops always look hard at the last person who is known to have seen the victim alive." He looked directly at her. "And, that would be...you."

She started to speak again and he held up his hand.

"Another thing the police look at is where the body is found. Correct me if I'm wrong, but wasn't it found in the trunk of *your* car?"

"I didn't kill him." She tugged her gown up. The concern in her voice sent an ounce of relief to his gut. "And you found his keys. That will explain how he got in there."

"That's going to help. However, innocent people are seldom caught driving around with a dead body in their trunks."

Those big angel eyes blinked. "Do you get a kick out of scaring people?" she asked, showing a little spunk behind her softer appearance.

"I do if the person is too stupid to realize she needs to be scared."

Her mouth dropped open. "Did you just call me stupid?"

"Depends. Did you change your mind about accepting my help?"

"Are you always so arrogant?" she came back, her spunk level up another notch.

"It comes and goes. But it mostly happens when I know I'm right."

She didn't reply, and he hoped that was because she knew he was right, too. But something about the tilt of her chin said she hadn't completely thrown in the towel, so he continued. "The only suspect that might trump one of those other situations is the person who was heard making physical threats to the victim. And damn, I think you were heard not once, but twice saying you wanted to kill him."

"I didn't mean it. I would never..." She pressed her palms against her eye sockets and moaned. "I use live mousetraps. I can't even kill a rodent."

"Really? By damn, make sure you tell that to the police," he said, and cut his eyes upward.

Her shoulders dropped in what he hoped was resignation.

"I already did." She brought her knees to her chest and wrapped her arms around her sheet-covered legs. "He wasn't too impressed."

Dallas almost laughed, imagining his brother's reaction. Especially because if there was one thing Tony hated, it was mice.

"I'm not a killer," she said. "Was I mad at my ex? Yes. And not just about him leaving me to pay the bill, but about... other stuff."

"What other stuff?"

She hesitated.

"It's all going to come out sooner or later," he insisted.

She let go of a breath. "A year ago, I caught him having sex with my part-time help on my office sofa." She sank her teeth into her bottom lip.

"Ouch. What did you do?"

"Fired her. Divorced him. And got rid of the sofa."

He grinned. "Bet you miss the sofa."

"Actually, I do." She frowned.

Dropping her head on her knees, she stayed like that for several minutes.

She finally raised her head. "I didn't kill him," she repeated.

He held up his hand. "You don't have to convince me, Nikki. I believe you." The moment he said it, he realized it was true. He believed her. Just like he believed Nance was innocent. "But when the cops and the DA look at this, I'm not so sure they'll see it my way. Not that their opinions are the end-all. The million-dollar question is: Do you think a jury of twelve of your peers will believe you?"

She stared at him, and he could see the doubt building in her eyes. "I'm not going to wake up and find out this is all a dream, am I?"

"Afraid not. This is a big mess you've got yourself into. The only thing that could make this case worse is if you're the beneficiary of your ex-husband's life insurance."

She blinked. "I think he changed that. Oh, hell, I don't know if he did."

Dallas crossed his arms over his chest and leaned against the bed. "Boyfriend?"

"Huh?" she asked.

"Do you have a boyfriend who maybe wanted to get back at your ex?"

"No," she said.

"Seriously?" He couldn't see someone like her not having men at her doorstep.

"Seriously."

"Lover?" he asked, not accepting that she didn't have some guy warming her sheets at night.

"I said I don't have a boyfriend."

"And I asked if you had a lover."

Her soft blond brows puckered ever so slightly. "And those are different, how?"

Damn, she was one of those women who looked cute when they got their feathers ruffled. He opened his mouth to explain the difference between casual sex and a relationship, knowing it would ruffle her some more, but he stopped. No doubt, Nikki knew the difference. She just didn't consider but one an option.

And what a shame. He continued to stare at her. "You need me, Nikki."

"Because I don't have a boyfriend?" she asked, her eyes tightening.

"No, because you're up to your pretty little eyebrows in trouble."

She let go of a deep breath and said, "How many paintings?"

Relief brought his smile back. "Maybe we should wait and see how much time I have to put into the case." In truth, he didn't give a flying flip about her paintings. The only reason he'd suggested it was because he sensed she had too much pride to accept his help for free. She could be painting Elvis on velvet for all he knew.

He let his gaze move over her briefly—gorgeous hair, expressive eyes, lips that could fuel wet dreams. Breasts—real breasts. Silicon didn't shimmy and shake like hers. And the softest skin he'd ever felt.

She wasn't tall. He did like long legs, but he had a feeling he wouldn't miss them if he got to check out the entire package hidden behind that hospital gown.

The tightening low in his gut sent his moral compass to full alert. The woman was in the hospital for Christ's sake—had been puking her guts out, and here he was getting hot for her. Telling his libido to take a hike, he ran a hand over his face and stared at the curtain to clear his head.

"My paintings usually sell for between eight hundred and three thousand dollars."

Forcing himself to look at her, he kept his eyes above her neck. "We'll work that out later."

She shook her head and the damn gown took another

slip off her shoulder. His moral compass got skewed again. He watched her pull it up.

"How much do your services run?" she asked.

"We'll work that out later, too." Oh, hell. He'd rather have what she'd first assumed he'd wanted to barter for, some no-strings-attached sex. Then again, hadn't he just come to the conclusion that Nikki Hunt didn't have no-strings-attached sex? While less than an hour ago, he hadn't known her well enough to say she didn't take her clothes off for a living, now he felt all the wiser. Something about her screamed pillow talk, slow walks on the beach, stay-overs, and commitment. All the things he'd given one woman, and vowed to never give another.

"So how do we proceed?" She nipped at her pouty bottom lip.

Carefully. The one word bounced around his head as he tried not to think about how he would like to be the one nibbling on her bottom lip. "That depends."

"On what?"

"On whether or not I arrest you," Tony answered, appearing at the curtained entrance. "Can I talk to you?" he asked Dallas. The clenched muscle in his brother's jaw told Dallas that something had happened. "Now."

Dallas looked at Nikki. Panic, no doubt at the thought of being arrested, rounded her blue eyes. Seeing her look so vulnerable and scared kicked his protect and serve instinct into high gear—never mind that he didn't carry the badge anymore.

He opened his mouth to tell her not to worry, to promise her he'd take care of everything. But that would have been a lie. First, Nikki Hunt was in a whole hell of a lot of trouble, and second...while Dallas might do everything humanly possible to prove her innocent, he didn't make promises he couldn't keep, especially to soft, angel-eyed women who would want more than he could give.

"I'll be right back," he said.

"You can be a bastard, can't you?" Dallas told Tony as soon as he cleared the curtain.

"Bastard?" Tony led him through a doorway to an empty corridor. "She's a murder suspect. Or have you forgotten what that means?"

"Yeah, well, seeing I was one of them myself not too long ago, it doesn't mean shit!"

His brother stopped walking and shook his head. "Okay, here's the thing. I get the fact that you are sympathetic. I'll even admit I see what you're saying about this Nance kid being innocent. But this is me. *My case.* Don't you know me well enough to know that I'm fair? That I'm not going to push for a conviction unless I believe it's warranted?"

"What I believe is that if she looks guilty, you'll do your job. And your job, the job I used to do, sometimes puts innocent people in bad situations."

"You don't know she's innocent," Tony snapped.

"My gut says she is."

"Your gut isn't the body part in charge right now. It's your dick. Admit it. You want to get in her panties."

"I don't want—"

"Bullshit!" Tony jabbed a finger at him. "If you believe that, then you're lying to yourself. I saw the way you were looking at her."

Dallas gritted his teeth. "Okay, she's hot. I wouldn't mind tapping it. But that's not why I believe she's innocent."

"Innocent? Are you sure about that?" Tony asked.

"Yeah. I am." His confidence rang in his voice, too.

His brother crossed his arms. His eyes pinched and his mouth pulled a little to the right.

"What?" Dallas asked.

"What, what?" Tony said.

"That's your negotiating face. The last time I saw that look I ended up taking Dad for his colonoscopy. What deal are you going to try to strike with me now?"

Tony continued to stare. "Do you know she told the waiter she was going to kill her husband?"

"Yeah, I know," Dallas said. "And do you know that she drove straight from the restaurant to the grocery store, which didn't leave her any time to kill him?"

"Not if she killed him immediately after leaving the restaurant."

"How would she have gotten him in the trunk?"

"He's wasn't that big of a man. I've seen smaller women handle that and more."

They stared at each other until Dallas finally asked, "So what are you chewing on right now?"

"Get her to voluntarily hand over her clothes to be tested for blood spatter."

"In exchange for what?" Dallas asked, suspicious.

"I won't arrest her and I'll keep looking for suspects."

Dallas crossed his own arms. "Two questions."

"Shoot."

"One: Why me? Why don't you talk her into giving up her clothes?"

Tony grinned. "I've haven't had much practice talking women out of their clothes. Besides, I thought you were helping her. Plus, it's like you said earlier: you two bonded." He held up one hand. "She could have puked on me. But she chose you."

Dallas didn't smile. "Two: What is it you're not telling me?"

Tony's brown eyes pinched tighter. "What do you mean?"

"Don't shit me. We both know she wouldn't be walking out of here unless you had a reason to think she didn't do this."

At least Tony had the decency to look guilty. "She thinks her ex was shot." He raised an eyebrow. "She could have been playing me."

"But you didn't think so," Dallas said.

"Right."

Dallas continued to stare at him and somehow he knew there was more. "And . . . ?"

Tony sighed. "I got a call from Juan. Ms. Hunt's an artist, owns a shop off the town square."

"And as Dad would say, what does that have to do with the price of tomatoes?"

"Juan's at her gallery now. The employee working at her place was found stabbed. It happened an hour ago. Nikki couldn't have done it."

"Told you she was innocent," Dallas said.

"Of this, yes. Of her ex-husband's murder, we still don't know."

"Come on," Dallas said. "Are you saying you think this is a coincidence?"

"I have to do my job," Tony insisted.

As much as Dallas hated admitting it, he knew his brother was doing what he had to do. It didn't change the fact that what he had to do could possibly put an innocent person behind bars. "Is the employee dead?" Dallas asked.

"Not yet, but Juan said the medics didn't seem sure she'd make it. The ambulance is bringing her here. That's all I know." Tony's expression hardened. "When she gets here, you stay out of my way. I accept that you want to help Ms. Hunt, but you need to know that if I find out she has something to do with this, I'm coming after her. If I have to barrel through you to get to her, so be it."

Dallas looked back toward the ER and wondered how close Nikki was to her employee. If he read her right as the type who treated everyone like family, they were probably close. "Are you planning on telling Nikki?"

"I thought you might like to do that?"

"That's your job." Dallas's gut knotted at the thought of being the bearer of bad news.

"Yeah, but remember I'm the mean bastard."

"You don't have to be," Dallas said.

"She's a suspect. I can't go soft on her. She'll take it better from you."

"You're just afraid she'll start crying."

"Guilty." Tony started walking back toward the ER. They continued in silence for the next few seconds before Tony asked, "Did you know LeAnn worked here now?"

"At this hospital?"

"I just spoke with her. When I heard her laugh, I swear I died and went to heaven."

Tony smiled—a smile like Dallas hadn't seen on his brother's face in a long time.

"So it went good?" Dallas asked.

"Not really." Tony's smile faded. "She was laughing

with some asshole doctor. But I think I know what I have to do."

"What's that?"

"Win her back." He inhaled. "She looked good. I'm getting her back." His smile returned, even bolder this time.

Dallas glanced at Tony and wondered if he had that goofy look on his face when he used to talk about Serena. Serena, the woman who'd walked out on him when he'd been accused of murder. Serena, who'd admitted to sleeping with her boss when they were married. God, was he ever one fucked-up idiot. He never wanted to smile like that again.

Never again, he thought. Not that he wished Tony bad luck, but love had made a fool out of Dallas once, and he wasn't going there again.

"And how do you plan to win her back?" he asked his brother.

"I'm still working on that, but I know this much. For nine months I've played by her rules. *Stay away. Give her time. Don't push.* It hasn't worked. Now, I play by my rules."

"And those are?"

"Anything and everything goes," Tony said.

They arrived back in the emergency room. Dallas looked at the curtained-off area where Nikki waited. "You said the ambulance's coming here?"

"Yep," Tony said. "And from what we know, she's still alive."

Dallas took a step then stopped. "I hate delivering bad news."

Tony nudged him. "I'll be right out here if you need me."

Dallas knew his brother was a coward. But when it came to dealing with emotionally distraught women, so was Dallas. He remembered the look in Nikki's big blue eyes when she heard his brother suggest he might arrest her. As the investigating officer, Tony's job practically mandated he be curt. Nikki Hunt would probably take the news better from him.

Dallas slipped between the curtains to face the music. Only problem, there was no music to face. Nikki Hunt wasn't there. The IV needle that had once been injected and taped to her wrist, now dangled downward and dripped onto the floor.

A woman's purse lay open on the hospital bed, some of its contents spilling over the mattress.

He stepped out of the curtained space. Tony met his gaze. "Problems already?"

"Yeah." Dallas looked up and down the hall. "Just a little one. About five-five, blond, and . . . very soft."

CHAPTER SIX

"SHE RAN?" TONY jerked the curtain back and stared at the empty hospital bed.

"We don't know that." But damn it if Dallas's mind wasn't moving in that direction. Not that running made her guilty—he still hadn't changed his mind about her being innocent. He personally knew how it felt to be accused of a crime you didn't commit. Hell, running had crossed his mind once or twice, too.

"Fuck it!" Tony snapped. "Let's break up and search for her."

Tony stormed off and Dallas could hear him drilling the nurses about Nikki's disappearance. That's when Dallas's eyes moved back to the purse and items on the bed. If the woman was running, wouldn't she have taken her purse or at least her wallet?

He picked up the red wallet and thumbed through it. *Does flat broke mean anything to you?* He recalled her earlier words. Good to her word, he found no cash, not even any loose change. But her debit and credit cards peeked out of the little pockets beside her driver's license.

He didn't know a woman alive who would leave home without her credit cards. He studied the purse's other contents: a tampon, a pen, a crossword puzzle book, a few receipts, a tube of lipstick and blush, a flash drive, a small can of Mace, and a pack of gum.

He snagged a piece of cinnamon gum, and started dropping the items back into her purse. That's when he realized the one thing that was missing. The thing most women kept as close as their credit cards. A cell phone. And that's when he pretty much figured what happened. Turning around, he walked out of the ER and looked for the first exit sign.

LeAnn O'Connor, on a much-needed short break, stepped outside of the hospital and walked to the small veranda where employees ate their packed lunches. The eight o'clock sun was gone, but its heat hung on, and the sky was still light. Half-afraid she'd launch into a stress-induced panic attack, she hoped the air outside would make breathing possible. Not that it was the inside air causing her lungs to fail. Nope. Her inability to breathe had nothing to do with air contaminants and everything to do with seeing her husband for the first time in nine months.

She knew facing him was inevitable. She just hadn't expected it to hurt this much. Or maybe she had. Maybe that's why she'd been avoiding him. Her hands shook and the hole that existed where her heart used to be seemed emptier, bigger and more painful than ever. Tears filled her eyes, but she refused to let them fall.

Heaven help her, but he'd looked good. And when he'd leaned across the counter and invaded her space, he'd smelled good, too. He'd smelled like...home. And that's what Tony had always been to her. Home. A sense of belonging, of believing she mattered, of having a special place in this big old world that hadn't felt so lonely.

Thanks to her sole parent, Colonel Becker, she'd seen a lot of that world. Texas, Florida, New York, California, even Germany and Japan. She'd moved a total of twenty-two times in her life. The day she graduated high school, her father had handed her a checkbook with enough money in it to cover her living expenses and college education. She got birthday cards, Christmas cards and an allowance until she finished college. She'd seen him three times since she'd graduated nursing school. He was, after all, a very busy man. LeAnn hadn't pressed for more than he'd been willing to give her. But make no mistake, she knew what she had never received from her father and it was the thing Tony gave her. Love and the feeling that she belonged, that she had a home. But then that, too, was ripped away from her.

Reaching up, she brushed a hand across her cheek, still feeling Tony's touch against her skin. When, she wondered, would she stop loving him? When would she stop missing what they had, and accept her life now? Hadn't she spent a lifetime accepting? She should be good at it by now.

She'd read about a dozen self-help books and all the bits of advice had started to sound the same. Move on. Let go of the past. Learn to live with the grief.

None of them, however, told her how to do it. How to forgive herself. How to forget.

I'm off Sunday. I'll be over around ten a.m. His words played like music in her head.

Closing her eyes, she knew Sunday couldn't happen. She wouldn't be there.

Something warm and wet hit the tip of her forehead. She reached up, touched the mess and pulled her hand back. Eww. Bird poo. Looking up, she saw a white pigeon perched on the limb of a tree. "You're kidding me?" she yelled at the bird.

The dang thing ruffled his feathers and went for a repeat performance. Stunned, she didn't move fast enough and the second drop of bird shit hit her on the cheek.

"Just freaking great!" She wiped it off, or tried to. More than likely she'd just smeared it across her face.

"Some people think that's good luck," a female voice said from behind her.

Swinging around, LeAnn eyed the woman standing there in a hospital gown with a cell phone held to her ear. She held up her finger as if asking for a minute and then spoke into the phone. "Nana? Pick up. Please," the woman said, sounding almost panicked and then she paused. "Nana, where are you? I didn't have good reception and the only thing I was able to hear was that there was lots of blood. Is someone hurt? I'm waiting to hear from you. Call me right back." The woman punched a button on her phone and dropped her hand.

LeAnn noted that the woman's complexion looked pale. Well, of course she was sick. She was in a hospital gown. The wind kicked up a bit and the woman's thin hospital gown shifted in the breeze. That's when LeAnn noticed the blood dripping from the patient's wrist.

"Are you okay?" LeAnn motioned to the bloody appendage.

"Just the IV," the woman said. "I sort of forgot about it when I left." She pointed back to the door. "The connection is bad in there." She pressed her thumb over her wrist to staunch the bleeding and then stared down at the phone.

LeAnn eyed the woman's hand and decided her bleeding wasn't fatal, but... "Maybe we should get you back inside."

"Not until I hear from my grandmother. I think something's wrong." The blonde looked up. "You have bird poop right..." She touched her cheek.

"I know," LeAnn said. "And you're still bleeding. We should get you inside."

"In a few minutes. I'm sure she'll call me back." The woman swayed and quickly sat down on the bench seat. The pigeon in the tree cooed extra loud. The blonde looked up and LeAnn took a step back, not chancing a third hit.

"I don't know why they think it's good luck." The blonde refocused on her phone.

"Me, either." LeAnn wondered if she should get someone to help convince the woman to go back inside. "But I could use some luck."

"Me, too." A hint of desperation sounded in her voice.

"Bad day?" LeAnn asked.

"Extra bad."

"Same here. I just had to face my estranged husband." LeAnn wasn't sure why she offered that information, other than she hoped to get the woman to trust her enough to come inside.

"I could top that." The woman closed her eyes. "I found—"

The door from the hospital building swung open. For a second LeAnn thought it was Tony stepping out the door. Her heart dropped to her stomach, but she quickly recovered when she realized it was Dallas, her bother-in-law. But why was he here?

"Dallas?" LeAnn said.

He turned his gaze away from the blonde to LeAnn. "Oh, hey. I was . . . looking for Nikki."

The blonde stood up. But then her phone rang and she whipped around and answered the call. "Nana? What's wrong? I only could hear part of what you were saying."

"You know her?" LeAnn asked Dallas.

Dallas nodded but his attention stayed on the blonde and her phone conversation. Right then, another gust of wind blew past and flipped open the back of the patient's hospital gown, exposing her backside.

LeAnn looked at her brother-in-law, who was staring at the blonde's ass. Then he glanced at LeAnn and shrugged as if to say he hadn't meant to see it. But then, in typical male fashion, he cut his gaze back to get a second eyeful.

Men! LeAnn cleared her throat. Dallas winced.

Fortunately, Nikki reached back and caught her gown while she continued talking. "What? I mean . . . is she okay?" The panic in the other woman's voice caught LeAnn's attention, or was it the fact that she swayed on her feet again? Either way, LeAnn, forever the nurse, moved in. But Dallas beat her to the woman's side.

"Where?" Nikki asked the caller, then holding a hand out to stop Dallas from grabbing her, she gripped the table. "What hospital?" There was a slight pause and then she turned around and dropped down on the bench's wooden seat. "Okay. That's where . . . I'm here now."

"How do you know her?" LeAnn asked Dallas, but he was too busy listening to the phone conversation to answer.

"Yes," Nikki continued. "I'll explain later. I'm fine." She disconnected. But she sat there and stared at the phone as if trying to cope with some terrible piece of news. Empathy filled LeAnn's chest. She knew all about trying to cope.

Nikki looked up at Dallas. "Someone...someone attacked Ellen, my friend. She's being brought—"

"I know." Dallas's gaze moved to Nikki's bloody hand. LeAnn saw Dallas's eyes fill with tenderness and concern. Her throat tightened, as she remembered when Tony had looked at her with the same caring O'Connor expression. *Home*, LeAnn thought. She missed it so damn much.

Dallas touched Nikki's arm. "We should get you back inside."

"Why would someone do this?" Nikki pressed two fingers over her trembling lips. "I don't understand any of this. Why?"

"I think getting her inside is a good idea." Knowing Dallas would help convince the escaped patient to return to her hospital bed, LeAnn moved in and helped raise Nikki from the bench seat.

Nikki eased away as if not wanting any help. And because LeAnn knew what it felt like to not want others to pity you or treat you as a basket case, she let go.

Nikki walked toward the door, but before she walked through, she looked back at Dallas. "You thought I'd run, didn't you?"

Run? LeAnn didn't understand, but decided now wasn't the time for inquiries.

"No," Dallas answered too quickly. "Not at all."

LeAnn didn't know her brother-in-law that well. He'd been sent to prison right after she'd started dating Tony.

But she knew him well enough to know he'd just lied. Plain and simple, O'Connors sucked at lying.

They walked down the hospital hall and into the ER unit. A familiar voice rang out. Before LeAnn could turn and run, Tony came barreling up.

"Damn it. Where did you..." He stopped bellowing at Nikki when he spotted LeAnn.

LeAnn stopped breathing again. Time froze and both Dallas and Nikki stared at Tony.

"She was making a call." Dallas broke the awkward silence, and shot Tony a back-off look. Not that Tony noticed. He was still too busy staring at her. And LeAnn's heart was too busy missing home for her to think straight.

Tony finally looked at Dallas and grimaced. "So she just yanked out her IV?"

Dallas frowned. "Maybe what happened was—"

"Maybe you should ask me," Nikki said.

"Okay, I will." The scowl line between Tony's brows tightened. "Why did you pull your IV out?"

LeAnn knew her husband could come off as a hard-ass, and perhaps Tony in cop mode was just that. But beneath that tough exterior was a man who cared deeply—a man who always tried to do the right thing. She knew, because she had been his right thing.

"I didn't pull it out," Nikki said. "I forgot it was in. I got a call from my grandmother and all I could hear was something about blood and then the connection went out. I panicked and left to find a place with better reception." Nikki frowned. "And I just learned that some-one attacked my friend. She's being brought here in an ambulance. Why is all this happening? You're a cop, you should—"

Tony's scowl line faded. "We're trying to figure it out."

That's when LeAnn finally figured it out herself. Nikki was the woman Tony thought had killed her ex-husband. LeAnn looked at the accused and decided she didn't believe it. And seeing as how she'd spent her entire life meeting strangers, she had a knack at reading people—distinguishing the good from the bad. It was part of basic survival. And LeAnn knew that Nikki wasn't bad. Tony's gaze landed on LeAnn again. Emotion tightened her chest. "I'm ... I need to get back." She walked away.

"LeAnn." Tony's voice stopped her. She turned around. He touched his cheek. "You have ... something."

"Bird shit," she said before she could stop herself. Then for some unknown reason, she continued, "It's supposed to be good luck."

Feeling her face heat with embarrassment, she met Nikki's gaze. "I hope things go okay." As she darted off to the restroom, one thing was clearer than before: she couldn't—wouldn't—do next Sunday. She wasn't emotionally capable of dealing with Tony yet.

And perhaps it was time to see a lawyer to get things settled so she didn't have to face him ever again.

Nikki saw the way the detective watched the nurse leave. Then she saw the way the PI—her PI—was watching the cop. If she wasn't so worried about Ellen, if she hadn't found her ex-husband dead in her trunk, if she hadn't been poisoned, she might have started wondering about the strange way everyone was behaving. But the hint of curiosity vanished when sirens echoed from outside the double doors leading out of the emergency room.

Nikki turned toward the sound.

Dallas caught her arm. "Let them see to her first."

Trying to think straight, she swallowed a deep gulp of air. "Oh God. Her family needs to be called. I don't have their home number."

"They've already been called," Detective O'Connor said, but he didn't look away from the nurse disappearing down the hall.

A few nurses ran out the double doors and Nikki's heart tightened for her best friend. She took a step closer to the door leading to the ambulance.

Dallas caught her arm again. "Why don't we—"

"I want to make sure she's okay," Nikki said.

"Tony can find out and let us know. Right?" Dallas looked at the detective.

"Yeah," his brother said.

Nikki stared at Dallas's face and then at the detective's serious expression. She got a terrible feeling. "How bad's Ellen? Do you know something you're not telling me?"

Dallas appeared to flinch, and the detective cleared his throat and answered, "All we know is that it's serious."

"Define serious." Fear bounced around her completely empty stomach then crawled up her throat and crowded her tonsils. "How serious?" When neither man answered, a vision of Ellen fluttering around the gallery filled Nikki's mind. Ellen—so filled with life, so upbeat, so positive, so caring. Ellen—the single parent to her little girl.

"Get back in the room!" A nurse ran to the unmanned desk and picked up a phone. She punched a few numbers and then started spouting out orders.

Dallas gave Nikki's arm a pull. Nikki stepped back. Three doctors sprinted down the hall to meet the arriving patient.

A gurney, surrounded by a crowd of people, came barreling through the doors. They all talked at the same time, calling out heart rate, blood pressure, O negative blood, stat.

Nikki stared, hoping to see Ellen. Just a quick glance to know she was okay. Just a tiny sign that told Nikki this wasn't as bad as the detective made it sound.

Dallas tried again to nudge Nikki back to her cubicle, but she yanked free. She had a mission and its name was Ellen. Finally, a small clearing appeared through the haze of the ER crew. But all Nikki could see was Ellen's arm. A very limp arm hanging down with blood dripping from the fingertips.

"No!" Nikki bolted for the gurney. Dallas caught her around her stomach and pulled her back a couple of steps. She yanked free, and took one step when a large male hand caught her arm and another hand moved down her lower back and she was swooped off her feet.

"Put me down!" She felt a cool breeze on her backside and realized Dallas's palm pressed against her bare bottom. She put a hand on his chest and looked into his dark blue eyes so he would know she was serious. "Put me down."

"Sorry." Ignoring her order, he carried her into the curtained-off room and carefully placed her in the hospital bed beside her purse.

Shaking, not so much from anger—though there was some of that, too—but mostly out of concern for Ellen, she stared up at him. Her gaze shot to the open slit in the curtain. She considered making a run for it, a run back to check on Ellen.

"Don't do it." From the way he stood at the end of the

bed, feet planted slightly apart, and determination etched onto his face, he looked capable of catching her.

That's when logic wiggled its way into her mind. She couldn't come between Ellen and her doctors—couldn't slow down whatever treatment Ellen needed.

Her insides started to shake again. "She's my friend," Nikki said around that knot in her throat and swatted a tear that rolled down her cheek.

"I know. And that's why you need to let the doctors do their thing. You understand?"

"No." She shook her head. "I don't understand. I don't understand why any of this is happening. Who would want to hurt Ellen?"

"We'll figure it out," he said calmly.

She bit down on her lip to stop herself from crying. *Crying doesn't solve anything. Crying is for the weak.* How many times had her mom told her that the first six years of her life? Enough that at twenty-seven, it was still tattooed on her memory.

She felt Dallas's gaze on her and for some odd reason she remembered his hand against her backside. Taking a deep breath, she swung her legs over the side of the bed and, reaching behind her to make sure the back of the robe was securely tied, she stood up.

"What are you doing?" he asked.

"Looking for something." She didn't glance at him as she opened the little cabinet beside the bed. Hadn't the nurse put the bag of her stuff in here?

"What are you looking for?" His voice came out soft, as if he was dealing with a child or someone who wasn't in their right mind.

And yes, she accepted that, for a second there, she'd

lost it. But for good reason. She'd wanted to make sure Ellen was okay. "Just...something."

"What?"

She turned around and stared at him. "My underwear." She wasn't sure why she'd had to remove them, but she recalled being told by the nurse that she had to remove *everything*. Now that she wasn't trying to throw up her heart, she realized that didn't make sense. She hadn't been here for a pap smear, so why had she needed to remove her underwear?

"I...have them," a male voice said at the opening of the curtain, and Detective O'Connor entered the small space.

Nikki looked at the detective and then at Dallas.

She recalled at some point thinking these two men looked alike. Now that they were standing shoulder to shoulder, she realized just how much they resembled each other. Not that the detective gave her the stomach flutters like Dallas did. Now she wondered if her recently hired PI—whose job was to prove her innocence—was somehow related to the detective whose job seemed to be to find her guilty.

Her mind went back to the problem at hand—her lack of panties—and she recalled what the detective had said.

"Why do you have my underwear?" she asked.

CHAPTER SEVEN

A KNOT FORMED in Dallas's stomach at the look on Nikki's face. His gaze shot to his brother, hoping Tony handled this well.

"Why do you have my underwear?" Nikki repeated when Tony didn't answer.

A few more seconds of silence ticked by. Dallas cleared his throat. "Evidence," he said.

"I thought you'd run," Tony answered.

Dallas wished he'd had a chance to explain without Tony's presence.

"Evidence?" she asked and then, shutting her eyes for a second, she muttered, "Oh yeah."

It was as if she'd forgotten she was suspected of killing her husband. How she could forget it for even a second was beyond Dallas. Then he recalled how upset she was about her friend. He didn't want to downplay that situation, but he worried that she didn't realize how serious her own problems were.

"He can only keep them if you agree to let him have them," Dallas explained.

Tony shot Dallas a frown. "I could get a court order and force you to comply."

"Just explaining her rights." Dallas looked back at her and continued. "However, I recommend you let him have them. If there is no blood splatter on the clothes, it'll corroborate your story."

Nikki stared down as if considering her options.

"Or I could obtain a court order," Tony said. "Place you under arrest and wait for the test results. The choice is yours."

Her gaze shot back to his brother. "So if I cooperate, you're not going to arrest me?"

"Correct," Tony said. "Of course, the investigation is still open, and if the evidence comes back—"

"Just say yes," Dallas said, stopping his brother from scaring Nikki more than he had. Couldn't Tony see the woman was at her wits' end?

An ER doctor, a tall, exhausted-looking brunette, popped in behind the curtain and looked at Tony. "I'm Dr. Rodriguez. You wanted an update on the stabbing victim's condition?"

"Yes. Thank you." Tony started to step out of the room.

"No," Nikki said. "Please, I need to know, too. She's my friend."

From the look on the doctor's face, Dallas worried it was bad news. But either way, Nikki deserved the truth. "She has a right to know," he said.

Fifteen minutes later, alone, worried and still sitting in the hospital bed, still hearing the words the doctor had confided in Tony, *They're doing all they can*, and *It's critical*, Nikki nipped at her lips and waited to hear news about Ellen's emergency surgery. A new nurse had come in and put a bandage on her wrist, scolding her about leaving her bed, but they'd decided she didn't need another IV.

Alone again, Nikki saw the curtain shift to the side ever so slightly. She sat up higher as a nose appeared, followed by an eye in the slit as if the person didn't want to make a commitment to enter. It was the nurse Nikki had run into while calling Nana. The one the bird had pooped on. And, if Nikki remembered correctly, she thought the detective had called her LeAnn.

After giving the small area a glance, the nurse stepped inside the curtain. "I come bearing gifts." She held out some folded scrubs. "Dallas called and asked if I could get you something else to wear besides a hospital gown to leave the hospital. It's not Valentino, but they're comfy."

"Thanks." Nikki inwardly softened at the thought of Dallas taking care of her needs, and she took the thin cotton uniform from the woman. "It's LeAnn, right?

"Yeah." She nodded. The room went quiet and LeAnn continued, "He also told me about your friend. I'm really sorry. Dr. Peters is the surgeon working on her and, believe me, he's the best we've got."

"I hope so." Nikki bit down on her lip again, found it sore, and inwardly scolded herself for doing it.

"I also heard about...your ex-husband. And that they think you were poisoned."

"Yeah," Nikki said. "It's been an all around crappy day."

"No shit," LeAnn said, and half-smiled. "I guess you were right, huh?"

"About what?" Nikki asked. Since she was feeling as if she was in a place where everything went wrong, if she was actually right about something she wanted to know what.

"You said you could top my bad day...earlier, by the picnic table."

Nikki sort of remembered them talking about that. Hadn't LeAnn said something about—

"If it makes you feel any better," LeAnn continued, "I know he can come across as a hard-ass sometimes, but my husband is good at his job. He'll take care of you."

Nikki tried to wrap her mind around exactly what LeAnn was saying. "Dallas is your husband?"

"Oh, no. Tony`is...was...soon to be was...my husband."

Nikka was curious about the whole is/was dialogue, but didn't feel comfortable enough to ask, so instead she asked for clarification. "Tony being...the detective?"

"Right," LeAnn said.

Nikki remembered something else she was curious about. "And that would make Dallas your...?"

"Brother-in-law."

"So they're brothers." Okay, Nikki shouldn't have been surprised, but she was. Dallas seemed eager to prove her innocent, while his brother seemed almost as eager to find her guilty. Or at least he suspected her of being guilty. She wondered if she could trust Dallas to help her when it appeared his brother was rooting for, and was the captain of, the other team.

She bit down on her lip, unsure what to say. Nikki didn't want to tell LeAnn that she was right—her husband was a hard-ass—or that she wasn't sure he was so eager to help her. Nor did she want to tell her that she was really happy Dallas wasn't her husband. Nikki didn't want to analyze her reasons for being so happy about his unattached status, either.

Then again, she'd already admitted to having a slight case of lust going on. However, she'd be stupid to even consider letting it go anywhere. And Nikki Hunt wasn't stupid. She might be weak on occasion. But—

"Hey?" A familiar male voice boomed from the curtain's entrance and when Nikki's eyes landed on all six feet plus of Dallas O'Connor, she was reminded of how weak she was. There was just something about a pair of wide shoulders and strong arms that said *lean on me*. Nikki knew she'd have to be careful not to do too much leaning.

He glanced at LeAnn and then at the folded scrubs Nikki held to her chest. "You found something for her to wear. Good." His half smile came off tender, and Nikki took another swipe at her sore bottom lip with her teeth.

"They aren't much better than a gown," LeAnn said. "But at least she won't be mooning anyone again." LeAnn cast a chastising look in Dallas's direction.

Nikki gulped. "Did I...?"

"No." Dallas frowned at his sister-in-law.

Nikki didn't know him well enough to swear it, but her gut said when his eyebrow twitched like that, he was probably lying. She was in the process of sticking that little piece of information into her memory for future use when voices exploded from the other side of the curtain.

"If Jack Leon is dead, I'll celebrate later. For now I want to see Nikki!"

Nikki's heart clutched at her grandmother's words. The curtain to Nikki's cubical was yanked back. Standing behind Dallas was Nana. Nana, all suited up in what looked like a dress from the eighteen hundreds. Nana with a cowboy hat hung down her back and fury in her eyes. It took a second for Nikki to remember that her grandmother was playing Annie Oakley at the local theater. And standing behind Nana was her contributing cast, four of the Ol' Timers group, all in western garb, and behind them was one very unhappy, hard-ass detective.

"You all can't be back here." A nurse popped into the scene and her eyes widened, right along with Dallas's and LeAnn's, at the garb of the Ol' Timers. But Nikki didn't flinch because Nana and this bunch were always up to something.

"Costume party?" the nurse asked.

"Dress rehearsal," Nana's friend Benny answered.

Nana, aka Annie Oakley, ignored the nurse and barreled past Dallas. "My gosh. What happened?"

The warm, aged hands of her grandmother came to rest on Nikki's face. The hands that had tenderly cared for Nikki since she'd been a child.

The warm loving touch on both her cheeks, along with the fear in her grandmother's expression, had Nikki's eyes growing moist. Damn it, she wanted to be the one taking care of Nana, not the other way around.

"I..." She tried to talk, but then had to swallow the need to cry.

Nana leaned in. "That piece of shit cop right there insinuated you killed your ex-husband. Then he said they thought you might have been poisoned. And now Ellen? What the hell is going on?"

"Some of you cowboys are going to have to saddle up and leave," the nurse said.

"Oh, goodness, Nikki, are you okay?"

Nikki opened her mouth to answer Nana, but her throat tightened and she couldn't talk.

"Nikki's fine, ma'am." Dallas took a step closer, and rested his hand on Nana's shoulder.

Nana looked first at Dallas's hand then his face. She did a double take to Detective O'Connor, and then settled her eyes back on Dallas. "I don't know you from Adam, young man, but I already don't like you just because you look too much like that bastard." She pointed to Dallas's brother.

Dallas's eyes rounded and his mouth went slack. Detective O'Connor cleared his throat, and looked about ready to read Nana the riot act or her Miranda rights—or maybe both—but then his gaze fell on LeAnn and his expression shot from anger to longing.

"I...need...to go." LeAnn swung around and ran face first into the curtain and fought with the thin material for a few long seconds before she finally managed to pull it over her head and disappear.

Everyone's eyes went back to Detective O'Connor. His scowl returned. "I didn't say she'd killed anyone."

"And I didn't say you said it," Nana said. "I said you insinuated it."

"And I said you can't all be back here." The nurse's voice grew louder. Another nurse stopped and peered in. "Rodeo in town?"

"Dress rehearsal," Nana said.

"I suggested we change clothes," said Helen, who had been Nana's best friend for as long as Nikki could remember. Helen met Nikki's gaze. "But your grandma was too worried about you."

"Took me fifteen minutes to lace up this western garb. I didn't have another fifteen to get out of it." Nana gave Nikki's hand a squeeze and then looked back at the detective.

"And for the record, Nikki couldn't hurt a fly. She even uses release traps to catch rodents."

Dallas coughed, but Nikki could have sworn it had only been to cover up a laugh. Not that she thought it was funny. The knot in her throat remained tight.

"Nikki informed me of that fact." The detective's frown deepened when he looked at his brother.

"Why, Nikki's an angel," said Helen with all the confidence she could muster while dressed like a nineteenth-century saloon girl, with her aged cleavage spilling out of her dress. "And whoever killed Jack Leon deserves a medal."

Nikki's heart did a quick jolt. Before, when anyone said anything bad about Jack, she secretly liked it. But now that he was...dead, well, it didn't have the same effect.

"Please," Nikki said. "Can we just—"

"If you have to have a suspect, then slap a pair of handcuffs on me. It's not as if I haven't had them on before," seethed Nana. "Seriously, I threatened to neuter his butt every time I laid eyes on him." She glanced at Nikki and then back at the cop. "And who do you think poisoned Nikki? Or hurt Ellen? Or have you been too busy accusing my granddaughter of a crime she didn't commit to go out there and find the real criminal?"

The nurse put her hands on her hips. "Do I need to call security?"

Nana scowled at the nurse again then glanced back at Nikki. "How's Ellen?"

"In surgery," Nikki said, finally able to talk.

"Can you people not hear me?" the nurse snapped.

Nana huffed and glanced back at the Ol' Timers. "Can

you guys go to the waiting room before this woman has an aneurism?"

A chorus of, "Fine," "Sure," and, "I guess," answered her.

They all nodded at Nikki. Well, everyone except Benny, the man who had a romantic interest in her grandmother. He stood there, dressed like an old lawman with a tin star pinned to his chest, and peered at the cop. Even though he was well into his seventies, his grizzly barrel-chested frame could still pull off the intimidating card.

"Walk the line," Benny said to the detective. "I have connections and I'm not above calling in favors."

"Just doing my job," Tony O'Connor said.

Nikki dropped back on her pillow. Would the craziness of this day ever end?

"Let's go," Helen said and motioned the other two to follow.

"Thanks, guys." Nikki waved at Nana's friends as they walked out, leaving Nikki with the detective, Dallas, and her grandma.

"There're still too many people in here." The nurse held up two fingers.

Dallas and his brother met each other's gazes and then the detective rolled his eyes and walked out. Nikki couldn't help but think the better man won. When Dallas looked up, Nana was giving him the evil eye.

"You, too, Buster Brown," Nana said.

Dallas stood there as if trying to decide whether he should chance going against Nana. Not many people chose to. Nana was only a few inches over five feet in height, but she had a big presence that screamed, *Don't mess with me*. Hence the reason she got the part as Annie

Oakley. And her strong personality was one of the reasons Nikki had walked a straight line in her younger years.

Not that Nikki had caused problems. She hadn't wanted to risk being given away again. And Nana never made her feel she'd do it. As a matter of fact, when Nikki had been seventeen and asked permission to skip school, Nana had rolled her eyes and suggested Nikki try just once to be a normal kid and do something rebellious without asking permission.

"Actually," Dallas said, "I'd like to introduce myself first. Name's Dallas O'Connor, I'm a private investigator and Nikki has enlisted my help with this case."

Nana cut her gaze to Nikki and then back to Dallas. "She's innocent, so why would she need your help?"

Funny how she and Nana thought alike. "Because..." Nikki's own words faltered. She remembered Dallas explaining those reasons—something about how she was the perfect suspect right now—and it had made perfect sense then, but now she couldn't recall exactly what he said. The fact that anyone would believe she would kill someone was...farfetched.

Dallas moved in a step. "Because sometimes even the innocent need someone in their corner."

"And you're in her corner?" Nana didn't sound convinced.

"Yes, ma'am." His gaze shifted to Nikki. "I'll do everything I can to prove she's not guilty."

"That O'Connor cop—is he your brother?" Nana asked.

Dallas nodded.

"He's an asshole."

"Nana," Nikki intervened. "Remember us talking

about you working on tact?" Nikki normally wouldn't call Nana on her bluntness. It was just part of who Nana was. But when Nana's lawyer called Nikki a couple of months ago and suggested she have a chat with her grandmother about being polite to the judge on court day, Nikki hadn't seen any alternatives.

"No," Dallas held up his hand to Nikki. "It's okay." Dallas's lips twitched as if he wanted to smile, but he held it back. "To be honest, I've called him that more times than I can count. However, of all the cops out there, we're lucky he's on the case."

"Then why does she need you?" Nana asked.

"Because his job is to find the evidence. Evidence can often be misconstrued. And his job demands he turn over the evidence to the DA—misconstrued or not. Then he has to listen to higher-ups, and they'll expect him to follow the political bull crap they call rules."

"And whose crap do you listen to?" Nana asked.

"You're looking at him."

Nana gave him another once-over. "Do you poach all his cases to see if you can get work?"

Dallas's eyes flinched at the insult.

"Nana," Nikki said. "It wasn't like that." At least she didn't think it was like it. But hadn't she asked almost the same question?

"It's good," Dallas said. "It's a valid question. I was with my brother when he got the call about the body being found. I sort of got caught up in the mess." He looked at Nikki, his eyes smiling, and she knew the mess he was referring to was her getting sick on him. "I offered my assistance. And no, I've never worked on one of my brother's cases."

For a minute, Nikki feared he would tell Nana he'd

agreed to barter with her because Nikki was broke...a fact she hadn't yet shared with her grandma. She relaxed when Dallas didn't seem ready to mention it.

Nana leaned back on the heels of her cowboy boots and held out her hand. "My name's Beatrice Littlemore. And to give you fair warning, I'll be in that corner with you."

Dallas smiled. "Fair enough. Nice to meet you, Mrs. Littlemore."

Nikki watched the tough-looking PI shake hands with Annie Oakley, and her respect for him inched up a notch. Then for some reason, emotion tightened her chest.

As soon as Nana pulled away, she waved toward the exit. "Now skedaddle so I can talk with my grand-daughter."

He looked at Nikki. "The nurse told me earlier that as soon as the doctor sees you, you'll probably be released. I'll see if I can find out how long it will be." He walked away.

Nana looked back at Nikki, crossed her arms over her chest and said, "I could be wrong, but I think I might like him."

And that, Nikki realized, was the problem. Even with her whole world shaken, her heart breaking for Ellen, Nikki thought she might like him, too. Too much.

"Now, young lady," Nana said. "What happened?"

An hour later, Dallas watched Nikki sitting in the waiting room to hear about Ellen's surgery. The dusty blue color of the scrubs made her eyes look bluer. And below those baby blues were dark circles, evidence of what she had been put through today. He'd heard the doctor tell her to go home and rest, that between the stress she'd suffered and what they thought was a dose of some strong ipecac, some kind of vomit-inducing medicine, she really needed to take it easy for a day or so.

Sitting in the operating waiting room wasn't taking it easy. Not that it was Dallas's place to say anything. His job was to prove her innocent, not to worry about those damn shadows under her eyes, or to dwell on the fact that she didn't have any underwear on under those cotton scrubs. And if he kept telling himself that, he might believe it. Running a hand through his hair, he couldn't explain the antsy feeling stirring in his gut.

Oh, hell, yes he could.

He'd already told himself to tread carefully. Nikki Hunt with her innocent blue eyes, soft skin and killer body, tempted him. And it wasn't just the temptation to strip her naked and screw her brains out. Not that he wouldn't like to do that, too. But he also wanted to be her hero. Hell, if there was anything his relationship with his ex had taught him, it was that heroes ended up with their pictures hung in the hall of fools. Serena had personally gotten his mug nailed on that wall.

His job was to prove Nikki didn't kill her husband by proving someone else did it. His job wasn't to take care of her. Staring at the door, he considered heading home. He could call Nikki tomorrow, set up a meeting to go over things. That fit the definition of his job.

"Hey." Tony stepped into the waiting room and they moved to the other side of the room to chat. "I think we should have this crowd moved up to the psych unit," he muttered.

Dallas frowned. "They were at a dress rehearsal for a play."

"It's not just the clothes. They just seem a little . . . over the top for senior citizens."

"Because they were in a play? Shit, I wish our old man would do something beside read the paper, watch the news, and call me up damning every politician to hell and back."

"He does do something else." Tony's tone changed. "He goes to the cemetery every day. Which reminds me—he wanted me to tell you that he wants us to—"

"He needs to stop doing that, too," Dallas interrupted. He knew what his dad wanted. And damn it, he didn't want to do it. Didn't see why he had to do it. His mom wasn't in that grave. He looked again at Nikki's grandma and, hoping to change the subject, he added, "Hell, maybe we ought to introduce them."

"God, no. The old woman reminds me of that ol' bitty on the greeting cards Mom liked so much—what's her name? Maxie or something?"

"Maxine," Dallas said. "I like her. She speaks her mind."

"Which one? The greeting card woman or Annie Oakley over there?" Tony motioned to Nikki's grandmother.

"Both." Dallas recalled his conversation with Nikki earlier when he'd had to twist her arm to get her to agree to accept his help. Nikki must have inherited some of her grandmother's "Maxine" gutsiness. Perhaps a little lower voltage of that personality trait, but it was there. Which explained the reason he found Nikki so damn attractive. Beautiful faces and sexy bodies were a dime a dozen. Spunk wrapped up in a beautiful package, however, was a rare find. He didn't just lust after Nikki—he liked her.

And wasn't that what had happened with his ex-wife?

Sexy, sultry, and sassy, Serena stole his heart on their first date. Yup, he really needed to tread lightly where Nikki was concerned.

"She called me a bastard," Tony said.

"You are." Dallas glanced at his brother's pinched expression. "Not that it's always your fault. It comes with the job." Looking back at the crowd, Dallas noticed the way Mrs. Littlemore kept glancing over at Nikki. "Besides, she's just looking out for her granddaughter."

Another frown pulled at Dallas's lips when he saw Nikki lean back in her chair as if exhausted. He wished her grandmother would do more than visually check in. Nikki needed to be carted off and tucked into bed. And before Dallas was tempted to do it himself.

The memory of picking her up and carrying her back to her hospital bed in the ER filled his head—again. He sure as hell hadn't meant to cop a feel of her bare ass. It didn't stop him from remembering how it had felt—round, soft—a perfect fit into his palm. If that made him a lowlife piece of shit, stamp the label on him now. Because about every two minutes he found himself savoring the memory.

"Don't let looks fool you," Tony said under his breath.

"What's that supposed to mean?" Dallas's gaze lingered on Nikki.

"She has a record."

Dallas's attention shot to his brother and then ricocheted back to Nikki, sitting in the hard hospital chair, looking as innocent as a newly hatched butterfly. "Nikki Hunt has a record?"

CHAPTER EIGHT

DALLAS STARED AT his brother. "What did Nikki do?"

Tony shook his head. "Not Nikki," he whispered. "She came back clean. Annie Oakley has a record."

Dallas relaxed. Okay... he could almost believe that. Almost. "For what, calling a cop a bastard?"

"Nope. Arrested for possession of an illegal substance. Caught trying to buy some pot."

Dallas studied Mrs. Littlemore. "Okay, I'll admit that's surprising. But I still like her."

Tony frowned. "I don't think she's the one you like, brother. And I'm not sure you want to go there."

His brother's attitude scraped across Dallas's last nerve. "You really think Nikki had something to do with her husband's murder?"

"If I *really* thought that, she'd be accessorizing those blue scrubs with a pair of handcuffs."

"Then what's your point?" Hell, Dallas already knew Nikki was hands-off for him, but he didn't like anyone telling him what he could or couldn't do. Especially his big brother, who always thought he knew best.

"My point is, where there's smoke there's fire. And right now there's a lot of smoke blowing around Nikki Hunt. She may not be responsible for her husband's death, but before this thing's over with, I have a feeling she's not going to come out of it looking as innocent as she is going in. Plus..." Tony motioned to the grandmother again and chuckled. "I hear the crazy gene is hereditary."

It was the chuckle that pushed Dallas over the edge. He spoke low, but the hard edge of his voice rang out. "Guess what else is hereditary? The judgmental stick-up-your-ass gene that you got from our ol' man. You're forgetting there was a hell a lot of smoke around me not too long ago."

Tony flinched. "I never doubted your innocence. I fought tooth and nail to—"

"I know that. But it's the same attitude you're using now that had my ass locked up for sixteen months."

His brother frowned. "Look, you and I both know that every cop who ever got involved with a woman from a case... well, it never ended well."

"Is that so?" Dallas almost asked how his brother's non-case-related relationship with LeAnn had turned out, but at the last minute he realized he wasn't that angry or that much of an insensitive asshole. "You're forgetting I'm not a cop anymore."

"Fine." Tony held up his hand. "I'm sorry I said anything."

"Yeah." Dallas looked away.

"Really," Tony nudged him with his elbow, "I'm sorry. It's just... seeing LeAnn has me tied in knots."

"I get it," Dallas said. And he did. He could still remember how knotted up he'd felt when he laid eyes on Serena for the first time after he'd gotten released. And he didn't even love her anymore—that much he was damn sure of—but seeing her still took him to an emotional place he didn't like. A place he didn't ever want to return to.

"To be honest…" Tony stepped closer. "She's hot. I don't blame you for going for her."

"I'm not going for her," Dallas snapped.

Tony's cell rang. As he reached for it, he said, "Then I can tell the guys who had the hots for her that she's free game, huh? Because several of them are interested."

Dallas shot his brother a go-to-hell look.

Tony laughed. "Not going for her, my ass. The only other time I've seen that look was when I told you I was going to ask out Jamie Wentworth in high school." Tony took the call. "O'Connor."

Dallas frowned at his brother. Yeah, but this wasn't high school. And no matter how much he might be tempted, he wasn't going after Nikki.

"Yes," Tony said to the caller. Then he turned his back to Dallas. "What did you get?" Pause. "You're shitting me. Okay, call me if you get anything else."

"What did they find?" Dallas asked as soon as his brother turned around.

Tony hesitated. His gaze shot to Nikki, then back to Dallas.

"Come on," Dallas said. "We've agreed we're on the same side."

Tony let go of a breath. "Only because I'm probably going to have to talk to her about it." He pushed a hand through his hair. "They checked Jack Leon's cell. Earlier today, he got two calls from a cell phone that belonged to an Ellen Wise."

"The same Ellen Wise in surgery?"

"One and the same." Tony arched a brow. "What's the chance that Nikki's good friend and employee was banging her ex?"

Dallas remembered Nikki telling him she'd already caught her ex screwing around with one of her employees. And yeah, if a guy found a sure-bet path to getting laid, he wasn't above trying again now that they were divorced.

Tony's phone rang again. "O'Connor," he said into the cell. As he listened, he glanced at his watch. "Is this a full moon, or what? I'm still at the hospital on the Wise case, waiting to see if the vic pulls through surgery. Can't you send Clark?" Pause. "Fine, I'll head over there now." Tony snapped his phone shut.

"What now?" Dallas asked.

Tony frowned. "Another homicide."

"Connected?"

"No," he said. "It's a convenience store robbery."

Dallas's interest instantly piqued. Not for Nikki, but for Eddie Nance, his other client. "Really? Where?"

"Victor and Holdensburg."

Dallas stored the info in his mind to tell Austin or Tyler. It wouldn't hurt to have one of them nose around the crime scene. If there were similarities to the robbery's MO they were accusing Nance of pulling off, this might be the thing that got the kid off.

"Clerk's dead," Tony continued.

"Damn." Dallas itched to ask what type of gun was used, but chances were Tony didn't have that info yet and if Dallas showed any interest, his brother would guess Dallas's reason and blow a gasket.

"What's happening to our town? I've never had this

many homicides in one night before." He glanced back at Nikki. "Looks like I'll have to chat with Nikki later." He started off then turned back. "Her car's going to be held for a while. If Annie Oakley leaves, can you make sure Nikki has a way home?"

Shit. That didn't follow Dallas's tread-carefully plan.

"Or . . . ," Tony continued. "I could call one of the other 'interested' guys to do it."

There was a teasing quality in his brother's voice that pissed Dallas off even more. "I'll do it," he growled.

Nikki sat with Nana and the Ol' Timers and Ellen's mother, taking a whole corner of the surgery waiting room. Nikki had only met Mrs. Wise once at an open house at the gallery. She had immediately liked the woman if for no other reason than, like Ellen, she was a warm and exuberant individual. Though none of that exuberance shined now.

Nikki couldn't help but wonder if Mrs. Wise held Nikki responsible for her daughter's attack. If not for Nikki, Ellen would probably have been home with her own young daughter and not holding the fort down at a dying art gallery.

Again, the questions started firing in Nikki's brain. Why was this happening? Who killed Jack? Was it just some freak coincidence that Ellen was also attacked? Nikki had asked the detective right before she'd been released if it appeared the motive had been robbery. He said that according to his men, the money was still in the register and Ellen's purse was still under the counter. So robbery didn't appear to be the motive. But what the hell was? It didn't make sense. Nothing made sense.

The mood in the waiting room could best be described as tensely optimistic—especially after a nurse had popped in and said they were still operating and it was touch and go.

Mrs. Wise passed around a picture of Britney, Ellen's six-year-old daughter, who was with her grandfather, probably asking for her mother.

Ellen had never said much about Britney's father, except to call him her biggest mistake. Nikki had to swallow several times to keep from crying when she looked at the little girl's picture. The thought that Britney might have to grow up without her mother ripped at Nikki's heart. And not just because her mother was Nikki's best friend. Nikki knew what it felt like to be that age and lose your parents. Not that Nikki's had died; they simply hadn't wanted her anymore.

Occasionally, someone waiting for another patient would ask about the vintage wear of Nana and the Ol' Timers. There had been some conversations about the Annie Oakley play, but then it got quiet again and the tension crept back into the room like a heavy fog.

Dallas and his brother, Detective O'Connor, were in and out of the waiting room taking phone calls. Nikki didn't know if they were about her but, because during those phone calls one or the other would glance over at her, she suspected they were. The detective's gaze was bothersome in that she could feel him measuring her for a pair of handcuffs. That would lead Nikki to thinking about Jack, and the vision of him dead in her trunk would flash in her head.

Dallas's gaze was equally disturbing. Not that he looked at her as if she was guilty. Nope, he looked at her with concern, as if she was his personal project and he had to make sure she was okay.

It wasn't that she didn't appreciate his help, but it reminded Nikki of how she'd felt for Jack in the beginning. She'd had her work for sale on commission at a small café, and when the business went bankrupt, her six paintings had somehow gotten caught up in the deal. When she'd gone to the law firm handling the case to explain, Jack had been all too eager to come to her rescue. He'd been a knight in shining armor. And Nikki had fallen right into the role of damsel in distress.

Almost as if her thoughts triggered his attention, Dallas looked over, concern etched deeper into his expression. He said something to his brother and then Detective O'Connor walked out of the room. Then, in all his knighthood, Dallas came over and dropped into the chair beside her.

"You're looking a little ragged around the edges," he whispered.

She gazed into his dark blue eyes. "I wouldn't recommend that as a pickup line," she whispered back, hoping to make light of his concern and determined not to act like a damsel.

"Don't worry." A smile appeared in the corners of his eyes. "I only use that one on women who puke on me."

"Why do I think you're not going to let me forget that?"

"A guy has to use what he can," he countered.

Realizing they were practically flirting in the middle of a hospital waiting room while her friend's life was on the line, she slumped back in the chair.

He leaned closer. "You should be at home resting."

"I've already tried to convince her." Nana, sitting to Nikki's left, leaned forward and invited herself into the conversation. "Don't let the angel face fool you. Nikki's got a stubborn streak in her wider than the Mississippi River is long."

"I wonder who I might have taken after," Nikki said.

"Your step-grandfather was a handful." Nana grinned and rested her hand on top of Nikki's. "Seriously, you've had a bad day. Let me take—"

"I'm fine." Nikki looked from Nana to Dallas. "I'm not leaving until I know Ellen's okay."

Dallas and her grandmother shared a look and then both leaned back in their chairs. Nikki went back to worrying—about Ellen, about who killed Jack, and about why the feel of Dallas's leg pressing up against hers sent tingles through her body.

Finally, she shifted her leg away and looked at Dallas. "Have you or your brother learned anything?"

He rubbed his finger under his lip and looked at her. "Not really." His right eyebrow arched.

"Are you lying to me?"

"There have been no developments that help us figure out who did this yet." His brow didn't arch this time. "We can talk later when we have a little more privacy."

"Wise family," a voice called out, and everyone sitting in the corner with Nikki rose to meet the doctor.

Holding her breath, Nikki moved over to the doctor, allowing Mrs. Wise to be in the lead. She kept telling herself the doctor's frown didn't mean bad news. She felt a solid body beside her and she looked over at Dallas. Then Nana came to her other side.

"How is she?" Mrs. Wise asked, tears rolling down

her face. Obviously, she'd noted the doctor's expression, as well.

"She came through the surgery. She's weak. She's lost a lot of blood. She's a fighter, though. We're keeping her in intensive care. The next few hours are critical. But if she pulls through that, I'd say there's a good chance of recovery." The doctor gave Mrs. Wise's arm a squeeze and then walked away.

Mrs. Wise swung around and hugged Nikki. Nikki embraced her back. "She's my baby, Nikki," Mrs. Wise said. "A mother should never have to sit shiva for her baby."

"And you won't," Nikki said, holding on tight and putting every ounce of emotion she had into the embrace. "She's going to be okay," she added and, with all her heart, she prayed she was right.

"I'll take care of her," Dallas told Mrs. Littlemore as they stood outside the intensive care unit's waiting room. It was after eleven and Nikki still refused to leave. He hadn't had a chance to talk to Nikki about the calls from Ellen to her ex-husband. Since Ellen's mom and Nikki had hugged, the two had been inseparable. Asking Nikki if her injured best friend might have been having an affair with her ex-husband in front of the friend's mom just didn't seem like a good idea. He valued his life more than that.

Mrs. Littlemore looked him directly in the eye. "She probably won't leave until she sees Ellen for herself. I tried talking to her. But the girl's stubborn." She huffed. "No, that's not true. She's only stubborn when it involves people she cares about."

"She and Ellen were close, huh?" Dallas asked, hoping to get a little insight.

"Yes. Ellen's the one who pulled Nikki out of Brokenheartville. I tried, but I think having someone her own age made a difference. Don't know why you young people think we don't know crap about heartbreak. I've lost two husbands."

Dallas hesitated, but decided to go for it. "Were Nikki and Jack getting back together?" From what Nikki had said earlier, he hadn't thought so. But for the last hour he'd spent time going over everything he knew, and the thing that kept poking at his mind was the question he hadn't asked Nikki. Why was she having dinner with her ex?

"God, no." Mrs. Littlemore hesitated. "I don't think so. I didn't ask why she agreed to meet him for dinner. She hasn't seen him since the divorce, over a year ago. And she brought the flowers he sent every week over to our retirement center. Said it was better than tossing them away."

"So he wanted to reconcile?" Dallas asked.

"Of course he did. He was a lowlife, cheating weasel, but he wasn't stupid. He knew what he'd lost. Nikki's a prize. Girl's got heart, and when she loves someone, they know it. Gives her all, that girl. But Nikki isn't stupid, either. She knew if he'd cheated once he'd do it again. She learned that from her own mother, I'm afraid."

Dallas wanted to ask her to clarify what she meant about Nikki's mom but didn't chance it. "Did you know Ellen well?" he asked instead.

"Well enough to know she's good people. I fill in at the gallery when Nikki needs someone. Why?"

He avoided her question, but asked another of his own

since the woman seemed willing to answer his first. "Did Ellen know Jack?"

She looked at him with a touch of suspicion. "Don't think so. Nikki didn't hire Ellen until after she filed for divorce. Ellen was the replacement for the little slut Nikki found Jack doing the goat's jig with on the antique sofa."

Goat's jig? Dallas had to bite back his smile.

"Why all the questions, Buster Brown?" A slight tease filled her voice, but he didn't miss the seriousness in her aged brown eyes.

He considered telling her what he knew, but decided it was best to talk to Nikki first. "Asking questions is my job."

"I thought proving her innocent was your job."

"It is, but I don't know where to start until I have some answers. That means asking questions."

She nodded but never looked away from his eyes. "Fine. Just you remember that Nikki's got me watching out for her. I may look like a crazy ol' bitty, but I can be a mean ol' bitty if I have to." She added a little smile to soften the threat.

"I'll remember that." He smiled back.

She continued to study him. "For the record, I think I like you. Don't go proving me wrong, because that would piss me off to no end."

"I'll try not to piss you off," he said.

"And you'll see to it that she gets home."

"I'll see to it." And for some crazy reason, he wasn't even dreading it anymore.

He watched the older woman walk away, trying to figure out how he could broach the subject of Ellen with Nikki without pissing Nikki off. Not that making her mad would stop him from doing his job. If he had to piss her off to prove her innocent, he would. And who knew? There might even be a legitimate reason Ellen had phoned Jack that didn't involve her screwing him.

He started back to the waiting room but his phone rang. It was Austin, calling from the crime scene at the convenience store.

"Learn anything?" he asked, hoping Austin had something to help clear Eddie Nance.

"I learned your brother's a bastard."

Dallas raked a hand through his hair. "I seem to be hearing that a lot lately."

"Maybe you should start believing it," Austin said.

"He's a good cop." Dallas defended Tony. It was the job that brought out the worst in him. A job Tony put on the line numerous times to come to Dallas's defense.

"Yeah, but the moment his good-cop ass spotted me at the crime scene, he had two of his minions chase me off."

Dallas knew Tony would figure out he'd been the one to send Austin there. He also knew Tony would give him hell for it later. Dallas felt the crease in his forehead pull. He dreaded that conversation, but not enough that he regretted his actions. He wasn't above upsetting his brother to clear Nance. And while Tony would get angry, he knew if the shoe was on the other foot, his brother would do the same.

"So you didn't get anything?" Dallas asked, his optimism waning.

"Not anything concrete, but it looks suspicious. They aren't releasing what type of gun was used yet. But when Detective Shane, the cop who arrested Nance, showed up, he and your brother had words. Whatever Tony said to

Shane got him ticked. I thought the two were going to go to blows."

"It must be the same MO," Dallas said. "I'll bet Tony pointed that out to Shane and he got hot under the collar."

"That's what I suspected, too. But damn it, if we knew for sure, we might be able to use that right now and get the DA to drop the charges against Nance."

"If it's really the same MO, Tony will speak up," Dallas said.

"To who? Shane? What good is that going to do? You think he'll admit at this point he arrested the wrong suspect?"

"If I ask Tony, he might give me something." Dallas knew he was grasping at straws. Tony was a by-the-book cop. "Do me a favor. Find Nance, see if he has an alibi for tonight."

"I already have," Austin said. "He's been home. The only person there has been his grandmother, asleep."

"Damn," Dallas said.

Tony stared at the body of the young store clerk as the coroners loaded it on the stretcher. For a homicide detective, death was a constant. But one or two a month he could deal with. Two a night, and two more victims possibly to follow, well…it would get to anyone. The ugliness of it filled his chest and he had to look away.

Wanting to wash the image from his head, he envisioned LeAnn…imagined how her soft hair shifted back and forth on her shoulders, the way she tilted her head slightly to the side when she listened to someone. She'd always been a good listener. Probably because she cared more than the average person.

Did she still care about him?

He'd noted that touch of interest in her eyes when she looked at him. Interest that, given the right conditions, he could turn to passion. However, he hadn't missed the pain in her soft green eyes. LeAnn was still hurting. That didn't surprise him. If he wasn't careful, he could go back there himself, to that emotional place where pain and guilt made it hard to breathe. A place where he almost felt losing LeAnn was his cross to bear. But he didn't want to go back there. He wanted to live life and, damn it to hell and back, but he wanted to live it with LeAnn. He wasn't giving up on them.

But could he convince LeAnn not to give up on them?

"Hey." Rick Clark, his friend and partner, joined Tony. "What the hell is it with tonight?"

"Tell me and we'll both know." Tony forced himself to look back at the body being moved out of the store.

"Shit," Clark said as the body passed by them. "How old was that kid?"

"Twenty-one," Tony muttered. "Just getting started."

"Did I hear there was another vic?"

"Yeah, an older woman. Shot in the chest. Ambulance left with her about thirty minutes ago."

"Damn. How's she holding up?"

"Not good," Tony said. "They don't think she's going to make it. She came to buy milk for her grandkids and it's probably going to cost her her life."

Clark looked around. "Cameras?"

Tony shook his head. "Have we ever gotten that fucking lucky?"

"Not working, huh?" Clark guessed correctly. Silence filled the room and then a woman screamed out front.

No doubt it was a family member of the vic. They both gazed through the glass to the woman sobbing on a cop's shoulder. "You ever think about quitting this gig?" Clark asked.

"Every time I'm called to a case," Tony said. But when he solved a case, he changed his mind. He loved that he caught the bad guys.

"I saw Detective Shane outside," Clark said, following Tony to the counter.

"And he can stay out there," Tony snapped.

"I heard you two nearly came to blows. What happened?"

Tony ran a hand through his hair. "A robbery took place several months back. Similar MO, black kid of average height and build and, according to the eyewitness, the same type of gun was used, only no one was shot. Dallas's PI firm is handling the case. He really believes the kid Shane fingered for it is innocent."

"Is the kid still locked up?"

"No," Tony said. "He's out on bail, but the moment I brought up the MO being similar, Shane accused me of trying to help Dallas."

Clark cut Tony an accusing look. "Are you?"

"Hell, no!" Tony snapped. "But neither do I want to see an innocent kid go to jail."

"I agree, but no cop wants a damn PI nosing around his case. Hell, I'd be pissed, too."

"I know." Tony glanced at the empty cash register and the baseball bat. "Looks like the kid tried to overtake the perp."

"And got himself killed." Clark leaned over the counter, looking at the blood pooled behind it. "From the blood splatter I'd say he was close to the counter when he took the bullet."

Tony walked around the counter and knelt down. "There's blood on the end of the bat and it wasn't near the blood pool that appears to be our vic's. The kid might have gotten in a hit before he got himself shot. Which means this really could be the same perp as the other robbery, and he only shot this time because he was provoked. Make sure CSU takes in the bat."

Clark nodded. They moved around a few minutes, figuring out how the crime went down. After taking notes, Clark asked, "Any news on the Ellen Wise chick?"

"She's going to make it," Tony said.

"You talk to her yet?" Rick asked.

"Doctors won't let us in until tomorrow."

"But it looks like I'm in the money, right?"

Tony looked up, confused. "Huh?"

"You know, the bet we took on the scene. If the suspect was guilty or not. Your brother put twenty on Blondie being guilty."

"He bet on her being guilty?" Tony asked, surprised.

"Yeah," Rick said, and chuckled. "That was before she puked on him."

Tony recalled his own initial reaction to Nikki Hunt and Dallas's accusation that he was like their old man and being judgmental. "You didn't think she was guilty?" Tony asked.

"I thought she was guilty as sin, but you make more if you take the long shot. I'm in the money, right?"

"I wouldn't count your money, but yeah, there's reasonable doubt." Tony recalled how Dallas had already grown attached to Nikki Hunt. For his brother's sake,

Tony hoped reasonable doubt was enough. This was one bet that he figured his brother wouldn't mind losing.

"I'll stay if you need me," Nikki told Mrs. Wise a couple of hours later, after one of the nurses had informed them that Ellen was doing great.

"You've been good to stay as long as you have. And with everything that happened, too. Please. Go get some rest. Ellen's father is going to relieve me in a couple of hours." She gave Nikki a hug. "My baby is going to be just fine."

Nikki pulled away, and when she saw tears of joy in Mrs. Wise's eyes, she got a little weepy, too. "I'll call in the morning."

"You do that," Mrs. Wise said.

Nikki went back to her seat for her purse. Dallas followed her out of the waiting room. Several times she'd told him he could leave. He shrugged and said he didn't have anything better to do and continued to read magazines.

As Nikki stepped through door, she opened her purse to look for her keys. She hadn't even gotten her hand past her wallet when she remembered.

Remembered she hadn't driven to the hospital.

Remembered why she hadn't driven to the hospital—because Jack had been found dead in her trunk.

Jack was dead. Dead. Dead. Dead.

Oh, and her car had been confiscated.

As had her clothes, down to her underwear.

Glancing downward, past the girls that hung freer than normal, she wiggled her toes in the rubber-footed hospital-quality socks and tried to keep the image of a dead Jack in her trunk from flashing in her head.

It didn't work.

The picture of him curled up, eyes open, staring at nothing, filled her head. She swallowed and slammed her eyes shut.

Go away. Go away.

"You okay?"

Drawing in a pound of oxygen, she opened her eyes and raised her head. She half-expected Dallas to be smirking because he probably knew she'd forgotten she didn't have a car and had been looking for keys. Half-expected him to have a touch of sarcasm in his blue eyes because, face it, she had told him to go home several times.

She blinked. No smirk. No sarcasm.

He had that look again, the knight-in-shining-armor look.

"I'm fine," she lied.

"I'll be happy to drive you home." His deep baritone filled her head and chased away the flashes of a dead Jack in her trunk.

She would have turned him down. Seriously, she would have in a second. But considering she didn't have a dime to her name, and considering she wasn't even sure taxis worked this late in her small town—and if they did come, would they accept overdrawn debit cards as payment? Considering all this, she bit down on her lip and did what she had to do.

"I'd appreciate a ride," she forced herself to say.

CHAPTER NINE

AT MIDNIGHT, AFTER her twelve-hour shift was over, LeAnn walked into the four-bedroom, single-story, white brick residence she used to call a home. Now it was just a two-thousand-square-foot structure. A place she slept, a place she drank coffee by the potful and nuked frozen dinners, a place for her to hide out.

Oddly enough, tonight was the first time she hadn't longed to run here and hide. The first time in forever that LeAnn hadn't wanted to leave work.

It wasn't about a sudden interest in her career, either. It was about Tony. She'd driven around the hospital's parking lot for ten minutes, searching for his car. She hadn't seen it. Why did she want to see him? Didn't it hurt too much? If one was on a diet, you didn't go hang out at a candy store, did you?

Nevertheless, she'd gone to check on Nikki Hunt before she'd left. The ER nurse had told her Nikki and her posse had moved up to intensive care where Nikki's friend was still listed as critical, but was now expected to pull through.

LeAnn was happy that Nikki's friend was okay. LeAnn

knew too well how it felt to lose a loved one. She found herself hoping everything went okay with the whole murder charge. Surely, Tony would uncover the truth, and the suspicions about Nikki would go away.

Closing the door and hanging her keys on the hook, she was struck by a surprise realization. Today was the first time she felt almost normal. Even with the pain of seeing Tony, reminded of all she'd lost, she'd managed to think about something and someone besides her own loss and grief. Was she finally on the road to recovery?

Dropping her purse, she walked past the living room, moved into the hall and stood in front of the door she hadn't been able to walk into for over nine months now. She reached for the knob but couldn't do it. Instead, she darted into the master suite.

Unfortunately, Tony's presence must have followed her home. She could see him stretched out on the king-size bed, looking all too sexy. In the snapshot appearing in her mind, he was shirtless and the bedcovers came low to his waist. Then the image shifted, and in this image he was still shirtless, but on his chest was their precious six-week-old daughter, Emily.

Tears filled LeAnn's eyes. She backed up against the bedroom wall and slid down onto the carpet, where she curled up in a ball and let herself weep.

She might be on the road to recovery, but she obviously still had a long way to go.

Dallas could tell Nikki was exhausted—mostly because she didn't say a word when they left the hospital—and he debated whether or not to broach the subject of Jack and Ellen Wise. But that was his job.

The night temperature, still running in the high eighties, made the walk to his car seem longer. Dallas opened the passenger door of his previously owned but new to him, red 2008 Ford Mustang GT. It had been the one luxury he allowed himself after he'd gotten out of prison. At the time, he'd been pretty sure he'd given up women and decided he needed something sexy in his life. Turned out, celibacy behind prison walls was a lot easier than outside them.

"Oh, just a second." He tossed a week's worth of fast-food bags into the backseat.

"Nice ride," she said when he stepped back.

"You into Mustangs?" he asked, not seeing her as a woman who would be. But a guy could always dream.

She made a cute face. "Sorry. I wouldn't know one if it followed me home and wanted to be fed. I just know it looks sporty and it's red. So I assume it's nice."

He grinned. "Is that your way of saying don't bore you about what I got under this baby's hood?"

"Bore away. Just don't expect me to respond intelligently." She yawned and, even in the dark, he could see the exhaustion in her face. The rings under her eyes were darker. "My mechanic is down to using terms like 'doo-hickey' and 'thingy' just so I'll understand."

She slipped past him and sank into the leather seat. Dallas stared down at her. There was something about the late hour, the fact they were really alone for the first time that made him even more physically aware of her. All he could think about was how pretty she looked sitting in his sexy Mustang. Not the kind of beauty one saw in magazines. But damn it if it wasn't a hell of lot more than girl-next-door pretty. She had that fresh, wholesome—he remembered how her ass had felt when he'd picked her up—hot, sex-kitten look that had a guy getting hard in seconds.

He shut the door before she noticed the growing wood behind his zipper. Jeezus, what was wrong with him? The girl was off limits.

Walking around his Mustang, he got behind the wheel and glanced over at her. Leaning back on the headrest, she gazed up at the roof of the car. The silence hummed.

"I doubt anything you would say would come off as anything less than intelligent," he said

She turned her head toward him. "You're forgetting I'm an artist. We're known to be ditzy."

"And you're blond, too," he teased. Then he reached around her and grabbed the seat belt. This close, only a few inches from her face, he caught a light fruity scent, and he found himself looking at her lips. His blood hummed with awareness. Pulling back, he handed her the buckle.

She took the buckle and secured it. "I gave you carte blanche with the artist angle." Belted in, she looked back at him. "But not on the blonde jokes." A slight smile touched her eyes, yet she appeared too tired to carry through with the gesture. She relaxed in the seat and her eyes fluttered closed.

He started the car and got some air going. The engine's purr reminded him of his sex-kitten thought. His gaze shifted back to her and his whole off-limit frame of mind flew out the widow. Her eyes were still closed, so he let himself enjoy the view. He took in her profile. The way her lips fell slightly open made him think of all the things she could do with that mouth. He took in the way her breasts filled out the top of the scrubs, and that made him think of things he could do with his own mouth.

He tightened his hands on the steering wheel and fought the urge to tug at his pant legs. "I know you're tired, but I have a couple of questions."

She opened her eyes. "Sure."

Before he got caught up in noticing things again, he pitched out the question. "Why were you meeting Jack at the restaurant?"

Her eyes shifted away so fast, he could tell she didn't like the question.

"Were you two getting back together?" He bluntly put it out there.

She stared at her lap. "Nana loves the cooking shows. After all she's done for me, that's the only thing she's ever let me do for her. The thought of letting her down, I…"

Dallas waited for her to continue. When she didn't, he said, "I'm not following."

She looked up. "I'm not her blood. When Nana agreed to take me in, he brought the DNA papers over to show her that I wasn't his. So I wasn't even her real grandchild. He told Nana that if she kept me, she'd lose him."

Dallas watched her nip at her bottom lip. "Who told her that?"

"My dad. Or I thought he was until that night."

"So why didn't you just go live with your mom?" he asked, almost afraid he'd pushed too far.

"You don't get it," she said. "He didn't want to divorce my mom. He just didn't want me. He said he didn't want to have to look at me anymore." Her voice shook and then she seemed to hold her breath. "Nana told him I was six and he was twenty-six, and he had a better chance of making it than I did."

Dallas got a vision of her as a little girl, all big blue

eyes and with her angel face, and having to hear the man she thought of as her dad say those things. His gut tightened. What kind of person did that?

"Nana gave up her own son for me." Nikki tightened her hands in her lap. "All she'd ever let me do was pay for the stupid cable." Nikki sighed. "So the answer is yes." She met his eyes. "I went there planning to say yes."

He was lost again, still thinking about her being six. "Oh, you mean to the restaurant."

She nodded. "Or I should say, I went there hoping I could say yes."

"Yes to what?"

"He wanted us to get back together. But, then I saw him and..."

"And what?" he asked.

She looked out the window. "I thought I would still feel...something. I wasn't expecting it to be like before, but I thought it would be enough. Then Nana would have her cable. I could pay Ellen. Life would be good."

"What happened?"

"I didn't feel anything," she continued. "Not love, anyway. And now..."

She brushed her fingertips over her face. His gut tightened when he saw a tear slip down one cheek. Considering what she'd been through, she had a right to shed a few tears.

Just don't let her start sobbing. He couldn't handle that.

"Now he's dead and on top of feeling bad about letting Nana down, I feel terrible because I was the last person he shared a meal with and all I felt was anger and resentment. I mean, if I had known he was about to die, I—"

"It's not your fault." The car's engine hummed and the AC blew out cool air as they sat in the unmoving car.

"I know that up here." She touched her head then placed a hand on her chest. "But not in my heart. I mean, if I'd known, I would have been nicer. I wouldn't have ordered the beer. I didn't even want the beer."

He mentally chewed on what she said and then had to ask, "What's wrong with ordering a beer?"

She didn't answer, just continued, "I could have waited for a bread plate. And God, I stuck my fingers in his gumbo just to make him mad."

Dallas could hear the guilt in her voice. "Didn't you tell me you caught him helping himself to your hired help in your office?"

She nodded.

"Well, I think that's a little worse than sticking your fingers in his gumbo. The guy got off fucking easy."

She stared at him, eyes wide, and bit down on her lip. "I didn't mean to..." She inhaled. "I'm sorry."

"For what?" Leaning closer, he brushed a curtain of her blond hair from her cheek and left his hand against her face. He was amazed again at how soft she felt. He ran the pad of his thumb down to her chin.

"You didn't ask about... I normally don't... babble. Well, just to myself. Which is a bad habit I'm working on."

She caught his wrist and moved his hand, letting him know his touch was unwelcome. Which was fine, he told himself. He shouldn't have crossed that line. She'd just looked as if she needed...

No excuses, he told himself. *She's off limits.*

He passed a palm over his face. "Are you always this hard on yourself?"

"Not always. Today's been a little tougher than most."
She smiled, just a slight one. Their eyes met and held.
The light humor seemed to change into something different, as if they were connecting on some other level. She
blinked and looked straight ahead.

He listened to his engine and the silence thickened
again. "You want to tell me where you live?"

She sighed. "I'm sorry I'm just so tired and…"

"And you've had a hell of a day," he finished for her.

"No shit."

For some reason it sounded funny coming from her
and he smiled.

"I live in the Knoll Apartments, 1350 Park Knoll. Just
take—"

"I know where they are." They were down the street from
the cemetery where his mother was buried. The cemetery
his father visited way too often, but that Dallas hadn't been
to since he watched them lower her casket into the ground
as he stood beside a deputy U.S. marshal. In handcuffs.

She leaned her head back as he pulled out of the parking space. The other question he needed to ask rested on
the tip of his tongue.

"What's going to happen next?" she asked.

He looked over at her. "I'm sure my brother will want
to see you tomorrow to ask you some more questions."

"When… when will I get my car back?"

She said the words as if they pained her, and he knew
why. She'd probably never forget seeing her ex's body in
her trunk. He'd seen things as a cop that he'd never forget,
too. Not that her ex would keep him awake. The ones that
nagged at him involved either women or kids. Stories like
her and her father. Or worse. Some of the tales he'd heard

in prison still haunted him. Hell, just being behind those bars haunted him.

"It won't take too long, will it?"

"Depends on how quickly CSU can go over it. I'll check with Tony tomorrow and see if he can't rush it."

They went back to silence and in less than ten minutes he pulled into the parking lot of her apartment complex. When he glanced at her, he expected her to be asleep. She wasn't. She sat rigid as if some demon chewed on her sanity. Damn if he didn't know about demons.

"Where are you in here?" he asked.

"Last apartment building on the left." She reached at her feet for her purse.

He drove to the building, pulled into a parking spot and cut off the engine. "One more question before you go."

She looked at him.

He debated how to say it, but as the silent awkwardness grew, he spit it out. "Did Ellen know Jack?"

"She knew about him, but didn't know him. Why?"

"You sure?"

"Yes." Nikki tilted her head to the side and studied him. "Why?"

If he didn't tell her, Tony would. And as Tony had said, any news coming from Dallas would probably be easier to take. "Maybe Jack came by the gallery while you weren't there."

"If he had, Ellen would have told me. And she'd probably have gone after him with a two-by-four or . . ." She bit down on her lip. "Not that I'm saying Ellen did anything. She was at the gallery when it happened. So don't even think about accusing her."

"I'm not," he said.

Nikki continued to stare at him. "Then why are you asking this?"

He gripped the wheel tighter. "Tony's men checked Jack's cell phone. He received two phone calls from a cell phone listed to Ellen Wise."

She shook her head. "They must be mistaken."

"It's no mistake, Nikki."

She sat there as if trying to understand. "You think... Ellen and Jack were seeing each other?"

"We don't know but I guess that's a logical assumption."

"Only logical if you don't know Ellen. There has to be some—"

"They wouldn't make that mistake," he said, hating to tell her but she had to hear it sooner or later.

"Maybe Jack called the gallery, and she thought he was a customer. But no way... no earthly way will I believe that Ellen and Jack were dating."

"Wasn't it one of your other employees that Jack cheated on you with?"

She frowned. Those big blue eyes no longer looked so exhausted, but angry. "That wasn't Ellen."

"I just think if Jack managed to convince one of your employees to jump between the sheets, then he might have gone after her the same—"

"I don't care what you think, or what the whole freaking police force thinks. Ellen wasn't seeing my ex-husband behind my back."

Dallas expected her to deny it at first. Then he'd expected her to get hurt, but he hadn't expected the absolute loyalty. Then he recalled what her grandma said: *Nikki only gets stubborn about people she cares about.*

She obviously cared about Ellen.

"Okay, but be prepared for Tony to assume—"

"He can assume what he wants! But if he upsets Ellen with this nonsense, I'll...I don't know what I'll do, but I won't stand by and do nothing."

"He has to talk to her," he said matter-of-factly, not to piss her off, but to prepare her.

"Not about this he doesn't!"

Dallas met her angry eyes. "Look, I'm not trying to upset you, but Tony has to ask questions. That's his job."

"Stop." She held up her hand. "I'm sorry, but...Look, you've been really nice. I mean, I puked all over you and you didn't even get mad, but...I can't take any more. I'm done. Done." She dropped her face into her hands and muttered something about crap quota for the day. Finally, she looked up. "Thanks for the ride." Her hand dipped into her purse and then froze and she slammed her eyes shut. "Shit! Shit! Shit!"

"What?" he asked but then figured it out. "No keys?"

She looked at him and those big blue eyes had tears in them. She blinked. "Wait. It's after eleven. It's okay. Bill's home. We're key buddies." She reached for the door handle. "Thanks."

Dallas couldn't help but wonder what other privileges key buddies got.

She stepped out of the car and so did he. She looked at him over the top of his Mustang. "You don't have—"

"I'll feel better if I make sure you get in, okay?"

"He's home. I can see his light on from here." She pointed back to the apartment on the corner.

Dallas walked around the car. "Humor me."

She frowned but started walking. He fell into step

beside her. She didn't look at him. But he couldn't keep his eyes off her. Measuring her height with his shoulders, he wondered if she was even five-five. She looked small. Vulnerable. His gaze shifted to her stockinged feet and, for purely male reasons, they reminded him that she wasn't wearing any underwear. He moaned inwardly and decided he really needed to get home, have a cold beer, a cold shower, and a long talk with his libido.

"Why is..." She stopped cold. "How could..."

He followed her gaze and saw a door to an apartment standing ajar. "Yours?" he asked.

"I know I shut it," she said. "And locked it."

He crouched down to reach his ankle holster. She took a step closer to the door. He yanked out his Smith, jerked up, hid the gun behind his back, and caught her by the elbow.

"Go to your neighbors." He gave her a nudge. "Now."

CHAPTER TEN

DALLAS STOOD NEXT to the door, with his back pressed against the side of the building. He noted the splintered wood around the lock. Someone had definitely broken in. He nudged the door open with his foot. The door creaked and a couple of splinters of loose wood fell to the concrete. In the distance, he heard Nikki knocking on the neighbor's door, but not a sound seemed to come from her apartment.

He moved in, gun held tight. He almost found himself yelling out "Police," but stopped himself at the last moment. Those days were over.

Good riddance, too.

Thinking someone had your back was nice, but when you found out the same people would turn their back on you so easily, it would make your head spin. And it hurt.

He blinked. His eyes adjusted to the next level of darkness. Books, magazines, and upside-down lamps littered the floor. Taking another step, he noted the small desk against the living room wall. On top lay some disconnected computer wires, but no computer. Had someone taken it? Was this your average break-in? If so, it was a hell of a coincidence.

He wasn't much of a believer in coincidences.

His gaze shifted back to the floor where the contents of the yanked-out desk drawers were strewn.

The place had been ransacked. Which usually meant someone was looking for something. But what? Of course, the most important question was if the "ransackee" was still present. He inhaled again, listening for any sign that he wasn't alone. He heard the hum of the refrigerator and the ticking of a wall clock. A light shined from an open doorway that led to a kitchen. He moved against the wall. When the only sound filling the dark apartment was the clock, he swung into the kitchen.

On the tile floor lay a few upside-down drawers, and scattered around was an assortment of utensils and kitchen paraphernalia. He moved his eyes and gun together, checking all corners of the room. No ransackee here.

Careful not to make noise, he moved back into the living room, stepping over a lamp, and started down the dark hall. A door off to his right stood slightly ajar. He backed against the wall, breathed in and out, and then nudged open the door. Bathroom.

The scent of some fruity soap or shampoo filled his nose and he remembered inhaling that same aroma on Nikki. His focus went to the empty shower. His mind, obviously more connected to his dick, created an image of Nikki standing under a warm spray of water, naked and... He sent that image packing. *Focus, damn it!*

Leaving the bathroom, he inched down the hall to what had to be the bedroom. Only his footsteps echoed in the silence. He nudged the door open. Gun clasped tight in his fist, he swung into the room. He swept the four corners with his gaze. Empty.

The air conditioner hummed to life and a spray of cold air hit his face. The closet door stood open. A light creaking sound filled the room. Maybe it was a water heater kicking to life, or someone hiding in the closet. He backed against the wall and then swung around, prepared to take aim. But the only things to aim at were the clothes lining the closet and the six pair of shoes neatly lined up like dominos. The creaking sound came again. This time he recognized it as some electrical appliance waking up from a nap.

Confident that whoever had broken in had left, he relaxed his stance and lowered his gun. Shifting slightly, he switched on a light. The fan above the bed whooshed to life and brightness chased out the darkness. He looked around at the scattered underwear—white, pink, red, black. The multicolored silky-looking garments weren't dumped out on the floor as if someone had emptied an entire drawer. They were strewn about as if someone had enjoyed the scavenger hunt with pleasure, fingered through each item, and then tossed them out one by one.

Was the perp a panty pervert? Hey, Dallas liked women's underwear as much as the next guy, but to really get excited, he needed the woman in them...or even better, out of them.

He looked at the bedside table. The drawer had been yanked out and dumped onto the cream-colored carpet. So the burglar hadn't only been looking for panties, he'd also gone for the small drawers. Whatever had been sought after in here must have been something that would fit in the more compact drawers. If there hadn't been a murder and an attempted murder connected with Nikki, he'd have thought this was just your average break-in, someone looking for quick cash and jewelry.

His gaze shifted and landed on the bed. The comforter was thrown back on one side, as if someone had slept there and slipped out hardly leaving an imprint. A sure sign Nikki had been sleeping alone.

He inhaled and caught the fruity scent again, along with something more. Sleepy, fresh-showered woman. His attention went back to the bed and his mind put Nikki in it...alone, wearing little or nothing—maybe the red panties about two inches from his feet—with her hair spread over the white pillow cases.

Scrubbing a hand over his face and the image from his mind, he turned to leave. And that's when he heard another noise. This one different. Not another appliance waking up.

Someone was in the apartment.

His gun came up right along with his alarm. He hit the light switch. Darkness crowded the space again. He moved out of the room, his gun pointing forward. He didn't see anyone through the doorway, but he could hear the sound of utensils clinking together in the kitchen as if someone was fumbling through a drawer looking for...

The image of Nikki's dead ex's knife wounds flashed through his mind. Determined he hadn't lived through sixteen months of prison for nothing, adamant he wouldn't die unless accompanied by the bastard who robbed him of those months, he shifted his finger to the trigger.

Hesitating at the end of the hall, he held his breath, felt his heart pound in his chest. Then he swung into the kitchen and tightened his finger on the trigger.

"Hold it right there!"

A scream ripped through the silence.

He recognized her. Too bad Nikki wasn't so quick to do the same. Armed with an eggbeater, she hurled the flimsy utensil at him.

It hit his chest. "It's me!" The eggbeater clattered to the floor.

She collapsed against the counter and stopped screaming. But when he realized how tightly he still held his gun, he suddenly wanted to scream. Damn it, he could have shot her.

He lowered his gun. "I told you to go to the neighbors."

"Bill wasn't...when you didn't...I thought...I..." She took a step, stumbled over something on the floor then caught herself on a kitchen chair.

He looked around for a light switch and hit it. When he saw her standing there looking scared, vulnerable, and so damn beautiful, his gut knotted again at the idea that he could have shot her. But jeezus, he wouldn't have been able to live with himself if he had.

"When a cop tells you to do something, you do it!" he snapped.

She wrapped her arms around her middle as if to protect herself from his anger. "You...you aren't a cop."

He ran a hand through his hair. The panic of what could have been faded, and he crouched down and holstered the gun. When he looked up, she stared down at him with confused blue eyes.

"You said you were a PI." Her eyes were bright, but from tears or anger he wasn't sure.

"I am. I used to be a cop." He stood and considered telling her how he'd been accused of murder and spent time in the pen. He'd never hesitated to tell other clients, but for some odd reason, he wasn't eager to spill his guts now. One look at her expressive eyes and he knew why. He'd seen it so often—the doubt, the hint of fear of dealing with an ex-con—that it didn't surprise him. He'd even seen it in some of the people coming to him for help. Truthfully, he hadn't given a damn.

Until now.

Hell, he'd been pretty sure his ability to give a damn had gone missing, but for some reason the thought of seeing any judgment, or doubt or even pity, in her eyes stung like fire. So he closed his mouth, and kept his dirty past to himself. At least for now.

The silence became the elephant in the room. "It's the same thing, though," he said, remembering what they were talking about. "When a PI tells you to do something, you should do it, too. I could have shot you." Saying it out loud brought another emotional jolt to his solar plexus.

"I didn't realize you had a gun. I was afraid if someone was in here they could have hit you over the head or something. I wanted to help." A touch of rebellion sounded in her voice.

He stood there, heart still on an adrenaline rush, and studied her. He noticed the little details, like how she chewed on her bottom lip out of some nervous habit, and how she twisted her right foot ever so slightly, and how she held her shoulders tight. That's when the complexity of this woman struck him again. She was soft, all innocent and sweet, but beneath that layer of gentle personality was the backbone of a fighter. She didn't give up her ground easily. He respected that.

"And what were you going to do if I was the bad guy?

Beat me to a froth with an eggbeater?" He smiled, hoping to ease the tension.

She didn't smile back. "I grabbed the first thing I found in the drawer when I heard you—or someone—walking down the hall." A frown pulled at her eyes. He could swear he even noted a sheen of tears. Considering the day she'd had, he couldn't hold her mood against her.

"Whoever broke in is gone." He looked at a clock on the wall and saw it was almost three in morning. It would be hours before this was over.

"Why?" she muttered. "I don't have anything really of value. Why would someone..."

"It appears as if they were searching for something. By the looks of things, it was something small. However, I think they got your computer." He stepped back into the living room. If he didn't believe this was a random break-in—and he didn't—then he couldn't help but wonder what she'd had on her computer that would provoke someone to steal it and not the TV and other small appliances. Had her ex sent her something?

"No, they didn't." She sounded drained.

He hit a light switch. Motioning to the desk where a few unconnected computer wires lay stretched out on top, he said, "I'm afraid they did."

She glanced at the desk and then met his eyes. "I didn't have a computer here. I mean, I did, but I...I sold it a few weeks ago." She glanced away as if embarrassed to have admitted that piece of information.

"To pay for your grandmother's cable," he said before he could stop himself.

"And...some other stuff. But it's not a big deal, I have one at the store."

She hadn't been kidding when she'd said she was flat broke. He had the craziest desire to check the fridge to make sure she at least had something to eat.

Pushing a hand through his hair, he saw her grimacing at the knickknacks littering the floor. The pile consisted of candles, books, a few small figurines, and a couple of framed photos, mostly silly stuff women added to their homes to make them cozy, things men considered dust collectors. But by the way she stared at the items, he could tell she considered her silly stuff important.

"I don't think this is your everyday burglary. Considering all that's happened, it would be too much of a coincidence."

She moved past him, dropped to her knees and picked up a photo frame as if she hadn't been listening. Cracked glass fell from the image and he heard her sigh.

"We need to figure out what the perp may have taken or what he was looking for."

She still didn't answer.

Dallas noticed a couple of disk holders had been emptied out. "Because whoever broke in went through the computer desk so thoroughly, I'm wondering if it wasn't someone looking for something computer related. A disk, or maybe before you sold your computer you had something on there."

She looked at him. Again, he noticed the purple circles under her eyes. They were darker. She appeared almost too worn out to think.

"Did your ex send you anything? A disk or an attached file?"

"No."

Now that the lights were on, he glanced around the

living room. It looked like a chick's place. Color, a lot of reds and light browns, dominated the room and the clutter on the floor appeared to match. However, the woman curled up on the floor, still wearing hospital scrubs and nothing else, seemed devoid of color. Her complexion looked almost chalky white.

"Why is this happening?" She hugged her knees closer to her chest. Sitting like that made her appear smaller, more vulnerable—a woman in need of a hero. Damn if he didn't want to apply for the job.

"I don't know." He took one step toward her then stopped himself. He was out of the hero business. "I'm calling Tony. He's going to need to come out."

She looked up at him. "Can't it wait until morning?"

He fought the desire to give in, then hit the button to call his brother's cell. "Sorry. It can't wait." He watched her drop her head on top of her knees. "Nikki, I need you to walk around the house and tell me if anything is missing. Can you do that?"

She muttered something and then rose in one fluid motion. Carefully, she set the broken picture frame on the end table and disappeared down the hall.

"O'Connor," Tony said. Then his tone changed as though he'd just read the caller ID. "Dallas. You fucking sent Austin here, didn't you?" Voices echoed in the background, telling Dallas his brother was still working the case at the convenience store.

"You know why I did it," Dallas said. "How similar is it to the Nance case?"

"Goddamn it, Dallas," Tony muttered. "If you want to do police work, then—"

"Hey," Dallas interrupted his brother, "I brought Nikki

Hunt home like you requested and discovered someone broke into her place. Ransacked it." Dallas walked over to the end table and picked up the picture that Nikki had so carefully put there.

"Shit," Tony said. "Is this night ever going to end?"

"I'm beginning to wonder." Dallas stared at the framed snapshot of a blond little girl standing beside an older woman. He recognized the woman as Nikki's grandmother and then focused on the girl. Nikki. Scared, big blue eyes and a forced smile stared up at him. Something about the insecure look on the young face told him the picture hadn't been taken too long after she'd been abandoned by her parents. His chest tightened.

"Did they take anything?" Tony asked.

"Not that she's noticed yet. She's just now going through the rest of the apartment. It appears as if they were looking for something."

"And I'll bet she doesn't have a clue what that could be."

"No, she doesn't," Dallas snapped.

"Where's her place?" Tony asked.

"Knoll Apartments, Park Knoll and—"

"By the cemetery?"

"Yeah," Dallas answered. "Apartment 605."

A light flicked on down the hall. Dallas stepped back and saw that Nikki had turned the bedroom light on, and she stood in the doorway staring inside the room. Then she leaned against the door frame, slid down to her ass and dropped her head on her knees again. He recalled her underwear being strewn all over the room.

"Do you think someone is after her, too?" Tony asked.

"I don't know." And Dallas didn't know, but the

possibility knotted his gut almost as much as the thought of him shooting her. He looked back at the front door still ajar, the lock broken. "Can you send someone out here ASAP? Nikki's had it. I'm taking her to my place."

"Your place?" Tony asked.

Dallas didn't answer. He was almost as surprised at his statement as Tony. Then he looked at the picture of a young and disheartened Nikki again and felt right about his decision. Making sure she didn't end up in someone's trunk or in the operating room, didn't make him a hero. It made him a decent person.

"I'll need to talk to her first," Tony grumbled.

"Talk to her tomorrow."

"Come on, Dallas. There's a reason people are dropping like flies around her and all this shit is happening. Chances are she knows something she's not telling us."

"See you tomorrow." Dallas hung up and went to check on Nikki.

A hand moved across Nikki's shoulder blades and lingered there. The touch sent shards of emotion charging right to her chest.

"Hey." His deep voice spoke close to her ear. "You gonna be okay?"

Biting down on her lip, she saw him kneel beside her. "It wasn't just computer stuff that interested him."

"Huh?"

"The jerk went through my panty drawer."

"Yeah, I noticed that." He gave her shoulder another light squeeze and stood. "Why don't you grab an overnight bag and I'll take you somewhere you can get some rest? Tony and CSU will be here and it could take them all night to check for prints and everything."

She wanted to argue, to tell him all she'd wanted to do was crawl into her own bed and sleep. However, knowing someone had broken in, that they'd gone through her underwear drawer gave her the creeps. Considering it was probably the same person who killed Jack and attacked Ellen, well, Nikki didn't love her bed that much. "Can you drop me off at my grandmother's place?"

He stared at her for several seconds. "Yeah, I could do that." He stood up and continued to look at her as if he had something else to say.

"Thanks." She started to get up, and he reached down to help her.

His hand stayed on her elbow, his thumb moving back and forth over the inside of her arm. It tickled and soothed at the same time.

"Of course, I'd think you wouldn't want to put your grandmother in any danger."

She pushed the feel of his touch from her mind to try and digest what he said. "What... What do you mean?"

"I mean that it appears as if someone could be after you. If you go to your grandmother's place, you might inadvertently bring trouble there. I have room at my place, and I'm better equipped to deal with any... problems."

Go home with him? She could still feel the tingle on her arm where he'd touched her. With clarity, she recalled earlier admitting to liking him... liking him too much. "No." *Heck, no.* "I don't... I couldn't impose on you to... that's too much to ask."

"You already barfed on me. Putting you up for a night is nothing." He chuckled.

She didn't see the levity right now. Tomorrow, she would probably laugh at the whole situation, but not tonight. "I'll just stay here."

"The lock's broken, Nikki. When Tony comes here, he's going to want to interrogate you. Nothing against my brother, but he's relentless."

The thought of having to face Detective O'Connor again had Nikki turning around, leaning her forehead against the hall wall, and giving it one light frustrated thump. "I need to sleep. I can't think right now." She closed her eyes.

"I know." His voice came at her ear again and she felt the heat of his body behind her. "That's why you should come home with me. Just until *we* get the locks fixed."

We? She didn't belong to a "we." She used to, but Jack wanted more than "we" and then he got himself killed. Killed. Jack was dead. The vision of him in the trunk flashed again. She jerked her eyes open.

She swung around. Dallas O'Connor stood so close she barely had room to do the complete turn. So close she could smell him, a musky spicy scent, as if he used one of those masculine make-women-notice-you scents of deodorant. The smell chased away the terrible vision, or maybe it was the soft way he studied her. The way his presence made her feel jittery, but safe. *We.* She missed being part of a we.

"I...don't think, I—" *I'm not having sex with you.* Was there a proper way of saying that? Her brain was mush and she wasn't sure. And face it, living with Nana all those years hadn't earned her an A-plus in diplomatic speaking. Nana said things the way they were and sometimes it was easier to follow Nana's path. "What I'm trying to say is..."

He pressed a finger over her lips. From the look in his

eyes, he knew exactly what she couldn't put into words. "It's three in the morning. You've had the day from hell. I promise you, I don't plan on seducing you tonight."

She bit down on her lip and, too tired to censor her thoughts, said the first thing that came to her mind. "What about tomorrow?"

He grinned and darn it if he didn't look sexy with his dark blue eyes and bedroom smile. "How about we take it a day at a time?"

We again. Then the between-the-lines suggestion of what he'd said sank in and she realized what he might have mistaken her question to mean. "I wasn't implying . . ."

"I know." His smile lessened and something even more dangerous filled his eyes. That soft, caring look that made her want to lean into him. "I'm just teasing you. Now, go get your things before Tony gets here."

CHAPTER ELEVEN

"WE'RE HERE." A voice intruded on Nikki's sleep a short time later.

She waved her hand, trying to send the masculine voice away. She wasn't ready to wake up. Tired. So tired. She only wanted to sleep. To forget about...

"Nikki?"

Hearing her name had her bolting forward and head-butting the owner of the deep voice right before a seat belt locked in place across her chest. Who? Where? Questions zipped through her sleep-dazed—and now jarred—brain. While the answers to her questions didn't come, all the things she wanted to forget about came hurtling at her. Jack, dead. Ellen, attacked. Her place, wrecked.

Then the answers to her questions quickly followed. Who? Dallas O'Connor. Where? His place.

She touched her sore forehead and looked at Dallas standing outside the open car door rubbing two fingers over his own sore spot.

"Sorry." Still not completely awake, she fought to release the seat belt.

"Need some help?" He sounded leery to lean down without permission.

"No. I can do it." She pushed down on what she thought was the release and nothing happened. She gave it a pull and tug. Still nothing. She twisted in her seat, trying to see what she was doing wrong, but the dang seat belt locked on her. She jabbed at what she thought was the latch again. Then jabbed harder. She gave it a frustrated yank, groaned, and then slammed back into the seat. "I'll just sleep right here."

He chuckled as he leaned down and, in one click, had her loose. She stepped out of the car. He put his hand on her back and led her forward. It took Nikki a second to realize where they were.

"Isn't this the old..." She put a hand over her mouth when she yawned.

"Funeral home," he finished for her. "Yup, I got it at a steal. I think the other potential buyers were afraid of ghosts."

"And you weren't?" Nikki watched him open the door. She wasn't scared of ghosts, but the idea of living—or in her case, sleeping—in a building that had been a funeral home, was a bit spooky. Of course, she was too tired to care. And right now her life was so scary, she wasn't sure a ghost could compete.

He cut his eyes down at her. "Let's just say I'm more afraid of the living than the dead."

She took one step in and stopped when she saw the coffin pushed against the wall. Maybe she wasn't too tired to care.

He chuckled again. "The prior owner was supposed to pick that up months ago."

She glanced at him over her shoulder. "Please tell me it's empty."

"I wish I could. Bud, get out of the coffin."

When Nikki heard rustling movement coming from the box, she jumped back and bumped into Dallas. His arm circled her middle, and his muscled torso pressed against her backside. He felt solid, strong, lean-on-me warm. She didn't pull away.

He laughed and called out again, "Bud, out!"

A round, white and tan canine head popped up and rested on the casket's lip. Its jowls flopped over the edge of the polished wood.

A little shocked, she giggled. Then realizing how close she was to the dog's owner—and that she hadn't been this close to a man in a long time—she shifted forward.

Dallas's hand brushed across her stomach as he released her. "He thinks it's his bed."

The dog spotted her and immediately leapt out of the box. His entire squatty, round body wagged as he came hurtling over to her. He stopped right over her stockinged feet and started sniffing and snorting at her legs.

"Bud, stop it," Dallas said.

"It's okay." Nikki knelt to pet him. Men she couldn't handle, but dogs were another thing. Nikki hadn't ever met a dog she didn't love. And as soon as she recovered from the loss of Chica, who'd died the same day her divorce was finalized, she was going to make a trip to the pound. Suddenly she felt a warm wet spray hit her right ankle.

"Uh-oh." She rose and stepped back.

"What?" Dallas asked.

"Happy sprinkles," she said and yawned again.

"Happy what?"

"He peed on me," she said.

Dallas laughed and apologized at the same time.

While too tired to think, and with one sock soaked in dog pee, she still liked hearing his laugh. "Happy sprinkles. That's what Nana calls it when her dog does that. Of course, Nana's Chihuahua doesn't sprinkle quite that much." Nikki reached down and took off her right hospital sock and suddenly wondered why she hadn't had the sense to change clothes at her place. Too much stress at seeing her apartment victimized, she guessed.

"My things." She remembered the bag she'd packed but hadn't brought in from the car. Her purse, too.

"Right here." He patted her bag where it was slung over his shoulder. "I put your purse in here, too." He motioned down the hall and they started walking. The English bulldog followed, his nails clicking against the wood floor.

"These are our offices." Dallas motioned to one large room that contained three desks and a television mounted on the wall. "Conference room." He pointed to a smaller room with a big table. He grinned and pointed at the door to the right. "My apartment."

He guided her through the doorway. A tan leather sofa centered the room, accompanied by a matching leather chair. A coffee table with a glass top centered the room and against the wall sat a large television. "Living room, kitchen." He motioned toward another shorter hallway. "Bedroom and bath. Nothing fancy, but home." He looked down at the dog, who now stood sniffing Nikki's bare foot. "Come on, Bud, I'll let you out."

Dropping Nikki's bag beside her, Dallas walked through the kitchen area and opened an exterior door for

Bud. The dog barked as if to say he'd be right back and then tore through the kitchen to the outdoors.

Dallas shut the door and turned back to her. That's when the awkwardness of this situation rained down on her. She was in the home of a man she hadn't even known for twenty-four hours. She wore hospital scrubs, no underwear, one sock and held a peed-on sock in one hand. "I think I'll use your restroom to wash off."

"Just one second." He hurried past her. "Let me…"

Nikki listened to him bumping and banging around in the bathroom. In less than a minute, he came out. "Lid's down now. There's soap in the shower, too. Clean towels on the counter."

Awkward. Very awkward. "Thanks." Bag in tow, she went into the bathroom. When she closed the door, she automatically locked it and then worried he'd heard the sound of the click and would realize how uncomfortable she felt. Then, too tired to care what he might think, she took several deep breaths.

It smelled as if someone had just spritzed the room with air freshener. The toilet lid was indeed down. A folded towel and washcloth were on the counter. She set her bag beside the towels and saw herself in the mirror. God, she looked like death warmed over. The word "death" brought it all back. Jack—dead. Ellen—attacked. Oh God!

Where was the logic in this? Why didn't anything make sense?

Almost too tired to take her clothes off, she glanced down at her one bare foot and decided a quick shower was in order. After figuring out how the shower worked, she disrobed, and then climbed in under the spray of warm water. While the water felt wonderful, she never relaxed.

A spicy male scent lingered in the foggy atmosphere, reminding her she was in a man's apartment.

When she left the steamy shower, she heard scratching and doggy whining at the door. In the distance, she heard Dallas scold the dog. For some reason she recalled Nana asking her if Jack had a pet. When Nikki had told her no, Nana had frowned and said having a pet was a sign of a decent man.

That thought took her back to opening her car's trunk, and the gruesome image filled her head once more. Attempting to push that thought back, she grabbed her bag. She couldn't even remember what she'd packed. She found a pair of boxer-style shorts and a tank top. What she didn't find was a bra. Obviously, her mind figured she'd gone without one for so long, it wasn't needed.

Not that it was needed to sleep in, but when she slipped on the tank top, she realized it was slightly clingy and accented the girls a bit more than her last scrub-style fashion statement. Too late to worry now. She finger combed her hair, stuffed her scrubs into her bag beside her purse and went to face the awkwardness again.

When Dallas heard the shower running, his mind started picturing her naked and his body hummed with anticipation. He knew damn well she wasn't showering to join him for a round of rambunctious sex, but certain southern body parts weren't convinced. Face it: He'd never brought a woman to sleep at his place when he hadn't indulged in some bedtime adventures.

Changing his sheets and preparing his bed for her, he recalled bits of the dialogue they shared before they'd left her place.

I promise you, I don't plan on seducing you tonight.
What about tomorrow?
How about we take it a day at a time?

Moving back into the living room, he dropped onto his sofa and passed a hand over his face. He'd told himself it couldn't happen. He'd told Tony it wasn't happening. And for damn good reasons, too.

If only he could remember them right now.

Shit! He was already wavering.

Staring at the blanket and pillow he'd already set out for himself, he tried to relax. But when the bathroom door opened, he popped up to meet her.

"Find everything you needed?" he asked. Bud danced at her feet with excitement.

"Yes. Thank you."

"I forgot to ask if you wanted something to eat or... drink." Damn! She looked...fucking great. All clean, wet, and ready to be stripped naked and sated. Her hair hung in wet wavy strands down to her shoulders. Unlike the hospital outfit, the tan and pink top hugged her form and showcased her breasts—a nice round set of C cups that had his jeans feeling tight again. The boxer-style shorts weren't nearly short or tight enough. However, what thigh he could see looked creamier than ice cream and he'd bet would taste a hell of a lot better.

"Uh. No, all I need is somewhere to lie down. I'm very tired."

"I...changed the sheets for you." He walked past her, aching to touch her, to pull her against him, to test his theory that she was as aware of him as he was of her. But he knew if he did, he'd be lost, so he kept going and pushed open the door to his bedroom.

She didn't follow him. "I . . . I can't take your bed."

"Yes, you can," he said, facing her. "I'm gonna hit the sofa for the rest of the night."

"I'll take the sofa." She headed to the living room.

He hurried past her and nearly tripped over Bud, who followed her every step. No way in hell was he letting her sleep on his crappy sofa. It was fine for sitting, but torture to sleep on. "I prefer you to take the bed. I always crash on the sofa. I probably wouldn't be able to sleep in the bed."

She cocked her head to the side and studied him. "Did you know that when you lie your right eyebrow arches up?"

He dropped down on the sofa, reclined back, and stretched his legs out. "Is that what happens?" He grinned and stuffed the pillow behind his head. "I never figured out how my mom knew it all those years."

She didn't respond to his humor.

"Okay, here's the thing." He purposely held his forehead muscles tight. "I don't sleep on it all the time, but I prefer the sofa." Damn if he didn't feel his brow arch upward.

"So do I," she said, and that sweet-looking mouth of hers bowed up and all he could think about was tasting it.

"Yeah, but . . . I'm already here and . . ." His gaze lowered to her breasts. Her mouth wasn't all he wanted to taste. "And unless you want to wrestle me for it—and I don't recommend that right now—then I suggest you head back to the bedroom and get some sleep. It's almost four in the morning."

Her eyes tightened. Her whole little body seemed to tense up and he'd kill to be close enough to feel it, too. Inside her being the ultimate proximity.

"If I wasn't so exhausted, I'd win this argument." She dropped both hands on her hips, giving him a good idea of just how small her waist was.

"I'll remember that." He folded his arms over his chest.

She swung around and hotfooted it down his hall.

"Let me know if you need anything." *Like a warm body to lie next to you and make you feel like a million bucks.* He shot up off the sofa to watch her move down the hall. Cute face, great breasts, and an adorable ass. And he was sleeping on the couch. What was wrong with this picture?

She stepped into his bedroom and shut the door with a whack. Not quite a slam, but close. Bud, a foot behind him, dropped down on his belly and whined like a big dog.

"Bud," he called. When the English bulldog trotted over, his head hanging with disappointment, Dallas reached out and gave him a good behind-the-ear scratch. "I know how you feel, buddy." Dallas looked at the door and imagined Nikki stretched out on his bed. "I really know how you feel."

At eight o'clock that morning, Tony, running on fumes, walked into Brian and Sterns Law Firm, and waited for the blond receptionist to acknowledge him. When she didn't move fast enough, he cleared his throat.

She looked up. "Sorry. Do you have an appointment?" She stood and slid a folder into a cabinet behind her. When she looked back, he noticed she had tears in her eyes.

Upset about Jack Leon? Tony wondered. And if so, what type of relationship did they have? She was thirty-ish and he supposed pretty enough to interest a single attorney.

Tony pulled back his suit coat to show his badge. "I'm with the Miller Police Department. Here about Jack Leon. My partner called."

The woman's eyes grew wetter. "Yes. Mr. Brian is waiting." She paused. "Jack was . . . a good man."

"Did everyone here feel the same way?" Tony pulled out his pad and pen. Normally, he relied on his memory but, exhausted, he wasn't taking chances.

"What do you mean?" she asked.

"I mean, did he play well with his work associates?"

"Of course he did."

"So, no office drama?"

She sat back down. "This is a law firm, detective. Lawyers are always dramatic."

"Good point, Miss . . . ?"

"Peterson. Rachel Peterson."

Tony jotted down her name. "Were there any hard feelings between Mr. Leon and anyone at the firm?"

She dropped her gaze. "Not really."

"You don't sound certain." He stepped closer.

"I'm just surprised. According to the news . . . it sounded as if you already knew who did this."

"We check all leads," Tony said. "Do you think anyone at this office would want to harm Mr. Leon?"

"No. There's always office politics, but nothing that would lead to . . . killing him."

"What kind of politics?"

She looked around as if she didn't want to get caught talking to him. "Brian Senior is about to retire. So someone is going to be promoted to partner. One slot, four lawyers."

Interesting. "What about Leon's personal life? Did he ever talk about anything? A girlfriend, his ex-wife?"

She hesitated. "Jack was a private person. He believed in following office protocol. He didn't share a lot."

"So he didn't have a girlfriend or..."

She tilted up her chin. "I was under the impression he was trying to get back with his ex-wife. He had me make dinner reservations for two yesterday at Venny's. He didn't say who he was taking but I assumed it was his ex-wife. And according to the news, it was her."

"Did his ex-wife ever call and speak with him at work?"

"Not that I'm aware of. But the lawyers use their cell phones for personal calls."

Tony decided to play his hunch. "How close were you and Mr. Leon?"

She looked taken aback by his question. "I respected him. He was a good lawyer. But nothing else."

"How about anyone else in the office? No romance in the workplace?"

"That's really frowned upon."

Tony nodded, too tired to know if he believed the woman. "Can you let Mr. Brian know I'm here?"

A few minutes later, Tony was met by a young man in his early thirties who introduced himself as Andrew Brian. He led Tony back to his office.

"You're retiring?" Tony asked.

"You must be thinking of my father."

"I see." Tony sat down in the seat across from the desk. His suspicion was piqued. "And you're not automatically in line to take his place as partner?"

Brian smiled. "It would appear that way. However... I'm not certain this is where I belong."

"Why not?"

"My father's footsteps are hard to fill and I guess you could say I'd like to blaze my own path."

Tony made some notes and got down to business. He asked Brian the same questions he'd asked the receptionist. Got the same answers, too. "Are you the Brian who handled Leon's will?"

"Yes. I'd just started here and Jack asked if I would fix it so his ex-wife remained listed as the beneficiary of his estate."

"Didn't you find that strange?" Tony asked.

"I have clients leaving fortunes to cats. There's nothing strange about Jack's request."

"Did he love her?" Tony asked.

"It would appear that way."

"Do you know if he was dating his ex again?"

"No, but like I said, he kept his personal life personal." The man leaned back in his chair. "Truthfully, I was shocked this happened. Jack was a well-liked man."

Tony leaned forward. "Well, I'd say someone didn't agree with you."

CHAPTER TWELVE

A LOUD SHRIEK jolted Dallas awake and he shot off the sofa.

Austin jumped back, laughing, bicycle horn in hand. Tyler stood at the door, laughing with him. Bud stood beside Tyler, begging to be let out.

Dallas, still foggy with sleep, stared at his two partners. He debated knocking the shit out of both of them, but then his gaze shifted to the sofa and he put what brain power he had to figuring out why had he'd fallen asleep there.

Dallas remembered Nikki at the same time Austin squeezed the horn again. Snagging the horn from Austin's hand, Dallas tossed it across the room. "Stop it! Nikki's asleep."

Bud bolted after the horn and caught it, sending out loud short blasts of noise.

"Shit!" Dallas started chasing Bud, Austin started chasing him, and Tyler stood there laughing. Finally, Dallas caught the dog, retrieved the horn and glared at his two partners.

"Who's Nikki?" Austin asked, a shit-eating grin on his face.

"Nikki Hunt, right?" Tyler asked.

Dallas nodded, ran a hand through his hair, and looked at the wall clock. It was eight thirty. He'd gotten less than two hours sleep. Damn it, but he was going to have to buy a sofa he could actually lay on. Bud, still in a playful frenzy, ran to the kitchen and pawed at the door. Having to piss himself, Dallas commiserated with his dog, and let him out.

"Who's Nikki?" repeated Austin.

Tyler chuckled. "The artist with size C breasts."

Austin looked down the hall with interest before turning back to Dallas. "You bring her home with you and you sleep on the couch? What's up with that? Does that mean she's free range? I mean, I'd rather have the stripper, but—"

Dallas pointed to the door. "You know better than to piss me off before I have my coffee."

Austin chuckled but he wasn't as stupid as he pretended to be, so he started out. Tyler, probably smarter than he and Austin put together, stayed at the door. "Your brother's called twice. And your dad called and said to remember what's coming up next week."

"Thanks." Dallas grabbed his cell off the coffee table. He'd turned it off, afraid Tony would be trying to find Nikki when he got to her apartment. And yup, two missed calls from Tony. One from his dad.

Looking down the hall that led to his bedroom, he considered it a miracle she wasn't awake.

"I made coffee in the office." Tyler still stood in the doorway. "I guess you'll fill us in as to why you brought her home with you, huh?"

You mean besides the fact that she's hot and makes me want to protect her from everything wrong in the world? Two images flashed in Dallas's head: one of her wearing that tight little tank top, still wet from the shower, and one of her at six years old, looking frightened as she stood beside her grandmother. One image made him want her. The other made him want to protect her.

Damn, he was so gone where Nikki was concerned. And maybe it was the lack of coffee, but right now he didn't want to fight what he felt. He recalled what he'd told her at her place, *How about we take it a day at a time?* At the time, he'd been joking, but now it sounded like a damn good plan.

He looked down the hall again. Had she slept better than he did? Between his unrelenting hard-on and the damn sofa springs, he'd barely closed his eyes.

He glanced back at Tyler, who was probably accurately reading every one of Dallas's internal thoughts. On top of a criminal justice degree, his partner had a degree in psychology.

Dallas sighed. "Give me a minute and I'll be in."

"Okay." Tyler started out the door.

"Tyler?" When Tyler turned around, Dallas asked, "Do I do something weird to my face when I lie?"

Tyler grinned. "You mean your brow thing?"

"Why the hell haven't you told me?"

"Because only the most observant person would notice. And I knew it would give you a complex." Tyler's gaze shifted to the hall that led to the bedroom. "She's an artist, so part of her job is to notice details. It makes sense she'd notice."

"You should have said something," Dallas muttered

and then said, "I'll be out in a few minutes." He ran a hand over his face. "I need to call Tony before he shows up on my doorstep with guns blaring."

"Too late." Tony's voice boomed from down the hall. "And the guns are loaded."

Tyler knew better than to come between two brothers talking about guns, so he went back to the office. Dallas watched his partner escape and hoped he knew to keep Austin cornered in the office. All Dallas needed was for Austin and Tony to get into it over last night.

Tony appeared in the doorway, looking as angry as he'd sounded. "We need to talk. You didn't answer my calls. I don't know if anything was taken from Nikki Hunt's apartment. And I'm only going to say this once: If you or one of your guys come sniffing around another of my crime scenes, I swear to God, I'll have your asses thrown in jail!"

Dallas groaned. He'd expected this much or more, but not before coffee. He moved to the door, hoping to stop Tony from coming inside his apartment. "Can you wait in the conference room? I'd like to take a piss and get some coffee, before you chew my ass out."

Tony frowned. "Why don't I chat with Nikki while you piss?"

"Why don't you let her sleep a few more hours?" His tone went deeper, implying it wasn't a request.

From the harsh lines on Tony's face and the wrinkled shirt he wore—the same one he'd been wearing last night—Dallas surmised Tony hadn't gone to bed. Just dealing with Tony was hard; dealing with a sleep-deprived Tony was like juggling sharp glass.

Not that Dallas was exactly a pushover himself, and

he didn't plan to back down, but...he needed coffee and a piss first. "She didn't get to bed until after four. Give her a couple of hours. Hell, go home and get some sleep yourself. I'll personally see that she gets to your office later."

His brother's scowl deepened. "Take your piss. I'll wait in your conference room."

Five minutes later, relieved, teeth brushed, and ready to get his ass chewed out—not that he didn't plan to chew back—Dallas walked into the conference room. He set two cups of coffee on the big mahogany table and pushed one across the top to his brother.

Tony, on the phone, nodded his thanks and pulled the cup toward his lips. "Tell them I just need five minutes. Damn it, get the doctor to okay it."

Did Tony mean Ellen Wise? Dallas sipped his coffee, grabbed a *Sports Illustrated* magazine from the table, flipped through the pages and feigned disinterest in the conversation. He wondered if his eyebrows went up when he did that, too.

"Did you get a confirmation from Brian and Sterns?" Tony asked the person on the line.

Dallas's interest was piqued even higher when he heard the name of the firm where Nikki's husband had worked.

Tony's frowned deepened. "I don't give a damn. You tell them I'll be there at two o'clock and somebody better be there to talk to me or the next court appearance they'll be making will be their own." He hung up and eyed Dallas with the same mood he'd offered the caller.

"What do you know?" Tony asked.

"What do *you* know?" Dallas countered.

"Don't fuck with me."

"Don't worry, you're not my type."

"I could go wake her up right now," Tony threatened.

Dallas almost got pissed, but then stopped himself. Knowing when to toss in the towel wasn't a sign of weakness, but intelligence. So he tossed it and hoped he got something for his trouble. "She didn't notice anything that was taken from her place."

"You believe her?"

"One hundred percent," Dallas said, meaning it.

Tony looked as if he knew something Dallas didn't, so he just waited for Tony to continue. Taking another sip of his coffee, Tony finally spoke, "It looked like a computer had been hooked up to the desk top, but it isn't there now. Did she bring it with her?"

Dallas shook his head. "I asked about the computer. She sold it a couple of weeks ago."

Tony leaned in. "That doesn't sound fishy to you?"

"Not when she'd already confessed to having money issues."

"So maybe she was doing something on the side to make a little cash. Drugs?"

"Christ, Tony. Does she look like a drug dealer?"

"Have you forgotten that the first thing they taught you at the academy was not to go on stereotypes?"

"It's not just how she looks. It's . . . my instincts."

"And like I said earlier, your instincts are being overrun by your dick. You're so hot for her you can't see how bad this looks. Hell, Rick Clark told me you bet on her guilt."

Dallas flinched. "So there's your proof. I see how bad this looks. But when I looked closer, I realized the truth. Why the hell do you think I'm representing her?

For Christ's sake, she's not the type of woman I want to get involved with, but I can't stop myself." He gut knotted when he admitted that truth. "Look, I know she's not guilty."

"We're cops. We're supposed to look at the evidence."

Dallas leaned in. "I *was* a cop. Look where the evidence got me. Or did you even look at the evidence in my case? My guess is that you didn't. You *knew* I was innocent."

"You're my brother."

"And I was innocent. But the evidence didn't prove that."

Tony shook his head. "Damn, you're right. You can't be a cop again. You'll never be able to let the evidence speak for itself."

"Good thing I don't want the job then," Dallas said. "And I still look at the evidence—I just know the evidence can lie."

Tony slumped back in his chair. "You, Austin, and Tyler were framed. Most people who look guilty are guilty."

"Yeah, we were framed. But Nikki's not being framed and she's a suspect. My other client, Eddie Nance, isn't being framed unless you blame Detective Shane for setting him up, and look what he's up against."

"No one is setting anyone up," Tony said.

The silence was heavy. Dallas wanted to ask about what happened between Tony and Shane, but he figured that would send Tony over the edge. Before he sent his brother there, he wanted more information about Nikki's case.

Tony picked up the coffee, sipped, and apparently

decided to clear the thick air with a change of conversation. "Did you mention Ellen's phone call to Jack to Nikki?"

"Yeah. She wouldn't even entertain the idea that Ellen was up to something with her ex." Dallas studied his brother's expression. Dallas's gut said Tony knew something else.

"What you got?" When Tony didn't answer, Dallas went for another question. "Have you talked to Ellen Wise yet?" Because he'd heard Tony's phone conversation, Dallas didn't think Tony had, but...

Contrary to what Dallas believed, Tony nodded. "Doctors let me see her at six this morning."

So who was it that Tony was going to see in a couple of hours? Was it about the robbery and shooting at the convenience store? If so, maybe a witness could help Nance. He stored that information to chew on later.

"And what did you learn?" When Tony didn't answer, Dallas decided to push. "Damn it, Tony, if you can't share anything, why the hell should I share with you?"

"Ellen didn't see the attacker," Tony offered. "She only remembers seeing someone in a ski mask. Bigger and taller than she was. But when I asked her if she knew of anyone who would want to hurt her, she said the only person she'd managed to piss off lately was Jack Leon."

"So she admitted to knowing him?" The thought of how Nikki was going to feel clouded his excitement at discovering something new.

"No," Tony added. "She said Leon had been calling Nikki at the gallery and sending flowers."

"Nikki told me that." She hadn't told him everything, but Tony didn't need to know that. And as soon as she woke up, Dallas planned to have a chat. He needed more information if he was going to do this job right.

"Ellen said Leon's last message sent her over the edge. She said Nikki was just getting over the jerk. So Ellen called Jack back and told him to stay the hell away from Nikki. Ellen said Jack got ugly, called her a bitch, and told her to get her nose out of his business. When he hung up on her, she called him back."

"Which explains the two phone calls," Dallas said.

"Yeah," Tony admitted. "So we're back to square one. We got fingerprints at Nikki's place and the gallery, but who knows if they belong to the perp? Other than a vague description of Wise's attacker, we've got nothing. We don't even know if the two crimes are connected."

Dallas set his cup on the table a little hard. "Oh, hell, they have to be."

"I know." Tony held up his hand. "It's coincidental otherwise, but..." He raked his hand over his face. "I keep thinking we're missing something. Something obvious. Something Nikki Hunt isn't telling us."

"We're probably missing something, but she's not hiding anything." He remembered the look in her eyes when she stared at the snapshot of her and her grandmother. "She's an open book, Tony. She's like Mom was. Remember how we could read her? Whatever she was feeling showed in her eyes." The words hadn't left his mouth when he recalled the sadness that played in his mother's eyes when she'd visited him in prison. His gut twisted as he realized how upset she'd been about him during her last year of life.

Tony chuckled. "You knew your ass was grass before she opened her mouth." He pulled his coffee to his lips and sipped. "Damn, I miss her."

"Me, too." Dallas sipped his own coffee and realized this was the first time they'd talked about their mom since he'd been out of prison. Probably because it hurt too much. Just losing his mom to cancer was hard. Losing her while he'd been unjustly put behind bars was hell. And while his mom had never questioned his innocence, she died not knowing he'd been cleared. How unfair was it that the last year of her life, when she'd been almost too sick to do it, she'd visited him once a week? For that reason alone, Dallas wanted to be the one to put a gun against the forehead of the man responsible for framing him, and Dallas personally wanted to pull the trigger.

"I hope you're right about Nikki," Tony said.

"I am." They stared at each other for a minute as if emotionally gathering their ground. As hard as talking about his mom was for Dallas, Tony had his own reasons not to want to go there. Less than two weeks after their mother had died, Tony lost his little girl. Then he lost LeAnn. The O'Connors had had some lousy luck lately.

Tony stood up. "I expect to see Nikki in my office by three this afternoon."

"She'll be there." Dallas met Tony by the door. "Why don't you go home and get some sleep? You look like shit."

"It's good to see you, too." Tony slapped Dallas on the back and started out.

Dallas remembered the potentially combative question he needed to ask. Not enjoying fighting with his brother, Dallas almost let Tony go, but he remembered nineteen-year-old Eddie Nance sitting across that same table, scared of what his future held. The kid didn't deserve to go down for something he didn't do, and if pissing off his brother was what Dallas had to do to get the kid off, he'd do it.

"Hey?" Dallas said.

Tony looked back.

"You wanna share with me what you and Shane nearly went to fist city over last night?"

Tony's eyes tightened. "I'm serious, Dallas. Stay the fuck away from my crime scenes."

"It was the Nance case that got him riled up, wasn't it? You saw something and mentioned it to him."

Tony stood stone faced. Dallas even watched his eyebrow, thinking maybe his brother suffered from the same infliction.

"Tell me it's not the same MO that Nance was arrested for. Tell me that and I'll drop this."

"I'm not telling you shit." Tony's eyebrow didn't budge.

"But you wouldn't let an innocent kid go down if you knew something, right?"

Frown lines deepen in his brother's face. "What I'm going to do is my job." Tony left.

Dallas let go of a deep breath. It wasn't the answer he'd hoped to get.

Before Dallas entered the office, he walked back into his apartment to let Bud in and to make sure Nikki wasn't up. With Bud inside, Dallas went to his bedroom door and listened and heard...nothing. Worried the horn or his brother's shenanigans had awoken her and she was in there chewing on her lip and fretting about what was happening out here, he cracked the door a bit to check.

She was still asleep. Resting on her side, her face toward the door, she had her hand tucked under her cheek.

With her hair scattered over his pillow, she looked...
warm, soft, and curl-up-beside-me beautiful. And what
he wouldn't give to be able to do that. Curl up beside her
and snag a few more hours of sleep. His gaze shifted to
the curvy figure under the sheet and he knew if he did
crawl in that bed, he wouldn't want to sleep.

A few very visual images of what he would want to
do filled his head. Suddenly Bud went charging into the
room and stopped by the bed.

"Shit," he muttered, and then whispered, "Bud?"

The dog looked at Dallas and shook his head as if saying no.

"Come here!" Dallas ordered, speaking low.

Bud's answer to that was to jump into the bed and ease
over to Nikki.

"Shit," Dallas muttered again. Thankfully Nikki
didn't budge. Obviously she was a deep sleeper. But deep
enough for him to grab the dog?

Still holding the doorknob, he debated whether he
should go snatch the dog away or just let him stay. He
imagined the conversation they would have if Nikki woke
up with him in the room, one knee on the bed. He snarled
at Bud, and swore to cut the dog's rations for punishment.

"Lucky dog," he muttered as he headed down the hall.

Walking into the office, Dallas found Tyler and Austin
arguing. It took all of two seconds to catch on to what the
argument was about: Tony.

"I just said it's not the time to start shit," Tyler snapped.

"I wasn't going to start shit. I wanted to ask a few questions about the crime scene."

"Tyler's right," Dallas said. "Wrong time. Tony was up

all night working and would've gotten pissed if he'd even seen you."

"I'm worried about a kid going to prison and you're worried that your sleep-deprived brother might get upset?" Austin snapped.

Dallas stared at Austin and fought with his own sleep-deprived patience. "If pissing Tony off would give us something to help get this kid off, I'd be first in line to shovel piss. But I know my brother, Austin. He's a good cop and a decent person, and I'm hoping he'll eventually give us what we need. But I know how far to push and when to back off. Let *me* deal with him."

"And how long are you going to deal with him while wearing kid gloves?" Austin asked, his frustration front and center in his voice. "Is your brother going to come around before Nance is in prison having to take it up the ass?"

A gasp echoed behind Dallas. The look on both Austin and Tyler's faces told Dallas whoever stood there was bad news. Dallas envisioned Nikki, but when he turned, he saw it was much worse.

CHAPTER THIRTEEN

SEEING EDDIE NANCE's scared face, Dallas winced.

"I didn't mean that," Austin said.

"Everything is going to be fine," Tyler added.

"We're on top of this," Dallas said, trying to sound more confident than he felt. But none of their words removed the look of total fear from Nance's eyes or the look of hopelessness in his seventy-five-year-old grandma standing behind him. She'd already lost three grandsons.

Right then, Dallas decided he had to hire a receptionist, someone to man the front and announce their clients' arrivals. He saw Nance swallow, his Adam's apple bobbing up and down with nervous fear. Damn it! Austin was right. Dallas had to get to the bottom of what happened last night at the crime scene. Tony would just have to understand.

"Tyler," Dallas said. "Show Ms. Nance and Eddie to the conference room and get them something to drink." He looked back at Eddie and his grandmother. "I'll be right in."

As soon as they were gone, Dallas faced Austin. His

partner held up his arms. "Don't tell me, I already know. I've gotta fucking watch what I say."

"Yeah," Dallas agreed. "But let's worry about that later. Right now tell me if you are still on speaking terms with that critical care nurse you banged a couple of weeks ago—the one who works at Methodist Hospital."

"I showed her a good time last weekend. Why?" Austin asked.

"Call and see if she can tell you who's on her floor. Tony mentioned going to see someone in a couple of hours. I think he meant Methodist Hospital and I have a feeling this is a witness of last night's convenience-store shooting. We need to know what this person knows."

"Won't that piss off your brother?"

"Hell, yeah. But I'll deal with Tony. You, however, avoid him at all costs. He said he'd arrest us for interfering and he means it." Dallas took off to try to help Tyler soothe Eddie and his grandmother.

Ten minutes later, the soothing wasn't going so well.

"I don't want to go to jail," Eddie said with so much emotion Dallas felt the kid's words slam against his chest. "I didn't do this. How did this happen?"

Dallas remembered asking the same damn question himself when he'd been called into the lieutenant's office and stripped of his badge and gun. But at the time, he hadn't been nineteen and still trying to figure out how to be a man. Prison was no place for a kid in his formative years. Prison could destroy a boy like Eddie Nance, and Dallas knew it.

"I know this is scary." Dallas pressed a hand to the boy's shoulder and wished he could promise the kid that nothing bad was going to happen. "We're doing everything we can to make this disappear." Dallas could see the kid working hard to keep it together.

"But what if you can't?" The boy swallowed. "You, all of you, went to jail for something you didn't do."

"We were framed," Dallas said. "You aren't being framed."

"It sure as hell feels like it," Eddie said, reminding Dallas he'd said much the same to Tony earlier. Tears filled the kid's eyes. He looked at his grandmother. "I did everything right. I did what you said for me to do. Kept myself clean. Finished high school. And where's it gotten me?" He wiped away tears he no doubt saw as a weakness. "Maybe I should just disappear."

"No," Dallas and Tyler said at the same time.

"We're not done fighting here," Dallas said. And he vowed to fight harder. Someone had to save this kid.

Eddie's grandmother looked at Dallas, emotion brightening her eyes. Dallas thought of his mom, how much she'd hurt seeing him behind bars. Blinking, he pushed that thought away. But another replaced it. He remembered another older woman who stood strong for someone she loved. Nikki's grandma.

Recalling Mrs. Littlemore led Dallas to thinking about Nikki. Someone else he had to save.

"Are they going to come after me for this last robbery?" Eddie asked. "Are they going to say that I killed someone? Try to give me the death penalty?"

"Slow down," Tyler added. "We don't know if they suspect you for this."

"The hell they don't. You weren't there when the cop came asking questions at two this morning."

"What cop?" Dallas asked. "Detective Shane?"

"Yeah, him. Why does he hate me?"

"Look," Tyler intervened. "This second robbery might work in our favor. If the MO is similar, we can use it to cast doubt on your case."

"He's right," Dallas said. "Right now we need you to stay calm. Let us do our job. We found the girl that saw you at the park the night of the robbery. That's going to help. I'll get with your lawyer and we'll go over the case."

Ten minutes later, Nance seemed more in control. He walked out of the conference room with Tyler. Mrs. Nance, the boy's grandmother, hung back.

She stared at her grandson's departing back, and then at Dallas. "He's a good boy." Her voice sounded ready to break.

"I know," Dallas said. "We wouldn't have taken the case otherwise." And they wouldn't have. But neither had Dallas expected to get so emotionally involved. In the beginning, opening the PI business had been something to do while the three of them hunted down DeLuna. Dallas didn't think any of them had lost their need for revenge by a long shot, but it wasn't the only thing that got Dallas up in the mornings anymore. He suspected it was the same with Tyler and Austin.

"He wouldn't last a month in prison," she said. "We both know that."

Dallas wished he could argue with her. "Let's hope it doesn't come to that."

"It won't come to that," she said. "I have a friend who lives in Mexico. She'd take Eddie in."

"If he runs, Mrs. Nance, he'll be running the rest of his life."

"But he'd have a life. I can't lose another one. I've buried too many of my boys as it is."

"Don't give up on us yet," Dallas pleaded.

"I haven't. But when you give up, when you know it's a lost cause, I want you to tell me...in plenty of time."

It was then Dallas realized how far removed he was from being the cop he'd been years ago, because he looked that grandmother right in the eyes and said, "You have my word."

With Nance and his grandmother gone, Dallas snagged himself another coffee and inhaled the last doughnut. Before he sat down with his partners, he checked on Nikki. He needed to shake off the doom and gloom he felt and, for some reason, even though Nikki's case wasn't a laugh a minute, thinking about her didn't get him down. Probably because he wasn't just thinking about her case. Anticipation. That's the feeling she inspired in him.

One day at a time.

He nudged open the bedroom door. She was sleeping, still looking too damn good in his bed, with Bud snuggled beside her and looking as happy as a pig in mud.

Realizing he was jealous of his dog, Dallas rejoined Austin and Tyler in the office. "Anything?" he asked as Austin hung up the phone.

"You were right. The new patient at Methodist is a second shooting victim. Fifty-year-old woman—in bad shape I'm afraid."

Dallas frowned. "Can you get in to see her?"

"I asked, but Karen said the doctor's not even letting the family back yet. It's bad."

Dallas dropped down in his desk chair. "Okay, but let's stay on top of it and, as soon as she's better, see if we can't get in."

"I hope we get in," Tyler said. "Because I'm reading

the news on the shooting now and the press didn't release shit. Except the shooter was described as a black male."

"By who?" Dallas asked.

"Witness," Tyler said. "That's all I've learned, but I've already posted it as a question to be answered." He tapped a pad with his pen. Tyler's question list was a daily ritual.

"Okay," Dallas said to Austin. "See if you can find out who their witness is. It could be the patient at the hospital or it may be that someone else saw something. I'll talk to my brother this afternoon when I take Nikki in. Hopefully, he'll give us something. Tyler, you call Nance's attorney and update him on the witness who puts Nance at the park the night of the first shooting. We gotta get this kid off."

They all nodded. After several seconds, Dallas's phone buzzed with an incoming text. He pulled it from his pocket and flipped open the lid.

The text was from Suzan Kelly, his biweekly sex partner. "Friday not happening. Rain check?"

"Bad news?" Tyler asked.

Dallas looked up. "No," he answered honestly. And that was what bothered him. He didn't care if Suzan couldn't make it Friday. He wasn't even eager to schedule a rain check. The sex was good. It suited his needs and he made sure he suited hers. So since when did he lose interest in a night of no-strings-attached, commitment-free sex?

Since you have a gorgeous blonde taking up residence in your bed.

He pocketed his phone without answering Suzan and decided to put it out of his mind for two weeks. He was dealing with Nikki and his mangled attraction for her a day at a time. "Did you get anything on Jack Leon?" he asked, remembering he'd put that bug in Tyler's ear yesterday.

"Mostly gossip, but it's interesting." Tyler thumbed through a stack of files on his desk.

"While he finds that, you wanna update us on your houseguest's case?" Austin asked.

Dallas leaned back in his chair. "You know about her ex being found in the car."

"Yeah, but you didn't fill us in on the best part."

"What part?" Dallas eyed Austin's shit-eating grin. Before the man answered the question, Dallas knew what it was.

"The part where she puked all over you." Austin let out a deep laugh and held up his hands. "Sorry, but I would have loved to have seen the look on your face."

Dallas rolled his eyes.

"She puked on you?" Tyler asked.

"The guys at the crime scene last night were talking about it," Austin told Tyler. "They said Dallas had her by the shoulders, when she bent at the waist and got his shoes. Then she rose up and she got him right in the chest. Which is the reason he came in without a shirt on yesterday." Austin laughed so hard he could hardly talk.

"I'm glad I gave you some comic relief," Dallas said. "Can we get down to business now?"

They both sobered, but humor lingered in their eyes. No doubt, they'd give him shit about it later. Not that he blamed them. If the shoe was on the other foot—if it had been their shoes to have been christened with barf—he'd be doing some shit-slinging as well.

"Anyway..." Dallas filled them in on everything from Ellen's attack to finding Nikki's apartment broken into. When he finished, he looked at Tyler, who was busy taking notes—or listing questions to be answered. "Now, what you got on Leon?"

Tyler picked up the file he'd found earlier. "I searched some court records and found Leon handled a few big cases last year. Won most of them. Then I called my contact at the courthouse."

"Who is that?" Dallas asked.

"My sister." He smiled. "She works as Judge Hardgrave's executive assistant and if there is one thing she excels at, it's courthouse gossip. If it involves a lawyer, judge, or a DA, that woman knows their dirty laundry."

"So does Jack Leon have dirty laundry?" Dallas asked.

"She said Leon was a lady's man, but serious about his career. Talk was he'd been up to make partner at his firm a year ago. Rumor was that Sterns only promoted family men. The divorce could have cost him that promotion."

Dallas wondered if this was the reason Nikki's ex was trying so hard to get her back, or if he really loved her. The man was dead and it shouldn't even matter. It didn't affect the case, but the question nipped at his mind.

"Oh, she also said Brian, the other senior partner, had a son working there. Andrew Brian is single, and not a great lawyer, but people were betting on who'd make partner first. Andrew or Leon."

"Was there bad blood between the two?" Dallas asked.

"Don't know, but I put it on my morning list of questions we need to answer."

While some people created a to-do list, Tyler created question lists. He claimed he hated chores, but loved finding answers. So if a chore could be written as a question he would get it done. Austin and Dallas had teased Tyler about the stupid head games he played with himself, but they had both learned the value of Tyler's oddball ways.

"Good question." Austin got up to get coffee.

"What are your other questions?" Dallas sipped his coffee and eyed Tyler over the rim of his cup. Oddball are not, of the three of them, Tyler was the best investigator. He saw angles and asked questions that Dallas and Austin didn't think of. Not that Tyler's angles were always right, but five times out of ten, one of his questions helped solve a case.

Tyler picked up his notepad. "Okay but these are for both cases and my...personal inquiries." The emphasis Tyler put on "personal" meant something, but Dallas ignored it.

"Just read the list," Dallas said.

Tyler looked back at the pad. " 'Who's the witness at last night's robbery homicide?' "

"Good one," Dallas said. "And hopefully Tony will help us answer that one."

Tyler tapped a pen against his list. " 'What was the relationship between Andrew Brian and Jack Leon?' "

"Another good one," Dallas said. "I'll see if Nikki knows anything about this man. And since Serena is using them to try to sue me for custody of Bud, I might go in and have myself a little chat with her lawyer."

"It might work." Tyler looked back at his list. "Number three, 'Why does Detective Shane have a hard-on for our boy Nance?' "

"What do you mean?" Austin asked, resettling in his leather chair. "Nance was Shane's arrest. He doesn't want anyone to prove he screwed up."

"Yeah. But Nance said it was Detective Shane who went to his house last night. That case was a homicide. It was Tony's case, not Shane's. It just seems as if paying Nance a visit after midnight goes above the call of duty."

Dallas chewed on that thought. "Maybe he feels it's

personal because we're trying to prove him wrong? But I see your point. Look into it?"

Tyler nodded.

"Is that all? No more questions?" Dallas asked.

"Just one more."

"Shoot," Dallas said.

"O...kay." Now it was Tyler who wore the shit-eating grin. " 'What is it about the blonde in Dallas's bedroom that has him so damn nervous?' "

Dallas rolled his eyes. "On that note, I'll go make a few phone calls." Coffee in hand, he went back to his apartment. He started into the kitchen, but detoured down the hall. He eased open his bedroom door. Bud raised his head, then plopped it back on the bed as if to say, "Don't even try to make me leave."

What is it about the blonde in Dallas's bedroom that has him so damn nervous?

It was a good question. And one Dallas hoped to answer soon.

Leaning against the door frame, he blew off the steam billowing up from the cup, and sipped at the hot brew. The desire to crawl in bed with Nikki and his dog was damn near irresistible.

Tony needed sleep, but with so much shit hitting the fan and slinging his way, if he took a few hours off, he'd be knee deep in crap. His cell beeped with a missed call as he walked into Methodist Hospital. He hoped it wasn't Dallas. His brother was going to blow a gasket when he learned what Nikki's ex in-laws had said. Sure, Tony had to tell him, but not now.

He pulled out his phone and saw it was Joe with CSU.

Tony had called Joe about seven times trying to get a report on the last two homicides, but Joe always took his sweet ass time.

Tony started to call Joe back but decided to do the interview first. Hopefully, Joe would have something that would help Nikki Hunt's case.

According to Mrs. Leon, Nikki Hunt was a gold digger from the wrong side of the tracks, who married their son for his money and then insisted on alimony when they divorced. Thankfully their son had been smart enough to have her sign the prenuptial agreement. However, her son hadn't been smart enough to cancel the quarter-million-dollar life insurance policy that listed Nikki Hunt as the sole beneficiary. In Texas, a divorce automatically removed an ex as the beneficiary, but not if a spouse had his ex reinstated afterward. Which according to Mrs. Leon, her son had done, because Nikki had insisted. Now Mrs. Leon wanted Nikki arrested.

Tony had called the insurance agency and confirmed the Leons' story. Although Tony suspected Nikki Hunt wasn't going to come out as clean she appeared, he'd been shocked by this. He'd learned a long time ago that most anyone could be provoked to kill, but to plan a murder for money, that took a special kind of lowlife.

With Dallas's evidence speech from this morning bouncing in his head, Tony wasn't ready to put a pair of handcuffs on Nikki. Tony just hoped Dallas realized that if something didn't turn up soon, he wouldn't have a choice.

The Leons were rich and influential people. Not that Tony would let that influence the case, but he'd made arrests on less probable cause. Still, things didn't add up.

Heading to the ICU unit, hoping to get in to see Marjorie

Brown, the second shooting vic from last night's robbery-homicide case, he paused at the hall where LeAnn had been working yesterday. Would she be here today? Hell, he went to see. The desk was unmanned and his chest ached with a flash of disappointment.

Whenever things got bad at work, LeAnn had been his touchstone to make things better. Just sliding in bed beside her, or watching her do silly stuff like rearrange the living room for the hundredth time, or watch her reading a book, made the ugly things he saw on the job less disturbing. The woman exemplified not just the good in the world, but its simple pleasures. And with the day and night he'd had, he could really use his touchstone now.

He missed her. Seeing her yesterday had made him realize how much. A nurse strolled out of a room and Tony walked over. "Is LeAnn O'Connor working today?"

The woman sized him up.

"I'm her husband," he added. He didn't say estranged, hoping that would change.

"She's on break."

The thought of seeing her filled his chest with joy. "Do you know where she goes on break?"

"The moon?" She offered him a smile. "Or maybe the cafeteria."

He smiled. "Where's that?"

She gave him directions.

"Thanks." He started to leave.

"How long have you two been married?" she asked.

"Over two years. Why?"

She grinned. "The way you lit up when I said she was here, I thought you were honeymooners."

"She's special." As he made his way to the elevator, he

decided to ask LeAnn out to dinner on Sunday. Take her somewhere nice. Maybe dancing. LeAnn loved to dance.

An image of her eight months pregnant dancing around the living room filled his mind. The pregnant part of the memory sobered his mood. He knew she was still hurting. Sooner or later, they had to talk about Emily. But not now. Now he just wanted to see his wife.

Nikki felt the wonderful peace of sleep being pulled out from under her. Resting on her side, she buried her cheek deeper into her pillow and tried to snatch back that sense of peace. However, the feel of the pillow against her cheek didn't help. It felt . . . different somehow. As a matter of fact, everything felt different.

The mattress. It was firmer than hers.

The smells in the room. Spicy male aroma—so totally not the way her bedroom smelled.

The sensation of brightness behind her closed lids. Her bedroom wasn't this bright.

However, she didn't feel alarmed until she noted the biggest difference of all. She wasn't alone on the firm mattress in the bright room filled with yummy scents.

The bulky, warm weight of someone at her back sent panic through her veins.

Oh crap! Her eyes popped open.

Completely disoriented, she didn't move anything but her eyes. Left to right, she took in her surroundings. The raw urge to scream crawled up her throat when she didn't recognize anything that her wide-eyed visual sweep took in. Not the gray walls, the huge pine dresser or the pair of jeans—a man's jeans—casually tossed over the top of that dresser.

The mental fog started to lift and bam, she remembered.

Jack, dead. Ellen, attacked. Her place, ransacked. And the good-looking, masculine-smelling PI who'd come to her rescue.

The bulky warmth at her back shifted ever so slightly. Had he... Had she...? *Oh, damn!*

Forcing her brain into recall action, she collected bits and pieces of data. He'd brought her to his place. She'd showered. He refused to let her sleep on the sofa. She'd gone to his bed. *Alone.* She was sure she'd gone to bed alone.

She recalled tossing and turning. His smell in the bed had been intoxicating. As aromatic and tempting as cupcakes in a bright yellow kitchen—Nana's old kitchen.

But this wasn't Nana's kitchen and Nikki prayed she hadn't already indulged in any—metaphorical—cupcakes. Taking a deep breath, she realized she was fully dressed. Well, as dressed as one could be when wearing boxer-style shorts and a tank top. She did one more lap around her brain, searching for anything that led her to believe she'd given into temptation.

Finally convinced that while he might have joined her in the bed, they hadn't done the deed, she took in a deep breath. The bulk against her upper back, possibly a shoulder, shifted again. Then she felt it... the rake of a warm tongue against her neck.

Nikki froze. He... licked her? What kind of a pervert was he? Sure, she was in his bed, but hadn't she argued to take the couch? Had he come in here with hopes of... Men! Dogs every one of them!

"You'd better retract that tongue, buster, before you lose it," she said in a justifiably bitchy whisper, and waited for his reply.

CHAPTER FOURTEEN

A DEEP, HALF SIGH, half moan was the only answer Nikki received. Was he not awake? Suddenly an obnoxious odor filled her nasal cavity. She covered her nose. Men were such uncultured beasts. She went to ease out of the bed when she heard a loud snore. Make that a snort.

"So you're not going to explain it, huh?" she asked.

"Explain what?" a deep voice replied. Only it didn't come from...

She raised her head off the pillow. Dallas O'Connor stood at the door. If he was... Who was...? She rolled over and stared at the dog.

"You mean Bud," Dallas said. "Sorry. He snuck in when I came to check on you,"

The canine opened his eyes, and proceeded to pass gas again. She actually heard it this time. Slow... and deadly.

The smell intensified. She pressed her hand over her nose and rolled out of bed.

The stench must have reached the doorway, because Dallas slapped his hand over his nose and looked mortified. "I'm sorry," he said, his hand still held over his nose as he walked into the room and pointed to the dog. "Bud, get out of here." Dallas's gaze shifted back to her. "I'll bet Tyler fed him people food last night. He can't do people food. But does Tyler listen? Hell, no!"

Nikki, still half-asleep, wasn't quite over the fact that she'd thought it was Dallas in bed with her, licking her neck and emitting the disgusting odors. A giggle started building in her chest. She shifted her hand over her mouth, but when the smell filled her nose again, she moved her hand back up.

"Out, Bud. Good Lord, what did Tyler feed you—dead skunk?" His gaze met hers again. "I'm sorry."

The giggle escaped. Dallas studied her and his eyes crinkled with grin lines. Even with half his face covered with his hand, he looked really good in grin lines. And the tight T-shirt and fitted jeans didn't look bad on him, either. She thought about cupcakes again and hard-to-resist temptations.

"Why don't we leave the room before that smell attaches itself to us?" He turned and walked out, Bud at his heels.

Nikki followed. "But aren't we bringing the source of the smell with us?"

He bolted out a laugh. It was deep and rich, and reached deep into Nikki's chest and made her want to hear it again.

It wasn't until they stood in the living room facing each other, that some of the awkwardness from the night before returned.

"You want some coffee?" he asked, still looking cupcake-good.

"That would be great. Thank you." Realizing her

hair was probably all over the place, that her breath was stale and her eyes were still morning puffy, she motioned toward the hall. "I'm...restroom."

"Yeah."

She felt him watching her as she moved down the hall. Awkwardness intensified with each step. The cloud of morning haze lifted and reality rained down on her like thumbtacks. She had to call and make sure Ellen was okay. She had to call Nana and see if she could borrow her car so she could visit Ellen. She had to get to the art gallery and see how badly ransacked it was. Oh, and she needed to clean up her place.

Instead of going into the bathroom, she darted into the bedroom, where she'd left her overnight bag, which had her purse and her cell phone. The smell still thrived in the room, but she ignored it. She found the cell phone then searched through her purse for the receipt where she'd written Ellen's mom's number.

It wasn't in the side pocket. It wasn't in the middle pocket.

What the hell had she done with it?

Suddenly realizing how bright the sun was streaming through the open blinds, she grabbed the phone and hit time. Twelve o'clock.

Oh shit. Her panic grew. She dropped on the floor and feverishly searched. Finally, she found it. She dialed the number.

It rang once. Twice. The image of Ellen's hand hanging from the gurney flashed in Nikki's head. Fear filled her chest. "Answer. Please answer."

"Hello, Nikki."

"Mrs. Wise." No time for pleasantries, she blurted out, "Is Ellen okay?" Nikki's voice shook, but she couldn't stop it. Her friend had almost died and she'd stayed in bed until noon without a care in the world. She couldn't believe she'd done this.

"She's fine."

"Thank God." Nikki pulled her knees up to her chest.

"I just talked to Milton and he said she was more alert than ever. I'm about to go to the hospital now."

"I'll see you there soon," Nikki said, her voice still shaky.

"You okay?" Mrs. Wise asked.

"I'm fine." Nikki batted back tears she hadn't known she'd released.

"I know you had a terrible day yesterday yourself. I'm sure you have to deal with...your ex-in-laws and their loss."

Nikki realized how totally, unforgivably neglectful she'd been. She hadn't called Jack's parents. How could she not have called them? Did they know? Surely, some-one had called them, right?

Emotion swelled in her chest. "I...need to go," she managed to say.

"Take care of yourself."

Nikki stared at the phone. Jack's parents had never been fond of her. They'd wanted Jack to marry well. In their opinion, a girl raised in a small house on the wrong side of the tracks by her grandmother—because her parents had abandoned their bastard child—didn't exactly meet their expectations. And those had been Jack's words, not Jack's parents' or her own. Of course, he'd laughed afterward and told her he'd been joking. When she didn't seem to think it was funny, he'd told her he didn't care what his parents thought of her. He'd married her, hadn't he? It still had hurt. Maybe in part because she'd begun to question if their dislike of her wasn't part of Jack's attraction to her. A rich kid, rebelling against Mom and Dad.

But their lack of affection, even Jack's lack of tact, didn't excuse Nikki's behavior now. How in God's name had she forgotten to contact them? Had Dallas's brother been in touch with them? Surely, he'd contacted the next of kin, right? Or had he expected Nikki to do that?

At the very least it was unforgivable for her not to offer her condolences. She'd been Jack's wife, their daughter-in-law. She'd gone out to eat with them once a week on the mandatory parents' night and she'd sat at their dining room table over three years of holiday dinners. She'd owed them the courtesy of a phone call and had fallen short.

Knowing their number by heart, she dialed, and prayed the right words would come to her.

"You!" A feminine shriek shook the line. "How dare you call!"

"Mrs. Leon," Nikki managed to say. "I'm sorry. I should have been the one to...tell you."

"Tell me what? That you murdered my boy? I hope that cop arrests you and you spend the rest of your life in prison!"

"I didn't—"

"I told him. I told that O'Connor cop everything. I told him how you tried to get my boy to pay you alimony."

"I didn't—"

"I told him how I'd reminded my son that he needed to change his will. I'll die before I let you get one cent." She started sobbing. "He was my son. My only son."

"I'm so sorry," Nikki said.

"Sorry that you killed him?"

"I didn't—" Her breath caught in her chest, followed by a big ache.

"You stay away from us!" Mrs. Leon snapped. "I told my boy you were nothing but white trash."

The phone went dead. Nikki sat in the middle of the floor and stared at her phone. The sobs came slowly at first and then began to gush out of her.

Tony spotted LeAnn right off—sitting at a lunch table by herself, picking at a bag of potato chips. His gaze shot to the table where an empty saucer sat. No doubt it had held her dessert. Which, more times than not, she ate first.

He recalled how hard it had been for her to eat healthy during her pregnancy. But she'd done it. *If eating green crap is what I have to do, I'll do it.* And she had. He remembered the night she'd held her nose and ate broccoli because she'd read it was good for the baby. He'd told LeAnn she didn't have to do everything the books said, but she wasn't taking chances. He felt so sorry for her that every time she'd looked away, he'd snag a bite of broccoli and eat it himself. He hated the shit, but would have eaten every bite for her.

Lunchroom noises brought him back to the moment. He watched LeAnn eat another chip. She hadn't had a mom to push the five food groups on her. To LeAnn, cake and a bag of potato chips were the perfect meal.

Walking over to the table, he longed to lean over and kiss her, to taste her lips. But instead, he pulled out a chair and snagged one of her chips. Shock filled her green eyes. She looked as tired as he felt.

He forced a smile. "Hmm, chocolate and potato chips, you've covered both your essential food groups."

"Yeah." She looked back at chips as if trying to collect her thoughts. "What are you doing here?"

"I had to talk to a witness," he said.

She nodded, but didn't look up.

"I was thinking maybe we could go out on Sunday. A nice dinner."

"I..." She looked back at him. "I was going to give you this on Sunday, but since you're here." She pulled a white envelope from her purse and pushed it to him.

His gut knotted with fear because he instinctually knew what it was. The knot rose to his throat when he saw the lawyer's name typed across the front.

"No." He pushed it back over to her. "I love you."

Tears filled her eyes. "You married me because I was pregnant, Tony. And now..."

Shock ripped through his chest. Was that what this was about? Holy hell, he'd counted his lucky stars, considered himself the luckiest man in the world when she came to him with that little stick with a pink line on it. He leaned in. "I married you because you totally rocked my world. You stole my heart. I would have asked you to marry me a month earlier if I thought there was a chance in hell that you'd say yes."

She sat there as if she didn't hear a word he said. "You did the right thing. You always do the right thing. So do it this time, too. Sign it, Tony. Let's move on." She got up and walked away.

His world, his touchstone just walked out. He swallowed the emotion down his throat.

"I don't want to move on," he said under his breath. And that's when he knew what he had to do. And while it involved moving, it wasn't on or away from LeAnn. It was back. He was moving back home.

Snatching up the envelope, he left. He was almost out of the hospital when he remembered he had gone there to interview someone. Folding the damn divorce papers, he stuffed them into his pocket, and went back to do his job.

Dallas let Bud out, started coffee, and then stood staring at his refrigerator trying to figure out what he could offer Nikki to eat. No eggs. Some bacon that had expired a month ago. He tossed that in the garbage.

Feeling anxious, he went back to the fridge and stared at the empty shelves. In the back of his mind he heard his mom's voice. *You know, staring in there won't make anything magically appear.*

I know, he would tell her. *This is where I do my best thinking.*

What on your mind, son? She would always come hug him from behind. Whatever dilemma he'd had, one trip to the fridge always led to problem solving with his mom. God, how he missed her.

And if she were here right now, he'd probably be telling her about his yin and yang feeling about the woman in his bathroom.

Shutting the fridge door, trying to shut off his thoughts, he moved his attention to the pantry. Those shelves were even emptier than the fridge.

Well, in addition to going out and buying a sofa that didn't give him a neck ache when he slept on it, he was going to buy some groceries. Feeling inadequate for not having a damn thing to offer Nikki, he slammed the pantry door.

Tyler's question popped in his head: *What is it about the blonde in Dallas's bedroom that has him so damn nervous?*

Why was he feeling like this? He hadn't bought groceries in over two months. Suzan had been over numerous times, and he hadn't once worried about offering her anything but a good time in the sack.

Bud scratched at the door. Dallas let him in, but eyed the dog in warning. "You fart again and I swear I'll look for a cork."

The dog turned his head as if to listen to something. Then he bolted out of the kitchen.

"Leave her alone." Dallas took after the dog before he started scratching at the bathroom door.

But Bud didn't stop at the bathroom—he rammed the half-closed bedroom door with his nose, and ran right in.

Dallas spotted Nikki on the bedroom floor, her face buried in her hands, crying. No, not crying. Sobbing. Deep heartfelt sobs.

Damn.

His first instinct—and Dallas generally followed his first instinct—was to run like hell. He could handle a few tears, was good at asking, "You okay?" and sounding sincere. And it wasn't even an act. He wasn't a jerk. He cared about people. But when it came to dealing with emotionally distraught women, well, Bud was probably a better man—better canine—for the job.

He turned around and had his foot in midstep when he heard another gasp and a hiccup. How that little sound could cause such an impact on his conscience he didn't know. But, accepting defeat, he took one deep breath, swung back around and walked right into the middle of an emotional storm.

"Hey." He knelt behind her and put a hand on her shoulder. "You okay?"

She shook her head no, but didn't attempt to answer. She didn't even remove her hands from her face. Another sob sounded behind her fingers. Bud walked circles around her and, looking at Dallas, he whined as if to say: *Do something.*

But what?

Dallas sat beside her and cautiously put his arm around her shoulders. He wasn't sure his help would be welcome. She twisted suddenly, and he thought she wanted him to let her go, so he pulled his arm up. But instead of yanking away, she pillowed her head against him.

Maybe he wasn't so bad at this after all. He lowered his arm again. "I know it's tough." And boy howdy, did he know.

He saw her phone on the floor and wondered if a call had upset her. "What happened? Is Ellen okay? Is that what's wrong?"

He heard her inhale. "No." She hiccupped and eased away. "It's my in-laws. Ex-in-laws. I forgot to call them yesterday. I can't believe I forgot to call them. That was so insensitive of me."

He studied her tear-streaked face. "You had a bad day yourself. Poisoned, found a body, had a friend of yours almost die, and then had your place broken into." Bud tried to lick Nikki's face. Dallas gave the dog a slight nudge.

"I still should have called them." She dropped her hands in her lap, and they landed on the hem of her shirt. The scooped neckline of her tank top scooped a little lower and Dallas had to work to keep his eyes from soaking up the view of her cleavage.

"You really are hard on yourself." He brushed her hair from her cheek. As emotionally hard as she was on herself, she was just as physically soft. And being this close to all that smooth feminine skin was wreaking havoc on his insides. He wanted to touch, to taste, to bring all that softness closer.

"They . . . they think I killed Jack." Pain thickened her voice and resounded in his gut.

Guilt for the direction of his thoughts pinched at Dallas's chest, and he mentally shot down his libido. "I'm sorry."

"I know your brother thinks I did, too. But he doesn't know me. I don't care what he thinks."

He almost told her she should care. Because Tony was the police and what he thought mattered a hell of lot more than what her ex-in-laws thought. But then he remembered how it felt to realize that people you thought believed in you, really didn't. People like Serena.

"They know me. I was . . . was part of their family for over three years. How can they think . . . I used to love him."

The "used to" in her sentence stuck in Dallas's head. He brushed a tear from her cheek and offered her the only words he could. "Your in-laws are hurting right now. They'll come to their senses." Most of them who'd doubted him eventually had come around. Serena had. What he didn't tell Nikki was that it didn't matter, because even if they decided they were on her side, she wouldn't be able to forget or forgive their betrayal. At least he hadn't.

She hiccupped. Dallas looked down at her bundled on his chest. He tightened his arm around her shoulders. She buried her face deeper into his shoulder and just cried. And he let her. Bud dropped down beside her and pressed his nose against her bare leg and occasionally gave the soft appendage a concerned lick of his tongue.

After a few minutes, she stopped crying. He felt her

coming to her senses. Felt her start to pull away. Oddly, enough, he wasn't relieved. Holding her had been...nice. And that's when the smell hit again. No, not her fruity sweet scent, but Bud's...

"Damn." He went to get up. With one knee still on the floor and one foot in the process of pushing up, he was off balance when Nikki bolted upward. She knocked him back then went to grab him and, instead of helping, she tumbled down on top of him. Right on top of him. Not that he was complaining.

Another sob left her throat. "Hey." He wrapped his arms around her waist.

She raised her face and rested her chin on his chest, and that's when he realized her last little noise wasn't a sob. "What did he eat?" The laughter in her voice sounded so sweet. If that's what it took to make her laugh, Bud might just be getting more people food after all.

Something about seeing humor in her eyes, her baby blues still moist with tears, made his chest feel tight. "I don't know." All he could think about was how perfect she fit on top of him. How happy he was that he hadn't followed his first instinct and run off instead of being here. Because being here felt...right.

She shifted as if to move off him, and he wasn't sure what provoked him to do it, but he raised his head an inch off the floor and pressed his lips against hers. It was just a kiss, he told himself. Probably wasn't the wisest move, especially considering her knee had optimum placement and could achieve a direct hit. And yeah, stealing a kiss had actually gotten him kneed in his youth. A guy didn't forget that.

But a little voice in his head said he probably should be

more worried about the direct hit to his heart. The second he tasted her mouth, he told the little voice to take a walk. Whatever happened, he wouldn't regret this.

Especially when her tongue slipped into his mouth and stroked his, proving that he wasn't the only one wanting here. Wanting to delve deeper into that sweet mouth of hers, he rolled her over without interrupting the kiss.

Not wanting to end it, he cupped the back of her head in his palm and leaned in to get closer.

Closer.

His mouth completely covering hers.

His chest against hers.

His thigh now tucked between her legs.

He was already hard—obviously his body hadn't gotten his "just-a-kiss" memo. Then her hand moved to his waist and slipped under his T-shirt and traveled up his side. Soft fingers, gliding over his bare skin making him harder.

Obviously, she hadn't gotten the memo, either.

Not that he was complaining. He'd never been fond of memos.

His breath caught at the feel of her touch sliding up to his chest. All he could think about was feeling her hand other places. And getting his hands on places—on her.

Getting his mouth on places—all over her.

He started lowering his kiss to her neck, nipping at the tender skin. Anticipation, eagerness, and need all came together in a big ball of hot want in his chest. He hadn't felt this much need, this much want, in ages.

CHAPTER FIFTEEN

THIS ISN'T GOOD. Gotta stop it.

Those words repeated in Nikki's head. But they just weren't getting through. Or maybe they did get through and she just didn't agree with them. *This is good.* It felt so...right. And so...delicious.

How long had it been since she'd had delicious? Too long.

So she went with it. Let it happen. And when just letting it happen wasn't enough, she encouraged it. She deepened the kiss and savored the texture of his masculine abs. The desire to move her touch downward brushed across her mind. But lower seemed hasty, a bit bold. She wasn't bold. So she let her fingers sweep all the way up to his chest. Over the hard, sculptured ribs to the tight little nubs of his nipples. She could feel his heart pumping and her own matched his.

The taste of his mouth still lingered in hers as his lips glided down, down her neck. Then he came back up to her lips. His mouth melted against hers, going from soft to firm, and then from slow to passionately fast. It was so... seductive.

She hadn't been kissed like this in a long time. Jack had stopped kissing her like this shortly after they'd been married. Stopped kissing her like he wanted to kiss her, and started kissing as it were just a chore he had to do before he got her naked.

Who wanted to be a chore? She wanted to be ... savored. She wanted to be desired. And that's what she felt right now. Desired. Oh, yes, Dallas knew what he was doing, but there was just a little something that said he really wanted to do this right. As if he waited for her to give him the slightest sign that it was okay to move onward.

And then he did it. His kisses moved downward again, past her neck to the top of her breasts. Pure delight.

That's when her sense of reason first hit. She had to stop this! She didn't need ...

"Cupcakes!" Temptation. She couldn't give in.

He muttered something, but the words were lost to her. His lips continued moving lower. His hand moved up under her shirt, a slow sweep upward of his palm on her bare stomach. A sweep that brought her shirt up with it.

She had to stop him. *Didn't she?*

The brush of soft cotton against her ribs tickled. Her nipples ached with anticipation. His hand found her breast, gently passing his fingers over tight nubs. He took her shirt up over her breasts and rose up on his elbow to see what he'd uncovered.

"Beautiful," he whispered. Then his lips melted back against her neck and continued downward.

She waited. Waited to feel his lips where his hands now explored. His pelvis lowered ever so slightly against hers. She felt the hard bulge behind the zipper of his jeans. The sweet ache tightened between her thighs. It was that deep, hot sweep of desire that jolted her into rethinking the wisdom of letting this happen.

"No cupcakes." She caught his face in her hand right before he took a nipple into his mouth.

The heat of desire brightened his eyes. He blinked. Swallowed—his Adam's apple shifted up and then down.

"I can't . . . We shouldn't," she said. Releasing his face, she yanked her shirt down. He rolled off her and lay back on the floor. She sank back onto the floor herself, wishing she could slip between the cracks of wood and disappear. "Sorry," she said. "I just . . . can't."

"Okay." His one word came out sounding deep and rusty. He was still so close. His shoulder touched hers. The heat of his body oozed into her arm. Neither of them spoke. The silence grew louder.

"I'm sorry. I shouldn't have . . . done that," she said.

"You didn't do it. I did."

"But I didn't stop you."

"True," he said. And they both turned their heads at the same time to look at each other.

Their gazes met—held. Neither of them spoke for long seconds. Then she said, "I . . . need to get to the hospital."

He nodded and his brow crinkled. "No cupcakes? What did you mean?"

"I said that?" Her chest instantly tightened with embarrassment.

He nodded.

She blinked. Her face grew hot.

"What did you—"

"Nothing. I just like cupcakes."

Confusion tightened his eyes. His gaze shifted to her chest. "So do I."

Did he think... "No. I wasn't calling..." She grabbed her boobs. "I didn't mean..."

His gaze shot to her hands that were giving her boobs a Wonderbra lift.

Now on complete overload of embarrassment, she let go of her girls and sat up. Her skin prickled from his continued stare. "I...I must be hungry," she lied, because she didn't want to talk about temptation.

Bud came over and butted her arm with his nose. She petted him, avoided looking at Dallas, and tried to find the right words to say. Finally, she took a deep breath and looked at Dallas. And boy howdy, did he look good. "I don't think it would be good if we complicate things by... doing that." Once again she envied Nana's say-it-like-it-is approach. Being diplomatic was hard.

"It didn't feel complicated to me." He ran a palm over his face.

"I've got too much on my plate right now."

He sat up and tugged at the legs of his jeans as if they were uncomfortable. She had to fight the urge to look and see how uncomfortable.

"I'm just not—" She swallowed hard.

"I get it."

"It would confuse things," she said.

He closed his eyes and pulled at his pants legs again. "You don't have to explain."

While his tone didn't sound angry, it was short and tense. He stood up and walked to the door.

Unable to stop, she blurted out, "It's not that—"

"You said no. Let's leave it at that, okay?" He shut his eyes again and then opened them. "I'm sorry. It was a mistake. A bad idea. I understand." The annoyance level in his tone had lessened. He said the words with conviction. And she didn't like it.

His understanding was nice, but calling it a mistake... Then again maybe she was confused. Who was she kidding? She was completely, over-the-top confused. She reached for her phone. "I'll call my grandmother to pick me up."

"No!" He inhaled. "I mean...we still need to talk about things. Tony came by earlier and I told him I'd bring you to the police station at three."

Her mouth went dry. "Is he going to arrest me?"

"No. He needs to go over a few things."

"Then I'll borrow Nana's car and drive—"

"I'd like to be with you when he talks to you. It might give me insight into the case."

She nodded. "But I need to see Ellen and—"

"Sounds good. Why don't we grab a bite to eat? We can talk and then I'll take you to the hospital. After that we can go see Tony."

"Okay," she answered. Then she recalled that she needed to stop using her overdrawn debit card. She had two hundred dollars in her change bank at the gallery, assuming the detective was correct that the intruder hadn't robbed the store. "Can we run by the gallery so I can grab some quick cash?"

He hesitated. "Sure."

Then, remembering she didn't have clothes, she frowned. "I also need to grab some clothes. I wasn't thinking when I gathered my things last night." Realizing how much she was asking, the awkwardness crept up in her chest again. "I should call Nana and borrow her car. And you can meet me at the police station. That way, you wouldn't have to—"

"No. I was going to suggest we go by your place and talk to the manager about getting your lock fixed anyway."

Their eyes met and held. Her mind took her back to how his lips had tasted and felt against her mouth, against her skin. Delicious didn't come close to describing it. Better than cupcakes. Her face heated up again.

She nodded. "Are you this accommodating to all your clients?" *Or does the fact that we almost got naked and ravished each other have anything to do with it?*

Biting down on her lip, she studied his expression—mainly, his left eyebrow—and tried not to frown. She didn't want to come off mad, just cautious. She couldn't be mad when she hadn't exactly discouraged him.

He might have started it, but she'd jumped in headfirst and into the deep end of the proverbial pool, too. Nope, she couldn't be mad, but she really needed to be careful.

Having sex with him would have been over-the-top crazy. And she couldn't afford any more craziness in her life. She'd already maxed out on craziness and didn't have overdraft protection.

"Of course, I'm this accommodating." His left eyebrow rose.

As if noting her focus, he ran a finger over his forehead and frowned. "Why don't you grab some coffee while I take a shower?" He turned and walked toward the bathroom, and she could swear she heard him mutter, "A cold one."

"How did it go?" Clark asked as Tony walked into the squad room and stored his gun in his desk.

"They wouldn't let me in to see her. They don't know if she's going to make it."

"Damn," Clark said leaning forward. His desk chair squeaked.

The noise raked over Tony's nerves. "Can you get a damn can of WD-40 and do something about that squeak?"

"In a good mood, huh?" Clark asked.

Dropping down into his own squeaky chair, Tony pushed a hand through his hair. It wasn't the noise chewing on his nerves. It was his lack of sleep and the envelope in his pocket.

Divorce my ass! The more he thought about it, the more he liked his plan. When he left this afternoon, he was grabbing a bag of clothes from his apartment and going home.

He knew she'd be madder than a wet hen hyped up on meth. But dealing with a mad LeAnn for a few days was better than losing her forever.

"Sorry. I just came from talking to Joey." Tony looked over at Clark.

"Bad news?"

"Yeah." Tony pulled the envelope out of his pocket and shoved it in his desk drawer. As close as he was with his partner, Clark wasn't the person to talk to about LeAnn. The man had gone through a nasty divorce three years ago and was still fighting for custody of his little boy. He hadn't gotten over the anger. His partner's advice for dealing with any woman issue was the same. *Fuck 'em. Just fuck 'em—that's all we should do with them. Not fall for them, not start caring, or giving 'em gifts. For God's sake, don't marry 'em. Just fuck 'em. As hard and as many of 'em as you can.*

Clark was one of the guys Tony had been talking about when he'd said nothing good came out of the relationships with people a cop met on the job. Clark's ex, Candy, had been a stripper. Clark had worked a robbery at the club— one look at Candy and he knew he could save her from the world she'd gotten caught up in. Didn't happen. You can't save somebody who doesn't think they need saving.

"Are you going to share what Joey said or do you want me to try to guess?"

It took Tony a second to remember what they'd been talking about. "Joey said that Jack Leon didn't have any defensive wounds. None."

"So." Clark leaned back in his chair again. "Either the killer walked up and surprised the hell out of him, or it was someone he knew and he didn't think she'd stab him."

"She?" Tony asked.

He leaned back and the damn chair squeaked again. "Didn't ya tell me Nikki Hunt had a quarter of a mil reasons for him to die?"

Tony nodded.

"Don't get me wrong, I got money riding on her being innocent, but I'd easily put a twenty in the pot if we could close this case. The boss has already scheduled a meeting with us tomorrow. My gut says he wants us to make an arrest. Supposedly, Leon's daddy is friends with the mayor."

Tony snatched up a pen and started clicking it. "I don't give a damn who he's friends with. I'm not making a bad arrest."

Clark stared at him. "What? You don't think she did it now?"

"I don't *know* if she did it. She couldn't have been the person who stabbed the Wise woman."

"So she had an accomplice. As hot as she is, she probably has men lining up to do her dirty business."

"But how does Ellen Wise fit into this? It made sense if the Wise woman was banging Nikki's ex, but—"

"Maybe the chick is lying," Clark said. "Maybe she was banging him and knew we'd trace the calls, and so she concocted the whole story."

"I don't think so."

Clark reached down to adjust the back of his chair. "Do we know if it was the same knife used in both stabbings?"

"Not yet," Tony said. "The hospital was supposed to e-mail over the pictures of Wise's wounds and information on the wound size this morning. When I spoke to Joey, he didn't have them. If they haven't sent them in an hour or so, I'll go raise hell."

"I can do that." Clark rolled back and tossed one foot on top of his cluttered desk. "I was going to talk to the Wise chick and see if she remembered anything else anyway."

"Fine." Tony clicked his pen, once, twice, three times. "Joey also confirms that Leon had a large amount of vomiting inducers in his system. But it wasn't lethal. And Nikki Hunt had the same thing. If she's responsible for giving him the ipecac, why take it herself? And why give him that if she was planning on killing him? Something isn't right." He clicked his pen three more times.

"Maybe she did all this just to throw us off."

"Did she ransack her place, too?"

Clark cut Tony an accusing look. "Is all this doubt because your brother has the hots for her?"

"Hell, no," Tony blurted out. "If I think she's guilty, I'm arresting her."

They both got quiet. Then Clark asked, "Do you believe her about selling her computer?"

"I don't know, I'm checking on it. She's supposed to be

here at three. And she's not leaving until I get answers."
Tony scrubbed his palm over his face, only to realize he
needed a shave.

Damn! He wished he'd remembered before he'd gone
to see LeAnn. She was a stickler for smooth cheeks, once
claiming he'd given her whisker burns between her thighs.
By damn he missed what they had—the friendship, the
laughter, the sex. He'd been with a lot of women before
LeAnn and not one of them compared to her. No one made
him feel the same. No one moved the same. No one…
tasted like LeAnn.

His dick twitched as he remembered those sweet little
noises she made when he was between her thighs. Nine
months of celibacy was a bitch. Sure, he'd had offers for
company—his neighbor at his apartment, the new clerk
here at the office. He didn't want sex. He wanted LeAnn.
He wanted his wife back.

"I heard CSU went over her car," Clark said. "They
didn't find shit so far. But they're going over it again
later."

Brought back to reality, Tony tugged at his pants
leg. "Where's Leon's phone records? Who else did he
talk to?"

Clark dropped his feet from the desk and started
thumbing through his stacks of papers. Tony almost
barked at him about not filing things, but at the last minute he held himself back. For all Clark's flaws, he was
actually a damn good cop and a decent guy. And Clark
wasn't responsible for Tony's bad mood.

Still shuffling papers, looking for the phone record
report, Clark asked, "Did you talk with the other lawyers
at Leon's firm?"

"Just the receptionist and one lawyer. He didn't give me shit. I've got meetings with the others tomorrow."

"Where the fuck did I put that phone record?" Clark paused in his search and looked up. "When you talked to Joey, did you get anything on the kid's body from the convenience store?"

"He was shot with a thirty-eight, like we guessed," Tony said. "And I was right. There was blood on the bat. O positive. Not the vic's."

"Have you told Shane? I'm sure he's gonna want to run a test on his robbery perp. He really wants to take that kid down."

"Not yet," Tony said. "I was planning on giving him the heads-up this afternoon."

Clark looked at him. "You mean after you give your brother the heads-up?"

Tony glared at Clark. "I didn't say that." But Tony wasn't denying it, either. But since Dallas's client could possibly be a suspect for this murder, if Tony chose to talk to him, it was within his boundaries.

"Here it is." Clark passed him the phone list. "But the only suspicious calls were those from the Wise lady."

The ride to her apartment was long and quiet. Nikki tried not to think about what almost happened between them. However, several times, the memory of how good his weight had felt on top of her, of how good his mouth felt, how his hands had held her breasts, would slip inside her head.

When he parked, she looked around to see where they were. They'd stopped in front of her apartment building at the manager's office.

"We should talk to someone about fixing your door," Dallas said.

Two minutes later, she stood in front of Mr. Wilde, the balding fifty-year-old manager whose straight-for-boobs stare always gave Nikki the heebie-jeebies. And while staring at her boobs, he told her she'd have to pay and arrange for the repairs herself.

Dallas, who'd remained quiet, walked right into the conversation. "You have a valid point," he told Mr. Wilde.

Nikki shot him a what-the-hell glance. Whose side was he on? He ignored her and continued, "Ms. Hunt will be happy to pay for the repairs."

Ms. Hunt nearly swallowed her tongue.

"Good." Mr. Wilde's gaze shot back to her unsupported girls.

"Excuse me?" Nikki said, and motioned for him to look at her eyes.

"But if she *does* pay for it," Dallas continued, "I'll see to it that every newspaper, radio, and TV station in town gets a report of every crime that has taken place near the apartment in the last five years. And I'll inform them how badly the parking lot is lit, about how the security gate is broken. And I promise not to forget to tell them how the management isn't doing anything about seeing to the safety of their residents."

Dallas shrugged. "Oh, and since I'm a PI, and an ex-cop, I have pull with media contacts." He motioned for her to leave.

She took one step, trying to figure out how she was going to pay for the door, when he swung back around. Nikki turned with him, and saw Mr. Wilde with his mouth agape and panic in his eyes.

In a confident voice, Dallas asked, "Don't you think the owners of the property would prefer you fix the damn door?"

Mr. Wilde muttered something about having someone out ASAP.

As they walked to the car, Nikki looked at Dallas. "Thanks."

He smiled, but when he glanced back at the office, a frown appeared in his eyes. "The jerk couldn't keep his eyes off your chest."

"I seem to have that problem lately," she said without thinking and immediately wished she hadn't.

"That was different." His frown deepened.

"Sorry. You are right. I didn't mean to lump you in the same category as... forget it." She hurried across the sidewalk.

He caught up with her. "It could have been good."

It had been good, she thought. "It would've been a mistake. You said so yourself."

She slipped into his front seat and shut the door, hoping to end the conversation.

He walked around the car, settled behind the wheel, and continued, "I'm not sure about it being a mistake now. For a while there, you seemed to be enjoying yourself. I know I sure as hell was."

She felt her face flush. "Do we have to talk about this?"

"You brought it up." His mouth spread in a sexy grin and his blue eyes twinkled with humor.

"Well, I'm ending it." She gave him a hard, firm look.

"Killjoy," he teased.

All she could think about was kissing him again. She looked away and reminded herself how dangerous just

being with him could be. She really should have called
Nana.

They drove around to the back to her building. Her
apartment door still stood ajar.

Seeing the mess wasn't any easier than it had been last
night. However, she managed to don some underwear,
slip on a pair of jeans and a pink blouse, put on a tad of
makeup, find her extra set of keys, and meet Dallas back
in the living room in less than fifteen minutes. She found
him sitting on the sofa.

He looked up and his gaze moved over her body.

"What?" she asked.

"Nothing," he said. "You look nice. Pretty in pink."

She noticed that he had her photo album in his lap.

"I hope you didn't mind." He held up the album.

"No." She didn't mind. Though why he'd want to look
through old family pictures was beyond her.

He glanced down. "You were a cute kid." He flipped
over to almost the back of the book. "And a beautiful
bride."

She glanced down at the eight-by-ten picture of her
tossing the bouquet, Nana at her side. Nikki had thrown
away the photos of her and Jack together, but she'd kept
this one. Her wedding had been one of the happiest
days of her life. Even if it had led to a broken heart and
a divorce, she hadn't wanted to forget everything. How
many happiest days in your lives did you get?

However, with Jack's death fresh on her mind, she
didn't want to walk down that memory lane. "We should
get going."

"Just one thing." Dallas stood and, this close, she realized how tall he was, and how small she felt beside him.

He looked at her desk. "Do you still have any paperwork on where you sold the computer?"

"You don't believe me?" Hurt curled up in her chest. His belief or disbelief in her shouldn't matter. But for some crazy reason it did.

"I do." His voice rang with honesty. And when she looked in his eyes she saw the same emotion there.

He set the photo album on the coffee table. "I wouldn't be doing this if I didn't. But as an ex-cop, I know my brother will want proof. He's big into evidence."

"I don't like your brother." And instead of just staring at Dallas and trying to figure out why his opinion was important to her, she started digging in the side pocket of her purse. She found the yellow piece of paper from the pawnshop.

"He's not all bad, Nikki."

"Couldn't prove it by me." She handed him the paper.

"The job makes him an ass sometimes."

"Did the job make you an ass?"

"Probably," he admitted.

"But you quit, which makes you less of an ass."

He stared at her as if he had something else to say, but her cell phone rang. Worried it could be news about Ellen, she grabbed her phone. The tightness in her chest lightened when she saw it was Nana.

After a conversation wherein she assured her grandmother she was fine, and hinted she might need to borrow her car, Nikki rode with Dallas to the gallery. Once there, she stopped at the unopened glass door. She looked past the closed sign and her breath caught. She'd expected there to be blood, but never this much. She gasped.

Dallas, standing at her back, moved in a little closer as if to say she could lean on him. Problem with leaning on someone was that one day, just when you were confident your wall of strength would be there, you found him screwing your hired help. Or you discovered you weren't his real daughter and he suddenly didn't love you anymore.

"You okay?" he asked.

She tried to take a deep breath, but only got down a swallow. "You ask that a lot." Her hands shook so hard, she couldn't fit the key in the lock.

"That's because you don't look okay...a lot." Humor laced his voice.

"You're a real champion with compliments, aren't you?" she countered, hoping to find some emotional footing in the lightness.

"I said you looked nice back at your apartment." He moved to her side and studied her. The smile in his eyes vanished as if he was seeing right through her attempt at humor. Frowning, he took the keys from her trembling fingers.

She thought he was going to open the door, instead he ran a finger over her chin. The sweeping touch reminded her how good his touch had felt in other places.

"You don't have to go in there right now," he said. "I'll pay for lunch. We can come back later. After you've seen Ellen, it'll be easier to take."

Not really, Nikki thought. She'd learned that postponing things didn't make them easier. Stiffening her spine, she took the keys from his hand and opened the door. As she walked inside, she heard him mutter something about her being stubborn, but she decided not to address it.

She wasn't stubborn. She was just...cautiously independent. Life had taught her to be.

Taking a deep breath, she found herself staring at one of her paintings—the one of a girl swinging on a tire swing with her father standing behind her. She wanted to lose herself in the painting and not look at the ...

Stop postponing it. She had to face this sooner or later. She would be fine, she told herself, and shifted her eyes back to the floor.

Wrong.

She wasn't fine.

Seeing Ellen's blood, so much blood—and this close up—sent a wave of nausea right to Nikki's stomach. Reminded of her hospital stay, she sucked air in through her nose. Where was her pink barf bucket when she needed it? She covered her mouth.

Dallas took her by the shoulders and turned her away from the scene. Not thinking, she buried her head on his chest. "Oh God. I can't believe this happened." She took another gasp of air in her nose and blew it out her mouth.

Don't puke. Don't puke.

Dallas's hand brushed over her shoulders. "Hey," he said, his voice low, soft and caring.

She felt herself leaning into him even more. The nausea started to fade, but she didn't pull away. She needed his wall of strength right now. Later, when the shock wore off, she'd cut the ties. Clean cut, too. She'd go cold turkey, no more wall. But now ...

"Nikki?" The warm whisper of his voice came close to her ear. How did he make saying her name resonate with so much concern? She waited for him to continue, to ask again if she was okay, or to tell her everything was going to be fine.

"You aren't going to puke on me again, are you?" he asked.

She pulled back and stared at him. "No."

"I mean, if you have to, I'll take one for the team. But you're gonna owe me big. And I like your work." He glanced at her paintings. Then he looked back at her and smiled tenderly.

"I'm feeling better," she told him.

"Good."

She suspected he'd teased her just to get her mind off being sick. And it had worked.

"Now, let's get out of here, okay?"

"But I need...the money."

He looked as if he was going to argue then stopped. "Is the money in the register?"

She nodded.

He held out his hand. "You got the key?"

She handed him her key ring and pointed to the key with a red dot.

"Wait here." He cupped her chin in his palm. "And breathe or you're going to pass out."

She wasn't going to pass out. But just in case, she breathed. He removed his hand and stepped away. She stared at the front door. All of a sudden her mind took her to what Ellen might have felt being here alone with a killer. Questions started bouncing around her head. Did Ellen see who did this? How long had Ellen been in the store alone and bleeding? How long had Ellen's attacker held her at knifepoint? Had Ellen screamed?

Fear crowded Nikki's chest and tears filled her eyes. She fought back the emotion and listened to the sound of the register drawer opening and closing. Dallas's footsteps neared and she waited for him, somehow knowing his nearness would make her feel safe again.

"Come on." He pressed his hand to the small of her back and moved her toward the door.

She stopped right before she walked out. "Wait? What am I doing? I . . . I should clean it up."

"You shouldn't." He paused. "Isn't seeing Ellen more important right now?"

"You're right." Nikki allowed him to guide her outside. When he locked the door, she couldn't stop from looking back one more time. She couldn't wrap her head around it.

Moving her gaze away from the blood-covered floor, she looked up at Dallas. "Has your brother talked to Ellen yet?"

He nodded. "This morning."

"Did she see who did this? Does she know who it was?"

"No. The perp was wearing a mask." He put his hand on her back again. "Come on, let's go."

Nikki hesitated. "I'm stuck in an old episode of *Law & Order*." She fought the wash of panic threatening to take over again. "I can even hear the music playing in the background."

"Yeah, but you're not alone." He put his arm around her shoulders and walked her to his car. His touch wasn't the least bit seductive as it had been this morning, but the light squeeze he offered and his not-alone comment came with genuine emotion. And that was even more of a lure than their little make-out session on his bedroom floor had been.

She liked this guy.

Cupcake or no cupcake.

CHAPTER SIXTEEN

LEANN STUDIED HER new patient's chart. *Ellen Wise*. Her heart lurched when she realized this was one of Tony's witnesses and the friend of Nikki, the woman Tony suspected of killing her husband. Damn. LeAnn didn't want to run into him again.

Closing her eyes, she pressed two fingers to her temple and wished she could run and hide. Alone. Not even at home. She needed to get away—somewhere her memories of Tony wouldn't haunt her.

She recalled the look on his face when he saw the envelope—hurt, disappointment, and guilt. It was the same look he'd had on his face when he'd packed his bag three weeks after the funeral and took off to San Antonio to do an undercover job. But how could he be disappointed in her now? Wasn't she giving him what he wanted? A way out without feeling guilty?

I married you because you totally rocked my world. You stole my heart. I would have asked you to marry me a month earlier if I thought there was a chance in hell that you'd say yes.

His words replayed in her head. Part of her wanted to believe them, *had* believed them, until she saw him pack his bags that day and leave for San Antonio. She'd been dying inside from grief and self-blame, but she hadn't considered that losing Tony was part of the deal. That was the day she realized that Tony probably blamed her, too.

She was a nurse, she knew SIDS wasn't a parent's fault, but hundreds of what-ifs had hunkered down inside her heart to live. What if she'd gotten up to check on Emily right when she'd stopped breathing? What if LeAnn let her sleep in the bassinet a month longer? What if LeAnn had eaten more vegetables when she was pregnant? If her own education hadn't stopped her from blaming herself, how could Tony *not* blame her?

"Something wrong?" Carolyn, her nurse tech, asked.

LeAnn looked up from the chart. "Just reviewing." She forced herself to smile and started moving.

"By the way...," Caroline said.

Nikki turned around.

"Did your hubby find you? Let me tell you, you are one lucky gal. I swear—"

LeAnn's throat tightened. "Yeah. He found me," she said and took off.

Dallas studied Nikki from across the restaurant table. The purple circles under her eyes had lessened. But the stress in her baby blues hadn't. Unfortunately, he needed to start asking questions, digging around in her past. He knew how hard this was going to be, but he needed to know things to do his job.

The fact that he wanted to know things for reasons other than the case shouldn't matter. He had to do his job.

"Tell me about Jack." He reached for the ketchup. He'd brought Nikki to one of his favorite hole-in-the-wall hamburger joints.

"I already did." She looked down at the plate.

"I need more, Nikki." Immediately the various truths of his statement filled his chest with a hot, raw desire. He needed more of what occurred between them this morning. Every few minutes, he'd remember how her hands had felt moving up his chest and how her breasts had looked and felt filling his palms.

"What kind of more?" she asked.

He reined in his wayward thoughts, but it wasn't easy because that pink top she wore did amazing things to her breasts. "What was he into?"

She smirked. "You mean besides my hired help?"

"Yeah, besides that." Dallas smiled, but he was beginning to understand her use of humor as a cover. Not that it was particularly a bad thing. He excelled at making light of things himself. But right now he needed the truth.

"Was he into anything illegal?" He squirted a mound of ketchup beside his onion rings and then ripped off a couple of paper towels from the holder on the table. "Drugs? Gambling?"

She appeared insulted at his question. "He was a lawyer."

"As if that makes a difference." Dallas picked up an onion ring and raked it through the ketchup and popped it into his mouth. As he chewed around the hot crusty piece of heaven, he noticed she still hadn't touched her food. Her stomach had to be gnawing on her backbone by now. He was starved, and he'd had a doughnut this morning and hadn't lost his dinner last night.

He wondered if her stomach was still knotted at the thought of the mess waiting on her at the gallery—an issue he planned to take care of, too.

He glanced up and remembered his quest for answers. "So Jack—"

"He wanted to make partner. That's what he was into."

He saw how hard this was her. "Man, this is good." He picked up another onion ring. "Try this." He held it to her lips.

He thought she was going to refuse, but then she took the offering from his hand and took a bite.

"Tell me that isn't heaven," he said.

"It's good." She finished off the second half.

He reached for a paper napkin. "How are your fries?"

"I haven't tried them yet." She stuck her fork into a fry, and took a bite. "They're good."

He felt better seeing her eat. Reaching over, he swiped one of her fries and popped it into his mouth. "They are good. I'll swap you half my onion rings for half of your fries."

She licked the sheen of oil off her lips. "No food-sharing issues," she said.

"Say what?"

She shook her head. "Nothing, I was just...thinking out loud again."

"So, is it a swap?"

"Sure." She handed him her plate.

He raked a few of her fries onto his plate and forked several of his onion rings onto hers.

"So Jack didn't make bets on the games or go to the horse races? Never indulged in casual drug use?"

"No." She picked up another onion ring and took a bite.

"So he had no hobbies, or passions...besides your hired help?" He picked up his hamburger and took a hearty bite. He hoped feeding his stomach would lessen the other hungers stirring in his blood.

She watched him eat, to the point he thought he had ketchup on his chin and picked up his napkin and wiped his mouth. Finally, looking down at her plate, she picked up a French fry, with her fingers this time, and started eating.

"Wine," she finally said. "That's what he was into. He belonged to six different wine clubs. He liked dining out at expensive restaurants, to be seen in the right circles. He played golf with the senior partners and sometimes his dad. But he hated golf. Called it a business requirement."

Dallas watched the sympathy play out in her eyes. For whatever reason, Nikki had cared for Jack Leon. Which meant the man had probably broken her heart.

"He was..." She took a breath. "He could be self-absorbed. But he wasn't a criminal or a bad person. He had a way of making people feel important. His clients... his work associates. People liked him."

"What about his wife?"

She looked confused. "I was his wife."

"I know. Did *you* like him? Did he make you feel important?"

She bit down on her lip. "Yeah, in the beginning he did."

"And then?"

"Then he didn't always approve of who I was. Like I said, he could be self-absorbed, wanted to always look good, but he wasn't all bad."

"You loved him?"

"Yes. But we all make mistakes, right?"

"Yeah." The conversation slowed and he finished of his hamburger.

"What about you?" she asked.

"What about me?" He picked up his iced tea and downed half the glass.

"You obviously aren't married." Her brow crinkled. " hope not." She looked worried and her gaze shot to his lef hand.

"Not married." He ran his thumb over his ring finger glad that the white line had faded. The whole time i prison, the white band had been a constant reminder o everything he'd lost.

"That means you're either divorced, or there's some thing wrong with you."

Dallas knew this was a ploy to change the subject, bu he still laughed.

He watched her pick up her hamburger and take a bite Her pink tongue slid across her bottom lip.

"Interesting," he said and tried not to think about he tongue sliding across him. But holy shit, what was wrong with him? He wasn't a horny sixteen-year-old virgin He was a co...—a PI working a case. And he needed to focus on that.

"What's interesting?" She dabbed her mouth with paper napkin.

"That you see a man who has never been married as flawed. I'd think it was the other way around. The divorced guy is the flawed one."

"Both have flawed possibilities. But at least the divorced guy had enough potential for a woman to take chance on him and he's not completely commitment pho bic. Of course, the flaw ratio changes if the guy's bee

arried more than once. Then he's like the fish people
ep catching and throwing back into the pond." She
cked up her hamburger again and asked, "So...what
e you? Divorced or terminally single?"

"Divorced," he admitted. "And only thrown back
ce."

"What happened?" She pulled another paper towel
om the roll and wiped her mouth. When he hesitated,
e shrugged. "You got personal first."

"Fair enough," he said, and it was fair. He opened his
outh with the intent of telling her everything. Hell, she
as going to find out anyway. But the answer that came
it was vague. Purposely vague. "I hit a rough spot at
ork. She...didn't like rough spots."

"Did that rough spot involve another woman?"

He admired her directness. "No," he said with a clear
nscience, and noticed her gaze shoot to his eyebrow.

He saw something akin to respect fill her eyes. But he
uldn't help wondering if he'd still see that respect if she
new that rough spot involved a murder conviction.

"Kids?" she asked.

"Just Bud." He ate another fry from her plate and tired
figure out how to tell her about his jail stint. Of all
eople, she should understand. But hadn't he thought that
ith Serena?

"Was Jack seeing anyone now?" he asked, not ready to
ake this about him.

"I don't know. Yet knowing Jack, yeah."

"You really haven't talked to him since the divorce?"

"Not once. Oh, he called almost every week. Sent
owers. I wouldn't take his calls and I took the flowers to
ana's retirement center."

"Did Jack have any enemies?"

She set her hamburger down. "Some of his client weren't happy when he lost their cases. Not that he los often. He was good at his job. People generally liked him He never got mad or lost his temper." Her brow crinkle as if she was remembering something. "Except…"

"What?" he asked.

"The phone calls."

"What phone calls?"

"At the restaurant. He was upset. I remember becaus he actually said 'fuck.' Jack didn't lose it like that. wasn't…politically correct."

Dallas leaned in. "Who was he talking to?"

"I don't know, but when I asked what was going on, h said it was something with work." She blinked. "Do yo think that has something to do with his murder?"

"Yeah, I do." Dallas recalled Andrew Brian, and th fact he and Jack Leon were both hoping to make partne "This is good." Dallas smiled, remembering Tony ha Jack's cell phone. For the first time, he thought this whol mess was going to be easier to solve than he'd originall thought. "Okay, try to remember everything you hear Everything."

Dallas's cell rang just as he and Nikki walked into th hospital. He pulled it out and frowned when he saw it wa his dad. Not that he didn't like hearing from the old ma but he knew what this conversation was going to be abou

He touched Nikki's arm. "I need to take this call. Wh don't I meet you at the ICU in a few minutes?" He looke at his watch. "But remember we only have an hour befor we meet Tony."

She nodded.

He met her big blue eyes and for some crazy reason he felt as if they were both searching for something in each other.

One day at a time. His phone rang again and he took the call. "Hey, Dad."

Nikki walked toward the elevators. His gaze fixed on the sway of her hips. Her jeans weren't too tight, but hugged her ass just right. Her fitted top hugged her waist and from behind showed off her hourglass figure. He shifted his gaze up to the way her blond curls stirred around her shoulders. Damn, she had gorgeous down both coming and going.

Then he noticed he wasn't the only one noticing. A doctor type wearing scrubs had stopped and was enjoying the view. A fleeting sensation of possessiveness filled Dallas's chest. He frowned and pushed it back.

"I left four messages on your phone," his dad said.

"I'm sorry. I . . . had a case fall in my lap." He watched Nikki disappear into an elevator.

"Too busy for your old man?"

"You got me now," Dallas said.

"Do you remember what next Wednesday is?"

His chest tightened. "I remember." Dallas wondered if that was why his mom had popped into his mind more than normal these last few days.

"I think it would be nice if we went to the cemetery together. She'd like that."

Dallas raked a hand over his face. "I'll see." He decided on a noncommittal answer because he didn't want to commit. Hell, he didn't want to go period.

"You'll see?" His father's tone deepened—obviously

not pleased with noncommittal. "There's no seeing about it. You'll be there. It's your mama's birthday."

Mom's gone, Dad. He almost said it, but couldn't spit out the words. "I know." There was a silence. "Did you go bowling with the guys today?" He went for the subject switch.

"Nah, I decided to skip."

"Didn't you skip last week?"

"I bought some beer and I'm grilling some chicken tonight," his dad said, leaving Dallas's question unanswered. "You wanna come to dinner? I asked your brother, but he said he couldn't make it."

"I'm sort of caught up with something, too. Don't know when I'll be done."

"I don't eat until seven. Just stop in. Eat and run is fine."

"Yeah." Dallas closed his eyes, feeling guilty. "I'll try to be there by seven."

"By the way, your wife dropped by yesterday."

Dallas snapped his eyes open. "What the hell did she want?"

"Said she was just in the neighborhood and wanted to say hello. We had a good chat."

"Next time don't let her in." Dallas started toward the elevators.

"Just because you two are having trouble doesn't mean—"

"Dad, we're divorced. And she's suing me right now."

"For what?"

"My dog."

"She wants that wrinkly ugly mutt?" His dad laughed.

"Bud's not a mutt." Dallas looked at his watch. "Look, I need to run. I'll try to see you tonight."

"Okay. Oh, make sure you mark your calendar for Wednesday. I'm serious."

"Yeah," Dallas answered without a lot of conviction.

As soon as he hung up, Dallas remembered the call he needed to make and stood by the elevator doors.

Austin answered. "What, you think she'll see a couple of real men and lose interest in you?"

He knew they'd give him hell about not bringing Nikki into the office earlier and making introductions. "Sorry, we were in a hurry," he said, but in truth he wasn't sure Nikki was up to meeting his partners. He sure as hell hadn't needed them giving him more crap about being nervous around her. He couldn't keep her from them for too long, but for now . . . he just needed to distant himself a bit before . . . before what, he didn't know.

"Is Tyler there?" Dallas asked.

"Yup."

"Put me on speaker phone." Dallas heard the click of the line. "Tyler?"

"Just added another question to my list," Tyler's voice came across the line. " 'Why wouldn't Dallas want us to meet our new client?' Nervous and possessive? This is serious."

"Knock it off," Dallas snapped. "Tyler, did you find anything else on Andrew Brian, the lawyer who worked with Jack Leon?"

"Just what I told you this morning. I've been working on setting up a meeting for us tomorrow with Nance's attorney. And I've been digging up some info on our good buddy Detective Shane. I think I've found something."

"What?" Dallas asked.

"Don't rush me. Let me finish my research before I start talking. I don't want to jinx it."

"Fine. Keep me updated. I'm meeting Tony at three. If something's up with Shane, I could use it to convince Tony to help us out."

"That's less than an hour from now," Tyler said.

"So get your ass to work. As soon as you get to the bottom of that, go after Andrew Brian. I'm thinking he might be the one who killed Leon. Nikki said Leon was arguing with someone on the phone at the restaurant and the only thing he would tell her was it was about work. Tony has the phone records. I'm hoping he'll tell me who Leon was chatting with then. But we'll need something more than a disgruntled conversation to throw suspicion off Nikki."

"I'll see what I can do," Tyler said. "By the way, Roberto called."

"Does he have anything on DeLuna?" Hope sparked to life in Dallas's chest. Roberto never called unless he had something.

"He has a lead on someone who may be one of DeLuna's dealers. It's a small operation. He needs money to throw at his source to get him to talk. And we'll probably have to make a buy."

"Give him whatever he needs," Dallas said. "I don't care how small the operation. We hit enough of his small deals, it'll add up."

"Yeah, I told him we'd have the money by tomorrow," Tyler said.

"Fine. Oh, Austin, remember the time I came over to your place and helped you snake out your toilet and you said you owed me?"

"Why am I not liking how this is sounding?" Austin asked.

"You don't mind getting your hands a little bloody, do you?" Dallas asked.

"Who do you want me to beat up? Because if it's one of DeLuna's gang, I'm not promising I can stop at just a little bloody."

Austin's voice had taken on a darker edge. Dallas felt his gut harden with his own old anger and need for revenge.

"Not DeLuna's man...Remember Roxie?"

"Oh, hell no!" Austin said.

CHAPTER SEVENTEEN

NIKKI SAT IN the ICU waiting room for five minutes before discovering that Ellen had been moved to the surgical floor. Tapping on Ellen's door a few minutes later, Nikki heard a soft, "Come in," and she moved inside.

Her gaze shot first to Ellen, asleep. She looked pale and small. Not anything like Ellen, who always wore a big smile and exuded a big personality. The vision of all the blood back at the gallery filed Nikki's head.

How could someone have done this?

And why?

Mrs. Wise, standing beside the hospital bed, quietly rushed over to join Nikki. "She's much better."

While locked in Mrs. Wise's embrace, Nikki spotted the nurse at the foot of the bed. It was LeAnn, Dallas's sister-in-law. Nikki nodded to her in greeting.

LeAnn's startled gaze shot to the door as if she was afraid someone, an unwelcome someone at that, might be following Nikki in. Recalling how LeAnn had run when her estranged husband, Detective O'Connor, had come into the emergency room, Nikki suspected the unwanted person was him. Nikki couldn't blame her; the man gave Nikki the same reaction.

"She's sleeping now," Mrs. Wise said. "But she was awake a few minutes ago."

"She needs rest." LeAnn marked something on the chart she held. "We've got a morphine pump hooked up. She might be groggy. If she wakes up in pain, remind her she has the pump and can push it for medication. And if you need anything, hit the nurse's button. I'm right outside."

LeAnn looked at Nikki. "Are you feeling better?"

Nikki nodded and looked at Mrs. Wise. "I met LeAnn while in the ER." Nikki wasn't sure if she should say anything about LeAnn being Detective O'Connor's wife, so she didn't.

Another tap came at the door. "Come in," Mrs. Wise said in a low voice.

LeAnn's gaze shot to the door again.

Dallas walked in. "Hello."

LeAnn relaxed. Mrs. Wise turned to greet Dallas. But Dallas barely gave the women a glance. He visually greeted LeAnn, then his gaze locked on Nikki as if he worried she might have fallen apart again. Embarrassment bounced like ping-pong balls through her chest. He probably had her down as a surefire basket case.

And why not? She'd done nothing but fall apart and wallow around in that basket since she'd met him. Well, when she wasn't upchucking on him, threatening to upchuck on him, or making out with him on his bedroom floor. Oh God, she really needed to pull herself together.

She made up her mind. She was calling Nana back and asking to borrow her car. Dallas O'Connor shouldn't be carting her around town. She'd hired him—well sort of hired him—to be her PI, not chauffeur or breakdown buddy. Nope, her breakdown buddy was asleep in the hospital bed. And until Ellen was back, Nikki was going to have to pull up her big girl panties.

Mrs. Wise moved closer to Dallas. "You were there last night with Nikki, weren't you? I'm sorry I didn't introduce myself."

"That's understandable." Dallas offered the woman his hand. "My name's Dallas O'Connor and I'm a private investigator looking into things. I'm happy your daughter is better."

"Aren't we all?" Mrs. Wise studied Dallas. "Are you related to the detective working the case?"

"Yes. He's my brother." Dallas's gaze flickered to LeAnn.

"No offense," Mrs. Wise said, "but I think I like you better. My husband said the detective came here this morning and was...gruff with his questioning."

"That's his job," Dallas and LeAnn blurted out at the same time. Their eyes met briefly. While Nikki was in agreement with Mrs. Wise, she saw a loyalty to the detective from both LeAnn and Dallas that was admirable. She wondered if Detective O'Connor deserved their faith.

Mrs. Wise looked embarrassed. "I didn't mean..."

"Don't worry," Dallas said. "To be honest, I'm definitely the better looking of the brothers."

Nikki saw LeAnn roll her eyes as if she didn't agree with Dallas's statement.

"Personally, I'd say it's about a tie." The weak voice came from the hospital bed.

Everyone's gazes moved to Ellen. "You're awake." Mrs. Wise hurried to Ellen's side.

"How's your pain level?" LeAnn asked.

"Is hurting like hell a level?" Ellen's gaze shifted to Nikki.

Guilt spread in Nikki's chest and tears filled her eyes. "I'm so sorry."

"For what?" Ellen licked her lips. "Is it true? Jack's . . ."

"Yeah." Nikki moved closer and squeezed her friend's hand. "I have no idea what's going on."

"You okay?" Ellen asked. "They really don't think you killed him, do they?"

Nikki's chest swelled with emotion. Ellen had almost died and she was worried about her. "It's you we need to think about right now."

Dallas stepped beside Nikki. "Ellen, are you up to telling me what happened?"

"I wish I could." Ellen looked at the water jug on her bedside table. LeAnn reached for the big cup and held it to Ellen's lips.

She drank then continued. "As I told your good-looking brother, I . . . don't remember much." Ellen flinched as if she had a pain. "I was in the office, and heard . . ."

"Remember what I told you," LeAnn said. "If you're hurting, press your pain button." She handed the pump to Ellen.

Ellen nodded, gave the button a push then refocused on Dallas. "When I went out front, I didn't see anyone. Then I heard something behind me. There was someone wearing a ski mask. I vaguely recall seeing the knife and feeling pain, but I must have passed out."

"The person wearing the mask . . . can you give me a description? Height, build, race? Was it a male?"

Ellen closed her eyes. "Bigger than me. Not too bulky, but I assumed it was a man. That's all I . . . know."

"Did he wear gloves?"

Ellen nodded, but didn't open her eyes.

LeAnn looked at Dallas. "Let her rest. Talking can wear her out."

Dallas glanced at Mrs. Wise, who was hovering over her daughter the same way Nana had hovered over Nikki last night. "Has Ellen told you anything else?"

"This is the most she's talked since I've been here. She asked about her daughter and Nikki." Mrs. Wise looked at Nikki. "She was worried about you."

"She nearly dies and she's worried about me." Nikki fought the sting of tears. Dallas squeezed her shoulder. Aware of how easily he touched her these last few hours—a brush across her face, a hand to her back—Nikki stepped away. She saw him glance at her, as if noticing her withdrawal.

LeAnn started to leave when another tap came at the door. She backed up and looked at Dallas with questions in her eyes. Nikki wondered what had happened between LeAnn and her husband that would allow her to defend the man so quickly, but to dread being near him.

The door nudged open and standing there was a tall man, early thirties, light blond hair. Nikki considered that it might be Ellen's ex.

"Can I help you?" Mrs. Wise asked, telling Nikki it wasn't the ex.

The man glanced over at Dallas. "I'm sorry, but I need to snag Dallas a second."

In a low voice, Dallas started introductions, "This is Austin Brook, one of my partners. Austin, this is Nikki Hunt."

Austin met her gaze and nodded, but Nikki got the

listinct feeling he was checking her out. Not necessarily
n a sexual way, but on another level.

"Good to meet you, Nikki," Austin said.

"Same here," she said.

"This is Mrs. Wise and her daughter, Ellen." Dallas
notioned to the patient who was awake again.

Ellen stared at Austin then looked at LeAnn. "Does
norphine make all the guys look hot? Because since I got
his thing, every guy I've seen has been a total hunk." She
ooked back at Austin. "You wanna marry me? I'm really
;ood in bed."

"Oh, my!" Mrs. Wise blushed. "Please forgive her.
That's the morphine talking."

Dallas and Austin chuckled. Nikki grinned at her
riend's bold statement.

Dallas, a smile still in his eyes, looked at LeAnn. "And
his is..."

"The nurse," LeAnn finished. "The nurse who's insist-
ng we let my patient rest."

Austin stepped back and gazed at Nikki. "Nice to meet
:veryone." His focus shifted to Mrs. Wise and then Ellen,
vho blew him a kiss. He grinned and started out of the room.

"Excuse me a second." Dallas followed his partner
)ut the door, but they hadn't gotten all the way out when
inother man walked in.

Seeing this new visitor—a tall, brown-haired man,
:arly thirties—Nikki thought he was another cop. Didn't
:he remember him from the grocery store parking lot? He
;poke to Dallas in a low voice. Whatever the newcomer
;aid, Dallas frowned. He looked over his shoulder at her,
ind then he walked out of the room.

The cop stepped inside. For a second, Nikki worried

he'd come to arrest her. She relaxed when he didn't star
reading her her Miranda rights.

"My name is Detective Clark, I'm working with
Detective O'Connor." He glanced at the hospital bed
"Ellen Wise, I assume?" When Ellen nodded, he contin
ued. "I'd like to go over your statement—"

"See what I mean?" Ellen tried to sit up a bit. "I'd do
him, too. I'd have sex with him in a New York minute."

The detective's eyes widened. Nikki bit her tongue to
keep from snorting out laughter.

"She doesn't mean that," Mrs. Wise informed the
detective. "She's a good Jewish girl."

"Yes, I do." Ellen dropped back on the bed. "Do you
know how long it's been since I got lucky?"

LeAnn chuckled and spoke to Mrs. Wise. "Maybe we
should see about changing her medicine." LeAnn looked
up at the officer. "Hello, Rick."

The detective nodded. "How are you, LeAnn?"

"Fine. But my patient is not up for an interview now."

"It would only take—"

"I said no." LeAnn's tone became firm. The detective
frowned, but bowed out of the room without a fight.

When the door swished shut, LeAnn looked back to
Mrs. Wise. "For sure, keep her away from that one. He's
bad news."

"He didn't look like bad news." Ellen closed her eyes.

"My goodness, I am glad her daddy's not here," Mrs.
Wise said. "Because I don't think any of those men would
even know what a bat mitzvah was."

CHAPTER EIGHTEEN

NIKKI WASN'T LOOKING forward to facing Detective O'Connor again. When Dallas pulled into the police station parking lot, he glanced at her. "Just be forthcoming. Don't let him rile you. He's going to push, hoping you'll give him something."

"So riling people is part of his job, like being rude, huh?" she asked.

"Yes, it is." While Dallas had sympathy in his eyes, he didn't attempt to soften his tone. "It's not going to be easy. I know you don't like it. I don't like it, either, but Tony's doing what every cop does. Just be honest."

"I haven't lied," she said.

"I know. I believe you. You do know that, right?"

She nodded. "Should I be...thinking about getting a lawyer?" Lord only knew how she would pay one, but...

Dallas leaned back and studied her. "If you brought a lawyer into this right now, it would make the cops that much more likely to arrest you. But don't worry, I know a couple of really good lawyers and if we need one I can call."

Her chest grew heavier at the realization of how easy it was to depend on him. Not wanting to fall apart again, she got out of his car. When he came around to walk her inside, his shoulder came close to hers. The closeness, her eagerness to lean even closer to him, were just more reminders that she needed some distance from Dallas O'Connor. Physically and emotionally.

When they got inside, they were asked to wait because Detective O'Connor had someone in his office. "I...need to run to the restroom," she told Dallas.

When Nikki walked back into the waiting room, Dallas was talking to the cop, Detective Clark, the one Ellen had wanted to have sex with. Nikki hung back, not wanting to intrude on their conversation. She obviously didn't hang back far enough.

Detective Clark's voice carried. "Come on, pay up. You put twenty bucks on her being guilty. I made it clear, if we were still looking for leads in twenty-four hours, then we would declare it a nonguilty bet."

Nikki tried to digest what she'd just heard. She didn't know what upset her more—that the cops were taking bets on her guilt or innocence or that Dallas had put money on her being guilty. Guilty?

I believe you. You know that, right? His words, spoken less than ten minutes ago, resounded in her head. She stared at the two men and waited for Dallas to deny it. Instead, he reached for his wallet.

Her chest grew heavy.

Suddenly, she couldn't help but wonder if they'd bet on anything else. Like the possibility of him getting her naked. Was that all she was to him? A bet?

Reaching into her purse she snatched one of the

twenties she'd taken from her emergency stash at the gallery, and hotfooted it over to Dallas and his cop buddy-bookie.

"Allow me." She glared at Dallas as she slapped the twenty into the detective's palm. Then, chin held high, she dropped into a nearby chair.

Dallas said something to the detective and the man left in a huff. Then Dallas came and sat down in the chair beside her. The side of his knee brushed against hers and emotional pain shot up her leg and punched her heart.

Staring straight ahead, she shifted over, refusing to look at him. But she could feel his blue-eyed gaze on her.

"Nikki?"

Distance. She needed some distance.

"At least look at me. That wasn't what it sounded like."

The tightness in her chest grew tighter. She wanted to believe him. "Really?" she asked.

"I swear," he said.

She tried to figure out how she could have misunderstood their conversation, but her figuring-out ability didn't offer up any possibilities.

When she didn't say anything else, he released a heavy sigh. "I..."

Swearing on everything holy that she was not going to break down, that she wouldn't let him see how much this stupid bet of his had hurt her, she forced herself to ask, "Did you make the bet?"

Regret filled his eyes. He looked poised to say something, but didn't. More importantly, he didn't deny it.

She tried to swallow the knot of hurt down her throat. It was stupid that this man's opinion, a man she hardly knew, could matter to her.

But it did.

It mattered a lot.

"You *did* make the bet, didn't you?"

He ran a palm over his face. "It happened right when I stumbled on the scene." He hesitated as if searching for the right words to say. "You hadn't even puked on me yet." He smiled as if humor would fix everything.

It didn't fix it. Her chest remained tight. She was just tired, she told herself, on emotional overload; later she would see how unimportant all this was.

But this wasn't later, and right now she had to get through this interview with Detective O'Connor. So she stiffened her spine.

"I was on the phone when Clark started the whole bet nonsense and I wasn't—"

"It's not important." She glanced away and told herself it wouldn't matter as soon as she got distance between herself and him. He reached for her hand, and a jolt of raw emotion came with his touch. She jerked away.

She felt him staring—heard him let out a gulp of air as if exasperated.

Then she heard a familiar voice from the doorway. A familiar, angry voice. She glanced up. Mrs. Leon—Jack's mother—passed by the door, and was giving someone hell. Detective O'Connor, from the looks of it.

He glanced her way. Mrs. Leon didn't. Realizing what a scene the woman could cause if she knew Nikki was here, she didn't move. Closing her eyes, she concentrated on not crying.

A minute or two passed until Dallas spoke up again. "It is important. Look, Nikki—"

"Hey," the deep male voice came from across the

room. She looked up at Detective O'Connor, thankful Mrs. Leon had gone. "Sorry, I held you up."

Nikki stood up. She felt Dallas beside her. "We'll talk about this later," he whispered.

Or not, Nikki thought.

The questions were grueling—over an hour of continuous gruel. Nikki was so tired. Tony wanted to know everything, from the name of Nikki's employee Jack had screwed on her antique sofa, to what the burglar had taken from her place. Dallas had cut him off several times, demanding he tone it down. When the detective asked about Nikki's missing computer, Dallas had slapped the paperwork from the pawnshop on the table and scowled at his brother.

That didn't slow Tony down, though. His questions grew more personal. "Why were you meeting your ex-husband for dinner?"

She told him the truth. "I thought I could go back with him, but when I saw him, I couldn't do it."

"Why?"

"Because I didn't love him, and I couldn't forgive him."

"So you were angry."

"Yes. No. I mean, I never really got angry at him before."

"You caught him screwing your employee and you weren't angry?"

"I was hurt. But when I saw him at the restaurant, that's when I got angry."

The detective leaned forward. "Angry enough to kill him?"

She blinked. "I'm not a killer."

"Did you know you were the beneficiary of his life

insurance? How long had you been planning on killing him? Since you didn't get the alimony you asked for in the divorce settlement?"

Nikki's backbone finally stiffened. "Jack set that insurance policy up when we got married. He also had one for the same amount on me. It was set up through his work, so I thought he'd cancel it. And I never asked for alimony. I signed the papers he handed me. I wouldn't let my lawyer fight it because I wanted it to be over."

Detective O'Connor eyed her with such intensity she felt like running. "You know we can request the court records and find out if you're lying."

"Maybe if you'd done that already I wouldn't have to go through this. I didn't kill Jack. I don't know why you refuse to believe me."

"You mean other than the fact that his body was found in your car after you told two people you were going to kill him?"

"Yeah...other than that." Feeling defeated, she dropped her head down on the table and swallowed hard to keep from weeping.

When she rose back up, he continued. "The Leons believe you killed their son for the insurance because you didn't get the alimony." His voice carried less conviction than before.

She forced words through her tight throat. "I know. I spoke with Mrs. Leon this morning. I have no idea why they think that. Except maybe...Jack lied to them. He placated his parents. Told them what they wanted to hear. I'm sure he wouldn't have told the truth of why we were divorcing. They never thought I was good enough for Jack. So maybe he made up a story for them."

The detective remained stoic for a few seconds. "I'm not sure anyone would have been good enough for them."

Nikki was so shocked at his statement she couldn't respond.

Dallas reached under the table and squeezed her hand. She pulled away.

"Tell him about the phone calls," Dallas said.

"What phone calls?" the detective asked.

Nikki told the detective about Jack arguing with someone on the phone at the restaurant. After that, the questions became less accusing and more about wanting insight into Jack. Many of the inquiries were the same ones Dallas asked over lunch, which made answering easier. She wondered if Dallas had done that on purpose.

After another ten or fifteen minutes of questions, Detective O'Connor stood up. "I appreciate you coming in, Ms. Hunt. We're done for now."

"My car?" she asked, and tried to keep the image of Jack in her trunk out of her mind, but it came anyway. She saw Jack's eyes open, empty, staring up at her from her trunk.

"Maybe tomorrow," the detective said.

Maybe tomorrow she'd be able to stop seeing flashes of her ex. Maybe tomorrow she'd understand why the hell all this was happening. Maybe tomorrow she'd be able to look at Dallas O'Connor and not want to beg him to hold her and help her forget.

"I need a word with you," Dallas said to his brother, then looked back at Nikki. "About another case. Can you give us a minute?"

She started out but as she got to the door, the detective spoke up again. "Ms. Hunt?"

Nikki glanced back.

"You're not under arrest, but I have to tell you not to leave town. The investigation is still ongoing."

Dallas studied Nikki. From the angst in her blue eyes, he knew how hard the interview had been on her. He could also tell she was still pissed at him over the bet thing.

Not that he blamed her.

From her perspective he came off looking like a jerk; from his perspective...he still looked like a jerk...but it had happened so fast. He hadn't been thinking and less than a minute after he'd done it, he was mentally kicking himself in the ass. Which was part of the reason he jumped on the case. So in the end, his being a jerk was the reason he was helping her. He wasn't sure how he was going to work all that into an apology, but he'd try. She had to understand, right?

Her eyes met his briefly, hurt and rejection playing in her baby blues, and then she walked out. Okay, so maybe the understanding wasn't going to happen all that fast. But damn it, he was on her side. She had to know that.

Dallas looked back at his brother. "Who was Leon talking to at the restaurant?"

"I'll have to check."

"Come on, Tony."

His brother hesitated. "The only people who spoke to him on that last day were Ellen Wise, his parents, and his office."

"Andrew Brian from his office has a motive," Dallas said.

"What would that be?"

"They were both being looked at for partner."

"And you know this how?" Tony asked.

"Connections."

"What connections?"

"It doesn't matter."

Tony stared him dead in the eyes.

"Fine," Dallas said. "It's a courthouse rumor. But I' n looking into it and I'm sharing it with you. And I expect you to share with me."

"Don't get in my way. This is my case."

"It's mine, too." He raked a hand through his hair. "She's innocent, Tony."

The stress lines on his brother's face deepened. "I'm leaning that way myself," he said. "But I need some-thing...something more than rumors. Right now, every new piece of information coming in is screaming that she's guilty. Then there're the vic's parents, screaming at my boss to arrest her."

Dallas threaded his hand through his hair. "What about Ellen Wise? You know Nikki couldn't have done that."

"I know, but I heard about an hour ago that it wasn't the same knife in both cases."

"Are you sure?"

"Completely different weapons. CSU said they weren't even close. And different weapons could mean different perps. It could mean they aren't even—"

"You know these two are connected."

Tony closed his eyes for a second. "Do I think they're connected? Yes. Do I think they were done by the same perp? Yes. Can I prove it? No. Right now, I have a dead man in the trunk of his ex-wife's car and two witnesses that will testify that she said she wanted to kill him. I need something else or I'm going to have to arrest her."

Dallas's gut knotted. "Get the court records of the divorce. At least that will weaken the Leons' story and maybe hold off your boss."

"I will, but I need more."

"I'll get it." Dallas decided to share a concern that had been gnawing at him since he'd met Ellen at the hospital. "You met Ellen Wise, right?"

"Yeah, why?"

"She fits the same physical description as Nikki. Blond, petite, pretty."

"What? You're going to go after them both?" Tony asked, and half-ass smiled.

"No. I'm wondering if whoever attacked Ellen thought she was Nikki?"

Tony's brow crinkled. "That's a possibility, but until we have a reason for any of this to have gone down, how is it going help us?"

"It helps me know that someone needs to watch out for her."

Dallas started to get up, but remembered what else he needed to talk to Tony about.

"Wait," Tony said, before Dallas spoke up. His brother passed a palm over his face. "Your other client...the Nance kid."

"I was just about to mention that." Dallas pulled out the copy of an old newspaper article that Austin had brought him at the hospital.

"Can you get the kid down here for Clark to talk to him?"

"You're going to try to pin last night's convenience store case on him?" Dallas didn't believe it. "Don't even tell me the second shooting victim identified him."

"The second victim died about an hour ago," Tony said. "And I'm not trying to pin it on him, I want to eliminate him as a suspect."

"How? I'm sure if you spoke with your buddy Detective Shane you'd know the kid was at home. Unfortunately, only his grandmother was there and she was asleep."

"I haven't heard that," Tony said, frustration heavy in his voice. "But it appears our perp from last night took a good hit with a baseball bat. If your boy doesn't have any marks on him, it might shed some new light on both cases."

Dallas studied his brother. "Does Shane know you're doing this?"

"No...not yet. I'm just eliminating suspects."

Dallas knew his brother was throwing him a bone. He appreciated it, but he still had to deliver the news. Shane's out to get the kid."

"He's just doing his job," Tony defended him. "The reason I'm doing this is—"

"No." Dallas handed Tony the proof that Austin had brought to the hospital.

"What's this?"

"Remember a few years back there was a drive-by shooting in Houston, and Shane's nephew was paralyzed? The main suspect, who they couldn't get enough evidence on to make the charge stick, was Nance's older brother. Shane wants to take Nance down for personal reasons. Somebody has to stop him."

"Whoa. You think Shane purposely went after Nance for this?"

"No, but I think once he realized who Nance was, he was dead set on bringing him down, and he didn't care

what the evidence said. Someone on the inside needs to
call Shane on this. Or we'll be forced to take it public."

Tony looked at the paper and his stress lines deepened.
"Fuck. I don't want to deal with this."

"And Nance doesn't want to go down for something he
didn't do, either."

Tony groaned. "Bring the kid in tomorrow. I'll talk to
him myself."

"And Shane?"

"I'll deal with that, too. Might as well piss him off
really good."

"Thanks." Dallas noticed his brother's tired eyes.
"You haven't been to bed at all, have you?"

"No."

"Is that why you told Dad you couldn't do dinner?"

"No, I'm moving tonight."

"Moving where?"

"Back home."

Contentment filled Tony's voice, and Dallas expected
there would be more if... "You and LeAnn made up?"

"No." Tony's ever-present stress lines deepened. "She
served me divorce papers."

"I don't understand," Dallas said.

"What's not to understand? She wants a divorce and I
don't. So I'm moving back home to prove to her it's a bad
idea."

Dallas held up his hands. "Maybe you should get some
sleep, think about this before—"

"I'm done thinking, it's time to act."

Dallas shrugged and started to leave.

"Hey." Tony's voice stopped him again.

"Yeah?"

"Since we're dealing out advice, let me offer this. Don't fall too hard for Nikki until the smoke clears."

"Yeah," Dallas said, but he wondered if the jittery feeling in his gut wasn't from the free fall he'd already taken.

Leaving his brother's office, he went to find Nikki, intending to do some serious groveling. He went to the waiting room. She wasn't there.

He walked outside into the main hall. She wasn't there. He shot off to the restrooms. A woman was entering the ladies' room, but Dallas stopped her. "I've lost someone. Can you check and see if anyone is in there?"

"Sure." She walked in and returned seconds later. "It's empty."

Getting a bad feeling, Dallas stormed back into Tony's office. "Do you have Nikki's cell number?"

"Yes, why?"

"She's gone."

CHAPTER NINETEEN

NIKKI'S CELL PHONE rang again.

"You gonna answer that?" Nana asked, as she stopped her Toyota at a red light. Nikki looked into Nana's worried eyes. Her grandmother had been worried ever since she'd picked Nikki up at the police station ten minutes ago.

"I didn't recognize the number," she told Nana.

"Someone must really want to talk to you to call three times."

"Probably a sales call." *Or Dallas.* Not that he had her cell number, but she'd given it to Tony. Nevertheless, she really didn't want to talk to Dallas.

Distance.

In a day or so, when she'd gotten over the shock of everything, gotten over the fact that he'd wagered on her being guilty, when she realized she didn't need to depend on a stranger for emotional support, then she'd meet with him.

She picked up her cell and looked at the call log again. "Oh crappers," she muttered.

"Crappers, what?" Nana asked.

"It's the Miller Police Department." Which meant it

could be Dallas or his brother. Ignoring Dallas was one thing. Ignoring the cop who suspected her of murder was another.

"Answer it. Maybe that cop finally pulled his head out of his ass and discovered who killed Jack."

She doubted that, but who was she not to hope? She hit the button. "Hello?"

"Where are you?" Dallas demanded. No hello.

No apology, either. She recognized his angry tone. He'd used it on her last night when she'd thrown the egg-beater at him.

"Nana picked me up. I'm borrowing her car."

"You can't just disappear like that," he said.

"I didn't. I told your bookie..." She paused just so he understood what she meant. "And I asked him to tell you I was leaving."

He exhaled loudly. "He's not...He didn't tell me."

"And is that my fault?"

"Why did you take off?" His voice boomed out of her phone and she knew Nana could hear every word.

I had to get away from you so I could think straight. "I didn't take off. I have things to do."

"The bet thing, right? You're still upset about that?"

She pressed the phone to her cheek, hoping to muffle the sound.

"That's what this is about, right?" he asked.

Yes. No. God, she didn't know. She just knew she couldn't be around him for much longer or she'd start counting on him. Like she'd counted on her parents and like she'd counted on Jack. She'd learned the hard way that counting on people got you hurt. She couldn't afford to be hurt now.

Nikki felt Nana looking at her, listening, and probably surmising what the conversation was about, too.

"You've carted me around all day. And I appreciate it, I do. But I've got things to do. We'll talk in a few days."

"Have they fixed your door?" he asked.

"I'm sure they have."

"What happened to your door?" Nana asked.

"But you don't know for sure?" He paused. "Where are you?"

"I should probably go."

"Nikki...if you'll give me a chance to explain—"

"Bye." She hung up and turned off her phone.

Nana turned into the parking lot of her retirement home condo complex, rolled real slow toward her building, studying Nikki every few seconds. "What's going on, Nikki?"

"It's nothing."

"You're upset."

"It's been a tough few days."

"What happened to your door?"

"The lock was sticking," she lied and did so with almost a clean conscience. She didn't want Nana worrying. "The apartment manager was supposed to fix it."

"Something happened between you and that PI, didn't it?"

"Nothing happened. He's just...I need to be alone."

"Sometimes a little company is nice."

"Not now." Nikki got out of the car and Nana did the same. She met her grandmother on the other side of the vehicle.

Nana reached up and pressed a hand on each of Nikki's

cheeks. "Come in for a bite to eat. I can whip up a batch of cupcakes."

The word "cupcakes" took her back to Dallas and their little make-out session on his bedroom floor. Heat immediately rushed to her cheeks. "I'd better head out."

"Are you okay...no issues with the poison?"

"Fine. I ate a big lunch."

Nana sighed.

Nikki decided to change the subject. "Are you sure you don't mind me borrowing your car? Mine should be ready tomorrow." She blinked away the image of Jack, and her heart raced. When was that going to stop happening?

"Lord, no. We're doing another dress rehearsal tonight. I'll ride with Benny and Helen."

Nikki hugged her grandmother, soaking up the love Nana offered. When she pulled back, Nana said, "You don't have to go through this alone. Stay here. Go see us practice. Have a few laughs."

Nikki remembered what Dallas had said about bringing trouble to her grandmother's door. "I'm fine. Besides..."—she plastered a smile on her lips—"I know Benny comes a calling at night."

"Nothing wrong with a gentleman caller every now and then." Nana pointed her finger at Nikki. "You should try it."

"I will when I find a guy as good as Benny."

"What about that PI? He seemed nice. Nice to look at, too."

"He's not my type," she lied. For some reason she remembered lunch when he'd swapped her fries for a part of his onion rings. It was stupid, but after spending years married to Jack, there was something refreshing about enjoying a meal with someone without worrying what fork she used or if the sandwich was too messy to eat with her hands.

Nana frowned. "You know, leaning on someone isn't a crime, child."

"I am leaning…leaning on you. I'm borrowing your car." And it pained Nikki to do it. She wanted to be the one Nana leaned on.

She gave Nana another hug. "Don't forget to take your blood pressure medicine. If Benny comes over, you'll need it." She sent her grandmother another smile and was hit with a wave of emotion. Somehow, Nikki had to get back on her feet—be the strong one in the relationship, and find a way to pay for Nana's cable.

Nana frowned as if seeing through Nikki's front. "Call me when you get home, okay?"

Nikki stopped at a stop sign and tried to decide. Go home and curl up on the bed and have that private meltdown she so deserved, or go to the gallery to take care of what had to be taken care of.

Only the weak cry. Her mother's voice played in her head. Biting down on her lip, she turned toward the gallery. Her stomach clutched at the thought of cleaning up Ellen's blood, but Dallas was right. It was easier now that she'd seen Ellen was okay.

She parked outside the gallery, moved to the front door, purposely not looking through the glass door at the blood, and started going through her purse for the keys. They weren't in the side pocket. They weren't in the middle, either. She pulled out her wallet. She really needed to clean out her purse. Shaking it, she didn't hear the keys jingle.

That's when she remembered she'd given Dallas the keys. "Shit." She leaned against the door. When she opened her eyes, another realization hit—the lights in the gallery were on. She distinctly remembered cutting them off when they'd left.

Her gaze shot to the tile floor and her stomach muscles knotted as she prepared to feel repulsed.

But...no repulsion.

No blood.

What had...How...?

She reached for the doorknob and when it turned in her hand, she fought the need to run. Instead, she reached back into her purse, pulled out her can of Mace and stepped inside.

The smell of some strong cleaner filled the air. Who had...?

The air conditioner spurted to life. She gripped the Mace. Her gaze shifted to the artwork, making sure none had been taken—though she supposed a thief wouldn't clean up and then rob her blind.

But then she heard footsteps.

Immediately her thoughts shot to Ellen's story of hearing someone in the gallery.

Nikki listened to the steps moving down the hall that led from the office at the back.

Her gaze shot to the front door. Without enough time to make it out without being seen, she backed up against the wall, so she wasn't immediately visible. The footsteps came closer.

Tap. Tap. Tap.

Is this how Ellen felt? Nikki's heart thumped so loud it echoed in her ears. Images of the blood flashed in her mind.

The steps drew closer—almost right beside her. Panic took over. Finger on the Mace nozzle, Nikki swung around, sprayed, screamed, and bolted for the door.

"Hello." Dallas walked into his dad's home. It didn't smell right. The house hadn't smelled right since he'd gotten out of prison. It wasn't that the house contained an odor. It was the lack of certain scents. It no longer smelled like Lemon Pledge or fresh-baked cookies. It no longer smelled like his mom.

When Dallas didn't see his dad right inside the door, he had the impulse to swing around, get back in his car and go to the Park Knoll apartments to check on Nikki. It had taken everything he had not to go straight there from the police station. What if her landlord hadn't fixed her lock? What if he was right, and someone was after her?

Dallas had called at least six times. Left five messages, all of which she hadn't answered. And not because she was in danger, but because she didn't want to talk to him.

You tried. She doesn't want you there. Leave her be. His brother's words of wisdom echoed in Dallas's head.

He had almost thrown those same words back at Tony about LeAnn. How crazy was it for his brother to move back home when his wife asked for a divorce? But Tony's problems with LeAnn were different. And Tony was right—Dallas couldn't force Nikki to accept his help. But he did have to return her keys. And as soon as he got the gallery key from Austin, he'd do so. Dallas had called Austin twice to see if the cleaning crew had finished, but Austin never answered his phone. So while he waited to hear back from Austin, Dallas felt obligated to have dinner with his dad.

Dallas took another step inside his parents' home. His dad sat in his old leather recliner, watching TV. Problem was, the screen was black. The thing wasn't turned on.

"Dad?"

His father jumped up as if he'd been in some kind of a daze. "Dallas. You're early."

Dallas spotted four beer cans on the coffee table. When his mom was alive, she'd allowed him a six-pack a week. No doubt, he was over his quota now.

"It's six-thirty, Dad."

"Oh. I must have dozed off. Let me get that grill going." He looked back over his shoulder as he walked into the kitchen. "So tell me about this new case."

His dad wasn't staggering, so he wasn't drunk, but the sad truth hit. He was lonely. Dallas could almost feel the emotion in the air. Sure, his dad could get out with his ol' buddies, but Dallas remembered his dad telling him once that all his friends did was complain about their old ladies. Did they know, his dad had asked, that he'd give anything if his own old lady was at home?

Dallas saw the photo albums on the coffee table. Was that what his dad did all day? Look at pictures and grieve? Guilt punched him in the gut. He'd been so wrapped up in his own grief that he hadn't considered how much his father must be hurting.

He stepped closer to the kitchen. "Instead of cooking, why don't we just go out? I have to pick up a key and return it to someone, then maybe we can go to that rib joint you like."

His dad paused. "You got the time?"

Dallas nodded. He'd make the time. "Yeah."

His dad chattered all the way to the car about how he

hadn't had ribs in a long time. How the dinner out was a great idea. Dallas was about to start the car when his cell rang. His heart gripped with hope that it was Nikki, returning his calls. While he didn't like the idea of groveling in front of his old man, it wouldn't stop him.

"Excuse me," he told his dad and looked at the call log.

It wasn't Nikki's number, but then he saw the name. "B. Littlemore." Nikki's grandmother. Could be Nikki.

"Hello?" Hope sounded in his voice.

"You said you'd take care of my girl," Mrs. Littlemore scolded. "And from what I can tell right now, you're doing a piss-poor job of it."

"What's wrong? Where's Nikki?" Dallas clutched the steering wheel, remembering how sweet she'd looked curled up in his bed this morning.

"She was supposed to call me when she got home. I called her and she didn't answer. Then I got Benny to stop by her apartment on the way to play rehearsal. Her door's been broken in. Where's my Nikki, Dallas O'Connor?"

Dread filled Dallas's chest. "I don't know. Look, I'll drive over to her place now. But calm down, the apartment was broken into last night, so I'm sure she's fine." He felt his left eyebrow arch upward. But damn he didn't want that to be a lie. "Wait. Maybe she went back up to the hospital to see Ellen."

"Nope, I called there. And I called the gallery. No answer."

"Does she have other friends?" He hated that he knew so little about her.

"Since the divorce, she's not been very social," Mrs. Littlemore said.

"Okay, you keep trying to reach her. I'll head out to

her place. If I find her, I'll give you a call. You do the same." He hung up his phone and looked at his dad.

"You want a rain check, right? Don't worry." His dad reached for the door handle. "I understand."

In honesty, that was exactly what he'd been going to say, but the disappointment in his dad's voice shot that idea to hell. "Or you could come with me."

A smile lit up his dad's eyes. "Let's go."

Dallas took off, and remembered another smile he'd grown fond of seeing. The thought that something bad could have happened had regret pulling at his gut.

CHAPTER TWENTY

"I'm so sorry," Nikki repeated for the tenth time, placing a stack of wet paper towels across Austin Brook's eyes. Then she scowled. "Why didn't Dallas tell me he was doing this?"

"I don't know," Austin growled then, yanking the wet paper towels off his face, he glared at her with bloodred eyes. "Goddamn it! I almost shot you."

"But you didn't," she said, hoping to soothe him. "And I really appreciate it, too."

He yanked the inch-thick stack of soggy paper towels back over his eyes and continued to mutter. She didn't understand everything he said, but most of it was four-letter words.

"If Dallas had told me about this, I'd never have sprayed you. It's his fault."

"Don't worry," he snapped. "He's gonna hear about this. You got a fan?"

"In the office," she answered.

"Bring it here and plug it in. Please." He motioned for her to hurry.

She took off to collect the fan. When she came running back in, Austin's phone rang. He dropped the paper towels from his eyes and stared at the cell, then answered it. "The next time you ask me to do you a damn favor, remind me to tell you to just kiss my ass!"

Tony dropped his bags so he could open the front door. It hadn't occurred to him that LeAnn might have changed the locks until he reached for his keys. Worry swelled in his chest that she might have tried to lock him out.

When his key slipped into the lock, he wanted to believe that her not changing the locks meant something. He grabbed his bags and held tight to his hope. Stepping over the threshold, he was surrounded by the feeling of coming home.

He belonged here. What's more, he should have never left.

Inhaling LeAnn's scent, he looked at the kitchen clock. He wasn't sure what time she got off, but if her hours were the same and she still worked twelve-hour shifts, he guessed she'd gone in at eight that morning and would leave at eight tonight. That meant he had a little over an hour to get his stuff unpacked, clean up, and emotionally prepare for the fireworks that were bound to happen when she found him here. He exhaled and hoped like hell his lack of sleep didn't hinder his ability to cope.

He dropped the bag of groceries on the kitchen table. He'd gotten a good bottle of red wine, a bag of the chocolate-covered peanuts she had a weakness for, her favorite coffee and hazelnut creamer, a pack of real butter, some croissants, and a bottle of the most expensive blackberry preserves his grocery carried. Expensive hopefully meant quality. LeAnn loved croissants and jam. Finding the wine opener, he popped the cork so it would have plenty of time to breathe. LeAnn also loved a glass of wine and a snack before bedtime.

He carried the other bags with him as he moved into the living room. His gaze fell to the empty corner of the room where the baby swing had once sat. He remembered coming home every evening, kissing LeAnn then walking to the swing and lifting his daughter into his arms.

His chest clutched when he recalled that only a week before Emily died, she'd learned to smile. And with that precious smile on her face, she'd looked so much like LeAnn. That was the day Tony had completely and wholeheartedly fallen in love with his daughter. Oh, he'd loved her before, but her first smile was a heart snatcher.

Determined to make his homecoming about good things and not about what they had lost, he shook off his grief, and went to store his things in the spare bedroom. He intended to let LeAnn know right off that his plan included joining her in their bed just as soon as she'd allow it.

He opened the third bedroom and dropped his bags inside. Then he walked back into the hall and stared at the closed door that led to the nursery. Curious to see what LeAnn had done with the room, he turned the knob. His breath caught.

The crib still had the pink sheet with teddy bears. The rocker still had a burping cloth thrown over one arm. There was even a little outfit set out on the changing table.

Had LeAnn even come in here since Emily died?

He'd been so grief stricken, losing his mom one week and then Emily the next, he hadn't stopped to consider what they needed to do with...her things. Or how they needed to go about healing from the loss. But standing here now, he knew they needed to clear out Emily's things. They needed to move forward.

But first he had to win LeAnn over. Prove to her that she didn't want this divorce. He shut the door and walked into the master suite. He stared at the bed where he and LeAnn had loved, played, teased, and laughed. That's what he needed to make LeAnn remember.

He went back to the spare bedroom and dug into his bags. He pulled out a pair of jeans and clean underwear; the shirt was optional. LeAnn had always loved him without his shirt. *You know what it does to me when you run around without a shirt on,* she'd said to him a dozen times.

Grabbing his leather bag that contained his razor, deodorant, and aftershave—the aftershave LeAnn had picked out herself—he started down the hall to the guest bath.

He almost made the door when he remembered—the guest bath only had one of those whirlpool tubs and no shower. He recalled debating with LeAnn about adding a shower when they had the extra bathroom remodeled. She hadn't wanted to have to hang a curtain rod. *You won't ever use this bathroom. You got the shower in the master bath.*

Smiling, he headed to the master bath. This just might work in his favor.

He stopped by the king-size bed and a memory from way back in the beginning tickled his mind. He and LeAnn had just started dating and he'd brought her to his new home to have dinner with some friends. He hadn't slept with her yet, because she insisted they hadn't waited long enough, and he'd caught her spraying his bed with her perfume.

"Just a little something to remember me by," she'd said, blushing.

"So you want me to lay here tonight and get hard thinking about you?" he teased her.

She laughed and confessed, "Yeah. That's sort of what I'd hoped."

It had worked, too. From the moment he'd gotten into his bed that night, all he could think about was her. That next morning, he'd gone to her apartment and convinced her he'd waited long enough.

Grinning, he took out the aftershave, splashed some on his hands and then ran his hands under her pillow.

Then he went to get ready, eager to start seducing his way back into LeAnn's arms, back into her bed, and back into her life. He'd waited long enough.

As soon as Dallas got off the phone with a very pissed-off Austin, he turned the car around and headed to the gallery. Then he called Mrs. Littlemore. "She's fine. She's at the gallery. Yes, I'll take care of her door. I promise."

"I still don't get it," his dad said when he hung up. "Who sprayed Austin with Mace?"

Dallas ran a hand through his hair. He'd tried to fill his dad in on what was going on, but it wasn't easy. "Nikki did."

"Nikki, the girl who killed her husband."

"Nikki didn't kill her husband. It was her ex-husband who was killed."

"So she killed her ex-husband."

"No, Dad." Dallas tried not to lose it. "Nikki didn't kill anyone."

"So who killed her ex?"

"That's what we're trying to find out."

His dad nodded. "So why did she Mace Austin?"

Dallas pulled up in front of the gallery. "It's complicated. Can I explain it later?"

His dad nodded again. "Is your job always this complicated?"

Being a retired plumber, his dad never had understood the whole law enforcement-PI appeal, and questioned how he could have raised two boys who did. "Not always," Dallas said, and realized his life hadn't felt this complicated until Nikki.

They got out of the car. "But just so I'm clear," his dad said right before Dallas grabbed the doorknob, "someone got the Mace away from her, right?"

"I don't think she'll Mace you, Dad." Dallas wondered if he should worry about himself. While he'd been on the phone with Austin, he'd heard her in the background muttering about this being his fault.

They walked into the gallery and Dallas looked at Austin, shirtless, sitting in a chair, holding a fan up to his face, and a dozen or more piles of wet paper towels at his feet.

"What? You bring your dad because you're scared I'm gonna whip your ass?" Austin asked.

There was humor in his partner's voice but, knowing how much Mace hurt, Dallas decided not to get too close. When he'd asked Austin to call Roxie, owner of CSCU, Crime Scene Clean Up, Austin hadn't been happy. Sure, Dallas knew Roxie was sweet on Austin. Which was why

Austin hadn't wanted to do it. But that was exactly why
Austin had to be the one to call her. She wouldn't have
been nearly as prompt to do the job if Dallas had called her.

"Scared of you?" his dad piped up, teasing Austin.
"You let a girl beat you up."

Austin turned his bloodred eyes back on Dallas, only
all the tease was gone. "I almost shot her. I had my finger
on the trigger."

Dallas remembered how he'd almost shot her last
night. "Where's she at?" he asked, worried she'd already
taken off.

"Getting more wet paper towels. She feels bad. But she
blames you."

Right then Nikki walked out from the back of the gallery. Her gaze slapped against Dallas. "This is your fault."
She walked over to Austin and plopped a handful of wet
paper towels over his eyes and then turned her angry blue
eyes full force on Dallas.

Austin snatched off the towels, wanting to see Dallas
get his comeuppance.

"What's his fault?" a familiar voice boomed at the
door.

Dallas looked back at Mrs. Littlemore and two of her
Annie Oakley crew—the sheriff and the saloon girl. They
were in costume again.

"It's his fault I sprayed Austin with Mace," answered
Nikki.

"Who are they?" his dad leaned in and asked.

"Who is Austin?" Helen, the saloon girl, asked.

"Who are you?" his dad asked Helen when Dallas
didn't answer soon enough.

Dallas ignored Helen and his dad and looked back at

Nikki. "I was only trying to help. But I probably should have told you what I was doing."

"What were you doing?" his dad asked.

"Why did you spray him with Mace?" Mrs. Littlemore asked Nikki.

Nikki looked at her grandmother. "Because..." Nikki's words faltered.

Dallas felt compelled to explain. "I had Austin call a friend of his who does crime scene cleanup to come here. Nikki didn't know anyone was here and she got spooked."

"You took my keys," Nikki accused.

"You took her keys?" Benny, the sheriff of the group, asked in his gruff voice—no doubt the one he'd practiced to use in the play.

"Oh, hell, just shoot him, Annie Oakley." Helen elbowed Nikki's grandmother and chuckled.

"I didn't take your keys." He looked from Helen and the rest of the Oakley group to Nikki and pulled her keys out of his pocket. "You left without telling me. I was going to drive you back to the gallery and get the keys I loaned Austin and then give them back to you. I was trying to help. I didn't want you having to clean up all that blood."

"What blood?" his dad asked.

"*You* should have told me," Nikki snapped.

"*You* should have told me you were leaving," Dallas countered.

"What blood?" his dad asked again.

"You bet twenty dollars I was guilty." Her words hit hard against Dallas's conscience. He'd hurt her and, damn, he hated it.

"He did what?" his dad and Austin asked at the same time.

"Okay, now I'm gonna shoot him," Mrs. Littlemore said.

"I'm sorry, I screwed up," Dallas said to Nikki, trying not to listen to the craziness going on around him. "Really sorry."

"You don't do that," Nikki said. "You don't make bets—"

"I made a mistake," he insisted. Everyone started chattering around him, making Dallas crazy. "You don't puke on people, either, but you don't see me holding it against you. And I said I was sorry. What do you want me to do?"

"She puked on him?" Benny asked.

"I'd give fifty bucks to have seen it." Austin laughed and then lifted the fan to his eyes.

"Fifty's too steep but I'd pay twenty." His dad chuckled. "Do you know how many times he puked on me when he was a boy?"

"I'm told she got him twice," Austin said. "When he came back to the office, he didn't have a shirt on." He paused for a second. "Can someone get me some more wet paper towels? My eyes are on fire."

"You don't have a shirt on," Helen said to Austin.

"She was poisoned when she puked on him," Mrs. Littlemore defended Nikki.

"And I was Maced," Austin said. "I could use some more wet paper towels."

Dallas stared at Nikki who stared back him. *I'm sorry*, he mouthed.

"Who poisoned her?" Dallas's dad asked and then looked back at Dallas. "You were right, son. This is very complicated."

"So you're Dallas's dad," Helen said. "I was wondering

who you were. Now, if I could just figure out who the shirtless Austin is."

"He works with Dallas at the PI agency," his dad explained, laughing. "He normally wears a shirt."

"Some wet paper towels would be nice," Austin said.

Nikki kept looking at Dallas, but he didn't know if the look meant forgiveness or not. "It happened so fast," Dallas said to Nikki. "I didn't mean it. I swear."

"What did he not mean?" Helen asked.

"I think he meant he didn't mean to make the bet," his dad answered.

"How does someone not mean to make a bet?" Benny asked.

"I made a bet I didn't mean to make at the horse races once," his dad said.

"Stop it!" Dallas yelled and held up his arms. "Would everyone shut up? Nikki and I are trying to have our first argument here."

He looked at Nikki. She laughed.

And then everyone in the room started laughing. Dallas stood there and stared at Nikki, her eyes filled with humor, and he prayed this meant she'd forgiven him.

An hour later, Nikki stepped out of the Ribs R Us restaurant bathroom, and found Dallas waiting for her. She still hadn't talked to him. Dallas's dad said something about going to eat ribs and invited everyone along and, before Nikki could say no, Nana and her group had agreed.

Nikki had purposely sat on the other side of the table away from Dallas. Not that she was still mad at him—well, maybe a little—but being close to the man was like being close to a live wire.

"You speaking to me yet?" Dallas asked her.

"Yes," she said, but she still needed distance.

He reached out to touch her and, before she could stop herself, she pulled back.

His blue eyes tightened with disappointment. "We need to talk."

"No, it's fine." He'd apologized, even done it in front of a crowd. Not many men would have done that. And she forgave him, or almost had. It still hurt. But she believed he was sorry. "Thanks for having the gallery cleaned. You should have told me, but I appreciate it."

"You're welcome."

"Just add it to what I owe you, and we'll figure it out when this is over."

"You're not big on letting people help you, are you?"

"It's not that," she said. "I just... like taking care of myself."

He smiled. "Which translates to, you're not big on letting people help you."

Laughter exploded in the restaurant. Dallas turned his head and looked out the door leading back to their table. "Damn."

"What?"

He looked back at her. "My dad. I haven't heard him laugh like that in a while."

"He's seems like a nice guy. I see a big resemblance in you two."

"He's difficult to take at times, but he's okay."

She grinned. "Like I said, I see a big resemblance."

He touched his chest. "Ouch."

Dallas's dad walked into the hall. "There you are. Look, I'm gonna go watch those crazy folks practice a few hours and Benny said he'd give me a lift back home."

"Sure." Dallas shrugged. "I'll talk to you tomorrow."

Nikki watched his dad leave then looked back at Dallas. "I should say good-bye."

He caught her. His touch sent a warm current up her arm and into her chest. "I'm going to follow you home."

"No, I . . ."

"Your grandmother said your lock wasn't fixed when she went by your place."

"I'm sure it is now."

"Just to be sure," he said.

"He's right." Nana had snuck up beside them. "It's either that, or you're coming home with me. I wouldn't sleep a wink if I thought you couldn't lock your door after all that's happened."

Nikki rolled her eyes and glanced back at Dallas. "Fine, follow me back to my place."

CHAPTER TWENTY-ONE

DALLAS WALKED UP to Nikki's apartment door, studying her as she moved. More than ever she seemed nervous. He suspected it was because she hadn't forgiven him. And that made him nervous.

"See I told you it would be fixed," she said. "Now you can go."

He tried to open the door. It was locked. "So how do you plan to get in?"

"He locked it?" She tried the knob and moaned. Then, snapping her fingers, she knelt and pulled up the runner in front of her door. Rising, she held out the key, and practically waved him away.

"That's really safe." Dallas hadn't realized how much he'd hoped the door wasn't fixed. He couldn't stop thinking about the coincidence that she and Ellen looked so much alike. The media had already gotten hold of the story, so if Nikki had been the intended victim, the attacker would know he'd missed his mark.

"We still need to talk." In the dark he couldn't read her expression, but he was guessing it wasn't happy.

Looking up at the dark porch light, he asked, "Blown bulb?"

"Electrical problem."

"You need to find another apartment," he said. "This isn't the best neighborhood."

"Can't this talk wait for a few days?"

"No." He took the key from her hand and unlocked the door. Nudging the door open, he waited for her to enter.

"You're pushy." She moved in and hit the light switch.

"You're stubborn," he countered, but smiled as he followed her inside. "I have a weakness for stubborn blondes."

She frowned. "Okay, make it fast. Start talking."

"Can we sit down?" He motioned toward the sofa.

She nodded. He moved around, careful not to step on the items still on the floor. When he sat on the sofa, he expected her to join him. But she took the chair across from him instead. He frowned. "You're still mad."

"I'm not mad."

"Then why won't you sit beside me?"

"Because...because I don't want to give you the wrong idea."

"What wrong idea?" he asked.

She hesitated. "I'm not going to...Oh hell, I'm not having sex with you. I'm not messing up the bedsheets, doing the tango, swapping bodily fluids. Not happening, got it?" She slapped her hands on her knees.

He leaned back on the sofa and laughed. "You missed one. I think your grandmother called it doing a goat jig."

Her eyes grew big. "You talked about sex with Nana?"

He laughed again. "No, she was...talking about your ex."

"Oh." She blinked and Dallas was sorry he'd mentioned it.

"Okay. Would you tell me why you're not going to have sex with me?"

She thought about it for a minute. Long enough for him to start thinking about messing up the bedsheets with her and about how they had come close to doing the tango this morning.

"Do I have to justify it?"

He saw that hurt in her eyes again. "It's because you're mad at me."

"No."

"Then why? We know you're attracted to me."

"We know that?" She leaned forward. "What makes you so certain?"

"Because you want to talk about sex. And because you're scared to sit next to me."

"I didn't want to talk about sex. You're the one who wanted to talk. And I'm not afraid to sit next to you."

"I wanted to talk, but I wasn't going to talk about sex. Not that I don't like talking about sex. I just prefer having sex to talking about it." He grinned. "But talking about it isn't bad."

"Okay, stop." She blushed.

"Stop what?"

"Talking about sex!"

"I didn't start the conversation."

"Well, I'm ending it." She crossed her arms under her breasts and made them even more noticeable. And damn, if he didn't feel something else becoming noticeable in his jeans.

They stared at each other. The tension between them

was sweet and hot. But he could still see it, that touch of something in her eyes that said he'd hurt her. "Can I get myself something to drink?"

"I don't have much," she said.

"Water is fine." Rising, he walked to the kitchen.

She followed him. "Let me." She pulled two glasses out of the cabinet. "Ice?"

"Please." He leaned against the counter and watched her move. He shouldn't be watching, noticing how snug the pink top fit across her breasts, but not noticing was impossible.

She opened the fridge and pulled out two bottles of water. His gaze shot to the fridge's contents. It contained less than his at home.

She filled the glasses and handed him one. "So what do you want to talk about?" Her eyes still contained the hurt.

"As soon as I made the bet, I wanted to kick myself."

"You don't have to—"

"Yes, I do." He paused. "Of all people, I should know better."

"Because you were a cop?"

"No." He looked at her. "There's something you need to know."

"About?"

"Me." The glass was cold against his palm. He took a sip.

"Is this about sex again?" She cut him a sharp look.

He smiled. "No." He waited for the humor to fade before getting serious. "I should have told you. I don't usually hide it."

Her eyes widened. "You aren't gay. I felt... I mean, you were interested when..."

He burst out laughing and had to set his glass down for fear of spilling it. "Oh, hell no. And yes, I was very interested. Uncomfortably interested."

She tilted her head to the side and studied him. "Oh God, you lied to me? You're married." She came closer and stared up at him as if trying to see the truth.

"No."

"Engaged?" She studied him closer.

"No."

"Involved?"

"No." Unable to resist, he caught her by the shoulders and pulled her against him.

"Then how is this about sex?" Her brow pinched with curiosity.

He started laughing again. "I told you it's not about sex."

She put her hands on his chest and pushed away a few inches. God, he wanted to kiss her again. She was so damn refreshing, so honest, so sexy. And so not the type of woman he needed in his life. Because she was the type a man didn't want to push away. And he'd vowed to always push.

The thought echoed in his mind and plunged into his chest. It felt as if the thought dropkicked his heart.

One day at a time. And then what? Damn it, he didn't want to analyze this.

"It's always about sex with men," she said.

"You're right. Most of the time it's about sex." As tempting as it was to forgo telling her the truth, and let this be about sex, he knew he had to do it. "But not this time." He forced himself to say it. "I was accused of murder."

"That's not funny." She took a step back.

That step hurt. "Which is why I'm not joking about it."

She moved close again as if to watch his eyebrow. "You're serious?"

He nodded.

"I was accused of murder and...arrested." Dallas looked into her eyes, trying to read her like she read him.

"That's awful," she whispered.

"Yes, it was. And that's why I feel terrible about judging you, even for a minute. I should never make rash assumptions. That's why I need to know you forgive me."

"Did you go to trial?"

"Yes."

"And they found you innocent."

He swallowed. "No. They found us guilty."

"Us?"

"Austin and my other partner, Tyler. We were accused of stealing drugs from a shipment. Then there was—"

"Glencoe police?" she asked.

He nodded. "You heard—"

"That was you?" She put her hand on his chest. There was no doubt in that touch. No judgment, no question of his innocence.

That's what he'd expected from Serena. What he'd gotten was questions. How did your fingerprints get there? How did the money get wired into Tyler's account?

"That was...terrible. They accused ya'll of brutally killing that couple. Ya'll went to jail until...someone proved you didn't do it."

"And that's the important part. We didn't do it."

"That's why you're helping me, isn't it?" She stood so close that her breasts nearly brushed his chest.

"Part of the reason."

"And the other reason?"

"It's probably to do with sex," he teased her and then leaned down to kiss her.

She put two fingers over his mouth. "Is this going to happen to me? Am I going to end up going to prison?"

"No." He knew he couldn't make promises, but he did it anyway. "I won't let that happen."

She dropped her head onto his chest and Dallas wrapped his arms around her. He leaned against the counter and she leaned into him. After a few minutes of just holding her, trying not to think about how it would feel to hold her like this without their clothes on, he brushed his hand over her back. She lifted her head and rested her chin on his chest and looked up at him.

"You should probably go," she said.

"Why?" He ran a finger over her cheek and then slowly moved it over her lips.

"Because this might end up being about sex."

"And would that really be a bad thing?" It was the question he'd been asking himself, too.

She gazed up at him, and he saw desire in her blue eyes. "No. Yes." She bit down on her lip. "I don't know."

He grinned. "I get the feeling you're indecisive."

"You got that, huh?" She smiled.

Damn if that wasn't the sweetest smile. Sassy and sexy. "Yeah, I got that. And I can't help wondering how easy it would be for me to help you make a decision." He leaned in, wanting to taste her. Wanting her naked. Wanting it even when wanting someone this much scared him. Because he knew where this kind of wanting could lead— to caring. Then the truth hit. He already cared about her. And not just in a client way.

"Too easy." She put a finger over his lips. "I just...I don't want to jump into something without thinking, Dallas."

And that was exactly what he wanted to do. Jump and not think, the consequences be damned.

He took in a pound of oxygen. Everything he was feeling, things he didn't want to feel zipping around in his chest like trapped bats. Maybe she wasn't the only one who needed to think this through. "Okay." He pushed a palm over his face. But he couldn't leave her. "Why don't you grab a bag for the night?"

She stared up at him. "Why would I do that?"

"Because you're staying with me for a couple of days to make sure you're safe."

She tucked a couple of loose curls behind her ear. "No, I'm fine. The door's fixed."

"You're not fine, Nikki. Someone broke in once, he can do it again."

"I have my Mace," she said.

"And they have a knife." When she didn't look convinced he decided to put it to her bluntly. "I think whoever got to Ellen thought it was you. By now the press is all over this. The attacker knows he got the wrong person. He could come back."

"But why? I'm not a bad person. I swear it." She paused. "What did I do that someone wants to kill me for?"

"I don't know, but I'd like to find out before he comes back to finish the job."

She looked down at her clutched hands. Dallas brushed her hair behind her ear. She glanced up. "I'll get a hotel room."

"Just come home with me. I promise I won't touch you." Realizing he was doing just what he said he wouldn't, he pulled his hand away from her face. "Okay, I won't touch you again. A hotel is going to run you at least a hundred bucks. You told me you were busted."

She appeared unconvinced, so he went for his trump card. "You could pay for Nana's cable with what it'll cost you to stay in a hotel."

She stared at him through her lashes and he saw her emotionally flinch. "Can you keep that promise?"

"I can." He smiled. "Unless you change your mind. Then we'll regroup."

She bit down on her lip as if considering. "For one night."

"Maybe two. Until we know it's safe."

She tilted her head to the side. Her soft hair swept across one shoulder. "I sleep on the sofa."

"No. I sleep on the sofa."

She snapped her chin up. "Then I'm not going."

He frowned. "You really are stubborn."

"I thought you liked stubborn blondes."

"I do, but I like them sleeping in my bed, not on my sofa. How about we flip for it?"

"Nope. And you sleep with Bud."

She wasn't going to give. He saw it in her eyes. "Deal."

She took off to get her bags and he went back into the living room. His gaze landed on the photograph of her and Nana. He picked it up and felt his gut tighten when he saw the pain in young Nikki's eyes.

How, he wondered, could her parents have done that to her?

At eleven that night, after LeAnn spent three hours at a bookstore looking for something that might hold her interest, she walked inside her house. She longed to fall into bed and read herself to sleep. Maybe tonight would be a good night. She'd had more good nights lately and really appreciated them. But after handing Tony the papers, she really doubted it. The look on his face kept flashing in her mind. For the life of her, she didn't know if it had been relief or hurt.

She stopped before she closed the door.

Something was wrong.

She sensed it. It wasn't just that the lamp was on and she never turned the lamp on because she never sat in the living room. It wasn't just the light scent of red wine and freshly ground coffee beans, it was... more. The air breathed different.

Tony was home.

The house had already taken on his scent and welcomed him back.

Panic sent her stomach fluttering. Had he come to hand-deliver the divorce papers? Was he that eager to get it over with? But would he have brought wine and prepared tomorrow's coffee to brew in the process?

Maybe. Tony was instinctively good. He was probably going to tell her to move out—it was his house. He'd bought it before they'd married. She'd known this would happen eventually, but damn, it still hurt.

Closing the door, she tiptoed inside. She looked off into the kitchen and saw a wine bottle opened and two glasses set out, waiting. Beside the wine was a candy dish. She didn't have to get closer to know it was filled with chocolate-covered nuts.

Breath held, she moved into the living room. Her heart lurched at the sight of him, asleep, stretched out on the sofa. The lamp cast a yellow glow over his bare skin. And wearing only a pair of unsnapped jeans, there was a lot of skin. Lord have mercy, the man could be in *Playgirl*. He had a washboard stomach, just enough chest hair to make him look masculine. The scar on his right shoulder added to the touch of masculinity. She looked at the coffee table, thinking she'd see the envelope and pen, but no, only a glass of tea...on a coaster. He never remembered to use a coaster.

Quietly, she lowered herself into the chair across from the sofa, and set her purse beside her. She felt herself trembling, felt the tears start to well up into her eyes.

"You want some wine?"

His voice startled her and she jumped. Her gaze shot to his face. He stared at her as he sat up.

She swallowed. "What are you doing here?"

CHAPTER TWENTY-TWO

TONY OPENED HIS MOUTH to give her the speech he'd practiced all night. He loved her, didn't believe she'd completely stopped loving him and he wanted to work it out. But suddenly he feared she'd shoot his idea down before he had a chance to set it in action. He needed a new plan. Fast.

"It's only for a while."

"What's for a while?" Suspicion colored her face.

"Me staying here. I couldn't believe it."

"Believe what?"

Believe that I don't have a freaking clue what I'm going to say. "They just . . . took over."

He ran a hand over his face. Delaying, desperately needing a second to regroup, he got up and walked to the kitchen to pour wine.

"What took over?" she asked.

He passed the television and recalled a news segment he'd seen tonight.

"Bedbugs." He didn't look back because LeAnn was good at seeing through him.

"What?"

"My apartment building. Well, six apartments." He filled both glasses and brought one to her.

"Your apartment has bedbugs?" She looked as if she didn't believe him, but she took the glass.

"Didn't you see the news? There's an invasion. There were guys there wearing hazmat suits and everything. Looked like a sci-fi flick."

"I heard it was hotels, not apartments." She stood up.

"I'm sure it'll be all over the news tomorrow." And tomorrow he'd better have a better answer.

She looked at the sofa, then back at him, and took a step back. "Have you been treated?"

"Me?" Friggin' great, now she wouldn't want to get close to him. Why the hell did he use bedbugs when that's exactly where he wanted to end up with her? "Yeah." But how did one get treated? He remembered a friend of his got lice as a kid. "Used the comb and everything."

"A comb? They get in your hair?" She passed a hand over her head.

"No. Yeah." *How the fuck am I supposed to know?* "But I didn't have any. I'm clean." He patted his chest.

He noticed her eyes followed his hands and stayed there for just a second. *That's right. Look all you want and forget about bedbugs.* He purposely ran his hand down his chest, stopping inches from his zipper.

Her gaze followed his hand, but then snapped back up. "And your things?"

"My things?"

"I heard they get in your clothes. Your bags. You didn't bring any with you, did you?"

"Just one."

Her gaze tightened. "One bug?"

"One bag, but...they freeze-dried it before I left." *Oh, he was so screwed.*

"Freeze-dried it?" She crossed her arms, disbelief pulling at the corners of her eyes.

"Crazy isn't it? That's how they kill them." He recalled bits and pieces of the news. "They have to either cook or freeze them. Nasty little creatures."

Some of her doubt seemed to fade. "Why didn't you go to a hotel?"

Oh shit. He had to think quickly. "You're kidding, right? How would I know if they didn't have bedbugs?"

"Why couldn't you stay with your dad?"

Tony hesitated. "He's afraid."

"Your dad's afraid of bedbugs?"

"Of getting them in his house." He drank a sip of wine. "I kind of feel the same way."

"Sorry," he said, but he knew LeAnn well enough to know she wouldn't toss him out to a possibly bedbug-infested hotel. Or at least he hoped she wouldn't.

She put the wine to her lips. "I'm not sure if this is a good—"

"Just a few days," he said. *Or until I convince you that you still love me.*

"You sure you're clean?"

"Not a bug on me." He did another swipe over his chest.

She nodded, looking at him somewhat suspiciously. "You do realize I can call your apartment and ask if this is...real?"

Totally *fucked.* "Do you want me to give you their number?"

She hesitated. "I'm going to bed."

"Sweet dreams." He watched his wife walk into the bedroom and shut the door. The bedroom they had once shared, a bed they had loved in, laughed in, and planned their life in. Hearing the click of the lock, Tony dropped down on the sofa.

Why the hell had he said bedbugs?

Nikki woke up with something pressing into her side. Dallas wasn't lying about the sofa being uncomfortable. She rolled over, stared at the ceiling, and remembered the look in Dallas's eyes when he'd offered to share his bed. Bud shifted positions at her feet. The dog whimpered when Dallas tried to take him to his bedroom, so Nikki had agreed to let him stay with her. She hadn't, however, agreed to share the couch with him.

"Why don't you go to sleep in my bed?"

Nikki rolled over so fast she nearly fell off the sofa. Dallas sat in a chair across from her. She blinked and noticed he was shirtless, wearing only what looked like a pair of long boxers.

She sat up and ran a hand through her hair. "What are you doing?"

"Watching you sleep."

"Why?"

"Because I couldn't sleep."

"Why?"

"Thinking too hard, I guess."

She swallowed a tightness down her throat. "About?"

"You really want to know?"

She pulled her knee up to her chest. "Is it about sex?"

He laughed. "Well, I thought about that, too." He paused. "Did you think about it?"

"No," she lied. She'd only spent a few hours remembering their make-out session on the floor, and remembering it fondly, too.

"Not even a little bit?"

She heard the hope in his voice and decided not to go there.

She hugged her legs. "What else were you thinking about?"

He hesitated as if he didn't want to answer. Then he finally spoke. "About your dad."

"*My* dad?"

"Yeah. I keep seeing that picture of you and your grandmother. You looked so scared, abandoned. I don't see how he or your mother could have done that to you."

Her chest tightened. "That was a long time ago."

"But sometimes things stay with us a long time."

She didn't deny it. Their eyes met and held. The room suddenly seemed smaller, quieter. Two people, alone. "What stays with you?" When he didn't answer, she guessed. "Prison?"

"Nah. It isn't prison."

"Then what?"

"It's the people. People who...who supposedly knew me. People who should have known I would never have done what they accused me of doing. People I lost when I was in prison. And then there's the bastard who framed me."

"Do you know who did it?"

"Yeah, just haven't caught him yet."

"I'm sorry." And she meant it. She heard the pain in his voice and ached to help him.

"Me, too. About your parents." He leaned forward in the chair. "Please sleep in my bed."

"I'm fine." The silence grew thicker.

"We could share it." His eyes met hers and she saw the heat of the invitation in his eyes.

She shook her head. But her heart screamed yes. She wanted to lie against him, to touch him, to be touched.

He stood up. "Good night, Nikki."

"Dallas?"

He turned back around.

"Thanks."

"Yeah."

She listened to his footsteps down the hall. She stood up, took one step toward the bedroom, then turned around. What was she thinking? She couldn't do this, could she?

Oh, but she wanted to.

Slow down, she warned herself. Think this through. Was she really ready for this?

Nikki felt the morning fog begin to rise. Not wanting to face the day yet, she pulled the covers over her head. She'd barely slept after she'd found Dallas watching her sleep. Of course, it wasn't just the sofa that kept her awake, but the sound of his voice when he'd talked to her last night. And then it was her own stupidity. Hadn't she already decided she needed distance from Dallas O'Connor? So why in God's name had she agreed to come here?

Because he reminded her about paying Nana's cable. Because she didn't want to get knifed to death. Because she liked him. Because she felt sorry for him because he'd been accused of murder. Because he made her laugh and feel alive for the first time in . . . a long time. Okay, she had plenty of reasons for agreeing to it, but that didn't make it right.

Did it?

There's nothing wrong with a little company every now and then.

Nana's words rang in her head. For a flicker of a second, Nikki considered it. Could she let herself get involved with Dallas O'Connor? Could she do it without losing herself? Could she do it without losing her heart? Without completely making someone her whole life as she had with Jack? Jack who had betrayed her. Jack who was now dead.

Now was not the time. But was there ever a good time?

Bud let out a loud snort from the end of the sofa.

Still beneath the covers, she heard a door open. Was that Dallas going into his office? She heard footsteps, only they seemed to be coming toward her rather than leaving. A deep laugh filled the room, but it didn't sound like...

"You still can't get her to sleep with you? Did you tell her you were hung like a racehorse?"

Okay, definitely not Dallas.

Unable to resist a grin, Nikki yanked the covers from her face. "He forgot to tell me."

Bud barked.

"Shit!" The man—dark black hair and warm brown eyes—took about three steps back, slammed into the coffee table, and sent the glass of water she had on the table crashing down to shatter by his feet. "I'm sorry. I thought...Oh shit!"

"Shit, what?" A deep voice boomed from behind her.

Sitting up, she looked away from the shocked man and shattered glass to where Dallas stood in the hallway wearing a...towel. Just a towel. And he wore it well. Lots of warm olive-colored skin, hard abs, a chest lightly dusted with hair, shoulders that begged to be leaned on, and thick dark hair that curled at the ends when wet. It took all of Nikki's strength not to sigh out loud.

"I... I thought. Nothing," the stranger said.

"You thought what?" Dallas asked.

"I... thought she was you," he confessed. "She was covered up—"

"What did you do?" Dallas glared at the man. "Not the horn?"

"No." He picked up the biggest piece of broken glass. "I'll get this up."

"Just go," Dallas said.

Obviously embarrassed, the man left Dallas's apartment. Bud jumped down and ran into the kitchen while Dallas looked at Nikki. Aware of how her body tensed beneath his gaze, Nikki drew the covers to her neck.

Bud barked. Dallas gripped his towel. "I need to..." He turned abruptly, walked into the kitchen and let the dog out. She watched him walk, taking in his bare feet and long thick legs, then averted her gaze when he sauntered back into the living room.

"That was Tyler," he said.

"The other PI?" She tried not to look below his chin, but it was hard to not look at perfection.

He nodded. "What did he do?"

"Nothing."

Their eyes lifted at the same time, met and held. "I'm gonna get dressed," he said.

"Good idea."

A grin tilted his lips as if he knew she liked what she saw. "The coffee's ready. Help yourself. Don't... cut yourself." He waved at the broken glass. "I'll get it in a minute." He tugged at his towel and walked away.

She watched him move down the hall, even leaned over the edge of the sofa to get a better view. *Hung like a racehorse, huh?*

"I said I'd get that." Dallas walked into the living room five minutes later.

Nikki looked back at him with what he hoped was appreciation, because she'd looked at him much the same way when he'd only had on a towel.

"Yeah," she said. "But Bud's barking to come back in and I didn't want him to cut himself."

She bent over to hold the dustpan, while attempting to sweep up the glass. Dallas lost himself for a second, appreciating her shapely backside encased in soft cotton pajama bottoms. When he caught himself, he took the broom. "Let me. You get yourself some coffee." He swept the last of glass into the dustpan she held.

"I will." She stood up.

He followed her as she went to empty the dustpan in the garbage. She stored the dustpan back in the pantry and he added the broom. Bud barked at the door.

He let the dog inside and Bud ran right up to Nikki and started wagging his entire body. "He really likes you." Dallas pulled two cups from the cabinet.

She knelt and Bud went up to her, all tongue. "I like him, too." She petted the needy dog, and damn if he didn't feel as needy as Bud. He swallowed hard.

"How do you take your coffee?"

"Black's fine." She stood up.

He passed her a cup. They both sipped, staring at each other over the rims. He'd lost count of the number of times he'd almost broken his promise and touched her.

Last night when she'd come out of the bathroom, smelling like toothpaste and soft woman, he'd ached to pull her against him and taste the minty flavor on her lips. And when they talked in the middle of the night, he longed to pull her up off the sofa and take her to his bed.

"We always have doughnuts in the office," he said. "I'll bring you one?"

"Just coffee." She pressed her lips to the rim. "This is good. Thanks."

He continued to stare. "How bad's your back hurting?"

She looked back at Bud. "It's fine."

He laughed. "What? Does your eyebrow jump when you lie, too?"

She glanced up and grinned. "The sofa wasn't that bad."

"I'll take it tonight."

"I probably should go home tonight."

He frowned at her over his cup. "Not yet." But he wasn't sure if it was for her safety, or if he just didn't want her to leave. "I kept my word and haven't touched you."

"I can't stay forever."

"I'm not asking for forever." He set his cup on the counter.

Her baby blues stared right at him. "So, what are you asking for?"

Suddenly he wasn't sure what they were talking about. The one-day-at-a-time speech he'd been giving to himself came to mind, but it didn't seem appropriate. "I just don't want anything to happen to you."

Something that looked almost like disappointment flashed in her eyes. Hell, what did she want him to say?

"I'm opening the gallery today. Fridays are good days for sales," she said as if throwing out words to help the help chase off the awkwardness.

"I don't know if that's a good idea," he said.

"It's broad daylight."

"Would you like to see the statistics of daytime crime versus nighttime crime?" he asked, not liking that he sounded so protective. But was it wrong to not want her to get killed before he proved her innocent?

"I'm not crawling in a hole and hiding," she countered.

He frowned and, because he understood how she felt, he tried to temper his tone. "Is someone going to be there with you? I'd go, but I have several appointments to keep."

"The stores on both sides of mine are open. I know the owners. As a matter of fact, I have voice messages from both of them."

"Were they not open when Ellen got attacked?"

"No. They close earlier than the gallery. But today I'll close the shop at five instead of seven."

He couldn't argue with that. "You have my number on your cell, right?"

She nodded.

"Will you take my calls this time?" he asked.

"If I'm not helping a customer."

Their eyes met again. "I'll come by when I get a chance. We'll do dinner out tonight."

"You don't have to."

"I want to. Is that okay?"

She hesitated. "Okay."

From that pause and the sound of her voice, Dallas knew she was just as conflicted as he was about where this was leading. The fact that he was willing to even consider that it led somewhere had him wanting to leave skid marks on his kitchen tile.

"I'll call you." He left for the office.

*   *   *

Nikki watched him leave. Her heart started racing. Had she just agreed to go out to dinner with him?

Yup, she had. But that wasn't the reason her heart was stuck in high gear. She knew if she went to dinner with him, if he brought her back here and made the tiniest advance on her, she'd be his for the taking. And maybe he didn't even have to make that advance, maybe she'd make it. Look how close she'd come to walking into his bedroom last night.

Would that really have been a bad thing? Wasn't everyone, Ellen, even her grandmother, constantly telling her she needed to stop taking life so seriously and just have some fun? Okay, her life was a screwed-up mess right now, but if she could just view this as something to help get her through a crisis, would that be so wrong?

Nikki looked down at Bud and dropped her butt on the sofa. The dog crawled up in her lap and nuzzled her neck.

I'm not asking for forever. Dallas's words whispered through her head. And that was fine. She didn't want forever. Frankly, she didn't know if she even believed in forever anymore.

Nikki took the dog's head in her hands and looked square in his big wrinkly face. "What should I do, Bud? Is it time I stop living on the cautious side and start playing with fire?"

He licked her face.

She pulled the big lug of a dog closer. "Will I get burned to a crisp? Or just singed a little bit? Because if it's just singed, it might be worth it."

"What did you do to her?" Dallas demanded as he walked into the office.

Tyler, sitting at his desk, ducked his head. "Nothing."

"Bullshit."

Austin laughed as he poured himself a cup of coffee. "You're just lucky she didn't Mace your ass."

"Spill it," Dallas said, stepping closer to Tyler.

"Oh, quit worrying." Austin smirked. "He did you a favor."

"What kind of favor?" Dallas asked Tyler.

"I thought it was you. She was under the covers." Tyler wiped a hand over his mouth as if to hide his smile.

"And?" Dallas asked.

"I might have mentioned something about you not getting lucky even though you were hung like a racehorse." Both Tyler and Austin belted out laughter.

Dallas couldn't help laughing, too. He dropped down in his desk chair and looked at Austin. "I'm sorry you got Maced."

Austin blinked his still-red eyes. "The Mace is nothing compared to the whole Roxie issue."

"What happened?" Dallas asked.

"She called me last night and asked me to go to her brother's wedding." He raked a hand through his hair. "A wedding invitation is like dinner with the parents."

Tyler snorted. "She has the hots for you. And let me tell you, I'd crawl under her skirt any day of the week."

"She's not my type," Austin snapped. "She cleans up body parts."

Dallas got the feeling that the truth was just the opposite. Roxie was too much Austin's type. The girl reminded Dallas a lot of Austin's ex-fiancée, Cara. Which meant Austin was afraid that he might actually like Roxie. Which also meant Austin was doing just what Dallas was doing—staying away from women he thought he'd have a hard time walking away from. Pure lust, no emotional attachment.

That's what he wanted. Wasn't it?

So what the hell was he doing toying with the idea of getting close to Nikki Hunt?

She had emotional attachment written all over her soft body and sassy smile. Even worse, she made him wish… Oh hell, no!

Dallas took a deep breath. *One damn day at a time.* He repeated the words in his head like a litany and then glanced over at Tyler. "Does your cousin still do that interior design stuff?"

"Which cousin? I've got like fifty."

"The one who offered to get furniture and decorate my place."

"Oh, Estella. Yeah, she's still doing it."

"See if she can get me a new sofa. Today."

Tyler started typing on his computer keyboard. "What kind of sofa?"

"Comfortable. It can be pink as long as it's comfortable to sleep on and here in my living room by this afternoon. And tell her to take the one that's in there when she leaves."

"Done," Tyler said, hitting one final key.

"Good," Dallas said. "Let's get to business. What's going on with Roberto?"

All traces of humor faded from Tyler's face. "He's coming by to grab the cash this afternoon."

"How much?" Dallas asked.

"He's not sure what he'll need. I offered five thousand, and we may have to buy that much in drugs to get them to talk to us."

"Do we have enough in the business account to cover it?"

"Yup, thanks to our resident clown." Tyler glanced at Austin. "Mrs. Mallard mailed us a nice little check."

"Did you call Nance and tell him to meet me here this morning?"

"He said he'd be here by nine. But he wasn't happy about making another trip to the police station."

"You explained this was to help him?" Dallas looked at his watch. He had an hour.

"Yup. Still wasn't happy. But he said he'd be here. I'm still waiting to hear back from Nance's attorney. It may be Monday before we can get in."

"Just make it as soon as possible. After I take Nance to see Tony, I'm going to the restaurant and see if I can find out who served Jack Leon his poisoned gumbo. Then I've got an appointment at Brian and Sterns myself to talk about Serena's custody battle over Bud. Hopefully, someone will give me something about Jack Leon or Andrew Brian."

"You going to let them know you're working on the Leon case?" Tyler asked.

"What they don't know can't hurt them." Dallas picked up a pen and rolled it between his palms. "Did you get anything else on Andrew Brian?"

"Just that he got into some trouble the first year in college. Drug trouble."

"How bad was it?"

"Don't know. I discovered it through an old newspaper clipping. Daddy got him off."

"That's the one kind of trouble that has a tendency to follow people. See if you can find anything on him having a drug habit now."

Austin put his empty coffee cup on his desk. "I'm going to hit the streets and see if I can uncover any more DeLuna deals in the making. I got a tip there's a new guy hanging out at the pool hall off Jefferson."

"You don't trust Roberto to keep us abreast?" Tyler asked.

"Yes. But why not do a little legwork myself?"

"Be careful," Dallas said.

Austin grinned. "I'm always careful."

Tyler laughed. "Which explains how you got Maced."

"If I don't get anywhere, I was going to snoop around Jack Leon's place and see if any of the neighbors are talkative. Maybe find out who he's been banging lately. I'm still betting this revolves around some woman."

"Good idea." Dallas looked at Tyler. "You got any new questions?"

"Just one," he said. "How come you two got women hanging all over you, and I don't? I mean it's obvious I'm the better-looking one."

"That's, easy." Austin wadded up a scrap piece of paper and tossed it at Tyler. "It's because we're both hung like racehorses."

CHAPTER TWENTY-THREE

FIVE MINUTES LATER, after snagging a doughnut, Dallas wondered if Nikki might have changed her mind about breakfast. Remembering how he ran out on her, he put the last chocolate-covered doughnut on a plate and took it to Nikki as a peace offering.

He stepped into his apartment and heard Nikki moan. She stood, holding on to the living room chair, one foot held up in the air.

"What is it?" he asked.

She grimaced. "Glass."

"Shit. How bad?" He dropped the doughnut on the coffee table and knelt beside her.

"It's nothing. Just hurts when I walk on it."

He wrapped his hand around her ankle and stared at the bottom of her foot. "No blood." He ran a finger down the arch. Even the woman's foot was soft. "Where's it at?"

"The heel." She looked over her shoulder and down at him. "You see it?"

"No. But the light's bad in here." He stood and scooped her into his arms.

"Whoa." She pressed a hand on his chest. "What are you doing?"

As he started down the hall, he remembered picking her up in the hospital and passing a hand over her bare ass. Something told him she was thinking about that, too. "Carting you off to my bedroom to play doctor." He grinned. "What I wanted to do last night." Damn, she felt good in his arms, light and feminine.

She rolled her eyes at him. "Seriously?"

"Seriously." He pushed the door open with his foot and Bud followed. "The light's better in the bedroom and I have tweezers in here."

"You didn't have to carry me."

"You said it hurt when you walked." Leaning down, he placed her on his bed. Bracing himself on one knee, and bracketing his arms on each side of her, he stared at her. "You look good in my bed." Grinning, and supporting himself with one arm, he decided the no-touching rule was null and passed a hand over her cheek. "Let me gather my supplies."

He ran to the bathroom to snag the alcohol and cotton balls, and then came back into the bedroom for his tweezers and a needle. She watched him. And he, her. The short time with her in his arms had gotten his blood singing.

"Do you know what you're doing?" She pushed up on one elbow.

"I was trained by the best." He sat down and brought her foot into his lap. "My brother and I hated wearing shoes. Mom was constantly getting splinters out of our feet."

"How long ago did she pass away?" she asked in a soft voice.

"About eleven months ago." He saw a flash of sympathy in her eyes.

"While you were in prison, right? She's the person you were talking about last night."

"Yeah." Leaning over, he opened the blinds for more light and held up her foot to study it. "I think I see it." He lowered her foot, dipped the tweezers and needle in the alcohol then splashed some on her heel. Gently running his hand over her ankle, he said, "It might hurt a bit. Do you need a bullet to bite on?"

"I think I can handle it." She smiled hesitantly. "But... hurt me too bad, and I'll kick you in the teeth. These are lethal weapons." She wiggled her toes.

"Thanks for the warning." He brushed a finger over the tip of her pink-painted toenails then passed the tweezers over the tiny cut. When she didn't flinch, he knew the glass had gone too deep to get it with the tweezers. Frowning, he reached for the needle.

"Hold still." He slipped the needle inside the cut. She flinched. "Sorry."

"I know." She dropped back on his bed and fisted handfuls of his blanket in her palms. "Just do it."

He pushed the needle to the side of the cut until he touched glass. She hissed. He hated hurting her, but he had to do it. He went deeper with the needle so he could force out the sliver. She hissed again, but didn't pull away. "Almost done." He saw the sliver of glass pop out. "I got it." He set the needle on the bedside table.

"Wasn't too bad, was it?" Still holding her foot, he pressed a kiss on her ankle.

"Terrible," she said in a teasing tone.

"Now, tell me if you still feel the glass." Running

his fingernail across the cut, he watched her face. "No pain?"

"No. I think you got it." She started to pull her foot away.

"Not so fast. I have to pour alcohol over it. And then the important part."

She rose on her elbow again. "What's the important part?"

He grinned. "Blow on it."

Her eyes brightened with humor. "You're gonna give me a blow job?"

He chuckled, admiring her daring sense of humor. Before he realized what he was doing, he brushed his hand under her pajamas and up her calf. The loose fit of her pants allowed plenty of room. Slowly brushing his hand back to her ankle, he picked up the alcohol and splashed a little on her foot.

"Ouch!"

He brought her foot to his lips and gently blew on it. Still propped up on one elbow, she met his gaze with hers and held it.

"Feel good?" His hand slipped up her leg again.

"Yeah." Heat flickered in her big blue eyes. Caught in her gaze, he pressed his lips to the side of her ankle again. "Is there any part of you that isn't soft?"

She didn't answer. His hand moved up her leg again. Noting the lack of stubble, he wondered if she'd shaved her legs for him. Anticipation set his blood afire and had his dick thickening.

She leaned back on his bed, but didn't stop staring at him.

"Soft feet. Soft legs." When she didn't pull away, he moved his hand higher, past the back of her knee.

She closed her eyes. Braver, he slipped his hand higher. The smoothness of her thigh took his breath away, and he heard her breath catch. She swiped her tongue across her lips. Her eyes remained closed and he noticed her nipples were tight and pebbled under her soft cotton top. Slowly, he reached his hand higher, inches from the treasure between her legs. He waited for her to tell him to stop, to catch his hand. She didn't.

Stretching out, keeping his hand inside her pajama leg, he rested on his shoulder beside her, and studied her face for the slightest sign that she didn't want this. The tips of his fingers touched the silkiness of her panties and his dick went from hard to rock hard. Running a finger over the top of the soft mound, he sensed the crinkle of hair beneath the smooth fabric of her panties. Lowering his touch, he felt sweet dampness behind the silk.

She moaned and her hips rose to deepen his touch. Deep was good. He pressed his lips to her closed eyes, and slipped his hand beneath the elastic band to touch moist skin.

"You're wet," he whispered.

"Feels . . . good," she said.

"Just enjoy it." He kissed the edge of her lips, and slipped his finger inside her tight opening. His dick grew harder, wanting to go where his hand was. But not yet. He wanted her wetter, lost in wanting him.

While his index finger moved in and out, he found the tight little nub and massaged it with his thumb. A light purr escaped her lips, and she tightened her thighs around his hand. "So good." She started to move against his hand.

"Not so fast." He moved his thumb from her hot button. "Let's make it last."

He started to pull his hand out and she muttered, "Don't stop."

"Not stopping. Just getting started." Panic stirred his chest when recalled he didn't have all day. He looked at the clock. His gut clenched. Twenty minutes before Nance showed up.

He slid a palm over her breasts. Caught her nipple between his fingers and tightened them. She opened her eyes and he saw the slightest flicker of doubt play in her baby blues.

"You okay with this?" he asked.

Nodding, she reached up and started unbuttoning his shirt from the bottom up. Loosening only one button, she ran her hand across his stomach then shifted lower. She slipped her hands inside his jeans. The tips of her fingers brushed against his aching dick, and it was his turn to hiss. "I think you're okay with it, too."

Working on losing the shirt, he smelled her scent on his hand. Unable to resist, he ran his thumb over his lips. When he saw her watching him, he took his finger deeper into his mouth. "You taste good."

Yanking his shirt off, he unzipped his pants. Then, wanting to see her, all of her—more than he wanted to lose his clothes—he changed directions. "You don't need this." He caught her shirt and pulled it over her head. Her breasts jiggled and while the idea of kissing his way down her body occurred to him, his patience—or time—didn't allow it. He lowered his lips to the round mounds of flesh, and took one tight pink nipple into his mouth. She moaned.

While his lips worked on her breast, he hitched his thumb in the elastic band of her pajama bottoms and lowered them, panties included. She raised her hips and, in one quick sweep, they were off. Pulling back, leaving her nipple moist and tight, he let himself savor the sight of Nikki, deliciously naked.

"God, you're beautiful." He ran a hand over one breast, down her tight abdomen, and to the curve of her waist.

"Ditto," she whispered, gazing at his torso.

He scooted down a few inches, leaned on one elbow and circled a finger around her tight nipple, still wet from his mouth. Then he touched her slow, easy, memorizing the dips and curves of her upper body. Finally, lowering his hand to the patch of blond hair between her legs, he slipped his finger inside her cleft. Her moan came louder and she tightened her thighs around his hand. He pulled his fingers from her moist center and gently opened her legs. "I like to watch what I'm doing."

When her thighs relaxed and he saw all that moist pink flesh, his dick slammed against his zipper.

His gaze shifted from her, completely naked on his bed, to the clock. Ten minutes. Not enough time to give her the slow first time kind of sex she deserved, but asking for a rain check was out of the question.

"Condoms are in the bathroom." He shot off the bed.

Nikki heard him walk out. She couldn't ever remember being this aroused, this totally not caring if it was right or wrong. "Hurry," she muttered.

He appeared at the door seconds later, a small foil pack in his hands. She watched him shuck off his pants. His sex, so hard, bounced up and slapped against his abdomen. Swallowing, she realized Tyler hadn't been joking. There was plenty of Dallas to love.

The mattress bounced with an unexpected canine visitor. Bud dropped down beside her, resting his wrinkly face on his paws and staring at her.

"Down, Bud," Dallas snapped. The dog must have heard the seriousness in his tone, because he jumped off the bed.

Dallas stretched out beside her. "We have a problem."

"Problem?" She glanced down at his sex, still standing completely erect.

He laughed. "Not that kind of problem."

Realizing he'd read her thoughts, she blushed. He kissed her cheek, then her neck. "We're short on time and I need to know how I can guarantee you'll be happy. Do I…use my fingers?" He ran a finger down her chest to circle her belly button. "B, use my tongue?" He leaned in and flicked his tongue at the edge of her lips. "Which I'm very good at," he added. "Or C, do you want me inside you?" He took her hand and wrapped it around him. She gripped the smooth, velvety organ and rubbed her thumb over its moist tip. He moaned and she loved knowing he was enjoying her touch.

"I've never been good at multiple choice questions." She moved her hand up and down his hardness, trying not to think and just act, to lose the embarrassment and replace it with boldness. "Is there not a D choice, all of the above?"

He grinned and caught her hand. "If you keep doing that, you're going to remove C from the option list."

"Wouldn't want to lose option C." She took the packet from him and ripped it open with her teeth. Then she rolled the thin piece of rubber over him.

As soon as the condom was in place, he rolled her

completely on her back and was on top of her. Keeping his weight on his elbows, he adjusted his legs until things down south lined up. She felt the cool tips of the condom at her center. Closing her eyes, she pressed her head back in the pillow and waited to feel him enter her.

"No. Open those baby blues. I want to see you when I first enter you."

She did as requested and he pushed inside. Slow, easy. Even wet with want, his fit was tight, hitting nerve endings she didn't know she had. Her breath caught.

"You okay?" he asked, his voice strained as he slowly pushed inside.

"Yeah." She managed to say, but she was better than okay. A sense of rightness filled her chest with every slow and measured in-and-out stroke. So right she knew it had to be wrong. Emotion swelled in her chest. Emotion she didn't want to feel. But the tight pleasure building between her legs chased away all negative thoughts.

She wanted this.

"Damn, you feel good." He dropped his forehead against hers, his gaze staying on her eyes, as his strokes became harder, deeper.

She raised her hips to meet his and the sweet ache intensified. The pace increased, and she heard a rumble come from his throat. She wrapped her legs around his waist, and his next thrust brought him deeper inside her, sending the pleasure higher. No awkward movements, they moved together like dancers who knew each other's exact steps. Pushing toward something wonderful, something blissful.

"I can't last much longer," he growled.

He didn't have to. Pleasure exploded inside her and her

entire body shook with sweet spasms of release. And with it came clarity. This was such a huge freaking mistake. His words from earlier rang in her head. *I'm not asking for forever.*

What was he asking for?

She'd played with fire and she hadn't just gotten singed. She was burnt. Burnt to a crisp.

He gasped, then rolled to the side, taking her with him. Neither moved for several seconds and then he put a hand on each side of her face and brought her lips to his. "That was—"

"A mistake," she finished. And instantly, for a thousand reasons, she wished she could take it back. And yet she meant it. She closed her eyes tight and vowed not to cry.

"No. Hell, no. Look at me, Nikki."

She opened her eyes.

"Why was this a mistake?"

Because I must still believe in forever.

She stared into his eyes. Because she was a smidgen away from falling in love with a guy who didn't want forever. "Because sex makes me ravenous and there's nothing to eat."

He laughed, and relief flashed in his eyes. "Would a chocolate-covered doughnut help?"

She forced herself to smile and lie. "Perfect."

Less than an hour later, Dallas was still reeling and almost giddy from the best damn sex he'd ever had. With a very nervous Nance at his side, he walked into the interview room of the Miller Police Department. His brother, sitting at the table, closed a file and stood up.

Dallas made the introductions. Tony, in complete cop mode, motioned for them to sit, and Dallas found his mood changing.

"Thanks for coming, Mr. Nance," Tony said.

"Your brother told me you were on my side," Nance said.

"Actually, I'm on the side of the law."

Nance looked at Dallas. "But the law thinks I'm guilty."

"Are you?" Tony asked.

"I haven't done shit," Nance said, his tone edgy, but honest. "I went for a jog at a park a few months ago, and the next thing I know I'm being slammed against the hood of a police car and told I robbed a store. And now you're trying to pin a murder on me."

"I just read your file." Tony tapped the folder. "Seems like your brothers have accumulated quite a rap sheet. Into gangs and everything. You gonna tell me you didn't get pulled into it?"

Dallas, seeing panic fill the kid's eyes, clenched his jaw to keep from telling Tony to back off. But down deep, Dallas knew his brother was doing his job, and today's meeting was intended to help.

"They're my half brothers," Nance said. "Ten years older than me. I was raised by my grandmother. But yeah, they tried to get me to follow in their footsteps, telling me I could have money and girls, but I didn't do it. I kept myself clean, sold ice cream at Baskin-Robbins and worked at a friggin' feed store, graduated and everything, and for what? To get accused of this shit anyway? And now 'cause of this, I lost my job. I got no money, no job, no girl, and I'm innocent."

Tony leaned back in his chair. "So you liked ice cream and loading seed better than girls and money?"

Dallas shot Tony a cold, hard look.

Nance scowled. "I liked it better than breaking my grandmother's heart. I watched my brothers and my own mama hurt her. I'm all she has left."

Tony glanced at Dallas, who could tell Nance had passed Tony's test. "Did my brother tell you why I asked you to come here?"

"You want to see if I had signs of being in a fight."

"Have you been in a fight, or injured in any way?"

"No."

"Will you consent to be checked by our CSU team? They'll want to take pictures and do a blood test to check your blood type."

"Will this clear my name?"

"If you don't have any signs of a struggle, it will help clear you of being involved with my investigation," Tony said. "And since the MOs are similar in both cases, it might help."

Nance looked at Dallas, who nodded. Nance nodded, too. "If your brother says to do it, I'll do it."

When CSU came in to do the search for open wounds and photos, Dallas and Tony stepped into the hall. Dallas leaned against the wall. "You talked to Detective Shane yet?"

"Not yet." Tony sounded frustrated. "I wanted to see how things here went first." He paused. "Did you ever catch up with Nikki Hunt?"

"Yeah." Dallas smiled when he remembered how she'd looked naked on his bed. Then, reminding himself to focus, he asked, "Did you get the court records on her divorce?"

"I have Clark on it now. She was telling the truth about er computer."

"I didn't doubt it." Dallas collected the mental list of uestions he had to ask Tony. "Did you check into Leon's hone records to see who he was talking to?"

"The last three calls late that evening were to and from is work. Unfortunately, CSU tells me the phone system's ot cataloged, so we can't identify an extension in an ffice because everything goes out from one trunk line, nd it's not labeled."

"So find out who the hell was in the office," Dallas aid.

"I already have. One of the lawyers admits to speaking ith Jack twice to discuss a case he was assisting him on."

"Who was it?"

Tony shook his head.

"Is it Andrew Brian?"

"Let me handle this," Tony said.

Which meant it was Brian. Dallas suddenly realized hat Tony had said. "You said there were three calls, and is person admits to speaking to him twice?"

"I can count. I'm checking into it, okay?" Tony let o of a sigh. "Look, I know this is important to you. I'm oing everything I can."

Dallas heard the sincerity in his brother's voice.

"So...how is Nikki holding up?" Tony asked.

"Better than expected." Dallas dropped his hands in is jean pockets, and reared back on his heels as his head eplayed that purring sound she made when she came.

Tony stared at him. "You slept with her, didn't you?"

"Why would you think that?"

"You got that just-got-laid look about you."

Dallas started to lie, but decided not to. His broth
always knew things. Not that he'd go into details. H
nodded.

"Was she good?"

"I don't kiss and tell." But he couldn't help smilin

"How was the homecoming with LeAnn?"

"Not as good as your night." Tony chuckled. "Yo
wouldn't know anything about bedbugs, would you?"

"About what?"

Tony explained and Dallas couldn't stop laughin
"You are so screwed. What if she calls your apartment?

Tony shrugged. "Hell. Chances are by the time she g
up this morning, she already figured out I was blowin
smoke. I'm hoping she sees the croissants and jam an
my note about cooking her dinner tonight and realizes sh
misses me."

"Or she decides to take you out for lying to her." Da
las chuckled.

Tony stared at Dallas. "How are you playing this wi
Nikki?"

"What do you mean?"

"You know what I mean. You keeping it light, or is
leading somewhere?"

"What kind of question is that?" Dallas pushed off th
wall.

"The kind you should be asking yourself right now
Tony stared down the hall as someone passed.

"What the hell is wrong with just enjoying what it is?

Tony cut his gaze at Dallas and frowned. "Nothing
wrong with it if you both know that's how the game
being played."

"I'm not playing games. We're two adults—" Th

or to the interview room shot open, and Dallas's words alled.

A frowning CSU officer and an unhappy Nance alked out. The boy's gaze shot to Dallas. "I got a fuck-g scratch on my knuckle. Does this mean I'm going own for this, too?"

CHAPTER TWENTY-FOUR

ON HER WAY TO WORK, LeAnn drove by Tony's apartment—admittedly not for the first time. At least once a week, she'd find herself cruising his street, hoping to get a glimpse of him. Today she wasn't looking for him, but for exterminator trucks or guys in hazmat suits. Not that she expected to see them. She might have been born yesterday, but it wasn't that early in the morning.

As expected, she saw no sign of bedbug extermination, and so she drove on to the hospital. What was Tony up to? Was he moving back in because he was afraid she'd try to take the house? Hadn't he read the divorce papers? She planned to move out in three months. She wasn't going to steal his house out from under him, but maybe he wanted her out sooner than ninety days.

No. That wasn't like Tony. Heck, every month when she sent in the mortgage bill, she'd get notified it was already paid. She'd told the bank to just let the check go toward the principal.

After clocking in at the hospital, she headed for Ellen Wise's room. Hearing laughter, she knocked and poked

:r head in the door. Nikki and Ellen's mom were in the
·om, visiting.

"Is this a party?" LeAnn asked.

"They're making me laugh and it hurts," Ellen said,
miling.

"She was in here." Nikki spoke to Ellen but was ges-
·ring toward LeAnn. "Ask her."

Ellen looked at LeAnn. "Did I really offer to have sex
ith a couple of guys yesterday?"

LeAnn grinned. "I'm afraid so." She moved in and fit
ie blood pressure cuff around the woman's arm. "But
on't worry. You explained yourself."

"That I was blitzed on morphine?"

"No, that it had been too long since you got lucky,"
eAnn said.

They all laughed again.

Once LeAnn updated her chart, she started toward the
oor. Nikki said her good-byes to Ellen and her mother
nd walked out with LeAnn.

"How are things?" LeAnn asked Nikki.

Nikki shrugged. "I haven't been arrested yet."

"Tony won't let that happen."

Nikki frowned. "I'm not so sure. I don't think he's on
ie pro-Nikki team."

LeAnn considered it. "If I can see you didn't do it, I'm
ire he can."

"Thanks. Maybe you could put in a good word for
ie...I mean, if you see him."

"I will." LeAnn paused by her next patient's door, but
er curiosity about Nikki kept her standing there. "You
on't have to answer me, but...are you and Dallas more
aan friends?"

After a brief hesitation, Nikki sighed. "If I told you
didn't know what we were, would you think I was crazy

"Not really. Life's peculiar sometimes." Tony w
back home, and LeAnn didn't know why.

"I just…everything is happening at once. And I'm n
sure what he wants…Crappers, I don't know what *I* wan

LeAnn grinned, but she felt the same stirring of pani
Did she know what she wanted? Somehow, she'd stopp
thinking about what she wanted and started doing wh
she thought was the right thing. "Sounds like you're co
fused." And LeAnn could really relate.

"I'd say." Nikki looked at her watch again. "I'
already late opening the store, so I'd better run."

Before Nikki could leave, LeAnn said, "Hey. Abo
Dallas. He's one of the good guys."

"Like his brother?"

LeAnn inwardly flinched, but it was a fair questio
especially considering she'd been the one to start the pe
sonal line of questions. "Yeah. Like him."

"Then why…" Nikki studied her and LeAnn cou
guess what she was about to ask.

"It's complicated," LeAnn answered, not wanting
say more.

"Yeah. The same here," Nikki said.

LeAnn hesitated and, while she wasn't ready to sha
her own issues, she did want to help Nikki. "I couldr
believe Dallas's wife divorced him when…Oh, you d
know about his being accused of—"

"Murder." Nikki nodded. "He told me."

"Dallas thought the sun set and rose on Serena. B
personally, I never liked her. She was just…I don't kno
too high falutin'."

"Then I'm really not Dallas's type," Nikki said and walked away.

LeAnn watched her. "I'd beg to differ," she said to herself. She'd seen the way her brother-in-law looked at Nikki. LeAnn remembered the same look on Tony's face when he'd sat beside her in the cafeteria.

Closing her eyes, she tried not to hope. What she needed to do was decide what she was going to do about tonight. Tony's note said he planned to cook dinner. Could she sit across a table from him and not break down because of all they'd lost—each other and Emily? Maybe she should just go to a hotel.

Dallas parked behind Venny's Restaurant, ran a hand through his hair, and tried to lose the frustration from the last half of the meeting with Nance and Tony. *You said coming here would help me!* Nance, who'd guessed he'd scratched his knuckle when he'd changed the oil in his grandmother's car, had left the police station more frightened than when he'd arrived.

The CSU officer had said it was unlikely a baseball bat had caused the scratch on Nance's knuckle, but nevertheless it would go into the report. Tony had even tried to calm Nance down, but he was scared and for good reason.

Dallas hoped that Tony would get Detective Shane to take another look at the case. If not, Dallas would take the story of Shane going after Nance for revenge to the press. But even that might not hold water. It depended on how the judge saw it. And if it didn't hold water...Dallas remembered the promise he made to Nance's grandmother.

"Shit." Could he give her the heads-up that Nance should run to Mexico and become a fugitive for the rest of his life? And if he ran, and they didn't find a suspect in the second robbery, the system would try to pin it on Nance just to close the case.

Dropping back in his car seat, Dallas released a gulp of frustrated air. He needed to get his mind off that case and onto Nikki. Or rather her case.

Every few minutes he'd think back to his bedroom—how soft she was, how it had felt when he'd first entered her and the sound she'd made when she came. But mostly he thought about her saying it had been a mistake.

Thinking about it, he didn't believe she'd meant his lack of food in the house. Hell, the more he thought about it, the more he wondered if she hadn't been right. One part of him said nothing that good should be considered a mistake. Another part of him said he knew it would be a mistake from the moment he found himself being pulled into her soft, blue eyes.

Then his brother's words played in Dallas's head. *Nothing's wrong with it if you both know that's how the game is being played.*

Christ! He wasn't playing games with Nikki. He liked her. Liked her a lot. If he didn't he wouldn't be so damn worried about her thinking their having sex had been a mistake.

His one-day-at-a-time approach felt weak. Frankly, he didn't know what scared him more, falling for Nikki and falling hard, when he'd vowed not to become another candidate for the fool-in-love award, or falling for a woman who very well might be going to prison. But holy hell, he knew she didn't see prison as a possibility. Decent people had a tendency to believe in the justice system. He knew differently.

He'd called her twice. Both times, the conversation felt awkward. He tried telling himself she'd had someone in the gallery. Everything was fine, but he wanted to see her. Mind made up, he decided when he was done here, he'd grab them some lunch and drop by the gallery.

Getting out of his car at Venny's, he looked around, his mind turned to another direction. What had brought Jack Leon back here?

Had the person on the phone asked to meet him here? Near the Dumpsters? Not likely. Did that mean Leon had come looking for Nikki's car? And if so, why? Leon had his own vehicle. Dallas recalled the cops having said his car had been towed from valet parking. Could Leon have wanted to hide something in Nikki's car?

Tony hadn't mentioned CSU finding anything in her car. Considering they planned on releasing it this afternoon, Dallas would bet it was clean. But damn, a piece of the puzzle was missing. He reached back inside his own vehicle for a pen and notepad. He saw the newspaper, which had a picture of Nikki in front of her store and named her a person of interest in the case. He'd already suffered through the article, but needed it as a conversation starter.

When he stuffed his pen in his shirt pocket, Dallas wondered if Leon had come back here to leave Nikki a note. Puking, the man wouldn't have wanted to go back into the restaurant. But why not call Nikki? Had she changed her cell number? A good question to ask Nikki later.

Walking past the Dumpster, he planned his approach. People didn't care much for talking to cops, or even PIs for that matter. But for some reason they loved talking to reporters. He just hoped the day employees weren't the same people who'd been there the other night.

Stepping inside the restaurant, relieved the hostess wasn't the brunette he'd already spoken with, he hesitated at the door. The hostess obviously didn't hear him walk in because she didn't take her eyes off the newspaper she held. No doubt, she was reading about Leon's murder.

Dallas waited patiently. She glanced up and quickly hid the newspaper. "Sorry," she said.

"No problem." He showed her his newspaper.

"Crazy, isn't it?" she said, and Dallas saw the way her green eyes swept over him with feminine appreciation.

He smiled. "You got that right."

"Table for one?" The flirty way her eyes moved over him told Dallas she might just be the person he needed to talk to.

"Unless you can join me," he said, upping his wattage of smile.

She grinned. "I'll bet you say that to all your hostesses."

"Only the pretty ones."

"Aren't you the charmer?" She started moving into the dining room.

Dallas glanced back at the bar. "Why don't I sit up there? The scenery is nicer." He let his gaze move over her again.

She smiled. "Fine with me."

She walked to a small table by the empty bar. "The bartender is running a little late setting up. Can I get you something to drink?"

"Coke would be nice. But do you know what would be even better?" He forced a touch of seduction in his voice.

She moved closer. "What's that?"

"A little information."

"About me?" she asked.

"And the interesting story you were just reading."

Suspicion colored her eyes. "Are you a cop? The boss said if you guys came in you'd have to talk with him first."

"Nope." He pulled out his pad and pen. "Just looking to add more to the story. Information that could be quoted as from an anonymous source."

"I wasn't here." She sounded disappointed.

"But I'll bet you've heard all about it."

"True." She perked up a bit. Glancing around as if to check for any of her managers, she started talking. She told him the cops had taken a bunch of knives to see if any of them were the murder weapon. And they were looking at waiters and the cooks for putting something in the guy's gumbo.

She shifted closer. "But all of them are willing to take a polygraph test. They're innocent. I don't know why the cops are doing this—the waiter told the cops that the man's wife admitted she was going to kill him. What else do they need?"

The right person, Dallas thought. Another customer came in and she stepped away.

Dallas got up and went to peek into the kitchen, hoping to see where the soups were located.

"You looking for something?" someone behind the stove asked as Dallas poked his head through the doorway.

"Bathrooms?" he lied, his gaze shifting around.

"To the left of the entrance."

"Thanks." Before he turned he saw two big soup warmers on this side of the kitchen, along with a stack of soup bowls. So anyone in the kitchen had access to the soup.

He went back to his table where a Coke now waited on him. The hostess looked over from her post as if she'd wondered where he'd gone. He smiled and, after glancing at her empty front doorway, she started over.

"How many people do you have working here on one shift?" he asked.

She hesitated. "Maybe twenty waitstaff. Two hostesses at night, and two bartenders on weekends. I think there're ten cooks and prep people in the back."

"Has anyone quit lately?"

"No . . . wait, there was that weird busboy."

"When did he quit?"

"All I know is he didn't show up yesterday."

The day after Jack was killed.

"I had to clean tables during rush hour," she said.

"Any chance you remember that busboy's name?"

She grinned. "As a matter of fact, I do." Reaching into her pocket, she pulled out a sticky note. "His girlfriend called today and wanted me to ask the manager when she could pick up his check."

He looked at the note. It had the girlfriend's name and the busboy's. More customers walked in. "Can I keep this?"

"Sure." She glanced at the waiting patrons. "And in case you need to ask more questions . . . or anything else." She snatched his pen and wrote her telephone number on his pad.

"Thank you." He pulled out his wallet. "For the drink?"

"It's on the house." She looked at the two twenties he placed in her hand.

"Nah. Keep the change for helping me."

"I'd rather you call me." She brushed her hand over his.

"As tempting as that is..." His eyebrow arched up. "You should keep the money."

Dallas hadn't gotten out of the restaurant before he'd dialed Tyler and given him the names to run down. Then he took off to pick up lunch. On the way, he found himself remembering this morning with Nikki and he smiled the whole way.

"I can't go lower," Nikki told Margo Preston with Preston Interior Designer as she added a shadow under the tree of her painting in process. Nikki had started the painting of two young boys fishing by a pond two weeks ago, but for some reason the boys now reminded her of Dallas and Tony. Was she subconsciously putting Dallas into her painting? Why? Because subconsciously she knew she'd have the picture longer than she'd have him?

"I'm offering you a twenty percent discount." *I'm not asking you for forever.* Dallas's words played in her head.

Nikki's cell phone rang, followed by her store phone. With the brush in her hand and a customer underfoot, she let both go to voice mail. Fridays were her busiest day, she didn't normally attempt to paint, but today she'd longed to lose herself on the canvas—to forget. She eyed the face of the littlest boy and confirmed her suspicion.

"Fine," Margo said. "I'll take it."

Setting her brush on the easel, Nikki felt the thrill of making her third sale for the day—Nana's cable was safe—even if the reason downright depressed Nikki. Who knew that being suspected of a murder made you a cause célèbre?

Her first customer had actually brought in the newspaper article for her to read—"Local Downtown Artist Person of Interest in Murder of Ex-Husband." The newspaper had run an old picture of her standing outside the front of her store when she'd first opened the gallery. Nikki was tempted to tell everyone the sale wasn't dependent on the guilty verdict.

As Nikki rang up Margo's purchase, her cell phone rang again. She ignored it.

"I need to hurry," Margo said. "Can you have it ready to pick up this afternoon?"

"I'm closing at five," Nikki told her.

The door to the gallery swished open and Dallas—an unhappy Dallas—stormed inside. Every nerve ending in her body jumped up and down with glee.

"You stopped answering your phone," he said, stopping just inside the door.

Nikki shot him a don't-be-rude look and tried to ignore the racing of her heart and hormones. "I've been busy."

Margo leaned in. "Is he the reason you're closing early? If so, I don't blame you."

Handing her the receipt, Nikki smiled. When Margo walked out of the shop, Nikki found Dallas studying her unfinished painting.

He looked up. "I was worried."

"I told you if I'm busy I don't answer my phone."

"It didn't stop me from being concerned." He gazed back at the painting and she feared he'd recognized her version of his younger self in her work. "You're really good."

"You're an art critic as well as a PI?"

"No, but I know what I like . . . when I see it." His gaze

shifted and he moved toward her—slow, sauntered steps, like a lion about to pounce on his prey. She was the prey and, in spite of the wisdom of doing otherwise, she wasn't running. She pressed her hands on the counter, wanting him to touch her, and afraid that he would.

He moved behind the counter and, glancing back at the door as if to make sure no one had walked in, he slipped his hand around her waist and pulled her against him. His lips found hers in a soft kiss that quickly went hot. His tongue slipped between her lips, and Nikki felt her nipples tighten against him when she recalled their morning rendezvous.

"Did you miss me?" he asked, pulling his head up but holding her against him. "Did you think about this morning?" His knee shifted ever so slightly between her legs. Instantly, the tightness in her breasts spread lower, which she suspected was his intent.

"Yes." She didn't lie. "But..." She put her hand on his chest to hold him off. Immediately she recalled touching him there this morning without a shirt. Then she recalled touching him without his pants, and she didn't have what it took to push him away.

Nikki wasn't what you'd call experienced. With fewer sexual partners than she had fingers on one hand, and two of them ending without... satisfaction, she wasn't exactly up on proper after-first-time-sex behavior—especially after the awesome sexual partner jumped in the shower and left her in his bed with only half a chocolate doughnut. Oh, he'd apologized profusely, both for leaving and eating the doughnut, and promised to make it up to her later. Some of the promises had included very explicit language of what he planned to do to her when he saw her next. Her cheeks warmed as she realized this was the next time. Surely, he didn't plan on...

"You know what I want?" he whispered.

"Not here," she said without thinking.

He grinned. "I was talking about lunch. I brought it—it's in the car."

Ten minutes later, they sat on the sofa in her office eating while Nikki kept one ear tuned to customers entering the store.

"Wow, that's you, isn't it?"

"What's me?"

He pointed to the plaster-of-paris bust in the corner. "I recognize those breasts."

"It was an art class I taught. Everyone did... self-portraits."

"Why is it hidden in here?"

She laughed. "It's not art, it's just—"

"It's beautiful. It belongs out there."

"Flattery will get you nowhere, Mr. O'Connor." She looked at her sandwich.

"You okay with turkey and cheese?" he asked. "I called to ask what you'd like, but someone wouldn't answer her phone."

"It's great. Thank you."

He rested his hand on her knee, sending a current of warmth up her leg.

"I sold three paintings today," she said, trying to chase away the memory of his hand moving up her pajama leg.

"I'm not surprised. You're good."

"Being a person of interest in a murder helps, too." She was going for humor, but fell short. "Imagine how many I'll sell if I'm actually arrested."

He frowned. "You saw the paper?"

"Yeah." She looked at the sandwich, her appetite vanishing as she remembered what else she'd seen in the paper. Jack's obituary. Tonight was the viewing at the funeral home. Nikki debated the wisdom of going. Would it enrage Jack's parents? If she didn't go, would it appear to be an admission of guilt?

He brushed a strand of hair behind her ear. "You shouldn't read it."

"I'll bet you read it when it was you."

"Then learn from my mistakes." He leaned in to kiss her.

She pulled back, not wanting to start things. "Speaking of mistakes..."

The heat in his eyes faded into a frown. "I'm sorry I had to leave like that this morning. There's this kid being accused—"

"I didn't mean that." She rolled her sandwich back up in its wrapper. The paper crackled in the silence.

He stared at her as if trying to figure something out. "I usually take more time." He ran a finger over her lips. "I promise tonight you won't have any complaints."

She felt her cheeks heat. "I didn't mean that, either."

"Then what's a mistake?"

"I meant the kissing...here." That was what she meant, but the word "mistake" brought up other things. She glanced away.

"You know you're not any better at lying than I am."

She looked at him and the words just came out. "I'm just scared, Dallas. My life's a mess."

"And I'm trying to help you."

But what about when this is over? What happens when I get used to you being there?

She dug deep for a way to say some of what she wanted to say without sounding like a psycho. "But you've done more than you should have. My staying at your place is too much."

"I'm not complaining."

"I know but...now that I've made some money, I can get a hotel room."

"Why?"

"I'm not saying we couldn't...see each other, but—"

"Someone may be trying to kill you, Nikki."

She cut him a get-real look. "I've been here all day and not one assault."

"I still don't like the idea of a hotel."

"Why?"

"Haven't you seen the news?" His brow tightened. "Hotels have bedbugs."

CHAPTER TWENTY-FIVE

OH, FRIGGIN' HELL. As soon as he'd said it, Dallas wished he could take it back. Now he was resorting to using bed-bugs, too.

"Bedbugs?" She looked at him as if he was crazy.

Maybe he was crazy. Maybe he was just crazy about her. No, he was crazy because he could feel her building barriers between them. Even to him, his feelings didn't make sense. By God, he didn't want her trying to be too clingy, but the idea of her putting up the barriers sure as hell didn't feel right.

He wiped a hand over his face. "Was the sex that bad? Because I could swear you enjoyed..."

She blushed again. "I did. We're just moving so fast."

"Okay, it's happening fast, and maybe it's a little scary, but..." *But what?* He searched for the right words, and was hit by the sudden realization of the truth. "But I like scary right now." Or at least he liked it a hell of lot better than he liked the idea of her pulling away. "Can't we just take this one day at time and see where it leads? Can't we just enjoy... this?"

There it was again. His one-day-at-a-time motto. But now it had another meaning. He was no longer scared of where it was leading—he was scared of it not leading anywhere.

She stiffened. "I didn't mean to imply that I expected forever, Dallas."

Caught up in his own thoughts, he tried to comprehend what she was saying. "What? You're losing me, here."

"This morning you said you weren't asking for forever and I'm saying I don't expect it. But I don't want to be hurt again like Jack hurt me."

He frowned. "You think I'd purposely hurt you?"

"Jack didn't do it on purpose. But—"

And Serena hadn't meant it, either. Bullshit! "So he accidentally screwed your hired help? What? Got a hard-on and just slipped and fell inside her?" Her eyes widened at his crudeness and, yeah, he knew he was being crude.

"He just..."

"What? His mama dressed him funny and that led to him cheating on you?"

"No, but...He's dead and I wasn't nice to him before he died."

"Dead or alive, I'm sick of people making excuses for people who go around doing others wrong. He cheated on you, Nikki. You didn't deserve that. Were you cheating on him?"

"No." She appeared insulted. "Look...this isn't about Jack. What I'm trying to say is that when you find yourself getting bored with me—"

"Bored?" He leaned in closer. "Are you kidding? Hell, you are all I can think about since you puked on me. I mean, I'm covered in it, it's oozing into my tennis shoes and I've got the instant hots for you. And today all I can think about is getting you naked again."

She laughed. "You're never going to let me forget that, are you?"

"Oh hell, no." He leaned in for a kiss. This time she didn't pull away. He actually felt her lean in. She put her hand on his thigh, and his jeans grew tight, and that was a damn good feeling. Good until the damn bell over the gallery door jingled.

She pulled back and brushed a finger over his lips. "I should..."

"Go." He watched her walk out and dropped back on the sofa waiting for the effects of her kiss to wear off. Head reclined, he tried to figure out the emotions doing laps around his chest. He didn't want Nikki to start talking about promises, but when he thought she was trying to pull back, the only thing he could think about was keeping her close. Hell, he was one mixed-up bastard. Closing his eyes, he listened to Nikki greeting her customer.

"So you're Nikki," the male voice said. "You're prettier than I expected."

Dallas stood and was out of the office and just about to clear the hall when the man spoke again. "And talented. I guess I should introduce myself. I'm Andrew Brian. I worked with your husband...ex-husband."

What the hell! Dallas stopped just before he stepped into the gallery. Reaching down, he pulled out his gun in case this guy turned out to be their suspect. Pausing, he could see Nikki standing behind the counter.

"Yes," Nikki said. "I think you started at the firm about the time we divorced."

"I remember," Andrew said. "That's why I'm here."

Dallas moved closer and could see Brian standing a foot away from the counter, but considering the way he eyed Nikki—as if she were a piece of candy—that distance wasn't nearly enough. Dallas debated making his presence known. Having an appointment at the law firm in about an hour, he hadn't planned to announce his involvement with Leon's case. So hanging back as long as he could to keep an eye on Nikki made sense.

"I don't understand," Nikki said.

"I handled your husband's will. You know Jack left everything to you, along with the life insurance policy."

"I'm sure his parents are having that changed," she said. "We're divorced."

"Yes, and in Texas, that means you were automatically taken off his policy. However, Jack had it reinstated. So they might want to fight, but legally it's yours."

Dismay darkened Nikki's face. "Why would Jack do that?"

Brian moved closer and Dallas's grip on the gun tightened.

"He told me he wanted to patch things up between you. He obviously cared about you. Not that I blame him." He smiled.

Dallas frowned. When Tony heard about this, no doubt it would only strengthen Nikki's motive for murdering her ex-husband.

"Anyway," Brian continued, "we are going to read the will next Monday. You should be present."

Nikki shook her head. "I . . . don't want Jack's money." She paused. "Wait. All I want is thirty thousand. That's what was in my account when we got married and when he left I had nothing."

"That's big of you." Brian sounded surprised by Nikki's answer. Dallas wasn't.

"So you'll be there on Monday," Brian said.

"No. If I need to sign something, I'll come in later. His parents wouldn't want me there. They don't really like me."

Brian shrugged. "To be honest, his parents don't like much of anything. Myself included. They ... stopped by the office earlier."

"I'm sure they're having a difficult time with this." Nikki spoke with sincerity.

Brian paused. "Are you going to the viewing tonight?"

"I ... haven't made up my mind."

Dallas frowned. She hadn't mentioned the viewing. And if she had, he'd have explained she wasn't going. She didn't need to rile up Jack's parents any more than they already were.

"If it will make it easier, I'll be glad to accompany you. We could do dinner before."

Dallas's gut clenched. The jerk was asking her out. He waited for Nikki to tell the guy to back off. To give him one of those no-nonsense blunt statements of hers.

"That's sweet of you to offer."

Okay, that wasn't what he wanted to hear.

"But," Nikki continued, "I'm not sure if I'll attend."

"How about I give you my card and you call me?"

"Thank you." Nikki took the card and her gaze shot to the hall. When she saw Dallas standing there with his gun out, her eyes widened, then she looked back at Andrew Brian. "Thank you ... for coming by."

Dallas waited for the jerk to leave. Instead, Brian looked around the gallery. "I love your artwork." He paused in front of a painting of a mother pushing a boy on a swing. "This would be perfect for my mom."

"Can I ring it up for you?" Nikki offered, sounding a bit nervous. Dallas didn't know if it was because Brian had asked her out or because Dallas was holding the weapon.

"Let me think about it. You'll be here on Saturday, right?"

"Yes," Nikki said.

And so will I, Dallas thought, and watched the man leave.

Nikki turned and looked at Dallas. "Why do you have your gun out?"

Dallas holstered his gun. "Because I think Andrew Brian killed Jack."

"Shit." Nikki dropped the card as if touching it repulsed her. Then she looked at Dallas. "But he seemed nice. Are you sure?"

"No," he admitted. "But he's on my list. Even more so now that he's hitting on you."

"He wasn't hitting on me."

"Yes, he was. So guilty or not, he's an ass. What kind of guy hits on a woman just after her ex-husband is killed?"

Nikki shot him a pensive look. "And what are you doing?"

"This isn't like that."

"Really?"

"I didn't go looking for you. We met."

"You came to the hospital." Smiling, she walked to him and put her hand on his chest.

"Because you needed me." And he couldn't say he was sorry about it.

The humor faded from her eyes. "And what happens when I no longer need you?"

"Then you'll stay with me for the sex." He kissed her before the conversation took a serious turn.

"I love you!" Nikki looked up from the plate of four cupcakes covered in yellow icing and pink sprinkles to Nana, who was holding it. The sandwich Dallas had brought her was still wrapped up in the bag in the office. She hadn't thought she was hungry until Nana walked in bearing gifts.

Picking up one of the cupcakes that almost still felt oven-warm, she pulled back the paper holder and sank her teeth into the sweet moist piece of heaven. "And cream cheese icing, too," she muttered licking the sticky sweetness from her lips.

"Here," Nana said and reached into a bag and pulled out a bottle of milk.

"Is it my birthday and I forgot?" Nikki asked and reached for the milk.

"No," Nana said and smiled. "I just...I know how much you like cupcakes."

Just a little less than she liked Dallas. Nikki remembered her whole cupcake issue that happened when she'd made out with him on his bedroom floor. Thinking about that led her back to what Dallas had said, *Then you'll stay with me for the sex.*

Not wanting to go down that mental path, she shifted gears. "I got a little something for you, too," Nikki said as the vanilla flavor tickled her taste buds.

"Me?" Nana asked.

"Yeah." Too busy eating to move, Nikki pointed to the book on the counter. "Mr. Pope had it for sale next door on his clearance table. I saw it when I popped in to just say hello this morning."

Nana picked up the book on Annie Oakley. "Wow. Maybe I can learn something that will help me play her." Her grandmother held the book to her chest. "That was so sweet of you."

"No, this is sweet," Nikki insisted, running her finger over her lips to catch a drop of icing. "That..."—she pointed to the book—"cost me a whole fifty cents." She grinned.

"Cost isn't important," Nana said and watched Nikki continue to eat. "I brought four thinking maybe...maybe I'd find your fellow here." Nana looked toward the back office. "Is he hiding out?"

"No. He...he was here. But he left." Left like he would do when the new wore off the sex. That's what men did, didn't they?

"Problems?" Nana asked, her right eyebrow arching up.

"Not really." Nikki filled her mouth with cupcake so Nana wouldn't expect more of an explanation. Unfortunately, Nana was a very patient person. Even when Nikki quickly took another big mouthful of cupcake and savored it for a good two minutes before swallowing.

No sooner than Nikki's mouth emptied did Nana pose her question. "What happened?"

"Nothing. I just...don't want to rush into anything." She ran her finger over the icing and popped it into her mouth. "How is Benny?"

"Don't do this, Nikki," Nana said.

"Do what?"

"Focus so hard on the potholes in the road that you run off the street and hit a tree."

Nikki rolled her eyes. "It was the pothole that made

me hit the tree," Nikki defended herself and her one accident. "I'd be a fool not to look out for them."

Nana shook her head. "Being careful is one thing. Being afraid to take a chance is another." She moved closer. "If you keep looking for bad things, sooner or later, you'll find them. You've proven that to yourself over and over again. Why not try to follow your heart on this one? Let it lead the way."

Nikki licked the corner icing off her second cupcake. "I'm afraid my heart's directionally challenged. It led me to Jack, didn't it?" And wasn't it just wise to look out for the potholes?

"Jack doesn't count. He fell into the asshole ratio." Nana reached up and smoothed back a tendril of Nikki's hair. "Trust me. There's nothing wrong with your heart, Nikki. If you'll take it off its leash, you might be surprised."

Dallas parked at the offices of the Brian and Sterns Law Firm two hours later and continued his phone conversation with Tyler. "Keep digging. I need an address." He needed to prove who killed Leon. And fast. His gut said something was about to happen.

"I'm working on it," Tyler said. "It's only been an hour since you gave me the names."

"An hour and a half. Have you heard from Austin?" Dallas had tried to call him, wanting him to watch out for Nikki. After the article in the paper, if the killer was after Nikki, he'd know he'd gotten the wrong person. But Austin's phone went to voice mail. He really needed to have a talk with Austin about answering his damn phone.

"He said he was going to snoop out a new dealer in town who might be connected to DeLuna."

For once, Dallas realized something in life mattered as much as catching the asshole who framed him. The realization was disconcerting. He liked being focused, knowing his priorities. But didn't he like Nikki more?

"If he calls have him contact me."

"Something up?" Tyler asked.

"I'm concerned about Nikki. Wanted him to keep an eye on her."

"After she Maced him…"

"I'm serious."

"Okay," Tyler's voice lost the humor, "you think she's really in danger?"

"I think it still bugs the shit out of me that Nikki and her friend Ellen look so much alike. If she had someone else with her I wouldn't worry."

"I could shut the office and go—"

"No, I need you to run down those names."

"I know a few cops who take babysitting gigs. Wouldn't tell them about Austin getting Maced, but…"

Dallas ran a hand through his hair. "I'm probably overreacting. Wait. What about Nance? See if he wants to hang out with Nikki. He said he was broke. Offer him a good hourly rate. And make sure he has a cell phone in case of emergency."

"He's not paying us and we're going to pay him," Tyler said. "You know we really suck at business."

"I think we can afford it."

"It wouldn't matter if we couldn't," Tyler said and Dallas knew his friend meant it. "Oh, you're going to tell Nikki that Nance is watching her, right?"

He considered it. "Yeah. She probably won't like it, but I think she'll accept it."

"Then I'll get right on it."

"And get me that info on the names. I want to go there after I'm done here." Dallas hung up and called Nikki. As he expected, she didn't like the idea of having a companion. However, when he explained it was a kid—also being framed for a crime—who needed to earn some money, she relented.

Happy, Dallas walked into the Brian and Sterns Law Firm. A tall blonde walked into the reception area from an office as Dallas stepped inside.

She gave him a puzzled look. "May I help you?"

"You sure may." He put on the charm. "I'm here to see Mr. Canton. To discuss my custody battle...over my dog. Can you really believe my ex is willing to take me to court for a dog?"

She grinned. "I heard about that. You have an appointment?"

"Sure do."

"Name?" she asked.

"Dallas O'Connor. Yours?" he asked.

"Rachel Peterson." She stared at the computer screen with a puzzled expression. Then she blinked and the look vanished. Dallas wondered if she was putting him together with Tony. It wouldn't be in his best interest if she were.

"Let me see if Mr. Canton is ready for you."

"I'd appreciate that, Rachel."

She made the call, exchanged a bit of conversation, and then hung up. "He asked if you can give him ten minutes."

"Sure. If you don't mind putting up with me." Dallas knew the support staff in an office—secretaries and receptionists—generally knew more about the goings-on than the higher ranked employees.

"That wouldn't be a hardship." She smiled the way a woman did when she approved of the merchandise. "Can I get you something to drink? Coffee?"

"Sounds good."

In a few minutes, she returned with coffee. "So why kind of dog is it?" she asked.

"English bulldog."

"I love them." She looked at him again in that puzzled way. "Do you have a brother?"

Inside he flinched, wondering how hard it would be to milk any information out of anyone if they put him and Tony together. "I do."

"Is he a detective?"

Dallas nodded, still trying to figure out how to work this now. "That's right. He's working a case about one of your partners here. The one who was killed by his ex."

"That's what they're saying. Your brother came here asking questions. Makes me think that...well, he suspects someone from here is guilty."

Dallas wondered if she was particularly worried. "He's just doing his job. Or do you think someone here did do it?"

"No. I mean, like I told him, when you get this many lawyers"—she leaned in—"this many egos in one building, it's not always friendly. But do I think anyone here killed him? No. My bet would be on the wife."

Dallas liked her desire to talk, even if he didn't like what she said. When she reached for her coffee, he noticed her extremely toned biceps. "You know, you look familiar to me, too. Do you belong to a gym? I used to go to one off Banker Road."

"I never went to that one, but I go to the Fitness Plus off of Cabot."

"I got a visitor pass there a while back. I'll bet I saw you. What's the name of that trainer, the dark-headed guy?"

"Larry?"

"Yeah, I think that was his name," Dallas lied and felt his eyebrow jumping up and down. "I almost joined just because of him."

"You should join." She smiled. "We could work out together."

"That would be nice."

"How about this afternoon? I get off at four and I go for an hour workout."

Dallas considered what he wanted to be doing around four—sweet talking Nikki—and came a breath away from asking for a rain check. Then again, wasn't getting information to prove Nikki innocent more important that taking her to bed? Hell, different parts of his body held opposing opinions.

Five minutes later, with a date to work out—and hope-fully to chat—with the fit receptionist, Dallas sat across from Mr. Canton, Serena's attorney.

"I'm glad you're willing to discuss this," Canton said. "We should settle this out of court."

Dallas fought the urge to tell the man he'd take this to the supreme court before he'd give up Bud. He'd given Selena everything, hadn't asked for one damn thing since he got out of prison, not even the twenty thousand they'd had in their savings account. Or the money she'd made sell-ing his truck. He'd give up his dog over his dead body.

But he hadn't come here to give the man a piece of his mind. He'd come hoping to get some information. And right now being cooperative seemed like the best way to reach his goal.

"I'm willing to talk. What kind of deal does my ex want?"

"Well." Canton pulled out his file. "Joint custody and..."

The man went on for about three minutes outlining all the crap Dallas would never agree to, and it was hell keeping his mouth shut.

"All I need is for you to sign here and—"

"First, I'd like a chance to go over it. I'll probably sign it, but I want to make sure Bud isn't getting shafted in this deal. He's a sensitive dog."

"Seriously?" Canton looked surprised. "I mean, sure."

Dallas leaned forward. "I heard my brother was in here earlier."

"Your brother?"

"Detective O'Connor. He's working the homicide case."

"Oh, I haven't seen him yet. I think I have a meeting with him on Monday."

"Sad thing about Jack Leon. He told me about it."

"Yeah." Canton picked up his pen. "Does he really think the wife did this?"

"You sound like you don't believe it. Surely, working family law, you've seen it all."

"Yes, but I've met the ex-wife. She doesn't seem the type."

"I got the feeling my brother thought that way, too. I think the whole wife-did-it is only one of his theories."

"And his other?" Canton asked.

"Well, he doesn't discuss his cases but, as an ex-cop, I'd guess his showing up here says something. You aren't going to get yourself arrested before you finish my case, are you?"

"Your brother suspects someone here?" Canton asked, avoiding Dallas's question.

"Something about office politics was mentioned. Making partner."

Canton frowned. "That doesn't mean one of us killed him. Hell, if they want to look at something, they should look at Jack's philandering. He may have come across all straight and narrow, but he didn't meet a skirt he didn't chase."

By the time Dallas left the law firm, Tyler had called him three times with updates. In the first call Tyler announced that he had an address for the busboy and his girlfriend, Angela Martina. Call number two reported the discovery that the busboy had a possession charge not too long ago. Third call was to report that Austin had checked in and was now trying to talk to Jack Leon's neighbors, and to let Dallas know that Nance was at the gallery keeping an eye on Nikki.

Checking his watch, Dallas figured he had an hour and half before he had to meet the receptionist for their workout-chat. He headed over to Angela Martina's apartment, a five-minute drive away, and dialed Nikki's cell. He hadn't been away from her for more than an hour but he missed her.

The moment she answered the phone, Nikki started talking. "I can't believe Nance did something wrong. He's not a bad kid, Dallas."

A sense of rightness filled his chest that Nikki agreed. "I know."

"You guys have to get him off."

"I'm doing everything I can." *And with you, too*, he thought.

"Did you know he was an artist and had an art scholarship before this happened?"

"I didn't know it was art, but I knew he had a scholarship. Hey, not to change the subject, but I was thinking about dinner. How about I cook steaks on the grill? We can hang out together. Alone." He put emphasis on the "alone."

"Okay." Her voice sounded a tad breathless.

"Maybe work on those multiple choice questions I gave you this morning. Adding that D, all of the above choice." When she didn't answer, he asked. "Are you blushing right now?"

"No."

"Liar." He could hear the embarrassment in her voice.

"You can't prove it," she countered.

He laughed and realized he'd laughed more since he met her than he had since he'd gotten out of prison. It was a good change, but change was always scary. But as he'd told her, in a lot of ways scary was good. Scary was invigorating.

"I have to do something at five. You go on back to my place. Austin's going to snag your car from the police station and bring it there. I'll swing by the store on the way home and grab a few groceries. I should be there by six thirty."

"I can get my car."

"I already talked to Austin."

"Okay, but why don't I just stay here until then?" she said, no doubt having reservations about staying at his place. Oddly enough, he didn't have any reservations. Not that this was permanent or anything. One day at a time.

"I guess," he said. "Oh, I forgot to ask you something earlier. Did Jack have your cell number?"

"Yes. But I never took his calls. Why?"

"He didn't try to call you after he left the restaurant?"

"No. Why?"

"Just trying to figure things out."

"What things?"

"What he was doing by your car."

"You mean besides getting murdered?" Her tone deepened.

"Yeah, besides that."

"Oh, I almost forgot. The viewing is tonight at the funeral home. I don't know if I should go."

"No," he said adamantly. "If you show up, it will just rile the Leons."

"That's sort of what I thought but..." Her line beeped. "I have a call coming in. It's probably Nana."

"Okay, I'll pick you up at the gallery. And tell Nance to stay until I get there."

Dallas knocked on Angela Martina's apartment door a few minutes later. He'd thought Nikki's apartment was bad. This complex looked like something from a third-world nation.

He heard a piercing cry. The door swung open. Standing in front of him was a dark-haired girl, who couldn't be over seventeen, holding a screaming baby.

"What?" she asked and the baby wasn't the only one crying. Tears spilled down the girl's face.

"I'm looking for Angela Martina."

"What for?" The baby let out another scream.

"Are you Angela?"

"If you're from the hospital, I told you I don't have the money." Another stream of tears rolled down her cheeks.

"I'm not from the hospital."

"Then who are you?"

He went with the truth. "I'm a private detective."

"What's Jose done now?" She swiped at her cheeks. The five- or six-month-old baby was red-faced from screaming. "Is he okay?"

"She. She's a girl and doctors say she's fine. Just a fussy baby. Does this sound like a fussy baby to you?"

Dallas looked at the child. "I...wouldn't know about babies."

"What do you want with Jose?"

"I just want to talk to him."

"Well, that makes two of us." She copped an attitude. "What do you need to talk to him about?"

"Someone got poisoned at his restaurant."

"Poisoned?" She shook her head. "You think he had something to do with it? No...if you said it was selling or smoking weed, I'd say yes. But that? No."

"Like I said, I just want to talk to him. So he's not here?"

"He hasn't been here in couple of days." Her eyes grew bright. "He was supposed to watch the baby while I work. He goes off and loses his job, and now I'm going to lose mine. The rent's not paid, they're going to cut off the power next week. My parents told me he'd do this, but did I listen? Hell, no!"

"Did he say why he lost his job?"

"He wouldn't tell me. He looked high again. I'm so sick of this. He promised he'd change. He'd help me take care of the baby. And now they won't even let me pick

up his check. The baby needs diapers and milk and..."
She took a shaky breath, as if realizing she was spilling
her guts to a stranger. She snatched a pink cloth from her
shoulder and covered her eyes.

Now Dallas didn't know who was crying harder, her
or the baby. Oh Lord, he wasn't good with crying females.
"Uh, I'm sure it'll be okay."

She took a few hiccuppy breaths. "No it won't, but
thanks."

He hesitated to ask but couldn't afford not to. "Do you
know where I might find Jose?"

"Maybe hanging out at his friends' place. I have their
address." She stepped from the door and motioned him
inside.

He took one step inside. She swung around and Dallas
knew he'd screwed up royally.

CHAPTER TWENTY-SIX

"OH, NO," DALLAS SAID, but she'd already dropped the unhappy baby in his arms. With a shitload of insecurities, he held the screaming little person about a foot away from his chest.

"Wait," he said. "I don't know how to hold it. Her. I don't know how..."

Angela was already across the room. She looked back at him. "Just pull her to your chest." She started thumbing through an address book with a pen and paper in her hand.

He brought the squirming child closer and she looked up at him and released another ear-piercing scream. "Don't cry. Mama will be right back." He tried to sound soothing, but he obviously failed.

The baby cried harder and started kicking her legs and arms. "I don't think she likes me. You might want to hurry."

"Don't take it personally. She does this all the time."

She finished scribbling down some information. He held the child out, ready to be relieved of duty. Right before

Angela took the baby, the child made a strange noise. Before Dallas could react, a milky-looking substance spewed out of the baby's mouth and soaked Dallas's shirt.

Angela burst out laughing. "The doctor calls her a projectile burper."

"Yeah." He handed the baby, still leaking projectile burp, to her mom.

Giggling, Angela handed him the pink cloth. "I'm sorry."

He looked at his shirt. "It's okay. I seem to have that effect on women lately." He returned her cloth.

She handed him the paper. "If you find Jose, tell him I'm going back to San Antonio to my parents."

Dallas looked from her to the child who'd finally shut up. And damn if the little toothless wonder didn't smile up at him.

"She's cute when she's not screaming," he said.

"She has her moments." The girl gently pressed a kiss to the child's head.

"If you hear from him, give me a call." Dallas pulled out his wallet to give her his card. He saw the stack of twenties and thought what the hell. He handed her both the card and some money. "For diapers. Call me if you hear from him."

"You don't have to do this," she said.

"I know." He smiled. "Take care of the projectile burper."

Dallas had just enough time to run back to the apartment, change his shirt, and grab some workout clothes before leaving to meet Rachel at the gym. On his way in, he stopped by the front office and updated the guys on what he'd learned. Austin agreed to try to locate the dead-beat dad-busboy before he picked up Nikki's car.

When he headed for the apartment, his shirt already off, Tyler yelled at him. Dallas popped back into the office. "What?"

Tyler eyed him. "You get puked on again?"

"As matter of fact, I did. What do you need? I gotta run."

"You had a visitor." Tyler grimaced. "Serena."

Fuck. "What the hell did she want?"

"She didn't say. I told her to call you."

"Why did you tell her that?"

"I thought it would be better than her showing up again later when...when you and Nikki are...getting to know each other."

"She better not show up." Dallas started off again.

"Wait," Tyler said.

Dallas swung around, losing his patience. "What?"

"My cousin was here."

"Your cousin?"

"To bring you a sofa."

That was before he convinced Nikki to sleep with him. "Fine." He started down the hall.

"I typed exactly what you said," Tyler's voice followed him. "You didn't care if it was pink as..."

Dallas didn't understand what Tyler was ranting about. Or he didn't until he opened his apartment door. A huge bright fuchsia-pink sofa sat in the living room.

"Shit," he grumbled and went to get dressed.

Nikki was giving Eddie Nance, the kid Dallas sent over, an art lesson when her cell rang. Because she'd just spoken with Ellen, who was doing well enough to gripe about going home, Nikki felt her pulse race. Hoping it was Dallas again, she stepped away from Eddie.

Meeting Eddie and realizing how genuinely good Dallas was had Nikki singing a different tune about the whole relationship issue. Or maybe she'd actually found a bit of wisdom from Nana's heart-off-the-leash talk. Then again, maybe she was just on a sugar high from having eaten four cupcakes. She was still scared, petrified actually, but had stopped thinking about trying to put distance between Dallas and her and started thinking about how to get closer.

And naked.

Which was hard to think about with a nineteen-year-old hovering over her. Not that she minded—Eddie was great. He reminded her of the art students she taught every June for the foster care program. Good kids cheated out of opportunities that other kids took for granted. A road Nikki herself could have gone down, if she hadn't had Nana.

Her phone rang for the third time and, not wanting to appear eager, she let it go one more. "Hello," she said seductively.

"Hello," an unfamiliar male voice answered.

Disappointment filled her. "May I help you?"

"It's Andrew Brian. I thought I'd remind you that I'd be happy to accompany you to the funeral home tonight."

Maybe it was because Nikki's mind was on sex, or because of what Dallas had said about him hitting on her, but she got the feeling that Brian's offer to go to the funeral home wasn't just out of the goodness of his heart.

"Oh, I'm sorry. I think it would cause a stir. It wouldn't be fair to his parents."

"What about what's fair to you?" he asked.

"I think they get the most consideration right now."

"That's big of you. Are you still at the shop?"

Chills ran up her spine. Dallas suspected this man of killing Jack and stabbing Ellen. "I'm about to leave, actually. I have a friend with me." Suddenly she was glad Eddie was there.

"I was hoping to run by and buy that painting."

"Sorry."

"Okay." He sounded almost annoyed.

She couldn't hang up fast enough. She looked at Eddie. "We should leave."

Dallas arrived at the fitness club three minutes late. Rachel Peterson stood by the door and she didn't look happy.

"I don't like to be kept waiting." She sounded like a class-A bitch.

Three minutes? What are you, the time police? "Sorry." She was already in her workout clothes. The sleeveless tank top and biker shorts made her muscular form stand out. While she wasn't butch-looking, Dallas couldn't help but compare her to Nikki. He'd pick petite and soft over Rachel's built form every time.

"You look like you spend a lot of time here." He worked to make it sound like a compliment.

"I'm a body builder on the side. Won some competitions." She ran her hand over his abs. "You could use some tightening."

Oh, she knew how to make a guy fall for her all right. "I'm working on it." Wanting to shift the conversation, he added, "I work out with my brother, but he's been busy lately."

"You two close?" she asked as they walked up to the check-in and got him a friend pass.

"Yup." He followed her to the hand weights.

"Has he mentioned the Leon case?" She started doing arm lifts.

"Some. He can't divulge too much." He picked up a weight set.

"Is he arresting the wife?"

"I don't think he's convinced she did it." He noticed the ease with which Rachel lifted her weights.

"She's gonna get off scot-free?"

"I think he's still looking at other suspects. Which is why he's nosing around your office...looking for a few answers."

"Good luck. Attorneys are famous for keeping their mouths closed."

"What about receptionists?" He tried to put some teasing in his tone.

"I need my job."

"There is that." He itched to ask why she thought her job might be in jeopardy, but didn't want to appear too interested.

She moved over to a machine and added two more cast-iron plates. She did ten leg lifts, of two hundred pounds. Impressive, Dallas admitted. He set himself up beside her to do his own. "As long as it's not Canton. I want this custody mess cleared up."

"Please, the man's a wimp. If it is someone at our firm, I'd have my bets on Andrew."

"Which one is he?" he asked, even though he knew exactly who he was.

"The senior partner's son. Let's just say he has a white powder problem."

"Really?" Dallas asked.

"I don't tolerate drugs. So if you're into that, you're not going to get any of this." She waved a hand down her body.

Holy shit, the woman moved fast. Little did she know he wasn't interested in any "of this"...or that, either. "I'm not into the drug scene."

"Good." She smiled. Dallas got a feeling she expected them to take this workout someplace else later. Not.

She did two more leg presses. "Is your brother coming by Monday to do more interviews?"

"I guess." Dallas suddenly found it interesting that getting her to talk was so easy. Was she just the type who loved to gossip? Or was there something more?

"Do you think you could give him a hint from me without it ever coming out?"

"Depends on how small of a hint it is."

"Like I said, I don't want to lose my job."

"I totally get that."

She sat up, reached for the towel, and wiped the sweat from her brow then stroked the towel down to her cleavage...no doubt for his benefit.

"On Tuesday, I left to go work out but forgot my suit coat. I went back inside." She watched him doing his leg lifts.

"When I went back in, I heard Leon and Brian Junior arguing."

"About what?" Dallas asked.

"Don't know. But it sounded...hostile. I grabbed my coat and left. With Brian being the senior partner's son, if I tattled, I'd be out of a job."

That did make sense, Dallas amended. Maybe Rachel

Peterson's willingness to talk wasn't so suspicious after all. Maybe her show of interest in him was more about him being Tony's brother than her wanting to take him home tonight. He could hope. If not, she was going to be disappointed.

His last hope was shot to hell when her hand landed on his thigh way too close to his crotch. "With a little work, I'll bet I can have you hard as a rock."

Dallas tried to think fast. "You know, there's something I need to tell you."

Thirty minutes later, earlier than he'd expected, Dallas aimed his Mustang toward Nikki's gallery. He'd never had to work so hard *not* to get lucky. When he'd been slow to explain his reasons, Rachel had been quick to guess. It had been easier to just agree, but he didn't like it. Then again, he did have a pink sofa!

Scary thought. Then a realization hit that was even scarier. He hadn't even been tempted by Rachel. And the reason was all too clear. Nikki.

Where was this thing between them leading? He remembered the conversation he'd had with Tony. Where did *he* want it to lead? Dallas pushed back into his car seat and decided he needed to put on some emotional brakes. Hadn't he promised to never commit himself to another woman?

But damn it to hell and back! He didn't want to start thinking about this tonight. He wanted to think about Nikki, getting her naked, keeping her naked all night long.

His cell rang. Temporarily distracted by his thoughts, he answered without checking the number. "Yeah?"

"Hello, Dallas."

Fucking great. If he needed a reminder of why he

didn't want to commit, the universe had just supplied one. "What do you want, Serena?"

"If I said you, what would you say?"

"I'd say go screw your boss again. Isn't he your fiancé now?"

"You can be an asshole, you know that?"

"Yeah, prison"—*and being married to you*—"will do that to you."

"I heard you talked to my lawyer."

"I heard you talked to my dad. I just suggest you don't do it again."

She ignored his comment. "Leo said you practically agreed to sign the papers."

"Leo? You mean Mr. Canton? What? You sleeping with him, too?"

"You're a bastard."

"A good reason not to want to deal with me, Serena. He's my dog. I'm not sharing him." Dallas hung up.

He pulled up at Nikki's gallery and saw immediately that the lights were out. Nikki's grandmother's car and Nance's green Saturn were missing.

Where the hell was Nikki? Had something...happened? Any thoughts of trying to establish an emotional distance were shot to hell and back.

He grabbed his phone and dialed her number. *"Pick up, damn it!"*

She didn't. The call went to voice mail.

CHAPTER TWENTY-SEVEN

"YOUR PHONE'S RINGING," Eddie said from the table.

"I'll call them back." Standing at the ice cream shop counter, Nikki glanced at the clock. She planned to call Dallas in a bit to let him know where they were and why they'd left the gallery. Maybe she was overreacting, but the call from Andrew Brian gave her the heebie-jeebies.

Snagging a couple of napkins, she took her order from the attendant. With the two ice cream cones in hand, she walked back to the table just as the phone rang again.

Passing Eddie his double dip of strawberry, she held tight to her one scoop of chocolate, and reached into her purse for her phone. Her one-handed attempt failed. Her purse and contents went scattering across the floor.

"Shit." She looked up at Eddie as she crouched to retrieve her stuff. "You didn't hear me say that."

"I'm about to be sent to prison and you're afraid the word 'shit' will be a bad influence on me?" Laughing, he knelt to help pick up her mess.

"You shouldn't curse," she said. "And you're not going to prison."

"Yeah, right."

She snagged a loose tampon and dropped it into her purse, along with her wallet, brush and almost empty can of Mace.

"Here." Eddie handed her a compact mirror and flash drive.

"This isn't mine." She returned the flash drive to him.

"It came out of your purse."

"You sure it wasn't just on the floor?" She stood and dropped her purse back on the table.

Eddie sat up and dropped the flash drive on the table. "It was with your other stuff."

"I never use 'em." Seeing a big drip of ice cream slipping down her cone, Nikki licked it. "Umm."

As she slid her purse away from the table edge, she pushed the napkins onto the floor.

"Ten-second rule." Eddie snagged the napkins and passed one to her.

"What's a few germs?" *Déjà vu* hit her. Jack had dropped his napkin when they met for dinner at Venny's. She remembered thinking how odd it was that...

Her gaze shot toward the flash drive. She didn't use the memory sticks, but Jack did.

Dallas and his brother had asked her if Jack had given her anything the night he was killed. Her purse had been under the table when he'd retrieved his napkin. "Shit."

"What?"

"Hold this." She passed Eddie her ice cream cone and called Dallas.

Dallas walked into the ice cream shop. The smell of cold, creamy sweet stuff filled his nose. Sitting at a nearby table, Nikki slowly ran her pink tongue up a cone. A pang of lust hit so hard Dallas had to concentrate to rein himself in. Still, he couldn't help watching her tongue slide over her ice cream.

Seeing him, she grinned, picked up the flash drive and held it out. She'd already told him about it on the phone and damn, he hoped she was right.

"I dropped my purse and it spilled out." Her tongue licked the side of the cone.

He nodded at Nance and took the memory disk. "I saw this the first night at the hospital." Then he snagged her cone and ran his tongue over the smooth chocolate, thinking about doing much the same to her when he got her back to his place. Just as soon as he plugged in the flash drive to see what was on it.

"So I was right." Nance chuckled.

Dallas returned Nikki's cone. "Right about what?"

"Right about you two being more than friends."

Dallas looked at the blush creeping up Nikki's neck, then glanced back at Nance. "Why would you think that?"

Nance laughed and Dallas realized it was the first time he'd heard the kid do that since he'd met him. Did Nikki have that effect on everyone?

"I used to work at an ice cream place. I know the language of ice cream sharing between a man and a woman. There's the nibble on the other side." He took a bite of his cone. "That means I haven't slept with you yet, but I really want to. Then there's this." He turned the cone around and slowly swiped his tongue across the ice cream. "That means—"

"It means you had way too much time on your hands when you worked at the ice cream shop." But Dallas couldn't help but smile and offer the kid a wink.

Less than twenty minutes later, he and Nikki stood peering over Tyler's back while he plugged in the flash drive. Dallas could have done it, but he would've needed to move his hands off Nikki and he hadn't wanted to do that.

With a few of Tyler's keystrokes, the screen changed. "One file, an Excel spreadsheet named 'Xfers.' Transfers." Tyler clicked on the file.

Seconds later, the file appeared. Tyler looked at Nikki. "You know what this looks like?"

"No."

"It looks like a list of amounts of cash. Maybe deposits," Dallas said.

"Over two hundred thousand," Tyler said. "Could Jack have been embezzling money from someone? The law firm?"

"No," Nikki said. "Jack wouldn't steal."

Dallas resisted the urge to point out that a man who cheats on his wife might have no problem cheating his employer. Instead, he decided to be diplomatic. "Well, since he's keeping tabs on it, maybe he considered it just borrowing."

"No," Nikki said again and her loyalty to her ex stung Dallas a little. "First off, Jack didn't need the money. His parents are super wealthy."

"Not anymore." Tyler looked at her. "Sorry to be the bearer of bad news, but my little Internet search says differently. Your in-laws lost their assets on the last stock market tumble. They're actually involved in a lawsuit against their broker for making bad investment recommendations."

Nikki's eyes widened. "Still, Jack would never take something that didn't belong to him." She stepped away from the warm place at Dallas's side.

"He took your hired help," Dallas insisted.

"That's different," Nikki said. "And if he had been doing this, why would he put the drive in my purse? Why would he want anyone to know what he was doing? I think he put it in there in case something happened to him."

"Okay, now I see your point." Dallas looked at Tyler. "Is there nothing else on there?"

"Just dates," Tyler said.

Dallas remembered Rachel Peterson saying Andrew Brian and Jack Leon had argued. He felt pretty damn certain he knew who was embezzling money from the firm.

"So this isn't going to help at all?" Nikki asked, sounding deflated.

"I didn't say that," Tyler said. "If these numbers and dates are compared to the records of a bookkeeper's files, even if the books were fixed, I imagine I'd be able to discover some missing funds."

"Right," Dallas said. "Now all we gotta do is figure out how we can get to look into those files."

LeAnn came home prepared to ask Tony why he was there and what he wanted, because if he really wanted her out of the house, she'd move.

However, the moment she stepped into the house and inhaled the scents of dinner, heard the soft music, and saw Tony—shirtless and barefoot—bebopping around the kitchen, she lost her nerve. Or maybe, it wasn't her nerve she lost. Maybe she didn't lose anything—maybe it was what she'd gained. Tony. He was home. With her. A part of her wanted to weep with joy.

Another part of her felt paralyzed with fear, afraid to hope what all this really meant.

"You're home," Tony said, wielding a spatula and a sexy smile.

Home. Her throat tightened. *This* was home again. She nodded, unable to talk.

"Good day?" He leaned against the counter. Why was he shirtless?

"It was okay," she said, forcing the words out.

"You hungry?"

"Yeah." They'd had several new patients added to her floor and she'd skipped lunch.

"Why don't you go take a shower? I'll get everything on the table."

Ten minutes later, showered and dressed in a simple yellow sundress, and vowing to get through the evening, she went back into the kitchen.

"Smells good. What are we having?" Her gaze kept slipping to his chest. All that bare skin begged to be touched.

He handed her a glass of wine. When his fingers touched her, it was like a thousand volts of electricity shot right to her heart.

"Why don't you sit down and I'll serve you?" he said.

She sat and Tony quickly placed a plate of tiramisu in front of her.

"Dessert first?" She brought a big spoonful of the fluffy sweetness to her mouth. The flavors, the different textures on her tongue, made her purr.

"It's what you like." He sat in his normal spot across from her.

God, she'd missed seeing him there. Missed eating tiramisu. Missed breathing the same air he breathed.

"You're not having any?" Unable to resist, she took another bite.

"I'm saving myself for dinner." He sipped his wine, watching her over the rim.

"Am I supposed to believe you made this?" The mocha flavor exploded on her tongue.

He grinned and put a hand on his bare chest. "Of course I did. I have no idea how the Little Italy box got in the garbage."

"Mm. I haven't eaten there in forever." She savored another bite.

He watched her and a slow heat built in his eyes, as if her eating was turning him on. From experience, she knew it didn't take much to arouse Tony. He liked sex. How could he not like something he was so good at? The thought brought a tightness low in her belly. Suddenly nervous, she put the spoon down.

He reached over and ran the tip of his finger over the edge of her plate and then tasted it. "Isn't that the restaurant where we went on our first date?"

"Yes." Memories of that night filled her mind. Had he chosen to buy the dessert from there because of its history? Was he sitting across from her without a shirt on to make her want him? If so, it was working.

He turned his wineglass. "Why don't we go there next weekend?"

Her pulse started racing. Did he plan on being here next weekend? What was his plan? What was Tony doing? "Won't your bedbug situation be cleared up by then?"

The moment the question slipped out, she wanted to take it back. She didn't want to talk about why Tony was here, because that conversation might lead to why he'd left. And she wasn't ready to talk about that.

She saw him studying her.

"You ready for the second course?" he asked, ignoring her question.

"Yeah."

Tony served her fried oysters, twice-baked potatoes, and candied carrots—one of the few vegetables she liked. They made small talk. She asked about his dad and about his work. He asked if she'd heard from her father lately and, when she said no, he frowned. Tony wasn't exactly a fan of her father. Not that she blamed him. She wasn't exactly a fan herself. She'd forgiven him for many things in her life, but not showing up for Emily's funeral was the last straw.

Trying to pull her thoughts from that path, LeAnn turned the conversation to Nikki. "You don't really think Nikki Hunt killed her ex-husband, do you?"

"My gut says no. But there's a hell of a lot of circumstantial evidence against her."

"Then follow your gut. It's always right."

He toyed with the stem of the glass.

"You could be nicer to her, too. She thinks you don't like her."

"I'm just doing my job, LeAnn."

"Do it nicer."

"I'll work on it." He stacked their plates and pushed them to the side. "You know Dallas has a thing for her, right?"

She smiled. "I kind of got that."

"Did you know she puked on him?"

"What?"

He told her the story and she couldn't help laughing. "How serious is it between them?"

"I know they're hitting the sheets already. I think the

thing with Serena made him gun-shy." Tony paused and stared at his wine again before looking up. "I think people sometimes let the past get in the way of the future. They let it stop them from moving forward."

Emotion caught in her chest. She knew he wasn't talking about Dallas anymore. "It's not always easy, Tony."

"Not easy. But I think it'd be worth it."

She knew where this conversation was leading. And like the door down the hall that she couldn't open, she wasn't ready to face it. Not with Tony. She was almost to the point where she didn't blame herself for Emily's death, and if she discovered Tony blamed her even the tiniest bit, she simply didn't think she could handle it.

"Thanks for dinner." She stood up. "Just leave the dishes and I'll wash them tomorrow. I'm tired."

"Well, I did ask you if you were gay." Nikki rubbed the arm of the pink sofa as Dallas returned from the kitchen where he'd drop off their plates. After Tyler left, they'd run to the grocery store for steaks. "You know, the only thing that keeps me from revoking your man card is your aptitude for grilling." She giggled.

"Hey, I'm so masculine that I can own a pink couch." He dropped down beside Nikki. "You have to admit it's comfortable."

"Very nice," she said.

"Let's see how it feels lying down." He pushed her back and stretched out beside her. "Hmm, not quite soft enough," he said and positioned himself on top of her. "Much better." His warm mouth, flavored with the wine they'd drunk, moved over hers in a soft, wet kiss.

He pulled back. "Do you have any idea how many

times I've gotten hard thinking about you today? In public. Once in an elevator in front of two nuns."

She laughed. "So sorry." She moved her knee slightly between his legs.

His expression turned serious. "Thanks for being nice to Eddie. He wouldn't even take the check Tyler tried to give him before he took off. He said you gave him art lessons."

"He's really a good kid. You're going to be able to get him off, aren't you?"

"Actually, I got a call from my brother while I was grilling our steaks. He seems to think Eddie's problems will go away. We should know something in a few days."

"Really? I guess I shouldn't judge your brother so harshly."

"He's a good guy, Nikki."

"Did you tell him about the flash drive?"

"Not yet. I wanted to talk it over with Austin and Tyler and hear their thoughts."

"Three heads are better than one, huh?"

"Yeah. In spite of how they act sometimes, they're really good guys, too."

"I don't doubt it." She ran a hand over his cheek. "Friends are important. I'm close to Ellen like that."

"She seems nice. A little frisky, but—"

"Hey, it was the morphine." Nikki giggled. "I went to see her before going to the gallery. She's better. Your sister-in-law was there."

"LeAnn's pretty cool."

"What happened between her and Tony? I mean, if you're not comfortable telling me, you don't have to."

"Nah, it's not a secret. Not that Tony or LeAnn talk

about it." He rolled to his side as if he worried his weight was too much for her. "They lost a child. Only a few months old. She died in her sleep, just stopped breathing. It was tough. I thought Tony was going to lose it. Mom had just died a week before. I don't know exactly what happened but, before long, Tony told me he'd moved out."

"That's terrible," Nikki said.

"Yeah. But he's trying to win her back."

"I hope it works out. I get the feeling she still loves him."

"I hope so. He's crazy about her."

Nikki's mind went back to the conversation they had about the busboy at Venny's. "I don't understand how the busboy could be involved if you think Andrew Brian did it."

"Someone had to put the ipecac in the gumbo."

"Yeah, but I just don't see a connection. And I don't understand why someone would give him something to make him throw up if they were planning on killing him."

"That's why we want to find the busboy. But why don't you let me worry about that?"

They lay there for long minutes, just being close.

"I bought some ice cream if you wanted dessert," Dallas said.

"I already had ice cream."

"I know." He smiled. "You really shouldn't have licked that ice cream like that in front of Eddie." Leaning closer, he ran his tongue over the edge of her ear.

She thumped him on his chest, but not hard enough to push him away. It felt way too good to do that. "It was you he was talking about, not me."

Dallas laughed. "I only licked it like that because

you did." He gently placed a moist kiss at the edge of her neck, and the warm feeling spread all the way down to her toes.

"It was my ice cream. I was eating it, not having sex with it."

"Speaking of sex..." He rolled on top of her again. It was amazing how every part of him fit perfectly on every part of her. "You still hoping for option D, all of the above?"

She studied him and grinned. "Are you trying to get me to talk dirty to you?"

He laughed. "Does that turn you on?"

"I... wouldn't know. I haven't tried it."

"Then you should try it," he teased. Heat and humor filled his blue eyes. "Tell me, Nikki. Tell me exactly what you want me to do to you."

A few very suggestive responses tickled the tip of her tongue, but she couldn't bring herself to say them. She blushed just thinking about them.

And he must have noticed, because he laughed. "I'm just letting you know what's on the menu so you can get what you want."

She swallowed a bit of embarrassment and tried to sound sexy. "How about I take whatever is on special for the evening?"

"All of the above, it is." He kissed her, slowly, thoroughly, and then stood up and pulled her up beside him.

"What?" She grinned. "I thought your masculinity wasn't threatened by the pink sofa."

"So you're into sofa sex?"

She cut him a coy smile. "I don't know. You'll have to define sofa sex."

"Define, it hell." He lowered her back on the pink leather. "I'll show you."

And he did. As well as option D.

For the record, she liked both.

An hour later, Tony was finishing the dishes and struggling not to slam pots and pans around. Damn it! Why couldn't he have kept it light, kept it fun? But holy hell, it had been going so well. They'd actually carried on a conversation. They'd laughed.

Moving to the living room, he looked at the closed bedroom door. Light spilled through the doorjamb. Maybe it was time to move to plan B.

He went to gather his deodorant, almost grabbed some clothes but that wasn't part of his plan. Heading back to the kitchen, he poured a glass of wine. Three glasses of wine and his wife usually got frisky. Not that he expected to get lucky tonight, but he sure as hell wanted her to start thinking frisky. Returning to the bedroom door, he knocked.

"Yes," she said hesitantly.

He opened the door. She lay in the bed, a book in her lap. He recognized the old nightshirt she wore. He'd taken it off of her dozens of times. The fact that he knew she didn't wear underwear to bed made his own underwear feel tight.

"I need to shower. You don't mind, do you?" He stepped inside, not giving her a chance to say no.

"Why can't you use the hall bath?"

Her long hair hung over her shoulders and brushed against her breasts, and his mouth watered. "No... shower, remember? I tried to talk you into putting one in there."

"Then why don't you just take a bath?" she asked, her brows tightening.

"I hate baths, you know that."

He set the glass of wine on her bedside table. "I thought you might want another." Looking down, he read the title of the book. "*A Hard Man.*"

"It's not what you think." She squinted at him.

"Isn't it a romance?"

"It still doesn't mean . . . He's a weight lifter."

He reached for the book and she jerked it back. "Come on, let me read a few pages. Sounds interesting."

"No." Her face turned red.

And he knew damn well why she didn't want him to read it. "It's not about a weight lifter, is it?"

"Is, too."

He laughed and, holy hell, but he wanted to fall in the bed beside her, to show her just how hard a guy could get. Nine months without sex could take a guy up a few notches. He started getting hard when she bent her knee and he got a peek at a creamy thigh. "I'm . . . going to take a shower." He got to the door. He wasn't sure what drove him to do it, but he turned around. "You want to join me?"

CHAPTER TWENTY-EIGHT

TEN MINUTES LATER, Tony turned the shower off and his hope went down drain with the sudsy water. Honestly, he hadn't expected her to join him, but damn he'd hoped.

Grabbing a towel, he ran a hand through his hair and wrapped the white fluffy cotton around his waist. He eyed himself in the mirror. Not bad for thirty-two years old. He flexed his muscles and loosened the towel so it draped a bit lower. He twisted the towel so the slit would offer the best opportunity, and then stepped out into the bedroom.

She sat there where he'd left her, her nose in the book. In her other hand she held the wine. Slowly, she lowered the book and looked at him. Shock widened her eyes.

"Sorry, I forgot to grab my clothes." He started toward the door, feeling her watching him. Reaching the door, he turned to find her gaze glued to him. "Good night. Enjoy your book." He stepped out and shut the door, but he heard her mutter,

"Forgot my ass."

He smiled. Then because he was having too much fun, he swung around and stepped back into the bedroom.

Cool air hit certain body parts down south, and he knew
the slit was exactly where he wanted it to be.

Her gaze shot down, then up, then down again.

"Are you sure you don't want to watch a movie?
picked up a couple from the Redbox. One of them migh
even be about a weight lifter."

Her eyes tightened with aggravation, but he knew
LeAnn well enough to know her eyes tightened long
before she acted on the emotion. She was easy and fur
to rile, but slow to real anger. It was only one of many o
things he loved about her.

"No." She waved him off, but not before her eyes low
ered one more time.

He shut the door, smiling. Oh, yeah, plan B was muck
more effective. All he had to do now was come with
plan C.

On Saturday, Dallas went with Nikki to the gallery
"You'll get bored," she'd told him. He insisted he wouldn'
and that leaving her alone when Brian had already show
up once was too risky.

Indeed, it was risk Nikki was worried about. But i
didn't involve Brian. Riskier was letting Dallas get close
to her than he already had. She tried putting up her barriers, but the more she was with him, the more she liked him

And it wasn't just about sex. Oh, the sex was awesome
but it was how he made her laugh even during the bigges
crisis of her life. It was how she could make him laugh
how he fit into her crazy world. Not having to apologize
that her family wasn't Norman Rockwell perfect. Nothing
against Norman—she liked to paint idealistic moments
that screamed emotion as well—but life wasn't about a

few captured seconds. It was about the seconds before and after.

On Saturday night, they'd visited Nana and the Ol' Timers to play board games. Dallas seemed to enjoy being around this odd group that made up a big portion of her life and a bigger part of her heart. He'd laughed, joked and she could swear he had a good time.

He'd even asked Nana if she might invite his dad to join them next time. Nana informed him that she'd already invited him, but he'd declined. Nikki heard the caring in Dallas's voice when he spoke about his father. She also heard it when he spoke to his father on the phone. She tried to remember ever hearing Jack talk to his parents like this, but she couldn't.

Sunday morning Dallas asked if she'd join him for lunch with his dad. How could Nikki say no when he'd gone with her to Nana's? Before they'd left, Dallas told her about his dad wanting him to go to the cemetery for his mom's birthday.

"You have to go," she'd said.

He appeared annoyed. "Do you have any idea how it felt going to my mother's funeral in handcuffs? Besides, my mom's dead."

"But your dad isn't," Nikki said. "This isn't for your mom. It's for him. And you're not in handcuffs now, Dallas. Maybe this time, it won't feel so wrong."

Dallas just stared. "Did I ask you to get logical on me?"

He'd put humor in his voice, but she knew he'd been serious. However, when eating burgers in Mr. O'Connor's bright red kitchen that day, Dallas told his dad he'd go. He even squeezed her hand when he said it. It wasn't that simple touch that sent Nikki's heart into emotional hiccups. It wasn't when Dallas's dad apparently noticed that emotional moment and asked. "So you two are serious, huh?"

It was Dallas's answer that did Nikki in. "No. Just taking it a day at a time, Dad."

Her heart started sputtering out emotional storm warnings, because she realized the truth. She was falling in love with Dallas. Head over heels in love with a man who wouldn't even promise her tomorrow. She told herself to pull back, and she tried. Really tried.

By Monday morning, Dallas had asked her about six times if something was wrong. A believer in honesty and confronting problems head-on, she did what she had to. She lied like a big dog with its paws crossed. It wasn't Dallas's fault her life was a mess, or that she was emotionally vulnerable. And heck, perhaps when all the murder suspect crap went away, she might realize it wasn't really love, just her drowning in problems and reaching out for a life preserver—needing someone to hold on to. And even with no promises for tomorrow, he was excellent at being a preserver.

And that night, after they'd made love, she rolled over and said, "Don't you think it's time I go home?"

"Nikki, I think in less than a week, I'll have Andrew Brian behind bars. Give me that time. Stay here. Can't we just enjoy this? Pretend we're on vacation or something."

"And after vacation we go back to a normal life?" She waited for him to define normal.

His hand came to rest on her shoulder. "Actually, I'd like you to find a different place to live. Your apartment's a dump. If I'm not going to be around, I want to know you're safe."

So he isn't going to be around. "Safe is important."

She put her head on his chest and tried not to start missing him already.

Later that morning, Dallas watched Nikki drive off and couldn't fight the dread pulling at his gut. And not because she might be in physical danger. Nance was meeting her at the gallery again, and Dallas planned to stop by every few hours, plus Tony had patrol cars driving by regularly. More important, Andrew Brian was going to be busy answering Tony's questions. Nope, it wasn't the danger that worried Dallas. It was more. The way she kissed him and even the way she'd made love last night. As if her heart wasn't in it.

She swore nothing was wrong, but hell, he could see it in her eyes. What had he done? Or not done? But friggin' hell, he liked Nikki. And the thought of her pulling away after having her close these last few days and making him happier than he'd been in forever, was a real kick in the balls.

He continued to watch Nikki's car get smaller. Then a realization took another swing at him. What the hell did he want? Wasn't it two days ago that he was frightened about where things were leading? Now he was worried about where they wouldn't lead. But shit, he was one fucked-up mess. Running a palm over his face, he knew he needed to figure some things out.

He shot off and went into the office to join Tyler and Austin for their daily meeting. Snagging another cup of coffee, he said, "Let's hurry this. I've got a busy day."

"Somebody's in a nasty mood. What, you didn't get any this morning?" Austin asked.

Dallas slammed his cup down so hard, half his coffee

sloshed onto the counter. He swung around. "Don't start that shit!"

Austin held up a hand. "Sorry. I..."

Tyler leaned back in his chair. "You aren't going to like what I have to tell you, either."

"Then don't tell me." Dallas felt like an ass, but was unable to stop himself.

"It's about Roberto," Tyler said.

"Tell me," Dallas said, trying to get his bad mood in check.

"The lead he was chasing wasn't DeLuna."

"And it cost us how much to find this out?" Dallas asked.

"He's bringing all but five hundred of it back."

"You sure he's not just playing us?" Austin asked.

"I trust him," Tyler said.

"Me, too," Dallas added, and his bad mood slipped another notch.

"Do you think this means DeLuna's pulled out of the Houston area?" Tyler asked.

"No," Dallas said.

"Do you think he already knows we were behind the last three shutdowns?"

"I wish," Dallas said. "But those operations were small time. Maybe he suspects he has a snitch. He'll show up. Shit like him never completely disappears. It might be a month or two, but he won't stay hidden too long."

They all seemed to take a minute to adjust to the disappointment of losing their lead on the man responsible for their prison time. Tyler spoke first. "When's your brother going to let you know what Detective Shane's doing?"

"I talked to him earlier this morning." A sense of

accomplishment wiggled into Dallas's mood. "Shane called him last night wanting to know the name and contact info for the witness who's willing to testify she was with Nance at the park. Tony thinks he's going to use this to dismiss the charges. He asked us to wait until tomorrow. I told him that was our cutoff date. If we hadn't heard anything at four that afternoon, we were taking it to the press. Tony assured me Shane is doing the right thing."

"You believe him?" Austin asked.

"Yeah, I do. I think we actually own this one."

"Well, damn!" Tyler let out a whoop.

"If this happens, we should celebrate," Austin said. "This will be our first case where we really save someone's ass from being wrongly convicted."

"We will," Dallas said. Would Nikki be around to celebrate with him? Shit. He hoped they'd be celebrating Nikki being let off the suspect list soon as well.

"Let's shift gears for a sec," Dallas said. "I went looking for the busboy yesterday. No one was home. I asked the neighbors and—"

"And they told you he must be on vacation, right? I went there four times over the weekend," Austin said.

Tyler opened a file. "I spent the weekend trying to break into Brian and Sterns files and searching for info on Andrew Brian. The firm obviously has a better computer system than they do phones. However, local rehabs don't. I found out Brian checked into a Cypress rehab two years ago."

"So Rachel Peterson was telling the truth." Dallas chewed on the new information.

Austin tapped a pencil on his desk. "I also went back to Jack Leon's place. According to a chatty neighbor, Leon liked blondes. She swears he had a blonde over a couple of weeks ago. She saw them jogging in the park. Unfortunately, she suggested that it was his ex-wife who killed him. I asked for a description and she said blond, fit and pretty. She said she'd seen the picture of the ex in the paper and thought it was her."

"It wasn't Nikki," Dallas said.

"I know, but if Tony finds this neighbor in the same chatty mood, she might tell him the same thing. I'm just telling you what I found."

"Looks as if I'm the only one who got lucky over the weekend," Tyler said, sounding proud of himself.

"Oh, hell, no," Austin chimed in. "I visited my nurse again and we know what Dallas was doing."

"I mean with the case," Tyler said. "I spent time looking at the flash drive. It belonged to Leon. I found a few deleted files, nothing of interest. But I found out that data on the flash drive had been downloaded on Tuesday. The day before Leon was killed."

"And the day Rachel Peterson heard Leon and Brian fighting," Dallas said.

"Right," Tyler confirmed.

Dallas tapped a pen on the desk. "I gave this some thought over the weekend. If we still don't have anything on the busboy by this afternoon, maybe we should give Tony the info. He might be able to find something we can't. But what I'd like to do is have a long talk with the senior partner, Sterns. Lay it on the table. Tell him I have proof someone was embezzling. He may just be curious enough to work with us."

"If you could get me into the office, I could probably tell him which computer this information was downloaded from."

"Good idea. I'll make that part of my pitch." Dallas stood up. "You know computer forensics should have been your specialty."

"That's boring. I gotta shoot at someone every now and then." Tyler grinned.

"Well if you feel the urge, make it Andrew Brian. I think he's our bad guy." Dallas raked a hand through his hair. "But add this question to your list," he told Tyler. "What's the connection between our busboy and Andrew Brian? If the busboy is involved—and at this point, I think he is—there has to be a connection. And we have to find it."

Nikki stopped by the hospital on her way to the gallery. LeAnn was in Ellen's room, checking on her. Ellen was better, bored senseless but, because of a slight fever, they wanted to keep her another day. Glaring at LeAnn, who stood at the foot of her bed, Ellen reached out and grabbed Nikki's hand.

"Please break me out of this place. I hate the white walls, the smell, the food."

Nikki pulled out a book she'd brought. "I brought you some entertainment."

"I hope it's hot. I swear I'm still feeling the residual effects of the morphine."

Nikki laughed and glanced at LeAnn. "How are you doing?"

"I'm...coping." LeAnn fit a blood pressure cuff on Ellen's arm.

"Is Tony still staying at your place?" Nikki asked.

"Didn't you hear? His apartment is overrun with bedbugs."

"Really?" Nikki grinned.

"Bedbugs?" Ellen asked.

"It's a boldfaced lie," LeAnn said.

"Hmm, I wonder why he's lying?" Nikki asked.

Ellen cleared her throat. "Why is it I feel as if I've missed out on something?"

Nikki looked at LeAnn. "Can I tell her?"

"Tell me what?" Ellen asked.

"Oh, hell, why not?" LeAnn said. "Maybe she'll stop telling me how gorgeous he is."

"Okay, now I'm really lost." Ellen sat up.

Nikki grinned. "Tony is LeAnn's husband."

"We're separated," LeAnn said. "Or we used to be. I don't know what we are now. Except flustered. The man walks around practically naked. It's...bad. Really, really bad."

"I'll bet," Nikki teased her.

Ellen flipped her focus from LeAnn to Nikki. "Who the hell is Tony?"

"Detective O'Connor," Nikki explained.

"You mean the hot detective?" Ellen grinned at LeAnn. "Oops."

"That's him," Nikki said.

"Oh, my." Ellen looked at LeAnn. "I can see why you're flustered. Wait. I didn't hit on him the other day, did I?"

LeAnn chuckled. "That was Dallas. And Nikki might have a thing or two to say about that."

Ellen stared at Nikki. "Who's Dallas?"

"Tony's brother," Nikki said.

"How did you meet—"

"Dallas is the PI who's working my case. You met

him," Nikki explained. But she hadn't told Ellen the details because she didn't want her worrying.

"That's not all he's helping you with," LeAnn said. "Or are you sleeping on his pink sofa?" When Nikki shot LeAnn a frown, she said, "Hey, you said you were going to tell her. I figured that meant everything."

Ellen's eyes widened. "Why, Nikki Hunt, are you staying at his place?"

"Someone broke into my apartment. Dallas thinks they might come back."

"Really?" She studied Nikki with laser-sharp green eyes. "Are you letting him take advantage of you and use you for his personal little bang toy?"

Nikki blushed. "Well, I..."

"Hot damn!" Ellen punched a hand in the air. "It's about time."

They all laughed. The ringing of LeAnn's phone brought a frown to her lips. "I'm being paged. Darn it, I know I'm gonna miss the best part, too." She grinned and walked out.

As the door closed, Ellen looked at Nikki and her smile faded. "Why am I just now hearing this?"

"You've had other things to worry about."

"Worry? I'm pissed you didn't give me the details of how good the sex is," Ellen said.

Nikki laughed then bit down on her lip. "It's crazy."

"The sex is crazy?"

Nikki smiled. "That, too. I'm scared. He's wonderful and, as corny as it sounds, he completes me. He makes me laugh, gets my jokes and...he eats French fries with his fingers."

"Wow. His fingers?" She laughed. "So what's scary?"

"I'm a breath away from falling in love with him. He

told me up front he wanted to take it a day at a time. I don't think he's what you would call a relationship person."

"But you're staying at his house. That doesn't sound like he's too scared."

"Only because he thinks someone is out to kill me. He even told me he wasn't asking for forever. And that this is like a vacation. It's temporary. I'm gonna get my heart broken, Ellen."

Ellen studied her. "You know what's really throwing me for a loop? You're more worried about your heart being broken than you are that someone might be trying to kill you—and let's not forget you're still the main suspect in a murder investigation."

Nikki dropped into a chair. "I'm worried about it all," she confessed. "But, I can't seem to do anything about the first two. Seriously, I can't believe they can blame his death on me. I didn't do it. Surely the evidence will prove that."

After another second Nikki continued. "I guess I'm trying to concentrate on the things I can change, the things that are in my control. And if I could walk away right now and save myself from pain."

"And what if he's right and someone *is* trying to kill you? It could be the same person who did this to me."

"I have Mace." Nikki looked at her best friend. "I'm sorry this happened to you."

Ellen frowned. "I'm fine now. It's you who could be in danger."

"Don't worry, I'm going to be careful."

The sounds of someone paging a doctor filled the room. Ellen continued to stare at Nikki. "About this guy. Maybe you shouldn't be so quick to...jump to conclusions. What if you walk away and it turns out he's just slow on the commitment thing?"

"What's the chance of that being true?" Tears tightened Nikki's throat, but she wasn't about to let them show. Ellen had all the whining rights. If anyone should be shedding tears right now, it should be her.

"I may be overstepping my bounds here, but I'm not certain he's the only one with commitment problems."

"That's not true." The room went silent for a several minutes. It wasn't true, Nikki told herself. Sure she was scared and hesitant, maybe she had a bad habit of looking for potholes like Nana said, but she wasn't commitment phobic.

Was she?

Ellen took Nikki's hand in hers. "Okay, I'm done acting like my mom. You have to do what you think is right. And you know if you really need a place to stay, you could go stay at my parents' house."

"Thanks," Nikki said, and somehow she suspected that Ellen's parents would honestly take her in. Not that she would go, but it was nice to have the option.

"What are you going to do?" Ellen asked.

"I don't know," Nikki said. "I really don't know. But I'll be fine." And she wished she could believe that with more conviction.

CHAPTER TWENTY-NINE

"YOU WANT ME TO do what?" Henry Sterns asked Dallas. "Turn my computer systems over to a stranger? Do you take me for a fool?" He waved a hand at Tyler, who sat quietly beside Dallas in a leather chair.

Sterns was in his early sixties, balding, about fifty pounds overweight and, if his red face was any indication, he suffered from high blood pressure.

"No," Dallas replied. "I took you for a smart man. If someone said they thought someone was stealing from me and had proof, I'd be interested in seeing it."

"Show me what you got."

"Sorry. It doesn't work that way."

"You think Jack Leon was stealing from me?" Sterns snapped.

"I didn't say that," Dallas said.

"Then what the hell *are* you saying?"

"We're saying someone in your office is stealing from you," Tyler chimed in.

"Who?" Sterns demanded.

"To answer that I'll need access to your computers," Tyler said.

"And you think this has something to do with Jack's murder?"

"Yes," Tyler and Dallas answered at the same time.

"How do I know you're not here to rob me blind?"

"By just having access to your computer?" Dallas asked.

"Oh, I could do it," Tyler said.

Dallas shot him a what-the-hell look, but he didn't flinch.

"But that's not my plan. We're here to help someone," Tyler said.

"Who?"

"Nikki Hunt," Tyler answered.

"Jack's ex?" Sterns asked.

Dallas nodded. "Yes."

"Look, I don't think she did it, but I can't turn over my computers to you without talking to someone."

"Then talk." Dallas passed him a business card then stood up. He and Tyler left the man to think over their offer.

As they walked out of Sterns's office, Rachel Peterson stepped in front of them. She looked angry, and ready to bench-press a couple hundred pounds, which was about how much Dallas weighed.

"Is this him?" she asked.

Oh shit.

"Is this your boyfriend?" Rachel demanded.

Tyler's mouth fell open. "Say what?"

Dallas answered, "I never said that. You assumed—"

"What?" she asked Tyler. "You haven't come out of the closet yet?"

"Oh, honey," Tyler said, getting into the story. "I came out of the closet, but sometimes I like to take this sweet hunk of man back into the closet. You wouldn't believe the toys I keep in there." He gave Dallas's butt a quick smack, and then dragged him away from Rachel.

As they walked outside, Dallas looked at Tyler. "I'll give you a thousand dollars to never repeat that. But if you do tell anyone you touched my ass, I will shoot you."

"Please," Tyler said. "You know me better than that." Reaching the car, Tyler continued, "It would have to at least be ten thousand. And you might as well load your gun."

Monday evening Tony watched LeAnn walk out of the kitchen with a lump of disappointment in his gut. Every night they ate dinner together, laughed, and talked about their day. She'd even started helping with the dishes.

And then she'd leave him.

It hadn't stopped him from trying, though. Every night, he'd use the shower, ask her to join him, but she never did. As he tossed the dish towel on the counter, he heard a door open.

He turned, hope filling him. "Change your mind about..." His heart stopped. Somewhere between his brain and lips the words got lost.

"Change my mind about what?" She sounded completely innocent—as if she wasn't standing there wearing nothing but a towel. As if her hair wasn't hanging around her bare shoulders, as if the towel didn't give him a generous view of her cleavage.

"About..." His gaze lowered. The slit came way above her thigh. He swallowed, and let himself enjoy the view. "About a movie."

"Nah, I'm taking a bath." She walked past and grabbed a wineglass. "Wine and a bubble bath."

His pulse doubled. She smiled and walked away. He stood there like a fool and watched her leave. Why hadn't he made a move? Tried to kiss her? Told her she looked sexy?

But damn. It had been so long since he'd seen that much of LeAnn's skin. He missed her skin. More than skin, he'd missed that smile. Missed the flirty way she looked at him. He suddenly realized what he hadn't seen just now on his wife's face. He hadn't seen the pain, the constant grief that had filled her eyes for so long. Were they finally moving on? Hope so intense that it almost hurt swelled in his chest.

He walked to the bathroom door and heard the water running. He smelled the scented bubble bath she used. His mind went back to the skin. He knocked. "Need someone to wash your back?"

"Nah. But thanks for the offer."

He leaned his forehead on the wood door that wasn't nearly as hard as he was. Then he grinned. Okay, so LeAnn wasn't quite ready for sex, but not only was she on to his game, she was playing right along with him. And that had to be good news.

"Bring it on, baby," he whispered. "Bring it on."

Later that night, Dallas watched Nikki get up and head toward his bedroom. What had seemed like a brilliant idea now suddenly felt foolish. A desperate attempt to fix something when he didn't even know what the hell was wrong.

She came to a sudden stop at his bedroom door and glanced back at him. "You do this?"

"Would you believe me if I said I opened the window and they just blew inside?"

She grinned as he approached her. "I've never made love on rose petals."

"I read it in a magazine and I thought…"

"It's sweet." She turned and kissed him, but it ended too fast.

He ran a finger across her wet lips. "What's going on inside that head of yours?"

"Nothing," she said.

He couldn't force her to tell him. And he didn't know what to say to change something he didn't understand. So he did what he did best. He undressed her, laid her back on the bed and brushed a rose petal over every inch of her soft skin.

When she came the first time, she called out his name, and that, Dallas decided, was the sweetest sound in the world.

Tuesday afternoon Dallas was at the gallery with Nance and Nikki when Tony walked in. Dallas saw Nikki look up and for a second she looked scared.

"It's okay," he whispered in her ear. "I think he's here with good news about Nance." He felt her relax against him and when she leaned on him, it felt so damn good. For some crazy reason, he recalled his dad telling him the thing he missed most about losing Dallas's mom was the feeling of her leaning on him. He said her weight balanced out his life. That without her occasional weight against him, he didn't feel grounded. At the time, Dallas thought it had been a sappy thing to say. Not anymore.

Dallas looked at Nance who now wore the expression

Nikki had moments earlier. Then Tony smiled and Nance's shoulders relaxed.

"How you doing, kid?" Tony asked.

"I've been better," Nance replied hesitantly.

"What if I told you it was over? All charges dropped."

Nance looked at Dallas. "Is he for real?"

Dallas nodded.

"Oh, damn!" Nance swung around and grabbed Nikki in a big bear hug.

Dallas watched the two embrace. "Remember, she's mine."

Nikki smiled and, for a flicker of a second, she looked at him without reservation.

"I do the work and she reaps the rewards," Dallas said to Tony.

"What's wrong?" Nance asked when he released Nikki. "You're jealous? You want a hug? Come here. Hell, I could kiss you for what you've done. But I'm not slapping you on the ass like Tyler did."

Dallas held out his hand. "A handshake will do."

"Whoa," Tony said. "Tyler slapped Dallas's ass? First a pink sofa and now this."

"He used the gay card to get out of sleeping with someone," Nance said.

"Did not. She assumed it. I just let her assume."

Nikki laughed. "I'll attest to Dallas's masculinity."

Dallas pulled her against him. "Thank you."

Nikki looked at his brother. "Maybe you're not so bad, after all."

Tony grinned. "I've been thinking the same thing about you."

Later, when Dallas walked Tony to his car, Tony's

body language changed. "I thought we were working together on the Leon case. On the same side—isn't that the way you put it?"

"We are."

"So would you like to share with me what you're hoping to find on Brian and Sterns computers? Mr. Sterns mentioned it during his interview."

"I was going to tell you if I hadn't heard anything by this afternoon." Dallas explained about the disk.

"Christ. I could've had those computers yanked yesterday."

"And they'd go into your CSU unit for a month before any one got to them. You know I'm right."

Tony's grimaced. "You could have told me."

"I told you about the busboy," Dallas said. "Have you located him yet?"

"No."

"Have you tried?"

"I sent a guy out. But that's not a viable lead. That kid probably just up and quit. We have no connection between him and Brian."

Dallas knew his brother had a point, but his gut said differently. "Did you question Brian?"

"Yeah. He swears he's innocent. Says he never left the office that night."

"And you believe him?"

"No, but I need to prove it. The Leons are getting impatient. They visited my boss yesterday."

"You can't arrest Nikki with other leads still pending."

"I still have two people willing to testify she told them she was going to kill him." Tony sighed. "I'm going to fight this. I've already pissed off my boss over it. But I need something concrete." Tony pulled out his keys. "Are things serious between you two?"

"Define 'serious.'"

"Dad thinks you're as good as married," Tony said.

"Married? Hell, no. Did that once. Didn't care for it."

"That was Serena." Tony opened his car door.

"Believe me, I know the difference. Nikki and I... we're good together. I like her... a lot. And if I can convince her, she'll be around for a long time."

"Convince her?" Tony asked. "What's wrong?"

"Nothing wrong," Dallas said. "We're just... just in this weird relationship place."

"Maybe because you can't admit what you want."

"I know what I want." And he did. He'd spent a lot of time thinking about it these last few days. He'd finally made sense of it all.

"And what do you want?"

"For her to stick around a while."

"Wow, with an invite like that I don't see why she's isn't chomping at the bit to say yes."

"What's that supposed to mean?" Dallas asked.

Tony just looked at him. "Not a damn thing. Good luck, brother." He got into his car.

"Everything is going to be fine," Dallas said. He watched his brother drive off and then reached up and touched his eyebrow, which kept jumping up and down. "Shit!" he muttered, wondering what his fucking eyebrow knew that he didn't.

The next day, Nikki poured herself a cup of coffee. Dallas was getting dressed to go to the cemetery for his mom's birthday. Dallas hadn't asked her to go. She

respected that this was a private event, but it was another
clue she longed to be a bigger part of Dallas's life than he
wanted.

Nursing her cup of coffee, petting Bud with her foot,
she tried to figure out her exit strategy. A knock came
on the door. She opened the door and Tyler stormed in,
picked her up and swung her around in his arms.

"I'm so damn good," he said.

Nikki laughed. "I don't think I can attest to that."

"Good thing, too, or you'd dump the gay guy with the
pink sofa."

Nikki laughed. When she'd first heard the story, she'd
felt jealous that another woman had approached Dallas.
Though it felt good that he'd turned her down, she and
Dallas didn't even have an exclusive agreement. Wasn't
that her number-one rule? Get an exclusive before sleeping with a guy? How did things move from puking on the
guy to being a breath away from blurting out "I love you"
when they made love?

Pretend we're on vacation or something. His words
played in her head. Vacations were fabulous, but temporary. Vacations always ended.

"So exactly how are you good?" Nikki asked, shoving
her problems aside.

"I don't care how good he is. He needs his own
woman." Dallas moved in from the bedroom.

Nikki looked over her shoulder at Dallas. "Tyler has
good news."

Dallas smiled, but he eyed Tyler's hands at her waist
with what looked like jealousy. Would a guy who didn't
want an exclusive be jealous?

Maybe she should stop guessing and start asking.

Soon, she promised herself. Instantly, she heard Ellen's voice of warning. *I'm not so certain he's the only one with a commitment problem.* Was Ellen right?

Tyler must have noted Dallas's look, too, because he dropped his hands from her waist. "Hey, I'm the one who should be jealous. You just up and went straight on my ass."

"Don't you think that story stopped being funny the third time you told it?" Dallas asked.

"I'm still laughing at it." Dallas's dad walked through the door.

Dallas nodded a quick greeting at his dad, whose phone rang, so he stepped back into the hall.

Watching his dad leave, Dallas frowned at Tyler. "Is there anyone in the state of Texas you haven't told?"

"If so, it wasn't intentional," Tyler said.

Dallas, in navy slacks and button-down light blue oxford shirt, turned Nikki's heart into a big gooey pile of emotion. How long could she let this vacation last? Was it wrong for her to draw it out?

"What's the news?" Dallas asked Tyler. "Did Sterns call and want us to check the computers?"

"Nope," Tyler said.

"Then what?" Dallas hooked a hand around Nikki's waist. It felt good to be close.

"I found the connection between the busboy and Andrew Brian."

"And?" Dallas asked.

"Drugs," Tyler said. "That's the thing they both had in common. I researched to see if the busboy and he attended the same AA meeting or rehab. I knew they traveled in different circles, but AA groups aren't class subjective."

"So they were in the same AA group?"

"Nope. That came up empty."

"So?" Dallas asked.

"I remembered that Andrew was new to Brian and Sterns. He worked for a small firm, Godfrey Law. I checked the public records and found out that busboy's drug case was handled by none other than—"

"Godfrey Law," Dallas and Nikki said at the same time.

"Nope." Tyler grinned. "I was very disappointed, too."

"You're losing me," Dallas said.

"Hell, I stay lost," Dallas's father said, walking back into the room.

Tyler continued, "He received free services from a nonprofit anti-gang group called Freedom."

Dallas shifted, obviously impatient. "The point?"

"Brian Senior is committed to the organization and he's twisted his son's arm to handle a few cases pro bono. The busboy's case was one of them."

Dallas picked Nikki up and kissed her. "I think we may have just cleared your name."

Five minutes later, after a mini-celebration, Dallas and his dad started out for the cemetery. Mr. O'Connor looked back at Nikki. "You're not coming with us?"

Nikki saw Dallas look at her in something that looked like surprise and then he said, "If Nikki would like to come, she's welcome."

"No," she said. "It's a private party." Besides, she had some serious thinking to do.

Thirty minutes later, dressed, and still unable to think, Nikki stopped by the office and waved good-bye to Austin and Tyler. "See you later."

"Be careful," they chimed out together.

Nikki went to give Bud, resting in the casket, a good-bye pat.

The front door opened. Nikki looked up, and stumbled back. Andrew Brian stood there staring down at her and he didn't look any happier to see her than she was to see him.

CHAPTER THIRTY

DALLAS SWALLOWED HARD. They stood in front of the gravestone, Tony on one side of his father and Dallas on the other.

"I sometimes talk to her when I come here," his dad said, his voice hoarse. "I know she's not really here, but..." He drew in a deep shaky breath. "I miss her so much."

"We all do." Dallas's own voice sounded strained.

His dad moved forward and placed the roses on top of the grave. When he stood up, he looked at his sons. "She loved you both so much. She said you were the best things she ever did."

"She was a hell of a mom." Tony passed a hand over his face.

Dallas's breath caught. "I'd give anything if she'd known that...that I was exonerated."

"She knew you would be," his dad said. "The day before she passed, she told me that she'd had a talk with someone..." He pointed to the sky. "Someone upstairs and He told her you were gonna be fine."

Dallas smiled and tears filled his eyes when he looked at his dad. "You picked us a damn good mom, old man."

"I did, didn't I?" He smiled and pressed his fingers to his lips. Taking a few steps, he pressed those fingers to the stone. "Love you, sweetheart. Happy birthday."

Dallas put a hand on his dad's shoulder. "You know, Dad, Mom wouldn't want to think you weren't taking care of yourself. Or that you weren't living life."

His father shook his head. "I know, and I'm working on it." He ran a hand over his face, then stared at Dallas. "Can you tell me you're doing the same?"

"I'm fine," Dallas said.

"I'll admit you've been happier these last few weeks than you have in months. But..."

"But what?" Dallas asked.

"Pull your head out of the sand."

"My head's not in the sand."

His dad shrugged and dropped his hands in his pockets. "Hold on to her, son. You'll regret it if you don't."

Dallas opened his mouth to argue, but didn't know what to say. Shit. His head wasn't in the sand. He knew what he wanted now. Why the hell did everyone keep saying he didn't?

His dad glanced at Tony. "We've all hit a rough spot. Thank God O'Connors are made of steel."

"Yeah." Tony's gaze shifted to the right, where Dallas knew his little girl was buried. "I'm going to go take a walk."

"Yeah," Dallas said and while he didn't want to rush his dad, Dallas ached to get back to Nikki.

*   *   *

Austin, looking panicked, met Dallas at the door to the office a short while later. "Andrew Brain is in the conference room with Tyler."

"What?"

"Yeah, it's fucked up. He wants to hire us to prove that he didn't do this murder."

"Where's Nikki?" Dallas asked.

"She left for the gallery. She was shaken when she saw him. But she's tough."

"She's not that tough." Dallas pulled out his phone and Austin walked away.

She answered on the first ring. "What does he want with you?" she demanded.

"Don't know yet. I wanted to make sure you're okay."

"I'm fine. Nance is here." She paused. "How did things go at the cemetery?" she asked.

He wanted to kick himself again for not inviting her. "Good. Thanks for talking me into going."

"You're welcome."

"Look, I'll call when I know something about Brian." He started to hang up, but paused, "Nikki…" He heard his old man's words. *Hold on to her, son. You'll regret it if you don't.*

"Yes?"

"I miss you."

"Me, too," she said, but it took her a long time to say it.

Getting off the line, feeling as if he'd screwed up again, he took off to talk to Brian.

"I didn't kill anyone," Brian's patience already seemed to be failing him and Dallas had just gotten started.

"What brought you to our door?" Dallas's own patience was in short supply, too.

"Sterns had you checked out. I read the report. It said you specialized in wrongly accused cases and I'm being wrongly accused."

"There's just one problem," Dallas said. "We're already working this case."

"So you're trying to pin it on me? Is that what you're saying?" Brian looked at Tyler sitting on the other side of the table.

"Goes back to the duck story," Dallas said. "If it walks like a duck, talks like—"

Brian slammed his hand on the desk. "I didn't kill Jack."

Dallas kept pushing the guy, hoping he'd crater. "Do you deny knowing Jose Garcia?"

The man's face went white. Oh, yeah, he was guilty. Dallas couldn't wait to hand him over to Tony.

"I didn't do it. Fuck!" He took several deep breaths. "If I tell you the truth, can you help me?"

"That depends on what the truth is," Tyler said.

Brian hesitated. "I knew Garcia."

"And you gave the kid the stuff to put in Jack Leon's soup, didn't you?"

"Yes, but it wouldn't have killed him."

"Did Leon discover you were cooking the books? Is that what happened?"

The man grew paler still. "I told him I was going to pay it back."

"What is it? Cocaine?" The muscles in Dallas's jaw tightened.

"At first, yes. But I stopped using. I hired this man

to...help me. He helped me kick the habit six weeks ago, but then he came back and said I had to pay him or he'd tell my dad. I took the money one more time. Jack found out. I tried to explain, but he wouldn't listen. I thought if I...threatened him, he'd back off. All I wanted was a chance to pay back the money. I've done some bad things but stealing from my dad's firm was the worst. I just wanted a chance to fix it."

"But he refused and that's when you decided to kill him, right?"

"No!"

"You broke into Nikki Hunt's apartment," Dallas accused.

"Jack had the information on a flash drive. I knew he'd seen her, so yes, I went looking for it. But I didn't kill Jack and I didn't attack anyone at that gallery. I'll take a polygraph, whatever, but I'm not going down for this." Brian shot his gaze to Tyler. "What do I do? How can I prove I'm innocent?"

Dallas folded his arms over his chest. He didn't believe Brian. "For starters, you turn yourself in."

"If I tell them about the money, they'll think I killed Jack."

"They already know. I handed all the evidence I have to my brother over an hour ago. He's probably already sent a squad car over to arrest you."

"Fuck!" Brian shot to his feet.

"Turn yourself in," Dallas said. "You'll look less guilty. Then get your daddy to find you a good lawyer."

"What about you guys? Will you help me?"

Before Dallas could say, "Hell no," Tyler said, "We'll look into it."

Dallas glared at Tyler. What the hell was he thinking? Then he saw it in his friend's eyes. Tyler believed Brian.

"It's really over?" Nikki asked Dallas that evening as she sipped from a glass of champagne. The cold bubbles danced on her tongue.

"You're officially off the suspect list, Ms. Hunt." He pulled her against him and kissed her so softly that she leaned into him and let herself enjoy being close. She'd planned on coming here, gathering her things and going home. Not angrily, not to call it quits, not even for a time-out. She just needed a slow down. Time to regroup her emotions.

"I figured we'd celebrate privately tonight." He ran his palm up her arm. "But tomorrow night, I thought we would take Nance and his grandmother, Tyler, Austin—hell, invite the Ol' Timers group, and let's all go out to eat."

"That would be fun." Nikki rethought her plans. Maybe she'd stay tonight. One last night. Bud came over and dropped at her feet, whining for her attention.

"She's mine tonight," Dallas told Bud and started swaying as if to a slow song. "You know, I've never danced with you. You like to dance?"

"Yeah," she said.

"How about I take you dancing one night? You can get all sexy, wear some of your colored underwear under something slinky and short and low." He ran his hand over the top of her breasts. "Drive me crazy all night."

"I'd like that." She brushed her free hand over his chest. "Thank you."

"For what?"

"For getting me off the suspect list."

"Oh, yeah. How does it feel?" He undid the top button on her blouse and they swayed ever so softly.

"Good," she said, unable to think about much more than his hands caressing her breasts. Then his thigh moved between her legs and she thought about that.

He undid another button. "Just good?"

She grinned and set her glass on a nearby table. "I had faith in you."

"That's nice. Have you ever slow danced naked?"

"I don't think I have."

"It's a lot of fun." He undid the last button on her blouse and slid it off her shoulders.

"You're going to have to pick out the artwork you earned."

"That's right, you owe me. Wanna barter for something else?" The edges of his eyes crinkled with a smile

"I'm serious."

"I told you what I want. The bust of you."

"You should take a painting."

"I want the bust. I like your bust." He undid her bra. Her breasts spilled out. "I really like your bust." He stopped dancing and slipped his finger in his mouth and then painted her nipple with cool wetness.

"Okay, take the bust," she said breathlessly, as her bra slid to the floor, "but . . . you get a painting, too."

"Fine." He undid her pants.

"It's only four in the afternoon," she said.

"Is there a four o'clock rule about sex?"

"No, but . . ." He slipped his hand inside her pants, under her panties and into the folds of her sex.

"But what?" He moved his finger deeper.

"I lost my train of thought."

"Then think about this." His finger moved deeper.

A loud bang on the door made Nikki jump.

"Dallas!" Tyler called out from behind the door.

Nikki pulled his hand out of her pants. "Maybe we should..."

"Not now!" Dallas yelled.

"Someone's here," Tyler said. "I think..."

Nikki snatched up her bra and top.

"Tell them to go away," Dallas called out.

"Take care of it," Nikki told him and smiled. "We can pick up later."

"Dallas?" a female voice called out.

Nikki looked at Dallas and saw his expression harden. "Who is it?" she asked.

"My ex."

"Oh." Nikki covered her breasts. "I should..." She motioned toward the bathroom and, at his nod, she hurried off.

After dressing, Nikki stood by the bathroom door, unsure if she should stay hidden, or go out. Oh hell. It wasn't as if Dallas was married. She didn't have anything to feel guilty about and she was curious to meet the woman Dallas had obviously loved at one time.

Opening the door, she heard Dallas say, "Yes, it's a pink sofa—so the hell what?"

"You told my lawyer you'd sign the papers," a woman said.

"You don't even like the dog. Why are you doing this? To make me miserable?"

"I like the dog."

Nikki bit her lip and remembered what LeAnn had said about Dallas's ex. Classy, pretty. And that Dallas had thought the sun rose and set on her. Jealousy tingled in Nikki's chest.

"Bullshit! He's been begging to be petted since you got here, and you haven't even acknowledged him."

"Fine," she said. "Maybe it's not the dog I want. I want you."

Wow! Nikki took a deep gulp of air and consider going back into the bathroom.

"You have to be fucking kidding," Dallas said. "You're engaged to another man."

"I'll break it off," she said. "We were good together, Dallas."

Nikki stayed where she was. Maybe she needed to hear this. In her head she heard Nana say, *If you keep looking for bad things, sooner or later, you'll find them.* She started to go back into the bathroom.

"No, we were not," Dallas countered. Nikki hesitated and listened. Not that she was looking for trouble or pot-holes, but . . .

"The sex is still good." Her voice went sultry. "We proved that."

Nikki's breath caught. Mentally she felt herself fall face-first into a pothole so big she didn't know if she could ever pull herself out of it. *They proved it?* When had they proved it?

Nikki's heart started racing and she flashbacked to walking into her office and finding Jack and her employee going at it. Hadn't Dallas told her it was over with his ex?

"Leave, Serena."

"Is that champagne? You have company, don't you?"

"Yes, and I'd like for you to get the hell out."

* * *

Dallas dropped onto his pink sofa and waited for Nikki to come out of the bathroom. He would have gone looking for her, but he was just so damn mad. Seeing Serena did that to him. She made him feel...betrayed. She brought back all the bitterness that had consumed him during his time in prison.

He breathed in. He breathed out. Realizing Nikki probably thought she was still here, he stood up and went to the end of the hall. "Nikki?" he called.

Nikki yanked open the bathroom door. She looked at him with blue fire in her eyes, fire that expressed both anger and hurt.

He stepped out of her way. "I'm sorry," he bit out, still trying to turn off his own emotional storm and unsure what hers was about. Then it hit. She'd heard Serena. Christ! *The sex's still good. We proved that.* Did she think he'd been with Serena since he'd met her?

"Whatever you're thinking, you're wrong," he said.

Her chin tilted up. "You said it was over between you."

"It is. Did that sound like sweet talk to you?"

She blinked and he could swear she'd been crying. "You said it was over when she divorced you."

"It was."

"So she lied about you two having sex?"

He ran a hand through his hair. "It happened once. Six months ago. I was drunk. It was a one-time mistake."

She dropped into his living room chair. He sank down in the pink leather sofa. "You can't be mad about this."

"I'm not. But it shows how little we know about each other."

"We're working on that," he said, somehow sensing

this wasn't just about Serena, but about what had bee
bothering her for the last few days.

"It's all happened so fast and..." A tear slipped fro
the corner of her eye.

"Hey." He went and knelt in front of her. "What
wrong with fast?"

"I need to move back home."

"I know that...eventually." His words came out easi
enough, but they seemed to hang in the air and he wishe
he could yank them back. *Hold on to her, son. You
regret it if you don't.*

"It's not supposed to work that way." Another te:
slipped out and she wiped that away before he could c
it for her.

"What's not supposed to work that way?"

"You're supposed to meet someone and eventuall
move in with them, not move in with them and eventuall
move out."

"What are you saying?" His breath seemed caught i
his lungs and a storm of emotions raged in his chest.

She gazed steadily at him. "After we have dinner wit
everyone tomorrow, I'll go home."

"Okay...," he said, finding complete relief that sl
wasn't walking away right now. And who knew, by tomo
row he could change her mind and talk her into hangin
around for while. He leaned in and kissed her. "In th
meantime, why don't we..." *pick up where we left of*
Something warned him she wasn't in the mood for th.
anymore. "Why don't we go dancing tonight?" He'd g
her in the mood slowly.

She touched his cheek. "No more surprises like thi
right?"

"No more." But as soon as he said it, he realized she meant no more surprises like learning he'd slept with his ex. That made him think of Suzan. He started to tell her, but saw the doubt in her eyes and he didn't want to add more.

Hold on to her, son. You'll regret it if you don't. Again his dad's words played in his head.

"What do you say? Go out on a date with me. Dinner...dancing?"

The smell of Chinese food greeted Tony when he opened the door that evening. LeAnn had said she'd do dinner since she didn't have to work. He grinned. Her idea of "doing dinner" had almost always consisted of ordering in. Not that he minded. She'd once told him she'd had to cook all her childhood due to the lack of a mom, and she'd decided she needed about ten years of ordering in to make up for it.

He'd give her twenty, or more. He'd give whatever she wanted.

Being home with LeAnn was heaven...and hell. Every night she teased him a little more. Her towels were getting shorter, worn lower, and every night he went to bed with a hard-on that could hammer nails. While he'd come within a breath of making a move, his gut told him she needed to take that first step. It didn't have to be a big step, it could be just a tiny one, and he'd be there with her.

"I'm home," he called out and purposely pushed the whole cemetery experience from his mind.

"Be right out," she called. His heart squeezed just hearing her voice.

He stored his gun in the cabinet beside the TV and kept his gaze on the hall, yearning to see her and wanting to tell her the good news. For some reason, LeAnn had instantly liked Nikki and was always asking him about how things were going. Today he could tell her that Nikki was pretty much off the suspect list.

She stepped out and his breath caught. She wore a peach-colored sundress, one of those dresses that made a guy wonder how little was worn beneath it. She had her hair pulled up with one of those clippy things that women loved and men loved to remove. Not that her hair didn't look nice. Several strands of warm brown hair hung down to tease her shoulders and led the eye to ample cleavage the dress revealed. Oh, hell, she was hot. And now he was hot. And hard.

"You look...," *sexy as hell*, "great."

"Thanks." Her smile came off all sass. "I ordered Chinese. I hope that's okay."

She walked past him and he got a whiff of something she was wearing, something that smelled like the color of her dress. Peaches.

"Yeah," he said, and repeated his vow that she would make the first move.

They ate, and over dinner he told her about Nikki. "Thank God," she said. "She didn't deserve that crap." She cut him a glance. "Were you nice to her?"

"I didn't see her today, but when I saw her and Dallas at her gallery a few days ago, I was nice."

"Good." She started stacking plates. When she reached, her scoop neckline scooped a little more and gave him a wonderful view of her breasts. Warmth caught in his chest and spread lower. He couldn't help but smile at how happy just...looking at her made him feel. Happy to be this close. Not that he didn't want to get closer.

They did the dishes. Several times, purposely or accidentally, she bumped into him. Sweet torture. When they'd finished, she looked at him as if she had something to say, but then she blinked and started out of the kitchen.

"I think I'll go read." She looked back over her shoulder.

"More weight lifter stories?"

She grinned. "Maybe." And then she sashayed her cute little, peach-covered ass out of the kitchen.

He counted to ten, begged for willpower and then went to the extra bedroom to get ready for his shower. Hell maybe ... just maybe tonight she'd join him. And if not, he was going to need a cold one. Of course, maybe it was time he take this game a step farther.

LeAnn plopped onto her bed and moaned into the covers. Would the man do it already? What did she have to do—put a sign on her back that said, "Will have sex, just try me?"

A knocked sounded at the door. She grabbed her book, yanked her dress top down a few inches and pulled up the hem a bit. "Come in."

He stepped in. She looked up and gasped.

"Gonna take a shower," he said, and walked his bareass self into the bathroom. "You're welcome to join me," he added over his shoulder.

As soon as the door clicked shut, she buried her face in a pillow and started laughing.

Then, feeling brave, she jumped off the bed, slipped the dress from her shoulders and went to see if he needed someone to wash his back.

CHAPTER THIRTY-ONE

Nikki had forgotten what it felt like to sit across the table from a guy who had eyes just for her. To feel the sting of embarrassment when her date looked at her like he was more interested in getting her naked than he was in eating.

She'd had him drive her by her apartment so she could get dressed. She had only one black party dress that suited the evening, but it fit really nice. She felt good in it. Dallas noticed, too. He hadn't stopped making love to her with his eyes. As conflicted as she was about where things between them were going, she decided that tonight she was going to enjoy herself.

But when dinner was finished and she stepped on the dance floor and into his arms, Nikki knew how imperative it was that she leave tomorrow. She wasn't falling in love with Dallas O'Connor, she was smack-dab in the middle of it. But for tonight she was going to pretend it wasn't going to end. Tomorrow, she'd pick up the pieces and try to put herself back together.

*　　*　　*

Tony heard the bathroom door open. He held his breath and prayed he hadn't imagined it. Seconds later, the door to the two-man shower squeaked open.

"Need someone to wash your back?" She sounded nervous.

He turned and saw her, naked and so damn beautiful it hurt to look at her. Warm steam rose around them, and the spray of water hit his lower back. His heart pounded as he reached out and pulled her against him. Her nipples were hard as they brushed across his chest. He removed the clip she still wore and her hair cascaded down around her shoulders.

"God, I missed you." His voice came out hoarse.

"Me, too," she said.

Leaning down, he brushed his lips against her mouth. He tasted the wine she'd drunk. He tasted the sweetness of the fortune cookie she'd eaten. He tasted LeAnn and nothing in his entire life tasted better. He wasn't sure how long they kissed—a minute, maybe five. Never long enough.

She ran her hand up his chest and touched the scar on the corner of his shoulder. He grabbed her hand and kissed her palm. Then he reached up and touched her breasts. They felt ripe and heavy and he wanted his mouth there. Then he knew what he'd missed more than anything. He knelt in front of her and kissed the top of her sweet mound.

He heard her moan. LeAnn had never been shy about letting him know what she liked, and she liked it when he used his tongue on her. He ran a finger down the sweet cleft of her sex. Felt the slickness of her wanting, and then touched her with his mouth.

He'd barely gotten started when she screamed out and collapsed against the tiled wall. Before he realized it, she'd slipped. He caught her, but they both went down, sitting on the floor of the shower.

"You okay?" he asked, laughing.

"Yeah," she said, breathing hard and grinning. "I think you knocked me off my feet."

She reached out and wrapped her hand around him, shifting it up and down, slowly. Then she leaned over. As her head came into his lap, he stopped her. "No, I want the first time to be inside you."

"Okay," she said. "But how about I just do this?" She leaned down and ran her tongue over the tip of his sex.

He caught her head and pulled her up. "Do that one more time and I swear I'll come."

"Poor thing," she teased and ran her finger over his tip again then popped the sweet little digit into her mouth and slowly pulled it out.

"You want me to explode right now, don't you?" Tony rose, turned off the water, pulled her up and carried her into their bedroom. And for the first time in almost nine months, he made love to his wife.

Slow sweet love that told her just how much he'd missed her. How much he loved her. How happy he was to be back in her life. And most important of all, that he would never leave her again.

Dallas couldn't wait to get that little black dress off Nikki. All night she'd teased him about what color her underwear was. He'd guessed black. He knew women liked matching things. But she swore she'd decided to be daring tonight. Maybe she'd worn red? Red was daring.

Oh, hell, he wanted to see her underwear, then he wanted to remove it and slide inside her. Him hard. Her wet. He wanted to make her scream his name—over and over again. Then he wanted her to promise him she wouldn't leave tomorrow. For a second, he considered asking her to move in with him, but that didn't feel right. Just thinking about it sent him into emotional overload.

He shoved that aside and tried to just think about the here and now.

When they stepped into his apartment, she spent way too long greeting Bud. "Hey, it's my time," Dallas complained.

Giggling, she stood and walked down the hall. "I'll be just a second."

When she stopped by the bathroom, he pulled her against his hard-on, letting her know how badly he wanted her. "Hurry."

Moving into the bedroom, he found the leftover rose petals he hadn't used the other night. He gave them a sniff test and then shook them over the bed. Dimming the lights, leaving just enough to enjoy the view, he removed his clothes and crawled in bed and waited. His dick saluted the ceiling. Damn, even he had to admit it was quite impressive. He thought he heard a door open, but he didn't see the light from the bathroom spill into the hall.

Footsteps sounded and he grew harder thinking about seeing her, wondering if she'd come in only wearing her underwear. Or would she save him the trouble of removing them? Either option appealed.

She appeared at the doorway, wearing something long.

"What you got on?" He leaned on his elbow and hoped she'd be impressed with the wood he was packing.

She moved inside the room. "Not very much."

The voice.

"Shit!" He sprang up and grabbed for the lamp switch. Right before he turned it, the bathroom light spilled into the hall. Both lights flooded the room. His gaze shot to the doorway where Nikki stood deliciously naked. His gaze cut to Suzan—also naked, a trench coat around her feet.

Nikki looked at Suzan, then at him. Her eyes widened in shock.

Suzan looked at Nikki and her eyes widened in something less than shock.

Dallas tried to breath. His lungs refused to work. Since he was fourteen, he'd fantasized about this happening. But this wasn't how it was supposed to go.

Nikki let out a jarring screech and covered herself with her hands.

Suzan smiled. "This could be fun."

Nikki looked at him with so much hurt, his chest gripped. Then she turned and ran. The bathroom door slammed.

Hold on to her, son. You'll regret it if you don't. His dad's words of wisdom played again in his head.

"Fuck!" Dallas jackknifed off the bed. His earlier hard-on was gone. Lost. Completely limp.

He ran to the bathroom door. "Nikki?" He tried to open it. It was locked. He could hear her breathing, as if she was hyperventilating.

Suzan, still naked, appeared at his bedroom door. "There's a problem, isn't there?"

"Yes! Get your coat on."

"I'm sorry," she said, but she didn't sound sorry. "I thought . . . we had a thing."

He tried to think how he could have let this happen. "Every other weekend," he snapped at her. "Your ex only gets the kids the first and the third weekend. You weren't supposed to be here." He had to work to keep from screaming.

"Since I didn't come last week, I found a sitter and thought I'd surprise you."

He raked a hand through his hair. "I want you to leave, okay? Leave the key. It's over. Got it?"

He tried not to sound furious at her, but he was. Or maybe it wasn't Suzan he was furious with, but himself. He'd fucked up. Royally.

When Suzan came out of his bedroom, she wore the trench coat. She looked at him and said, "Sorry." This time it sounded real. Not that it helped.

"Me, too," he said and he meant it, too.

"She's leaving, Nikki." He leaned his head on the door.

"She doesn't have to," Nikki called back. "I'm out of here."

About twenty minutes later, Nikki realized she couldn't stay in his bathroom forever, so she took a deep breath and walked out.

He stood leaning against the hallway, still naked. "That wasn't what it seemed."

"Really," she said, swearing on everything holy that she wasn't going cry. "Did I just imagine a naked woman standing in your bedroom?"

"No, but—"

"Then how is it not what it seemed?" Storming past him, she snagged her purse.

He moved in front of the door. "I haven't slept with her since I met you. You can't hold this against me."

"You told me you weren't involved."

"I wasn't involved."

A knot of emotion built in her chest. "How long have you been seeing her?"

He raked a hand through his hair. "Four months. But—"

"She had a key, right?"

"Yes, but it wasn't a relationship."

"What defines a relationship in your screwed-up testosterone-soaked brain?"

"It was...sex, Nikki. Just sex."

The words rolled over with the subtlety of a dump truck. She jerked her chin up higher and poked him in the chest. "Let me tell you something, buddy. I'm sick and tired of how 'just sex' has screwed up my life. I was abandoned by my own parents because of 'just sex.' And I found my husband humping my hired help and I lost my marriage, my sense of self-worth, and most everything in my bank account, because of 'just sex.' I'm sick of it. And I'm sick with myself because I realize that this is what we're all about. Just sex." She stormed out.

She cried all the way to her apartment. She cried all the way to her bed. She cried all the way until sunrise. It was after twelve when she opened her eyes, remembered, and started crying again.

How had she let herself get back in this situation? After a fifteen-minute pity party, she rolled out of bed, dried her eyes, and vowed not to crater. She heard her apartment phone beeping when she passed it on the end table. She'd taken it off the hook last night when it had started ringing as soon as she'd gotten inside.

She went to her kitchen table, sat down, realized she

didn't even have any coffee, and dropped her aching head down on the table. It throbbed harder. She almost succumbed to tears, then decided she couldn't let herself do that. So she stood, mentally pulled up her big girl panties, and made herself a cup of decaffeinated tea.

Hearing her cell phone beep with missed calls, she almost ignored it. Then, realizing it could be Nana, she dug it out of her purse.

She hit the call log to see who'd called. Dallas. Dallas. Dallas. Dallas. Dallas. Dallas.

Her head throbbed each time she read his name. Ah, finally Nana.

Taking a deep breath, she hit redial. "You called?" she asked.

"Dallas called," Nana said.

"Sorry. Unplug your phone or just leave it off the hook. That's what I did."

"What happened, Nikki?"

"I don't want to talk about it"

"You went looking for potholes, didn't you?" Nana asked.

Nikki hiccupped. "Wasn't looking for it. But I fell in it. And it's the size of Houston, Nana." She bit down on her lip to stop her voice from shaking.

She heard Nana sigh. "If I need to go neuter that boy, you just say the word."

"No, let him keep his balls," Nikki said. "It's all he has going for himself."

Someone banged on her front door. "Uh, I'd better go. I'll call you later."

The pounding got louder.

"You sure you're okay? You want me to come over?"

"I'm fine." She hung up.

The pounding came again, followed by his voice. "Nikki, I know you're in there. Your car's here. Please open the door."

Only when hell starts growing snowmen.

"I'm not going anywhere. I'm sitting right here until you open this door. I don't care if it's all day."

Reaching for her purse, she dug out a certain business card, picked up her phone and made a call.

Dallas, sitting on his ass beside Nikki's door, heard footsteps and looked up. His butt was sore, his gut hurt, his head was pounding, and his heart felt as if some rottweiler had used it for a chew toy.

He so was not in the mood to face his brother.

Tony folded his arms over his chest and looked down at him. "Hey."

"Please tell me she didn't call you."

"You want me to lie?"

"Fuck." Dallas got to his feet. "Just leave."

"She said if I didn't get you out of here, she was calling the real police. Obviously, I'm not the real police."

"She won't do that."

"I wouldn't bet on it. She sounded really pissed. I mean she never got that mad when I was accusing her of murder. What the hell did you do?"

Dallas's chest tightened. He started pacing. "I think I love her. No. I *do* love her. And now I look back at the last few days and I see every fucking time I screwed up. It's just like you and Dad tried to tell me. I had my head buried in the fucking sand. I didn't want to admit what I was feeling. Anytime I was tempted to take a step closer,

I'd shut down and convince myself that what I was doing was enough. Enough to convince her to hang in there with me. Why the hell didn't I listen?"

Dallas stopped walking and Tony stepped closer. "Nobody listens until they're ready to hear. Your ex did a number on you. You had to get here on your own time."

Dallas raked a hand over his face again. "I didn't invite her to go to the cemetery. I told Dad it wasn't serious—in front of her. Can you believe I did that? Then I told her she'd eventually have to move out. What the hell was I thinking?"

"You weren't thinking," Tony said.

"Yeah, but..." He pressed a hand to his forehead. "How do I fix it?"

"For starters, let her calm down."

Dallas started pacing again. "She's not going to forgive me. And I don't blame her."

"Tell her you were scared and didn't mean it. Women love it when we admit our mistakes."

"I don't know. This was...bad." He went back to pacing. "Suzan showed up."

"Suzan?"

"I told you about her. My fuck buddy." Just saying it made him sound like a cold bastard. He was a cold bastard!

Tony's brow pinched. "She actually showed up when Nikki was there? Ouch."

"Nikki will never understand. Suzan came in wearing nothing but a damn trench coat and then Nikki came out of the bathroom and...and..."

Tony's eyes widened. "They were both naked."

Dallas looked at his brother's expression. "If you as so much as grin, I swear I'll knock you on your ass."

Hold on to her, son. You'll regret it if you don't. His dad's words never felt truer than right now.

Later that afternoon, Tony parked in front of his house and sat in his car a few minutes. Running his hand over the steering wheel, he stared at the house and a sense of rightness filled his chest. How many times had he parked at his apartment and sat there feeling empty, alone. This was home. And it had nothing to do with the structure, the brick, the walls or the furnishings inside the house. It was the person waiting for him. Her touch. Her smile. Her kiss.

LeAnn had called and said she'd be home early because of a scheduling mix-up. She wanted him to know she'd be waiting on him. *Impatiently.* She wanted him. And more importantly, he knew she loved him. Had never stopped loving him.

He remembered them showering together last night. And making love in the bed afterward. And the three times after that. It had been so damn perfect. It had been so damn right.

And so damn wrong.

Not once had they mentioned Emily.

Going to the cemetery with his dad and Dallas had been hell. He'd left them alone and forced himself to walk over to his daughter's grave. He ended up going to his car and weeping. It had hurt, but it had also somehow helped. And that's what he and LeAnn needed.

And this morning when he'd left LeAnn in her bed, he'd stood outside that nursery door and he knew they needed to talk. They needed to put away the bed. They need to move past this. And the only way to move past it was to face it.

But what if she refused to cooperate? What if it pushed LeAnn away?

He reached into his backseat and snagged a couple of tools he'd need to disassemble the crib he'd worked so hard to put together eighteen months ago. Tucking the tools in his back pocket, he prayed he wouldn't lose LeAnn a second time, and opened the front door.

LeAnn popped off the sofa and ran into his arms. She wore another sundress, similar to the one she'd worn the day before. This one was pink. He loved her in pink. She kissed him, softly, seductively, the kind of kiss that a woman meant to lead somewhere.

Closing the front door, he took her by the hand and started walking. "We have to do something."

"Eager, aren't you?" she teased.

His chest felt heavy. He stopped in the middle of the hall and then turned and looked at her. "You know I love you, right?"

She looked at him. "Of course I do."

"We have to move past it."

"Move past..." Her gaze shot to the nursery door. He pulled the wrench from his pocket. She started shaking her head. "No, Tony."

"Yes."

"No!" She swung around to walk away, but he caught her around her middle and pulled her against him.

"No!" she screamed and tried to get away.

He didn't let her go. He held her against him, and waited for her to stop fighting.

He listened to her sobs. Big and deep, they ripped at his heart. Then she stopped struggling.

"I love you," he whispered. "We can do this together."

She turned in his arms and looked at him. Tear stained her face.

"Together," he repeated.

He opened the door. She hesitated but finally walke inside with him.

"I'm so sorry," she whispered. "I should have save her. I'm a nurse. That's what I do. I should have saved her! She fell to the floor and rocked herself back and forth.

"No!" He dropped down beside her and dragged he into his lap. Tears rolled down his own cheeks. "LeAnr look at me." He pulled her hands from her face. "This isn' your fault. We lost something precious. I blamed mysel for a long time, too. I should have checked on her befor I went to bed. I should have been a better person. No worked so much." He breathed in. "I was eaten alive wit guilt. But it wasn't our fault."

She buried her head on his shoulder and he just hel her. They stayed like that for the longest time. Tim enough that sunlight that once brightened the room fade to a purple glow.

"You ready to help me?" he asked.

She nodded. They both got up and, together, they too apart the crib they had once put together. Piece by piec They both cried. And they talked about Emily. Abou how sweet she was. About how they would never stop lov ing her.

When they finished, they put the bed in the attic unti they decided what to do with it, then went to bed. The didn't make love. They were both too emotionally spen But she held on to him the whole night and he held he and Tony knew everything was going to be okay.

*   *   *

On Monday, Nikki decided to take a mental health day. The fact that she'd done the same on Saturday and Sunday was unimportant. So instead of opening the gallery, she stayed in bed until ten. Then she got up, brushed her teeth—which hadn't been brushed in two days—drank another decaf tea, ate the last of sixteen cupcakes Nana had dropped by, and opened a can of tuna and called it breakfast. After managing only a bite, she phoned Nana and set up a lunch date.

At lunch at her favorite restaurant, Nikki ordered enough for an army and didn't eat enough for a bird.

Seated across from her, Nana didn't eat much more. "You gonna spill the beans, child?"

"No beans to spill," Nikki said.

Nana shot her the parenting scowl that still held weight. Giving in, Nikki told Nana the truth. The whole truth.

"That jerkwad wanted you to have a threesome?" Nana asked.

"No. From what I overheard he didn't know she was showing up."

"But he confessed that he'd been having sex with her since you two met?"

"No, it's not that."

"Then what is it?"

"He lied to me. He said he wasn't involved. And then he said it was just sex."

Nana placed a hand on Nikki's arm. "Sweetheart, from a male perspective *involved* takes on a whole new meaning. I'm not saying it's right. What I'm saying is maybe he wasn't lying. Have you considered that you might be punishing Dallas for something your parents and dumbass ex did—God bless that dead man's heart."

Nikki went on the defensive. "Dallas never wasted an opportunity to let me know that we weren't serious."

"Sounds like he was as scared as you are," Nana said, pouring herself a cup of hot tea.

Nikki stared at her grandmother. "You're supposed to take my side, not his."

"Oh Nikki, I'm not taking his side. I told him if he came within ten feet of you I was taking a pair of wire clippers to his balls. Funny thing is, usually that keeps a guy from calling back. Not Dallas. He's called twice a day asking if you were okay. And each time he asked me to tell you that he needed to talk to you."

"No," Nikki said and had to swallow to keep from crying.

"Just think about it, Nikki. Just think about it."

Tuesday was another mental health day. And her last, she swore. Nikki called Eddie Nance and offered him a part-time job at the gallery. It made her happy hearing the excitement in his voice...not so happy when he said, "Dallas misses you."

Then she went to see Ellen who was finally out of the hospital and spending a week or so with her parents. Nikki had avoided Ellen since the whole Dallas disaster. Her friend deserved to recover in peace and not be dumped on. All Nikki had to do was keep from dumping.

Nikki had worried for nothing. Dallas had already dumped. "How dare he come to you with this!" she said to Ellen.

"He didn't. I called him looking for you when you wouldn't answer the phone. And he sounded like warmed over baby poo."

"I'm sorry. Not for him, but for worrying you." Nikki sat down at the kitchen table beside Ellen. The sun streamed in through the large window looking out at the backyard pool.

"You should be. I was concerned," Ellen said.

"Well, I'm fine."

"Don't lie to me."

"Okay," Nikki confessed. "I'm hurting like hell, but if I keep faking it, I should get better in about..." Nikki looked at her watch. "Eleven months from now."

"What happened?" Ellen picked up her diet soda.

"I thought Dallas told you."

"He told me his side." She giggled. "Sorry, I know it's not funny, but it was."

Nikki gave her the short version and, when Ellen appeared confused, she asked, "What? Was his version different?"

"No, actually that's exactly how he told it."

"Then why are you confused?" Nikki turned her drink in her hands.

"Are you sure you're not letting your past issues cloud your judgment here?"

Nikki frowned. "Have you been conniving with Nana?"

Ellen picked up her soda. "Nikki, you're mad at a guy because he slept with someone before he met you."

"No, I'm mad at him because..." Nikki had to work to remember. "He lied."

"Okay, he should have told you when you asked about surprises, but is hiding one's sexual past from their new sexual partner a breakup offense? When I was dating— eons ago—I never told my new boyfriend about my old one. I mean, when a guy's...going there...you don't want him thinking about another guy having been there."

"I hate it when you do that!" Nikki dropped her head on the table.

"When I do what?" Ellen asked.

"Make sense."

Before lunch on Wednesday, Dallas and Tyler were summoned to Brian and Sterns Law Firm by Mr. Sterns. Dallas went but only because Tyler insisted.

Sterns sat behind his oversize desk. "The cops aren't sharing the information with us that you found. Can we pay you for it?"

"Sorry," Dallas said.

"How much?" asked Tyler, always wanting data before making a decision.

Sterns named an impressive number, but Tyler didn't bite. "You know, you had your chance to work with us."

Sterns frowned. "I can't believe my partner is still standing behind that murdering, thieving son of his."

"Actually, we're not certain Andrew is guilty," Tyler said. "Of the murder that is. He is definitely a thief. Has a drug problem, and made a couple people sick, but—"

"I thought you were the guys who had him arrested for murder because you're now banging Leon's ex." Mr. Sterns looked at Dallas.

Dallas stood up. "What did you say?"

"Sorry," Sterns said. "That was a tad crude."

"It sure as hell was."

"However," Tyler continued with his own agenda, "we think the murderer works here."

"Here?"

"Could be you," Tyler said. "You see, Leon argued with someone at this office three times the night he was killed. Brian Junior admits to only two of those calls."

"I told the police I never spoke to Jack Leon that night."

Five minutes later, not having learned anything more, they started out of Sterns's office. They got as far as the front door of the building when Rachel Peterson met them. The look in her eyes was one hundred percent pure bitch.

"So you're screwing Leon's leftovers, huh?"

"I'm sorry if I hurt you," Dallas said, trying to play it nice.

Rachel muttered something under her breath and stormed away.

"Damn," Tyler said, grinning. "She must have really wanted your body."

Later that afternoon, Dallas and Tyler went to the police station when Andrew Brian was being reinterviewed. They stopped by Tony's office when he finished talking to the lawyer.

"I don't get it," Tony said. "You hand me Brian on a silver platter and now you don't think he's guilty."

Dallas hesitated to answer, but Tyler jumped in. "We're just saying the guy agreed to do a polygraph," Tyler said. "And we think you should do it."

Tony nodded before looking at Dallas, "How's Nikki?"

Just hearing her name brought Dallas pain. "She still won't talk to me."

"Do you want LeAnn to talk to her? They hit it off."

"I don't think it'd help." Then something about the

way Tony said his wife's name seemed different. "You and LeAnn...?" Dallas asked.

A smile parted Tony's lips. "Yup. She couldn't resist this body."

Tyler laughed out loud.

"Congrats," Dallas said and meant it. One of the O'Connor men deserved to be happy. Or make that two. His father had been hanging out with the Ol' Timers club. He was even talking about selling his house and moving into the same retirement community.

"Okay," Tony said, getting back to business. "If Brian didn't kill Leon, who did?"

"Someone at his office," Dallas answered. "That third phone call on Wednesday evening is still not accounted for. If they are telling the truth, there was Canton, Sterns, and Brian Senior in the building."

Tyler sat forward. "Maybe Andrew's dad figured it out and killed Leon to protect his son?"

Tony sighed. "I guess I could talk to Brian Senior again. But if he killed to protect his son, it doesn't seem likely he'd let him go to jail."

Driving back to his place alone, Dallas kept going over everything Brian Junior had said. Something about the story didn't sit right, but he couldn't put his finger on it. Then his mental finger finally pointed out the problem. Brian had said it was Wednesday night when he and Leon had argued. Rachel had specifically told Dallas it had been Tuesday. And if Brian was right, and Rachel had overheard the argument, that meant that she was in the office Wednesday evening. She could have been the person arguing with Leon on the phone. Or perhaps she just had her days mixed up.

Her earlier words rolled through his head. *So you're screwing Leon's leftovers, huh?* The anger in her tone had sounded venomous. Angry enough to kill?

"Shit." Suddenly it became clear. Everyone said Jack Leon had a problem chasing skirts. Leon had been having a fling with Rachel. When she found out he was trying to win Nikki back, she became furious. After she'd killed Jack, she went after Nikki and got Ellen instead.

Not sure where Nikki was, he grabbed his phone, and called her. She didn't answer. So he phoned Nana. "Where's Nikki?"

"The gallery. Crawling back to her on your knees, huh?"

"Yeah." He hung up, turned the corner and pushed the Mustang as fast it would go.

Nikki missed the call and now stared at Dallas's number. They needed to talk. She'd accepted that. She'd accepted that perhaps she'd overreacted. Not that it was all on her. Dallas hadn't been the best communicator, except to make it clear he wasn't promising anything serious. Still, the man had been her anchor since everything had happened. Thanks to him, she was no longer considered a cold-blooded killer.

He didn't deserve her scorn. She didn't deserve to have her heart broken, but that wasn't exactly his fault. For that reason, she'd decided to apologize—in person—pay him for his services, and say good-bye. As badly as she wanted to believe that they could fix things, it didn't seem fixable. Yeah, she'd been looking for potholes, and maybe that was her flaw, but no matter how she turned and tried to see things from a different viewpoint, there was one truth that remained. Dallas had been upfront with her from the beginning. He was a one-day-at-a-time guy.

She wanted more. The longer she postponed the inevitable, the harder it would be.

It was gonna hurt like hell, but she'd survive. She'd survived worse. Right?

It didn't feel like it right now, but time would make it better.

Walking into her office, she picked up the bust that Dallas had said he wanted, to take it her car. The dang thing weighed at least twenty pounds. She was also going to give him the painting of the two boys fishing, the one that brought to mind Dallas and Tony. Even if she had to say so herself, it was one of her better works.

She was only a few feet out of her office when someone stepped into the hall from the gallery. Someone wearing a ski mask. Nikki's breath caught. When she saw the knife in the person's hand, she let out a scream worthy of a horror film. Too bad no one was around to hear it.

"Bitch." The attacker, obviously female from her voice, lunged forward. Nikki jumped to the left. The knife scrapped across the plaster-of-paris bust, carving a small chunk out of the right breast.

The attacker muttered a curse, obviously angry that she'd missed her target. Nikki, fear short-circuiting rational thought, was furious about her bust. "This doesn't belong to me anymore."

"Neither did Jack, but you took him anyway." The words seethed from beneath the mask, and the intruder lifted her knife. "I'm sick and tired of men leaving me for someone prettier. First my husband, then Jack. You bitches are all the same, taking whatever you want."

Nikki backed away. "I didn't want Jack back."

"What is it that you have that I don't?"

A sound mind, Nikki thought, but didn't say it.

"I tried to just forget about it. But then, even the PI... He was interested in me and then you came along. Why?"

"Dallas?" Nikki asked, now confused.

The woman lunged again. Nikki screamed and used the bust to ward off the knife. The weapon took a chunk out of the bust's left breast. This time Nikki didn't care about the artwork, what infuriated her was that this was the person who'd hurt Ellen and killed Jack.

"You're sick!" Nikki screamed, courage rising unexpectedly from deep inside her.

The woman lunged again. Nikki faked a move to the right then darted left. The knife missed the plaster of paris, and came within millimeters of Nikki's real bust. Way too close for comfort.

"You wanna piece of me?" Nikki leaped back. "Take this piece." With all her anger, all her fear, she threw the bust at her attacker.

Everything seemed to happen in slow motion.

The bust slammed into the attacker's upper chest and head. A loud thunk sounded.

The attacker slammed against the wall. Another loud thunk sounded.

The artwork shattered on the tile floor, one breast went rolling down the hall.

Nikki followed it.

Imagining the knife-wielding woman behind her, Nikki ran with everything she had. She screamed like there was no tomorrow, because frankly she didn't know if there would be one.

She cut the corner, bolted past the checkout counter, and ran smack-dab into another wall.

A wall of hard, warm muscle. Dallas grabbed her by her shoulders and she saw his gun in one hand.

"You hurt?" His gaze flickered over her and then back to the hall door.

"No." Her whole body shook.

He pushed her to the side, pointed his gun down the hall and started moving.

"She's got a knife!"

"I've got a gun." He took another step. Nikki grabbed his arm to stop him.

"Let go." His dead serious tone brought reason and reality to her mind. Her hands started shaking again, and her knees wobbled.

Dallas, moved past the cashier's desk, gun held tight. He stopped at the hall door.

"She's down. Call 911," he told Nikki.

Forcing herself to move, she bolted for the phone as Dallas moved into the hall. Not wanting to lose sight of him, she snagged the phone and darted to the doorway.

The ski-masked woman lay crumpled on the floor. Dallas kicked the knife away from her hand, knelt and put two fingers to her neck.

"Oh, God. Did I kill her?" Tears filled her eyes and she couldn't catch her breath.

"No." Dallas looked up. "But call 911. Do it, Nikki."

An hour later, Nikki sat on the sofa in her office, staring at the wall and focused on breathing. She couldn't stop shaking. Every few minutes Dallas would look inside to check on her. He smiled, nodded, then left again. The police had arrived. Tony had arrived. The paramedics had arrived. One of them took her blood pressure, made sure she hadn't been cut then insisted she sit down and focus on breathing. Hence, her being in the office . . . breathing.

Earlier, Nikki had prayed her attacker would wake up, then when she did, Nikki realized she should be more careful what she prayed for. The woman started fighting. They had to put her in handcuffs. Dallas had already explained who the woman was, and what had motivated her to do this. Rachel confirmed her motivation and even more when she screamed the whole time about her husband cheating on her, leaving her for another woman. Nikki knew how much it hurt to be cheated on, but not once had she considered going on a murdering rampage.

Tony came in and talked to Nikki. He was really nice and when she thanked him for it, he grinned, and asked her to make sure to tell his wife he hadn't been rude.

Nikki hesitated to ask, but then went for it. "Why did she put Jack's body in my trunk?"

"The only thing she said was that Jack was in your car trying to find a piece of paper to leave you a note when she found him. I assume Jack had the keys in his hand and your trunk just seemed to be the best place to hide the body."

When Tony left, Dallas came back in. "Everyone's gone." He sat beside her, put his arm around her shoulder and pulled her against him.

Immediately, Nikki forgot about breathing and started crying. She cried because someone had almost killed her. She cried because she could have killed someone. She cried because the piece of artwork Dallas wanted was shattered all over her hall.

After a while, she stopped crying, but she didn't pull away. Sitting beside Dallas, his arm around her, her head partially buried on his shoulder, felt good. Right. Safe.

He pressed a kiss to the top of her head. "Will you please listen to me?"

She nodded.

"I've spent the last five days kicking myself for things I said, for things I didn't say, and for some things I let happen out of sheer stupidity. I made so many mistakes, Nikki. But I didn't sleep with anyone since I met you. I did not know Suzan was coming over. Not that it excuses the other things I did."

Nikki heard his heart racing.

He took a deep breath. "I was scared, Nikki. And after really giving this some thought, I realized, I'm not the only one who's scared. We were both hurt by people we cared about and that's hard to move past."

She pulled back and looked at him. "I was looking for potholes."

"Potholes?" he asked.

"In the relationship. Nana says I do that. Look for problems until I find one."

"She probably has a point," he said. "And I made it easy for you to find one. It's the hole that I had my head buried in." He touched her cheek and shook his head. "You were looking for problems, and I was creating them by not admitting to myself how I felt, not wanting to see that I was screwing up the best thing that ever happened to me."

"So we're both to blame," Nikki said.

"Yeah. Though, I'm big enough to admit that I probably contributed more than you. I'm surprised you didn't get my gun and shoot me when Suzan showed up. But yeah, refusing to talk to me, calling my brother on my ass—that might have been a tad much. Not that I didn't deserve it. But you have no idea how miserable I've been these last few days. Forgive me, Nikki. Please."

Her heart swelled with hope. "We should start all over, try dating, and just see—"

He put a finger over her lips. "No."

Her chest grew tight.

"I don't want to start over. I want you back at my place. Bud hasn't been the same. He's not eating right. I carried him to the vet and he said he's depressed. He's farting like crazy and there's no one there to laugh with me about it. It's pathetic."

She chuckled. "This is supposed to make me want to go back?"

He smiled. "You love Bud. Don't deny that."

She took a deep breath and decided to be honest. "He's not the only thing I love, Dallas. And that scares me because if you don't feel the same way—"

"For God's sake, Nikki, what the hell do you think I just said?"

She considered his question. "Saying you want me to share your dog's farts is not saying you love me." She laughed.

He dropped his head back on the sofa and laughed with her. Seconds later, he looked at her. "Then let me say it. I love you." He kissed her nose. "I love all of you. There's nothing I don't love about you. The way you talk to yourself. The way you care about your crazy grandmother and her friends. The way you accept people and make everyone happy. Including me. You make me happy, Nikki. Do you know how long it's been since I've been happy? Oh, and I love your body. I really love your body."

She smiled. "I love you, too."

"And my body?" he asked, his blue eyes twinkling with sexy humor.

She laughed again. "I love your body, too." She pressed a quick kiss on his lips. "No more one-day-at-a-time crap?"

"Oh, hell no." He pulled her close again. "We're going for the long haul."

Zoe Adams has memories of
a life that couldn't be hers...
or could it?
Sexy PI Tyler Lopez is
helping her unravel the secrets
of her past, one by one.

Please turn this page
for a preview of

BLAME IT ON TEXAS

CHAPTER ONE

"SPIDERS. DEFINITELY SPIDERS."

"Don't forget snakes."

"Trust me, it's clowns." Zoe Adams removed her waitress apron and added her two cents to the conversation the other waitresses of Cookie's Café were having on their biggest fears. She plopped down on one of the stools lining the breakfast counter, and pulled out her tips to count them. She hoped she had enough to pay the rent. Looking up at the other diner employees, she added, "And considering my regular gig is that of kindergarten teacher, I've had to face that fear more times than I care to admit."

"I'd take a clown over a spider any day of the week," said Jamie. Like Zoe, she was in her mid-twenties.

"I can step on a spider," Zoe said looking from Jamie to Beth and Melinda. "Clowns are too big for my size sixes." She held up her foot. "I don't know what it is, but I see one and it's like I hear scary music and my mind starts flashing *Friday the 13th* images." In truth, clowns weren't her biggest fear. Small, dark places scared Zoe more than anything. Not that she'd ever share that with the ladies at

Cookie's, or anyone else for that matter. Some things Zoe didn't talk about. Especially the things she didn't understand. And lately her life was filled with a lot of those things. Crazy how watching an episode of the TV series *Unsolved Mystery Hunters* had turned her life upside down, and sent her from Alabama to Texas in search of . . . the truth.

"Roaches. The kind that fly. I hate 'em," Dixie Talbot said, joining in on the conversation. In her early sixties, Dixie was the matriarchal cook, waitress, and part-owner of Cookie's Café. "Years ago, I was standing right over there by booth two and one of those nasty creatures flew into my shirt."

Zoe stopped counting her money and laughed. "Yeah, Fred told me about the little striptease you pulled, too."

"Honey, he'd better be glad that roach flew off my right boob once the top came off or I swear to everything holy I'd have been standing there naked as a jaybird."

"Was that the day he proposed to you?" Zoe asked.

They all laughed. It was the laughter, the camaraderie of Dixie and the other diner employees that kept Zoe from looking for a higher-paying gig while in Texas. God knew she could use the money. Kindergarten teachers in Alabama didn't rake in the big bucks.

Oh, it was enough to get by, but not enough to fund this research trip to Miller, Texas, when she now had to pay for two apartments. Not to mention the entire month off from work—a month she only got because the principal had been friends with her mom. But truthfully, more than money, she needed companionship. Since her mama died two years ago, and especially for the last year since Chris, her live-in boyfriend had decided he'd rather date a stripper than a kindergarten teacher, Zoe had spent way too much time alone.

And lonely.

Hey, maybe she should get Dixie to teach her a few moves. Not that Zoe wanted Chris back. Nope. For four years, she'd given her heart and soul to that man. She'd already had names picked out for the two kids she was sure they'd give life to, thinking any day he'd pop the big question. And he had popped a big one. It just wasn't the question she'd expected. *Do you mind if I bring home my stripper girlfriend to live here until you can find another place?*

Okay, he hadn't actually worded it like that, but he might as well have. He'd taken Zoe's heart, and returned it, along with her self-esteem, in a big mangled mess. Not so much of a mess that she hadn't reminded him that she'd been the one to rent the apartment, and he could just grab his stuff and get the hell out. Nor had he been so shocked at her suddenly found backbone that he hadn't called her a bitch for not being understanding. Didn't she understand it wasn't his fault he'd fallen in love with someone else?

What she understood was that she'd been played for a fool—paying most of the bills, being his personal house cleaner, trying to be the perfect little Alabama housewife. Even a year later, it still stung like a paper cut right across her heart.

Zoe's cell rang. Considering she'd gotten all of two calls in the four weeks she'd been in Texas—one from her principal back in Alabama confirming she'd be at work on September 25, and the other a wrong number—a call was a big thing. Zoe checked the number. Unknown caller.

"Hello?" Zoe answered. And while she hated it, there

was a tiny part of her that hoped it would be Chris, wanting her back, telling her he'd screwed up. Not that she would ever take him back, but it would still be nice to know he missed her.

She heard someone breathing, but nothing else. "Hello?" A click sounded. Stashing her phone back in her apron, a tad disappointed, she looked up at Dixie. "Can I use your computer for a bit?"

"You betcha. Just stay off those porn sites," Dixie teased.

"Just can't help myself," Zoe shot back as she scooted her butt off the stool. "I haven't had any in a month of Sundays."

"I could remedy that," offered Peter, the new fry cook who couldn't be more than seventeen.

"I'll consider it as soon as you get written permission from your mama," Zoe said and while all the employees snickered, she grabbed her canvas bag with a change of clothes, and went back to the office.

Five minutes later, Dixie brought two big bowls of chicken and dumplings into the office and set one down in front of Zoe on the oversized and timeworn oak desk. "Eat lunch before you go."

Zoe looked up and smiled. It had been a long time since she'd had anyone looking out for her. She was going to miss Dixie when she went back home.

"Thanks. I've been smelling these cooking all morning." She dished a big spoonful into her mouth and moaned as the savory taste exploded on her tongue. "My mama used to make these."

"Mine are better," Dixie teased and dropped down into the worn desk chair beside Zoe and started eating.

After a few minutes of silence, Dixie asked, "You miss her—your mama, I mean?"

"Like the dickens. She was special." But if what Zoe suspected was the truth, her mama had a side of her Zoe never knew. In the pro-con list Zoe had made before she decided to actually come here, uncovering her parents' ugly secrets had been the only con.

Dixie's gaze shifted to the computer monitor.

Zoe felt the need to grab the mouse and delete the screen. But, realizing it would be rude she forced herself to just keep eating. Besides, Dixie had already gotten a peek at what Zoe was researching last week when she'd stepped out of the office for a potty break and forgotten to close the screen. When she'd returned, Dixie was reading the article Zoe had found at the library and had download onto a flash drive.

"The Bradfords again?" Dixie asked. "Is there a reason you're intrigued with that rich family?"

Zoe glanced at the screen. She couldn't divulge everything. People would think she was crazy—hell, sometimes she considered the possibility herself—but she could tell Dixie part of it. "There was a story about them on that *Unsolved Mystery Hunters* show a couple months back. I guess I just love a good puzzle."

"About the murder of that kid?" Dixie asked.

Zoe nodded and her chest constricted.

"I remember when it happened. They never did find out who killed her. Sad stuff."

"Yeah." Zoe spooned another bite into her mouth and stared at the picture of Thomas Bradford. It was as if Zoe felt by staring at the man, she could discover the truth. But no such discovery came.

"I heard that the old man isn't doing so well. The kids and grandkids are already fighting over his inheritance. Lucky for me, all I've got is this run-down café, and neither of my kids want anything to do with it."

"It's not so run-down," Zoe said. "Best food in town." She spooned another dumpling and a big chunk of stewed chicken into her mouth.

Dixie chuckled. "That's because you're not a citified gal like my kids. My son ran off to California to learn to talk like they do on the six o'clock news. Works for a radio station out there. Boy's ashamed of his southern roots. And my daughter—you wouldn't catch a dumpling within six feet of her lips. Says she's allergic to carbs."

Zoe frowned. "I haven't met a carb I haven't loved. Guess it shows, too. I'll bet I've gained five pounds since I started working here."

"And you're wearing it well, too, honey. You should see the guys checking out your butt when you walk away." Dixie looked back at the computer screen. "If you're real curious about the Bradfords, you should ask those PIs who come in for my chili cheeseburgers on Tuesdays. They do something for the Bradfords."

Zoe's interest peaked. "What PIs?" She surely didn't have money to hire a private investigator, but if they had knowledge of the Bradfords, she could at least ask them some questions. How much would they charge just to talk to her? Nothing, she hoped.

"Those three hunk-a-hunk men, two dark haired and one blond. All of them drool worthy, especially that Tyler Lopez. They own that PI agency, Only in Texas." Dixie shook her head. "Are you seriously telling me you haven't noticed them?"

Zoe tried to think. "They only come in on Tuesdays?" While she didn't recall them, she mentally stored away the title of the agency.

Dixie dropped her spoon in her bowl. "Girl, you are either blind or a lesbian not to have noticed them."

"Neither. Self-preservation. Just mending a broken heart," Zoe said honestly. "I'm not sure men are worth the risk so I've trained myself not to notice things like sexy bedroom eyes or wide shoulders." But she was getting a little breathless just thinking about it. Maybe she should reconsider dating again. If for no other reason than to have someone call her every now and then, and make her cell phone worth its monthly charge.

"Oh, honey, these would be worth it. Then again, 'cause I like ya, if you noticed them too much I'd reel you in so fast you'd leave skid marks on my linoleum."

"What's wrong with them?" Zoe tried to feign only a mild curiosity while she pushed another dumpling around her bowl. But on the inside she was chomping at the bit and felt her excitement growing by leaps and bounds. This might be her one big break. The one that answered the questions Zoe had been looking for all her life—questions that had exploded after seeing the special on the unsolved mystery on the Bradford kidnapping and murder.

God knew all her other plans had seemed to fail. Phone calls to the Bradford businesses, a visit to their lawyer, and even a couple of drop-in visits to the mansion—not that she'd gotten past the security gate. The last time she'd been told by one security guard that if he saw her there again, he was calling the cops.

Heck, she'd even tried following the limo when they'd left the house, and got herself a nice little ticket for running a red light that she didn't run. The cop who gave her the ticket suggested she go find another old fart to attempt to seduce because Mr. Bradford wasn't in the market for an Anna Nicole.

"Nothing wrong with them if you like suspected murderers." Dixie arched her painted brow.

"They're murderers?" Zoe asked.

"I said suspected. They used to be cops. Supposedly they got involved in some seedy drug deals, and then they got arrested for brutally murdering this couple. Practically decapitated the woman." She ran a finger across her neck. "It was big news in town. Then they got convicted and went to jail."

Zoe reached up to touch her neck and felt her jaw fall open a bit. "And what? They escape every Tuesday just for your chili cheeseburgers?"

Dixie laughed. "Hey, my cooking's that good. But actually, they got let go."

"So they're not guilty?" Zoe really hoped that was the case. If she was going to look them up, and you could bet she was, she'd like it if they weren't really murderers.

"Well, that depends on who you talk to. You know small towns, folks around here get one thing in their mind and changing it is about as easy as chewing glass. My neighbor has a son-in-law who works for the Glencoe Police Department where they worked. According to him, they had those three down and dirty. But then they got themselves . . . What you call that when the governor lets someone go?"

"Pardoned?" Zoe asked.

"No, the other word. Oh, yeah. Exonerated. That's what they got."

"Dixie," Jamie called from out front. "Lunch crowd is dripping in."

"Guess I'm on again." Dixie stood up and pressed a hand on Zoe's shoulder. "I like you, kid. I really wish you'd stick around here."

Emotion filled Zoe's chest. Reaching back, Zoe put her hand on top of Dixie's. "I like you, too. But I've a job waiting for me in Alabama."

As soon as Dixie disappeared, Zoe sat there a few minutes letting that wonderful feeling of hearing Dixie's words stir in her chest. Nothing like feeling someone actually cared about you.

Then she shifted her thinking gears and wondered if she should wait until Tuesday and hope the PI threesome showed up, or if she should take matters into her own hands. A surge of impatience stirred inside her and she hit the Google search engine. Typing in the agency name, she whispered, "Come to Mama." Then she reached up and touched her neck again, hoping her impatience didn't lead to her losing her head. Figuratively, of course.

Less than thirty minutes later, Zoe parked in front of the Only in Texas building. The sign in the window read they were open. The fact that her little Google search informed her that until recently the place of business had housed a funeral home almost seemed absurd. Convicted—albeit exonerated—murderers had bought an old funeral home to house their business. Was there not something slightly off about that? Maybe three angry ex-cops making a point to the townsfolk who'd judged them unfairly?

But slightly off, or angry men or not, she wanted

answers. So she grabbed her purse, climbed out of her dependable silver Chevy Cobalt and went to see if she could find them. Stopping at the door of the large red brick building, she released her shoulder-length auburn hair from her ponytail and shook it out. Her hair, a tad too thick and too curly for her tastes, usually caught a man's eye and if it took letting her hair down for a bit to encourage one of these men to talk with her, she wasn't above doing it.

All she had to figure out was how much to tell the PIs. She knew sooner or later, she was going to have to trust someone. She just wasn't sure who or when. Stepping inside the business, leaving the bright sunshine for a dark room, she allowed her eyes a few seconds to adjust. And when they did, her gaze caught on the only piece of "furniture"—if you could call it that—in the room. She took a quick step back. A coffin, yup, an honest to goodness coffin with a raised lid, bracketed the back wall.

"Hello?" she muttered in the dead silence. And it did feel dead. Like a funeral home felt. She'd been in too many already in her life. First her dad at age sixteen, her best friend who'd been killed in a car accident their senior year of high school, and then her mom. Personally, she preferred not to ever have to visit another one.

A noise, a slight moan, echoed from the room. No wait...not from the room, but from the casket. *Shit!* Her heart started racing. Her eyes shot back to the casket, and her hands jerked behind her, feeling for the doorknob. Then another snortlike noise came from the coffin. Suddenly a big canine face popped up and rested its round head on the coffin's wooden edge.

Zoe let go of a nervous chuckle. "A vampire dog, huh?"

The dog stretched its neck—what little neck it had—and then leapt out of the casket and came sniffing around her feet.

"So, you're the official door greeter?" She knelt to pet the English bulldog as it started sniffing her up and down. "You smell Lucky on me? Or is it the Slam Dunk, Three-Egg Dollar Ninety-Nine special you smell?" It usually took two or three shampoos to get the smell of bacon from her hair. After a couple of seconds of giving the animal attention, she stood back up.

"Hello?" she called again.

And again no one answered. She walked down the hall. The dog followed at her feet, his paws clicking on the wood floor, but the lack of noise filtering into the building seemed louder than the clickity-clack of his paws. The first door to the left was a large office. Three unmanned desks filled the room. She stepped inside.

A sign hanging from the front desk said, "If no one is here, press the button."

Zoe looked for a button to press. The desk was covered with various files and papers. Was the button under those? Moving in, she looked around the desk. She started to raise a big pile of files when a name on one of the files caught her eye. Bradford.

Was this the same Bradford?

Zoe reached for the file then pulled her hand back as if it might bite. Then she reached for it again and pulled back again. Yanking her purse higher on her shoulder, she stood there while her conscience played tug-of-war with her desire for answers. She gave the room a good look-see for anyone who might tattle if she . . . took a small peek.

Looking down at the dog, she asked, "You wouldn't tell on me, would you?"

When he shook his head back and forth, she laughed.

Finally, her desire for answers won over. She reached down and flipped open the file. Less than a dozen sheets of paper took up residence there. The first one looked like a résumé. She picked it up to read it when the sound of a door opening filled the quiet office.

The dog barked and took off running.

Feeling as if she'd been caught doing something really bad, she dropped the papers back on the desk, and slapped the file closed. She stepped away from behind the desk, but in her haste to move quickly, her purse knocked the folder off, and the file and all dozen or so papers scattered on the floor.

"Damn," she muttered and dropped to the floor on her hands and knees to gather the evidence of her wrongdoing. She heard footsteps moving closer and her heart pounded.

Snagging the folder and papers, she threw them on the desk. She was about to stand up when she heard the footsteps enter the room, followed by the sounds of clicking paws.

Friggin' great.

Now all she had to explain was why she was down on all fours behind someone's desk. Her heart did another flip-flop when she remembered she was possibly dealing with angry ex-cops, now ex-cons who'd been accused of murder.

The dog pranced around the desk and gave her a big lick right on the lips then started sniffing her bacon-scented hair. Those footsteps moved closer still, and her mind raced right along with her heart.

The deep masculine sound of a man clearing his throat came from behind her. "Nice view."

She looked back over her shoulder, praying she'd come up with a good excuse for being in this ridiculous position. But the moment her gaze landed on the clown, the only thing she came up with was a scream. A loud one.

THE DISH

Where authors give you the inside scoop!

♥ ♥ ♥ ♥ ♥ ♥ ♥ ♥ ♥ ♥ ♥ ♥ ♥ ♥

From the desk of Christie Craig

Dear Reader,

As an author of seven humorous suspense romance novels, I'm often asked how I come up with my characters. Since the truth isn't all that fun to describe—that I find these people in the cobwebs of my mind—I usually just tell folks that I post a want ad on Craigslist.

One of those folks replied that she'd be checking out my ad and applying for the position of romance heroine. Right then I wondered if she'd ever read a Christie Craig book. Well, it's not just my books—every good story is really a triumph over tragedy. (Of course, I have my own lighter spin of tragedy.) And by the ending of my books, my heroines have found a man who's smoking hot and deserving of their affection, and they've experienced a triumph that's sweeter than warm fudge. Friendships have been forged, and even the craziest of families have grown a whole lot closer. And I do love crazy families. Probably because I have one of my own. Hmm, maybe I get some of my characters from there, too.

Point is, my heroines had to earn their Happily Ever After. The job requires a lot of spunk.

Take poor Nikki Hunt in ONLY IN TEXAS, the first book in my Hotter in Texas series, for example. Her cheating ex ditches her at dinner and sticks her with the bill. She then finds his dead body stuffed in the trunk of her car, which makes her lose her two-hundred-dollar meal all over his three-thousand-dollar suit. Now, not only is Nikki nearly broke, she's been poisoned, she's barfing in public (now, *that's* a tragedy), and, worse still, she's a murder suspect. And that's only the first chapter. Nikki's fun is just beginning. You've hardly met Nikki's grandma, who epitomizes those family members who drive you bonkers, even though you know your life would be empty without them.

As we say in the south, Nikki's got a hard row to hoe. For certain, it takes a kick-ass woman to be a Christie Craig heroine. She's gotta be able to laugh, because sometimes that's all you can do. She's gotta be able to fight, because life is about battles. (I don't care if it's with an ex-husband, a plumber, or a new puppy unwilling to house-train.) And she's gotta be able to love, because honestly, love is really what my novels are about. Well, that and overcoming flaws, jumping over hurdles, and finding the occasional dead body.

So while in real life you may never want to undergo the misadventures of a Christie Craig heroine, I'm counting on the fact that you'll laugh with her, root for her, and fall in love alongside her. And here's hoping that when you close my book, you are happy you've met the characters who live in the cobwebs of my mind.

And remember my motto for life: Laugh, love, read.

Christie Craig

www.christie-craig.com

♥ ♥ ♥ ♥ ♥ ♥ ♥ ♥ ♥ ♥ ♥ ♥ ♥ ♥ ♥ ♥ ♥

From the desk of Isobel Carr

Dear Reader,

I've always loved the "Oh no, I'm in love with my best friend's sister!" trope. It doesn't matter what the genre or setting is, we all know sisters are forbidden fruit. This scenario is just so full of pitfalls and angst and opportunities for brothers to be protective and for men to have to really, really prove (and not just to the girl) that they love the girl. How can you not adore it?

Add in the complications of a younger son's lot in life—lack of social standing, lack of fortune, lack of prospects—and you've got quite the series of hurdles to overcome before the couple can attain their Happily Ever After (especially if the girl he loves is the daughter of a duke).

If you read the first book in the League of Second Sons series, you've already met the sister in question, Lady Boudicea "Beau" Vaughn. She's a bit of a tomboy and always seems to be on the verge of causing a scandal, but she means well, and she's got a fierce heart.

You will have also met the best friend, Gareth Sandison. He's a committed bachelor, unquestionably a rake, and he's about to have everything he's ever wanted—but knew he could never have—dangled in front of him... but he's going to have to risk friendship and honor to get it. And even then, things may not work out quite as he expected.

I hope you'll enjoy letting Gareth show you what it means to be RIPE FOR SCANDAL.

Isobel Carr

www.isobelcarr.com

♥ ♥ ♥ ♥ ♥ ♥ ♥ ♥ ♥ ♥ ♥ ♥ ♥ ♥ ♥ ♥ ♥

From the desk of Hope Ramsay

Dear Reader,

In late 2010, while I was writing HOME AT LAST CHANCE, something magical happened that changed the direction of the story.

A friend sent me an email with a missing pet poster attached. This particular poster had a banner headline that read "Missing Unicorn," over a black-and-white photograph of the most beautiful unicorn I have ever seen. The flyer said that the lost unicorn had last been seen entering Central Park and provided a 1-800 number for tips that would lead to the lost unicorn's safe return.

The unicorn poster made me smile.

A few days later, my friend sent me a news story about how hundreds of people in New York had seen this poster and had started calling in reports of unicorn sightings. Eventually, the unicorn sightings spread from Manhattan all the way to places in Australia and Europe.

At that point, the missing unicorn captured my imagination.

The worldwide unicorn sightings proved that if people take a moment to look hard, with an innocent heart, they can see unicorns and angels and a million miracles all around them. As we grow up, we forget how to look. We get caught up in the hustle and bustle of daily living, and unicorns become myths. But for a small time, in New York City, a bunch of "Missing Unicorn" posters made people stop, smile, and see miracles.

The missing unicorn and his message wormed its way right into my story and substantially changed the way I wrote the character of Hettie Marshall, Last Chance's Queen Bee. Sarah Murray, my heroine, tells Hettie to look at Golfing for God through the eyes of a child. When Hettie heeds this advice, she realizes that she's lost something important in her life. Her sudden desire to recapture a simple faith becomes a powerful agent of change for her and, ultimately, for Last Chance itself. And of course, little Haley Rhodes helps to seal the deal. Haley is a master at seeing what the adult world misses altogether.

I hope you keep your ability to wonder at the world around you—to see it like a child does. You might find a missing unicorn—or maybe a Sorrowful Angel.

Hope Ramsay

❤ ❤ ❤ ❤ ❤ ❤ ❤ ❤ ❤ ❤ ❤ ❤ ❤ ❤

From the desk of Dee Davis

Dear Reader,

Settings are a critical part of every book. They help establish the tone, give insight into characters, and act as the backdrop for the narrative that drives the story forward. Who can forget the first line of *Rebecca*—"Last night I dreamt I went to Manderley again." The brooding house in the middle of the English moors sets us up from the very beginning for the psychological drama that is the center of the book.

When I first conceptualize a novel, I often start with the settings. Where exactly will my characters feel most at home? What places evoke the rhythm and pacing of the book? Because my books tend to involve a lot of adventure, the settings often change with the flow of the story. And when it came time to find the settings for DEEP DISCLOSURE, I knew without a doubt that Alexis would be living in New Orleans.

One of my favorite cities, I love the quirky eccentricities of the Big Easy, and I wanted to share some of my favorites with readers, including the Garden District and the French Quarter. Of course, Alexis and Tucker don't stay in New Orleans long, and it isn't surprising that they wind up in Colorado.

We moved a lot when I was a kid, and one of the few stable things in my life was spending summers in Creede. But because I've used Creede already in so many books, I decided this time to use the neighboring town of South Fork as the place where George has his summer retreat. And Walsenburg—one of the places we often stopped for groceries on the way to Creede—as the scene of Alexis's family's disaster.

I confess that Redlands, Tucker and Drake's home, is a place I've never actually visited. But a dear friend lived there for several years and tells such wonderful stories about it that it seemed the perfect place for my boys to have grown up and developed their love of baseball.

And of course Sunderland College, while fictional, is indeed based on a real place: Hendrix College, my alma mater. I spent a wonderful four years there, and I hope you enjoy your time at Sunderland with A-Tac as much!

For insight into both Alexis and Tucker, here are some songs I listened to while writing DEEP DISCLOSURE:

The Kill, by Thirty Seconds to Mars
Breathe (2 am), by Anna Nalick
Need You Now, by Lady Antebellum

And as always, check out deedavis.com for more inside info about my writing and my books.

Happy Reading!

Find out more about Forever Romance!

Visit us at
www.hachettebookgroup.com/publishing_forever.aspx

Find us on Facebook
http://www.facebook.com/ForeverRomance

Follow us on Twitter
http://twitter.com/ForeverRomance

NEW AND UPCOMING TITLES

Each month we feature our new titles
and reader favorites.

CONTESTS AND GIVEAWAYS

We give away galleys, autographed copies,
and all kinds of exclusive items.

AUTHOR INFO

You'll find bios, articles, and links to personal websites
for all your favorite authors—and so much more.

GET SOCIAL

Connect with your favorite authors, editors, and
other Forever fans, and share what's important to you.

THE BUZZ

Sign up for our monthly romance newsletter,
and be the first to read all about it.

VISIT US ONLINE AT

WWW.HACHETTEBOOKGROUP.COM

FEATURES:

OPENBOOK BROWSE AND
SEARCH EXCERPTS
•
AUDIOBOOK EXCERPTS AND PODCASTS
•
AUTHOR ARTICLES AND INTERVIEWS
•
BESTSELLER AND PUBLISHING
GROUP NEWS
•
SIGN UP FOR E-NEWSLETTERS
•
AUTHOR APPEARANCES AND TOUR
INFORMATION
•
SOCIAL MEDIA FEEDS AND WIDGETS
•
DOWNLOAD FREE APPS

BOOKMARK HACHETTE BOOK GROUP
@ WWW.HACHETTEBOOKGROUP.COM